Hidden Desire

CATHY WILLIAMS

MAISEY YATES

KAREN ROSE SMITH

MILLS & BOON

First Published in Great Britain 2020
By Mills & Boon, an imprint of HarperCollins*Publishers*
1 London Bridge Street, London, SE1 9GF

HIDDEN DESIRE © 2020 Harlequin Books S.A.

Enthralled by Moretti © 2014 Cathy Williams
A Game of Vows © 2012 Maisey Yates
Fortune's Secret Husband © 2016 Harlequin Books S.A.

Special thanks and acknowledgement to Karen Rose Smith for her contribution to the *Fortunes of Texas: All Fortune's Children* continuity.

ISBN: 978-0-263-28110-1

MIX
Paper from
responsible sources
FSC
www.fsc.org
FSC™ C007454

This book is produced from independently certified FSC™ paper to ensure responsible forest management.

For more information visit: www.harpercollins.co.uk/green

Printed and bound in Spain
by CPI, Barcelona

ENTHRALLED
BY MORETTI

CATHY WILLIAMS

To my three wonderful daughters.

CHAPTER ONE

CHASE EVANS PUSHED aside the folder in front of her and glanced at her watch. For the fourth time. She had now been kept waiting in this conference room for twenty-five minutes. As a lawyer, she knew what this was about. Actually, even if she hadn't been a lawyer she would have known what this was about. It was about intimidation. Intimidation by a juggernaut of a company that was determined to get its own way.

She stood up, flexed her muscles and strolled over to the floor-to-ceiling panes of glass that overlooked the teeming streets of the city.

At this time of year, London was swarming with tourists. From way up here, they appeared to be small little stick figures, but she knew if she went down she would join foreigners from every corner of the globe. You couldn't escape them. You couldn't escape the noise, the crowds and the bustle although here, in the opulent surroundings of AM Holdings, you could be forgiven for thinking that you were a million miles away from all that. It was deathly quiet.

Yet another intimidation tactic, she thought cynically. She had seen a lot in the past few years since she had been a practising lawyer, but the antics of this company took some beating.

She thought back to meeting number one, when they

had imagined that buying up the women's shelter would be a walk in the park. For meeting number one, they had sent their junior lawyer, Tom Barry, who had become embroiled in a tangle of logistics with which he had patently been unable to cope.

For meeting number two, they had dispatched a couple of more experienced guys. Alex Cole and Bruce Robins had come prepared, but so had she. Out of all the pro bono cases in which she specialised, the women's shelter was dearest to her heart. If they had come prepared to wipe it out from under her feet, then she too had upped the stakes, pulling out obscure precursors and covenants that had sent them away scratching their heads and promising that they would be back.

Chase had had no doubt that they would. The shelter, or Beth's House, as it was nicknamed, sat on prime land in West London, land that could earn any halfway canny speculator a great deal of money should it be developed. She knew, through contacts and back doors, that it had been targeted for development by the AM group. An ambitious transformation—from a women's shelter to an exclusive, designer shopping mall for the rich and famous.

Well, over her dead body.

Staring down as the minutes of the clock ticked past and no one appeared, she knew that there was a very real possibility that she would have to let this one go, admit defeat. Yet for so many reasons she refused to let herself think that way.

After Alex and Bruce, her next meeting—this time with her boss by her side—had been with their top guy, Leslie Swift. He had cleverly countered every single magic act they had produced from their rapidly shrinking hat. He had produced by-laws, exemptions and clauses that she knew had been designed to have them running back to the drawing board. Now, alone in this sprawling conference room, Chase knew that she was in the last-chance saloon.

Once again she glanced at her watch before moving back to her seat at the thirty-seater table. Lord only knew who they would send this time to take her on. Maybe they would realise that she was mortally wounded and see fit to delegate her right back to the junior lawyer so that he could gloat at the woman who had sent him packing.

But she had one more trick up her sleeve. She wasn't going to give up without a fight. The memory of giving up without fighting was too embedded in her consciousness for her ever to go down that road again. She had dragged herself away from a dark place where any kind of fighting had never been a good idea and she wasn't about to relinquish any of the grit and determination that had got her where she was now.

Banishing all thoughts of a past that would cripple her if she gave it a chance, Chase Evans returned her attention to the file in front of her and the list of names and numbers she had jotted down as her final attempt to win her case.

'Shall I tell Ms Evans how long she might be expected to wait?'

Alessandro Moretti glanced up at his secretary, who stared back at him with gimlet-eyed steeliness. She had announced Chase Evans's arrival half an hour ago, longer, and had already reminded him once that the woman was waiting for him in the conference room. From anyone else, a second reminder would have been unthinkable. Alicia Brown, however, had been with him for five years and it had been clear from the start that tiptoeing around him wasn't going to be on the cards. She was old enough to be his mother and, if she had never tiptoed around any of her five strapping boys, then she certainly wasn't going to tiptoe around anyone. Alessandro Moretti included. He had hired her on the spot.

'You can't keep her waiting for ever. It's rude.'

'But then,' Alessandro countered drily, 'you've been with me long enough to know that I'm rude.' But he stood up and grabbed his jacket from where he had earlier flung it on the long, low, black leather sofa that occupied one side of the office.

In the concrete jungle where fortunes were made and lost on the toss of a coin, and where the clever man knew how to watch his back because the knives were never far away, Alessandro Moretti, at the tender age of thirty-four, ranked as one of the elite pack leaders.

Well, you didn't get to that exalted position by being soft and tender-hearted. Alessandro understood that. He was feared and respected by his employees. He treated them fairly; more than fairly. Indeed they were amongst the highest paid across the board in the city. In return, the line they trod was the line he marked. If he wanted something done, he expected it to be done yesterday. He snapped his fingers and they jumped to immediate attention.

So he was frankly a little put out that his team of lawyers had, so far, singularly failed in nailing the deal with the shelter. He couldn't imagine that it was anything but routine. He had the money to buy them out and so he would. Why then, four months down the line, was he having to step in and do their job for them?

He had elaborate plans to redevelop the extensive land the place was sitting on. His price was more than fair. Any fool should have been able to go in, negotiate and come out with the papers signed, sealed and delivered.

Instead, in a day which was comprised of back-to-back meetings, he was having to waste time with a two-bit pro bono lawyer who had set up camp on the moral high ground somewhere and was refusing to budge. Did he really need to take valuable time out to demolish her? Because demolish her he most certainly would.

He issued a string of orders as he left his office and threw over his shoulder, as he was about to shut the door behind him, 'And don't forget how good I am at sacking people! So I'd better not find that you've forgotten any of what I've just told you! Because I don't see your trusty notepad anywhere...' He grinned and shut the door smartly behind him before his secretary could tell him what she thought of his parting shot.

He was carrying nothing, because as far as he was concerned he didn't need to. He had been briefed on the woman's arguments. He didn't anticipate needing to strong-arm her at all into giving up. He had managed to unearth a couple of covenants barely visible to the naked eye that would subvert any argument she could put forward. Additionally, she had now been waiting for over forty minutes in a conference room that had been deliberately stripped bare of anything that could be seen as homely, comforting, soothing or in any way, shape or form, designed to put someone at ease.

He briefly contemplated summoning those losers who had not been able to do their job so that they could witness first hand how to do it, but decided against it.

One on one. Over and done with in fifteen minutes. Just in time for his next conference call from Hong Kong.

Having had plenty of time to mull over the intimidation tactics, Chase was standing by the window waiting for a team of lawyers. In bare feet, she was five-eleven. In heels, as she was now, she would tower over her opponents. The last one had barely reached her shoulders. Maybe, as a last resort, she could stare them down into submission.

She was gazing out of the window when she heard the

door to the conference room opening behind her and she took her time turning round.

If they could keep her waiting in a room that had all the personality of a prison cell, then she could take her time jumping to attention.

But it wasn't a team of lawyers. It wasn't Tom Barry, Alex Cole, Bruce Robins or Leslie Swift.

She looked at the man standing by the door and she felt the colour drain from her face. She found that she couldn't move from her position of dubious advantage standing by the window. Her legs had turned to lead. Her heart was beating so violently that she felt on the verge of a panic attack. Or, at the very least, an undignified fainting spell.

'You!' This wasn't the strong, steady voice of the self-confident twenty-eight-year-old woman she had finally become.

'Well, well, well…' Alessandro was as shocked as she was but was much more adept at concealing his response and much faster at recovering.

And yet, as he moved slowly towards her, he was finding it almost impossible to believe his eyes.

At the speed of light, he travelled back in time, back to eight years ago, back to the leggy, gloriously beautiful girl who had occupied his every waking hour. She had changed, and yet she hadn't. Gone was the waist-long hair, the jeans and sweater. In its place, the woman standing in front of him, looking as though she had seen a ghost—which he supposed she had—was impeccably groomed. Her shoulder-length bob was the same blend of rich caramel and chestnut, her slanting eyes were as green and feline as he remembered, her body as long and willowy.

'Lyla Evans…' He strolled towards her, one hand in his trouser pocket. 'Should I have clocked the surname? Maybe I would have if it hadn't been preceded by Chase…' He was standing right in front of her now. She looked as though she was about to pass out. He hoped she wouldn't expect him to catch her if she fell.

'Alessandro… No one said… I wasn't expecting…'

'So I see.' His smile was cold and devoid of humour. Of their own accord, his eyes travelled to her finger. No wedding ring. Not that that said very much, all things considered.

'Will you be here on your own, or can I expect the rest of your team…?' Chase tried desperately to regain some of her shattered composure but she couldn't. She was driven to stare at the harsh, sinfully sexy contours of a face that had crept into her head far too many times to count. He was as beautiful as she remembered. More so, if that were possible. At twenty-six, he had been sexy as hell but still with the imprint of youth. Now he was a man, and there was nothing warm or open in his face. She was staring at a stranger, someone who hated her and who was making no attempt to mask his hatred.

'Just me. Cosy, as it turns out. Don't you think? So many years since last we saw one another, Lyla…or Chase, or whoever the hell you really are.'

'Chase. My name is Chase. It always was.'

'So the pseudonym was purely for my benefit. Of course, it makes sense, given the circumstances at the time…'

'Lyla was my mother's name. If you don't mind, I think I'll sit.' She tottered over to the chair and collapsed on it. The stack of files in front of her, her briefcase, her laptop, they were all reminders of why she was in this conference room in the first place, but for the life of her she couldn't focus on them. Her thoughts were all over the place.

'So, shall we play a little catch-up, Lyla? Sorry…Chase? A little polite conversation about what we've been doing for the past eight years?' Alessandro perched on the edge of the sprawling conference table and stared down at her:

the one and only woman he had wasted time chasing, only to be left frustrated when she'd failed to fall into his bed. For that reason alone, she occupied a unique spot in his life. Add all the other reasons and she was in a league of her own.

'I'd rather not.'

'I bet. In your shoes, I'd plead the fifth as well.'

'Alessandro, I know what you must think of me, but—'

'I really don't need to hear any sob stories, Lyla.'

'Stop calling me that. My name is Chase.'

'So you became a lawyer after all. I take my hat off to you—although, thinking about it, you did prove you were the sort of girl who would get what she wanted whatever the cost...'

Chase's eyes flickered up to him. The expression on his face sent the chill of fear racing up and down her spine, yet how could she blame him? Their story had been brief and so full of things that had to be hidden that it was hardly surprising.

'And I notice that there's no telling wedding ring on your finger,' he continued in the same mildly speculative voice that wouldn't have fooled an idiot. 'Did you dispose of the hapless husband in your ever-onwards and upwards climb?'

When he had met her—sitting there in the university canteen with a book in front of her, a little frown on her face, completely oblivious to everyone around her—she had knocked him sideways. It was more than the fact that she'd stood out, that she possessed head-turning looks; the world was full of girls who could turn heads. No, it had been her complete and utter indifference to the glances angled in her direction. He had watched as she had toyed with her sandwich before shoving it to one side and heading out. She had looked neither right nor left. The canteen could have been devoid of people.

Standing here now, looking at her, Alessandro could recreate that feeling of intense, incomprehensible attraction that had swept over him then as though it had been yesterday.

Significantly, she hadn't been wearing a wedding ring then either.

'I'm not here to talk about my past,' Chase said, clearing her throat. 'I've brought all the paperwork about the shelter.'

'And I'm not ready to talk about that yet.' He sat on one of the chairs alongside her and angled it away from the table so that he had a bird's eye view of her as she stared down at the bundle of files and papers in front of her and pretended to concentrate. 'So...' he drawled. 'You were about to tell me where the wedding ring's gone...'

'I don't believe I was,' Chase said coolly, gathering herself. Eyes the colour of bitter chocolate bored straight through her, bypassing the hard, glossy veneer she had taken so much time and trouble to build like a fortress around herself. 'You might be curious about what I've been up to for the past few years, Alessandro, but I have no intention of satisfying your curiosity. I just want to do what I came here to do and leave.'

'You came here to lose to me,' Alessandro told her without preamble. 'If you had any sense, you would recognise that and wave the white flag before I start lowering the price I've offered to pay for that place.' He drew her attention to the clock on the wall. 'With every passing minute, I drop my price by a grand, so make sure your argument's a winning one, because if it's not you're going to find that you're not working on behalf of your client.'

'You can't do that.'

'I can do whatever I like, Lyla...Chase...or shall I call you Mrs Evans? Or perhaps *Ms*...?'

'This isn't about *us*, Alessandro.' She tried to claw the

conversation back to the matter at hand, back to the shelter. 'So please don't think that you can use empty threats to—'

'Look around you,' Alessandro cut in lazily. 'And tell me what you see.'

'Where are you going with this?'

'Just do as I ask.'

Chase looked around nervously. She could feel the jaws of a trap yawning around her, but when she tried to figure out what sort of trap she came up empty. 'Big, bland conference room,' she told him in a voice that hinted that she was already bored with the subject. When she looked around her, her eyes kept wanting to return to him, to look at his face and absorb all the small changes there. Seeing him now, she was beginning to realise that she had never entirely forgotten him. She had buried him but it had obviously been in a shallow grave.

'I like it bland. It doesn't pay to provide distractions when you want the people seated at this table to be focused.'

'*You* like it bland…'

'Correct. You see, I am AM Holdings. I own it all. Every single deal is passed by me. What I say goes and no one contradicts me. So, when I tell you that I intend to drop my price by a grand for every minute you argue with me, I mean it and it's within my power to do it. Of course, you're all business and you think you can win, in which case my threat will be immaterial. But if you don't, well, after a couple of hours of futile arguing… Do the maths.'

Chase looked at him, lost for words. In view of what had happened between them, the deceit and the half-lies that had finally been her undoing, she was staring at a man who had been gifted his revenge. She should have done her homework on the company more thoroughly, but she had been handed the case after her boss had done the preliminaries himself, only to find that he couldn't follow through for personal reasons. She had focused all her energies on trying to locate loopholes that would prevent the sale of the shelter to *anyone* rather than specifically to AM Holdings. Even so, would she have recognised Alessandro had his name cropped up? They hadn't afforded much time for surnames.

'Sounds ungentlemanly.' Alessandro gave an elegant shrug and a smile that was as cold as the frozen wastelands. 'But, when it comes to business, I've always found that being a gentleman doesn't usually pay dividends.'

'Why are you doing this? How could you think of punishing those helpless women who use the shelter because we…we…?'

'Had an ill-fated relationship? Because you lied to me? Deceived me? Does your firm of lawyers know the kind of person you really are?'

Chase didn't say anything but she could feel her nervous system go into overdrive. She had inadvertently stepped into the lion's den; how far did revenge go? What paths would it travel down before it was finally satisfied? Alessandro Moretti owned this place. Not only was it within his power to do exactly as he said, to reduce the amount he was willing to pay for the shelter with each passing minute, but what if he decided actively to go after *her*?

'Things weren't what they seemed back then, Alessandro.'

'The clock's ticking.' He relaxed and folded his hands behind his head. Against all odds, and knowing her for what she really was, he was irritated to discover that he could still appreciate her on a purely physical level. He had never laid a finger on her but, hell, he had fantasised about it until his head had spun, had wondered what she would look like underneath the student clothes, what she would feel like. By the time he had met her, he had already bed-

ded his fair share of women, yet she had appealed to him
on a level he had barely comprehended.

He hadn't gone to the university intending to get involved with anyone. He had gone there as a favour to his
old don, to give a series of business lectures, to get students inspired enough to know that they could attempt to
achieve in record time what he had succeeded in achiev-
ing. Six lectures charting business trends, showing how
you could buck them and still come out a winner, and he
would be gone. He hadn't anticipated meeting Lyla—or,
as she now called herself, Chase—and staying on to give
a further six lectures.

For the first time in his very privileged life, he had
found himself in a situation with a woman over which
he'd had little control and he had been prepared to kick
back and enjoy it. For someone to whom things had always
come easy, he had even enjoyed the hard-to-get game she
had played. Of course, he had not expected that the hard-
to-get game would, in fact, lead nowhere in the end, but
then how was he to know the woman he had been dealing
with? She had left him with the ugly taste of disillusionment in his mouth and now here she was…

Wasn't fate a thing of beauty?

'You're not interested in reliving our…exciting past.
So, sell me your arguments… And, by the way, that's one
minute gone…'

Feeling that she had stepped into a nightmare, Chase
opened the top file with trembling fingers. Of course she
could understand that he was bitter and angry with her.
And yet in her mind, when she had projected into a future that involved her accidentally running into him somewhere, his bitterness and anger had never been so deep,
nor had he been vengeful. He could really hurt her, really
undo all the work she had done to get where she had.

She began going over some of the old ground covered

in the past three meetings she'd had with his underlings, and he inclined his head to one side with every semblance of listening, before interrupting her with a single slash of his hand.

'You know, of course, that none of those obstructions hold water. You're prevaricating and it won't work.'

Chase involuntarily glanced at the clock on the wall and was incensed that the meeting—all the important things that had to be discussed, things that involved the lives of other people—had been sidelined by this unfortunate, unexpected and worrying collision with her past.

And yet she lowered her eyes and took in the taut pull of expensive trousers over his long legs, the fine, dark hair that liberally sprinkled his forearms… Not even the unspoken atmosphere of threat in his cool, dark eyes could detract from the chiselled perfection of his face. He had the burnished colour of someone of exotic blood.

When she had first laid eyes on him, she had been knocked sideways. He hadn't beaten about the bush. He had noticed her, he said, had seen her sitting in the university canteen. She had instinctively known that he had been waiting for a predictable response. The response of a woman in the presence of a man who could have whoever he wanted, and he wanted her. She had also known that there was no way she could go there. That she should smile politely and walk away, because doing anything else would have been playing with fire. But still she had hesitated, long enough for him to recognise a mutual interest. Of course, it had always been destined to end badly, but she hadn't been able to help herself.

She tightened her lips as she realised just how badly things could go now, all these years later.

'Okay, so you may have all the legalities in place, but what do you think the press would make of a big, bad company rolling in and bulldozing a women's shelter? The public has had enough of powerful people and powerful companies thinking that they can do exactly as they like.' This had been her trump card but there was no hint of triumph in her voice as she pulled it out of the bag.

'I have names here,' she continued in the gathering silence, not daring to risk a glance at him. 'Contacts with journalists and reporters who would be sympathetic to my cause...' She shoved the paper across to him and Alessandro ignored it.

'Are you threatening me?' he asked in a tone of mild curiosity.

'I wouldn't call it threatening...'

'No? Then what exactly *would* you call it?'

'I'm exercising leverage.' It had seemed an excellent idea at the time, but then she hadn't banked on finding herself floundering in a situation she couldn't have envisaged in a million years. His dark eyes focused on her face made her want to squirm and she knew that her veneer of self-confidence and complete composure was badly undermined by the slow tide of pink colour rising to her face. 'If you buy the shelter in a cloud of bad publicity, whatever you put up there will be destined to fail. It's quite a small community in that particular part of London. People will take sides and none of them will be on yours.'

'I bet you thought that you'd bring that out from up your sleeve and my lawyers would scatter, because there *is* such a thing as bad publicity being worse than no publicity. It's a low trick, but then I'm not surprised that you would resort to low tricks.' He leaned forward, rested both arms on the shiny conference table and stared directly at her. 'However, let's just turn that threat on its head for a minute...'

'It's not a threat.'

'I have offered an extremely generous price for the purchase of the shelter and the land that goes with it. More than enough for another shelter to be built somewhere else.'

'They don't *want* to build another shelter somewhere else. These women are accustomed to Beth's House. They feel safe there.'

'*You* can wax lyrical to your buddies at the press that they're being shoved out unceremoniously from their comfort zone. My people will counter-attack with a long, detailed and extremely enticing list of what they could buy for the money they'll be getting from me. A shelter twice the size. All mod cons. An equal amount of land, albeit further out. Hell, they could even run to a swimming pool, a games room, a nursery...the list goes on.

'So, who do you think will end up winning the argument? And, when it comes to light that I will be using the land for a mall that will provide much-needed jobs for the locals, well, you can see where I'm going with this...' He stood up and strolled lazily towards the very same window through which she had been peering earlier.

Chase couldn't tear her eyes away from him. Like an addict in the sudden presence of her drug of choice, she found that she was responding in ways that were dangerously off-limits. She shouldn't be reacting like this. She couldn't afford to let him into her life, nor could she afford to have any deep and meaningful conversations about their brief and ruined past relationship. Heck, it had only lasted a handful of months! And had never got off the starting block anyway.

'So.' Alessandro turned slowly to face her. With his back to the window, the light poured in from behind, throwing his face into shadows. 'How are you feeling about your ability to win this one now?'

'It's Beth's place; she's comfortable there. Why do you think people fight to stay in their homes when a developer comes along promising to buy them out for double what their place is worth?' But he would be able to sell it across the board. He had the money and the people to make sure that whatever message they wanted to get across would be successful. She knew Beth. Was she fighting to preserve something for reasons that were personal?

'I can tell from your expression that you already know that you're staring defeat in the face. By the way, it's been nearly forty-five minutes of unconvincing arguing from you... So how much have you lost your client already? The games room? The nursery? The giant kitchen with the cosy wooden table where all those women can hold hands and break bread?'

'I never thought that you were as arrogant as I now see you are.'

'But then you could say that we barely knew anything about each other. Although, in fairness, I didn't lie about my identity...' He was unconsciously drawn to the way the sunlight streaming through the panes of glass caught the colours of her hair. Her suit was snappy and business-like and he could tell that it had been chosen to downplay her figure. In his mind's eye, he saw the tight jeans, the jumpers and trainers, and that tentative smile that had won him over.

Chase stared down at the folder in front of her. There was nothing left to pull out of the hat. Even if there was, this was personal. He was determined to win the final argument, to have the last word, to *make her pay*.

'So I'm guessing from your prolonged silence that you'll be breaking the happy news to... What's her name? Beth?'

'You know it is.'

'And can you work out how much I'll be deducting from my initial offer?'

'Tell me you don't really mean to go through with that?'

'Lie, in other words?' Alessandro walked towards her and perched on the edge of the table.

'You can't force them to sell.'

'Have you had a look at their books? They're in debt.

Waiting to be picked off. It may be a caring, sharing place, but what it gains in the holding hands and chanting stakes it lacks in the accountancy arena. A quiet word in the right banker's ear and they'll be facing foreclosure by dusk. Furthermore, if it becomes widespread knowledge that they're in financial trouble, the vulture developers will swoop in looking for a bargain. What started out as a generous offer from me would devolve into an untidy fire sale with the property and land going for a song.'

'Okay.' Chase recognised the truth behind what he was saying. How could this be the same man who had once teased her, entertained her with his wit, impressed her with the breadth of his intelligence...driven her crazy with a longing that had never had a chance to be sated?

'Okay?'

'You win, Alessandro.' She looked at him with green eyes that had once mesmerised him right out of the rigidly controlled box into which he had always been accustomed to piling his emotional entanglements with the opposite sex. 'But maybe you could tell me whether you would have been as hardline if I hadn't been the person sitting here trying to talk you out of buying the shelter.'

'Oh, the sale most certainly would have gone ahead,' Alessandro drawled without an ounce of sympathy. 'But I probably wouldn't have tacked on the ticking clock.'

He strolled round to his chair and sat back down. His mobile phone buzzed, and when his secretary told him to get a move on because she could only defer his conference call for so long he informed her briefly that she would have to cancel it altogether. 'And make sure the same goes for my meetings after lunch,' he murmured, not once taking his eyes off Chase's downbent head. He signed off just as Alicia began to launch into a curious demand to know why.

'I don't want to keep you.' Chase began stacking all her files together and shoving them into her capacious brief case. She paused to look at him. *Last look*, she thought. *Then I'll never see you again.* She found that she was drinking in his image and she knew, with resignation, that what she looked at now would haunt her in the weeks to come. It was just so unfair. 'But I would like it if you could reconsider your...your...'

'Lower offer? And save you the humiliation of having to tell your client that you single-handedly knocked the price down?'

Chase glared at him. 'I never took you for a bully.'

'Life, as we both know, is full of cruel shocks. I'll admit that I have no intention of pulling out of this purchase, but you could recoup the lost thousands.'

'Could I? How?' She stared at him. At this point, the images of those wonderful additions to any other house Beth might buy vanishing in a puff of smoke, because of her, were proliferating in her head, making her giddy. She knew that the finances for the shelter were in serious disarray. They would need all the money they could get just to pay off the debts and wipe the slate clean.

'We have an unfinished past,' Alessandro murmured. 'It's time to finish it. I wouldn't have sought out this opportunity but, now it's here, I want to know who the hell you really are. Satisfy my curiosity and the full price is back on the table...'

CHAPTER TWO

So WHERE WAS the jump for joy, the high five, the shriek of delight? For the sake of a little conversation, she stood to claw back a substantial amount of money. He might have expected some show of emotion, even if only in passing.

Alessandro didn't take his eyes off her face, nor did he utter a word; the power of silence was a wonderful thing. Plus, he didn't trust her as far as he could throw her. If she thought that she could somehow screw him for more than the agreed amount, then let her have all the silence in the world, during which she could rethink any such stupid notion.

'I would need any assurances from you in writing,' Chase finally said. He wanted to finish business between them? Didn't he know that that was impossible? There were no questions she could ever answer and no explanations she could ever give.

'You will be getting no such thing,' Alessandro assured her calmly. 'You take my word for it or you leave here with your wallet several shades lighter.'

'There's no point rehashing what happened between us, Alessandro.'

'Your answer: yes or no. Simple choice.'

Chase stood up and smoothed down her grey skirt. She knew that she had a good figure, very tall and very slender. It was a bonus because it meant that she could pull off cheap clothing; she felt she needed simply to blend in with the other lawyers and paralegals in the company where she worked. Fitzsimmons was a top-ranking law firm and it employed top-ranking people; no riff-raff. Nearly every-one there came from a background where Mummy and Daddy owned second homes in the country. She kept her distance from all of them, but still she knew where they came from just by listening to their exploits at the week-ends, the holidays they booked and the Chelsea apart-ments they lived in.

Thankfully, she was one of only two specialising in pro bono cases, so she could keep her head down, put in her hours and attend only the most essential of social functions.

She didn't want her quiet life vandalised. She didn't want Alessandro Moretti strolling back into it, asking questions and nursing a vendetta against her. She just couldn't afford to have any cans of worms opened up.

Likewise, she didn't want to feel this scary surge of emotion that made her go weak at the knees. Her life was her own now, under control, and she didn't want to jeop-ardise that.

But where were the choices? Did she make Beth pay for what *she* didn't want? Did she risk her boss's disapproval when she turned up and recounted what had happened?

More than that, if she kept her lips tightly buttoned up, who was to say that Alessandro would conveniently disappear? The way those hard, black eyes were watch-ing her now…

She sat back down. 'Okay. What do you want to talk about? I mean, what do you want me to say?'

'Now, you don't really expect us to have a cosy little chat in a room like this, do you?'

He began prowling around the conference room: thick cream carpet aided and abetted the silence; cream walls;

the imposing hard-edged table where the great and the good could sit in front of their opened laptops, conversing in computer-speak and making far-reaching decisions that could affect the livelihoods of numerous people lower down the food chain, often for the better, occasionally for the worst.

'I mean, we have so much catching up to do, Lyla... Chase...'

'Please stop calling me Lyla. I told you, I don't use that name any more.'

'It's approaching lunchtime. Why don't we continue this conversation somewhere a little more comfortable?'

'I'm fine here.'

'Actually, you don't have a vote. I have five minutes' worth of business to deal with. I trust you can find your way down to the foyer? And don't...' he positioned himself neatly in front of her '...even think of running out on me.'

'I wouldn't do that.' Chase tilted her chin and stood up to look him squarely in the eyes. As a show of strength, it spectacularly backfired because, up close and personal like this, she could feel all her energy drain out of her, leaving behind a residue of tumultuous emotions and a dangerous, scary *awareness*. Her nostrils flared as she breathed in the clean, woody, aggressively masculine scent of his cologne. She took an unsteady step back and prayed that he hadn't noticed her momentary weakness.

'No?' Alessandro drawled, narrowing his eyes. 'Because right now you look like a rabbit caught in the headlights. Why? It's not as though I don't already know you for a liar, a cheat and a slut.' He had never addressed a woman so harshly in his life before but, looking at her here, taking in the perfection of a face that could launch a thousand ships and a body that was slender but with curves in all the right places, the reality of their past had slammed into him and lent an ugly bitterness to every word that passed his lips.

'I notice you're not defending yourself,' he murmured. He didn't know whether her lack of fight was satisfying or not. Certainly, he wished that she would look at him when he spoke, and he was sorely tempted to angle her face to him.

'What's the point?' Chase asked tightly. 'I'll meet you in the foyer but...' she looked at him with a spurt of angry rebellion '...I won't be hanging around for an hour while you take your time seeing to last-minute business with your secretary.'

Alessandro's eyes drifted down to her full, perfectly shaped mouth. He used to tease her that she looked as though she was sulking when it was in repose, but when she smiled it was like watching a flower bloom. He had never been able to get his fill of it. She certainly wasn't smiling now.

'Actually, you'll hang around for as long as I want you to.'

'Just because you want to...to...pay me back for...'

'Like I said, let's save the cosy chit-chat for somewhere more comfortable.'

Only when he left the room did Chase realise how tense she had been. She sagged and closed her eyes, steadying herself against the table.

She felt like the victim of a runaway truck. In a heartbeat, her life seemed to have been derailed, and she had to tell herself that it wasn't so; that because Alessandro was the man with whom she was now having to deal, because their paths had crossed in such a shadowy manner, it didn't mean that he was out to destroy her. His pride had been injured all those years ago and what he wanted from her now was answers to the questions he must have asked himself in the aftermath of their break-up. Not that they had ever really had a *relationship*.

Of course, she would have to be careful with what she told him, but once he was satisfied they would both return to their lives and it would be as if they had never met again.

She left the conference room in a hurry. It was almost twelve-thirty and there were far more people walking around than when she had first entered the impressive building. Workers were going out to lunch. It was a perfect summer's day. There would be sandwiches in the park and an hour's worth of relaxing in the sun before everyone stuck back on their jackets and returned to their city desks. Chase had always made sure to steer clear of that.

In the foyer, she didn't have long to wait before she spotted Alessandro stepping out of the lift. As he walked towards her, one finger holding the jacket that he had tossed over his shoulder, she relived those heady times when she had enjoyed kidding herself that her life could really change. Every single time she had seen him, she had felt a rush of pure, adrenaline-charged excitement, even though all they ever did was have lunch together or a cappuccino somewhere.

'So you're here.'

'You didn't really expect me to run away?' Chase fell into step alongside him. It was a treat not to tower over a guy but she still had to walk quickly to match his pace as they went through the revolving glass doors and out into the busy street.

'No, of course I didn't. You're a lawyer. You know when diplomacy is called for.' He swung left and began walking away from the busier streets, down the little side roads that gave London such character. 'And, on the subject of your career, why don't we kick off our catch-up with that?'

'What do you want to know?'

Alessandro leaned down towards her. 'Let's really get

into the spirit of this, Chase. Let's not do a question-and-answer session, with me having to drag conversation out of you.'

'What do you expect, Alessandro? I don't want to be here!'

'I'm sure you don't, but you're here now, so humour me.'

'I…I…got a first-class degree. In my final year I was head-hunted by a firm of lawyers—not the ones I work for now, but a good firm. I was fast-tracked.'

'Clever Chase.'

Chase recognised that it hadn't been said as a compliment, although she could only guess at what he was implying. He loathed her so, whatever it was, she had no doubt that it would be offensive.

Yet, she *was* clever. In another place and another time, she knew that she would have been one of those girls who would have been said to 'have it all': brains and looks. But then, life had a way of counter-balancing things. At any rate, she had relied far more on her brains than she ever had on her looks. She had worked like a demon to get her A-levels, fought against all odds to get to a top university, and once there had doggedly spared no effort in getting a degree that would set her up for life. And all that against a backdrop that she had trained herself never to think about.

'Thank you.' She chose to misinterpret the tone of his voice. 'So, I got a good job, did my training, changed companies…and here I am now.'

'Fitzsimmons. Classy firm.'

'Yes, it is.' She could feel fine prickles of nervousness beading her forehead.

'And yet, no designer suit? Don't they pay you enough?'

Chase cringed with embarrassment. He had never made any secret about the fact that he came from money. Was that how he could spot the fact that her clothes were off the peg and ready to wear from a chain store? 'They pay me more than enough,' she said coolly. 'But I prefer to save my money instead of throwing it away to a high-end retailer.'

'How noble. Not a trait I would tend to associate with you.'

'Can't you at least try and be civil towards me?' Chase asked thinly. 'At any rate, most of my work is pro bono. It's sensible not to show up in designer suits that cost thousands.' It was what she had laughingly told someone at the firm ages ago and her boss had applauded her good sense.

They were now in front of an old-fashioned pub nestled in one of the quieter back alleys. There were gems like this all over London. When they entered, it was dark, cool and quiet. He offered her a drink and shrugged when she told him that she would stick to fruit juice.

'So…' Alessandro sat down, hand curved round his pint, and looked at her. He honestly didn't know what he hoped to gain from this forced meeting but seeing her again had reawakened the nasty questions she had left unanswered. 'Let's start at the beginning. Or maybe we should pick it up at the end—at the point when you told me that you were married. Yes, maybe that's the place we should start. After we'd been meeting for four months… Four months of flirting and you gazing at me all convincingly doe-eyed and breathless, then informing me that you had a husband waiting in the wings.'

Chase nursed her fruit juice. She licked her lips nervously. Her green eyes tangled and clashed with cold eyes the colour of jet. 'I don't see what the point of this is, Alessandro.'

'You know what the point of it is—you're going to satisfy my curiosity in return for the full agreed price for your shelter. It's a fair exchange. Tell me what happened to the husband.'

'Shaun…was killed shortly after I got my first job. He… he was on his motorbike at the time. He was speeding, lost control, crashed into the central reservation on the motorway…'

'So you didn't ditch him in the impersonal confines of a divorce court.' Nor would she have. Alessandro downed a mouthful of beer and watched her over the rim of the glass. Not, as she had told him on that last day in exhaustive detail, when he'd been her childhood sweetheart and the love of her life. 'And I take it you never remarried.'

'Nor will I ever.' She could detect the bitterness that had crept into her voice, but when she looked at him his expression was still as cool and unrelenting as it had been.

'Is that because there's no room for a man in the life of an ambitious, high-flying lawyer? Or because you're still wrapped up with the man who was…let me try and remember… Oh, yes, I've got it: the only guy you would ever contemplate sleeping with. *Sorry if you got the wrong idea, Alessandro. A few cappuccinos does not a relationship make, but it's been a laugh…*'

'We should never have seen each other. It was a terrible idea. I never meant to get involved with anyone.'

'But you didn't get involved with me, did you?' Alessandro angled his beautiful head to one side as he picked up an unspoken message he wasn't quite getting.

What was there to get or not get? he thought impatiently. The woman had strung him along, led him up the garden path and then had casually disappeared without a backward glance. Hell, she had made him feel things… No, he wasn't going to go there.

'No! No, I didn't. I meant…'

'I'm all ears.'

'You don't understand. I shouldn't even have even to you. I was married.'

'So why did you? Were you riding high on the knowledge that you'd managed to net the rich guy all the groupie students were after?'

'That's a very conceited thing to say.'

'I value honesty. I lost track of the number of notes I got from girls asking for some "extra tuition".'

If there hadn't been notes, she thought, then he surely would have clocked the stares he'd garnered everywhere he went. The man was an alpha male with enough sex appeal to sink a ship. Throw in his wealth, and it was little wonder that girls were queuing up to see if they could attract his attention. She'd never, ever been at the university longer than was strictly necessary but, if she had been, she knew that she would have become a source of envy, curiosity and dislike.

'So was that why you decided to keep your marital status under wraps? To take the wedding ring off? To string me along with the promise of sex?'

'I never said we would end up in bed.'

'Do me a favour!' He slammed his empty glass on the table and Chase jumped. 'You knew exactly what you were getting into!'

'And I didn't think... I never thought...'

'So you lied about the fact that you weren't single or available for a relationship.'

'If I remember correctly, you once told me that you weren't interested in commitment, that you liked your relationships fast and furious and temporary!'

Alessandro flushed darkly. 'Weak reasoning,' he gritted cuttingly. 'Did you lie because you thought that you might try me out for size? See whether I wasn't a better bet than the stay-at-home husband? Is that why you strung me along for four months? Were you hedging your bets?' He shook his head, furious with himself for losing control of the conversation, for actually caring one way or another what had or hadn't been done eight years previously.

'No, of course not! And Shaun was never a *stay-at-*

home husband.' Again, that bitterness had crept into her voice.

'No? So what was he, then?' Alessandro leaned forward, the simple shift of body weight implying threat. 'Banker? Entrepreneur? If I recall, you were a little light on detail. In fact, if my memory serves me right, you couldn't wait to get out of my company fast enough the very last time we met.'

Alessandro was surprised to find that he could remember exactly what she had been wearing the very last time he'd laid eyes on her: a pair of faded skinny jeans tucked into some cheap imitation-suede boots and a jumper which now, thinking about it, had probably belonged to the 'childhood sweetheart' husband. On that thought, his jaw clenched and his eyes darkened.

It hadn't taken her long to spill out the truth. Having spent months of innocent conversation, tentative advances and retreats and absolutely no physical contact—which had been hell for him—she had sat down opposite him at the wine bar which had become their favourite meeting place; at a good bus ride away, it was far from all things university. With very little preamble, and keeping her eyes glued to his face while around them little clusters of strangers had drunk, laughed and chatted, all very relaxed in the run-up to Christmas, she'd informed him that she would no longer be seeing him.

'Sorry,' he recalled her saying with a brittle smile. 'It's been a laugh, and thanks for all the help with the economics side of the course, but actually I'm married...'

She had wagged her ring finger in front of him, complete with never-before-seen wedding band.

Shaun McGregor, she had said airily. Love of her life. Had known him since they were both fifteen. She had even pulled out a picture of him from her beaten-up old wallet and waxed lyrical about his striking good looks.

Alessandro had stared long and hard at the photo of a young man with bright blue eyes and a shaved head. There was a tattoo at the side of his neck; he'd probably been riddled with them. It had been brought home to him sharply just what a fool he had been taken for. Not only had she strung him along for fun, but he had never actually been her type. Her husband had had all the fine qualities of a first-rate thug.

'Shaun did lots of different things,' Chase said vaguely. 'But none of that matters now, anyway. The fact is, I'm sorry. I know it's late in the day to apologise, but I'm apologising.'

'Why did you use a different name?'

'Huh?'

'You used the name Lyla. Not just with me, with everyone. Why?'

'I…' How could she possibly explain that she had been a different person then? That she had had the chance to create a wonderful, shiny new persona, and that she had taken it, because what she could create had been so much better than the reality. She had still been clever, and she had never lied about her academic history but, she had thought, what was the harm in passing herself off as just someone normal? Someone with a solid middle-class background and parents who cared about her? It hadn't been as though she would ever have been required to present these mysterious and fictitious parents to anyone.

And she had always made sure never to get too close to anyone—until Alessandro had come along. Even then, at the beginning, she had had no idea that she would fall so far, so fast and so deep, nor that the little white lies she had told at the beginning would develop into harmful untruths that she'd no longer be able to retract.

'Well?' Alessandro prompted harshly. 'You lied about your single status and you lied about your name. So let's take them one at a time.' He signalled to a waitress and ordered himself another glass of beer. There went the afternoon, was the thought that passed through his mind. There was little chance he would be in the mood for a series of intense meetings and conference calls later. He was riveted by the hint of changing expressions on her face. He felt that he was in possession of a book, the meaning of which escaped him even though he had read the story from beginning to end. Then he cursed himself for being fanciful, which was so unlike him.

'Lyla was my mother's name. I like it. I didn't think there was anything wrong in using it.'

'And so you stopped liking it when you decided to join a law firm?'

'You said we weren't going to do a question-and-answer session!' Her skin burned from the intensity of his eyes on her. Alessandro Moretti, even as a young man in his mid-twenties, had always had a powerful, predatory appeal. There was something dangerous about him that sent shivers up and down her spine and drew her to him, even when common sense told her it was mad. He certainly hadn't lost that appeal.

'It was easier to just use my real name when I joined Edge Ellison, that first law firm. I mean, my Christian name.'

'Why am I getting the feeling that there are a thousand holes in whatever fairy story you're spinning me?'

'I'm not spinning you a fairy story!' Chase snapped. Bright spots of colour stained her cheeks. 'If you want, I can bring my birth certificate to show you!' Except that would suggest a second meeting, which was not something that was going to be on the cards.

But what would he do if he found out where she really came from? What would he do if he discovered that the solid, middle-class background she had innocently hinted at had been about as real as a swimming pool in the middle of the Sahara?

He might be tempted to have a quiet chat with the head of her law firm, she thought with a sickening jolt. Of course, she hadn't lied about any of her qualifications, and she knew that she was a damned good lawyer. There was no way she could be given the sack for just allowing people to *assume* a background that wasn't entirely true, yet...

Wounded pride and dislike could make a person do anything in their power to get revenge. What if he shared all her little white lies with the people she worked with— the posh, private-school educated young men and women who weren't half as good as she was but who would have a field day braying with laughter at her expense? She was strong, but she knew that she was not so strong that she could survive ridicule at the work place.

'I should be getting back to work.' She drained the remainder of her orange juice and made to stand up.

Without thinking, Alessandro reached out and circled his hand around her wrist.

Chase froze. Really, it was the most peculiar sensation...as if her entire body had locked into place so that she was incapable of movement. His fingers around her wrist were as dramatic as a branding iron and she felt her heart pick up speed until she thought it might explode inside her.

'Not so fast.'

'I've answered all your questions, Alessandro!'

'What the hell was in it for you?'

'Nothing! I...just made a mistake! It was a long time ago. I was just a kid.'

'A kid of twenty and already hitched. I didn't think that kind of thing happened any more.'

'I told you...we were in love...' Chase looked away and

shook her hand free of his vice-like grip. 'We didn't see the point of waiting.'

'And your families both joined in the celebrations?'

She shrugged. 'He's dead now, anyway, so it doesn't matter whether they joined in the celebrations or not.'

'Spoken like a true grieving widow.' Why did he keep getting this feeling that something was out of kilter? Was his mind playing tricks on him? Had his ego been so badly bruised eight years ago that he would rather look for hidden meanings than take her very simple tale of treachery at face value?

'It's been years. I've moved on.'

'And no one else has surfaced on the scene to replace the late lamented?'

'Why is this all about me?' Chase belatedly thought that she might turn the spotlight onto him. If there was one thing to be said for going into law whilst simultaneously detaching yourself from most of the human race, it was that it did dramatic things to your confidence levels. Or maybe it was just her 'flight or fight' reflex getting an airing. She stared him squarely in the face and tried not to let the steady, speculative directness of his gaze get to her.

'What about *you*?' she asked coolly. 'We haven't said anything about what *you've* been up to…'

'What's there to say?' Alessandro relaxed back, angling his body so that he could cross his legs. She really did have a face that made for compulsive watching. It was exquisite, yet with a guarded expression that made you wonder what was going on behind the beautiful mask. Even as a much younger woman, she had possessed that sense of unique mystery that had fired his curiosity and kept it for the duration of their strange dalliance.

And now, yet again, he could feel his curiosity piqued. 'I'm an open book.' He spread his arms wide. 'I don't hide who I am and I don't make a habit of leading anyone down the garden path.'

'And is there a special someone in *your* life? Is there a Mrs Moretti dusting and cleaning in a house in the country somewhere and a few little Moretti children scampering around outside? Or are you still only into the fast and furious relationship without the happy ending?'

'My, my. You've certainly become acid-tongued, Chase.'

Chase flushed. Yes she had. And there were times when she stood back and wondered if she really liked the person she had become. Not that she had ever been soft and fluffy, but now…

'I don't like being trampled.'

'And is that why you think I brought you here? To trample over you? Is that what you think I'm doing?'

Chase shrugged. 'Isn't it?'

'We're exchanging information. How could that possibly be described as trampling all over you? And, in answer to your question, there is no Mrs Moretti in a country house—and if there were, she certainly wouldn't be dusting or cleaning.'

'Because you have enough money to pay for someone to dust and clean for you. Are you still working twenty-four-seven? Surely you must have made enough billions by now to kick back and enjoy life?'

She used to listen, enraptured, as he'd told her about his working life: non-stop; on the go all the time. The lectures, he had said, were like comic relief, little windows of relaxation. She had teased him that, if giving lectures was his form of relaxation, then he would keel over with high blood pressure by the time he was thirty-five. She was annoyed to find herself genuinely curious and interested to hear what he had been up to. Having anything to do with Alessandro Moretti was even more hazardous now than it had been eight years ago.

'None of my business,' she qualified in a clipped voice. 'Am I free to go now?'

Alessandro's lips thinned. He had found out precisely nothing. None of his questions had been answered. His brain was telling him to walk away but some other part of him wanted more.

'Why did you decide to concentrate on pro bono cases?' He asked softly. 'Surely with a first-class degree, and law firms head-hunting you, there were far more profitable things to do?'

'I've never been interested in making money.' He had stopped attacking her and she realised that she had forgotten how seductive he could be when he was genuinely interested in hearing what she had to say. He would tilt his head to one side and would give the impression that every word she uttered was of life-changing importance.

'I'd always planned on becoming a lawyer, although the two other options that tempted me were Social Services and the police force.' She blushed, because she didn't think that she had confided that in anyone before—not that she did a lot of confiding anyway.

'Social Services? The police force?'

'So please don't accuse me of being materialistic.'

'I can't picture you as a social worker, even less a policewoman.'

'I should be getting back to work. I have a lot to do, and I'll have to visit the shelter later today and tell them what the outcome of my meeting with your company was. They'll be disappointed because they honestly don't want to move premises, not when they've been such a reliable fixture in the area for such a long time, and not when the majority of the women who use their services are fairly local to the area. A big place with a swimming pool and a games room in the middle of nowhere is no good for anyone.'

'What made the decision for you?'

Hadn't he been distracted from asking her personal questions? Having lowered her guard for three seconds, Chase now felt as though she was handing over state secrets to the enemy, and yet what was the big deal? Was she so defensive because Alessandro was on the receiving end of her confidences? And wasn't it possible that, the more secretive she was, the more curious he would become? She forced herself to relax and smile at him.

'The hours,' she confessed in a halting voice. 'I didn't want to think that I might be called out at any time of the day or night. I might work long hours at Fitzsimmons but I can control the hours I work.'

'Makes sense. More to the point, I suppose both other options would have involved an element of danger, and even more so for someone like you.'

'Someone like me?' Immediately, Chase bristled at the implied insult. 'And I suppose you're going to launch into another attack on me? More criticism of me that I'm a liar and a cheat? Although I have no idea how that would have anything to do with being in the police force or working for the council! I get it that you're angry and bitter about what happened between us, but attacking me isn't going to change any of that!'

'Actually,' Alessandro murmured, 'I meant that those two professions are the ones that are possibly least suited to a woman with your looks. You're sexy as hell; how would that have played out for you if you had found yourself in a dangerous situation…?' The lips he had never kissed and the body he had never touched…

Suddenly, his body jackknifed into sudden, shocking arousal. The sheer force of it took him by surprise. It pushed its way past his bitterness and anger and made a mockery of the answers he had told himself he demanded to hear. As his erection throbbed painfully against the zip of his trousers, his mind took flight in a completely different direction. He imagined her hand down there, her mouth wrapped around him…

Who the hell cared about answers when he was consumed with lust? He had to shift in the chair just to release some of the urgency that was becoming painful.

He was suffused with anger at his physical response to her. She represented everything he found most repellent, yet how was it that she could still manage to turn him on? Was his libido so wayward that it could defy cool judgement and rise to the challenge of the unavailable, the unacceptable…the out of bounds? He had never lost control when it came to any woman and he had dated some of the most spectacularly beautiful women in the world. So what the hell was going on here?

'I never gave that side of things any thought at all.' Chase was determined not to let that description of her take their conversation in a direction she most certainly didn't want.

Her voice was cool, Alessandro noted, yet her colour was up. And she couldn't meet his eyes. Now, wasn't *that* telling?

He knew that the last thing he should contemplate doing was to pay any credence to whatever her expression was saying or, more to the point, whatever his disobedient body was up to, and yet…

'You know what? I think I might like to see this shelter. Evaluate just how the land will play out for what I have in mind. I'm taking it you'll be my escort…?'

CHAPTER THREE

FOR THE FIRST time in years Chase felt helpless. Three days ago she had walked into the imposing glass building that housed AM Holdings with a simple mission: save the shelter. She had been in control—the career woman, successful in what she did, in command of the situation. She had hoped for a favourable outcome but, had there not been one, she would have left with a clear conscience—she would have done her best.

And now here she was, hanging around by the window in her house, peering out at regular intervals for Alessandro, who had made good on his request to be shown the shelter.

'What for?' she had demanded at the time. 'I don't see the point. You're just going to demolish it anyway so that you can put up a mall catering for rich people.'

'Be warned,' he had said, eyebrows raised, those midnight eyes boring straight through her, making her feel as though her whole body had been plugged into a socket. 'Do-gooders and preachers have a monotonous tendency to become self-righteous bores. Naturally, I have details of the land somewhere but I want to see for myself what the layout is. Since you're the one handling the deal, I can't imagine that would be a problem. Or is it? Does our past history make it a problem for you?'

Yes. Yes, it does, she had thought with rising desperation. 'No. Of course not. Why should it?' she had answered with an indifferent shrug.

So here she was now and she felt as though control was slipping out of her grasp. She knew that under normal circumstances a lapse in her self-control would be easily dealt with but with Alessandro…

Her frustration and anger was underlined by a darker, more insidious emotion, a swirl of excitement that scared her. It felt like a slumbering monster slowly reawakening. Even though she had taken care to dress as neutrally as possible, in a navy-blue suit that was the epitome of sexlessness—and an impractical colour, given the wall-to-wall blue summer skies and hot sunshine—she still felt horribly vulnerable as she hovered in the sitting room waiting for him to show up.

She had informed him that she would meet him at the premises, but he had insisted on collecting her.

'You can fill me in on the history of the place on the way,' he had said smoothly. 'Forewarned is forearmed.'

She had bitten her tongue and refrained from telling him that there was no point being forearmed when the net result would be a demolition derby. He was the guy with the purse strings and she had already seen first-hand how he could use that position to his own advantage. She had no desire to revive the ticking clock.

A long, sleek, black Jaguar pulled up outside the house just as she was about to turn away from the window and her attention was riveted at the sight of him emerging from the back seat, as incongruous in this neighbourhood as his car was.

He was dressed in pale-grey pinstriped trousers, which even from a distance screamed quality, and a white shirt, the sleeves of which he had rolled to the elbow.

For a few heart-stopping seconds, Chase found that she literally couldn't breathe, that she was holding her breath.

The mere sight of him was a full-on assault on all her senses. She watched as he looked around him, taking in his surroundings. She felt sure that this was the sort of neighbourhood he would be accustomed to telling his chauffeur to drive straight through and to make sure the car doors were locked. By no means was it in a dangerous part of London but neither was it upmarket. Well paid though she was, she wasn't so well paid that she could afford to buy a house in one of the trendier areas and, unlike many of her associates, she didn't have parents who could stick their hands in their pockets and treat her to one.

She dodged out of sight just as he turned to face the house and, when the doorbell rang, she took her time getting to it. Her heart was beating like a sledgehammer as she pulled open the door to find him lounging against the doorframe.

'Right. Shall we go?' she asked as her eyes slid away from his sinfully handsome face, returned to take a peek and slid away again. She gathered her handbag from where she had hung it on the banister and bent to retrieve her briefcase from the ground.

'In due course.' Alessandro stepped into the hallway and shut the front door behind him.

'What are you doing?'

'I'm coming in for a cup of coffee.'

'We haven't got time for that, Alessandro. The appointment has been made for ten-fifteen. With rush-hour traffic, heaven only knows how long it will take for us to get there.'

'Relax. I got my secretary to put back the visit by an hour.'

'You *what?*'

'So this is where you live.'

Chase watched in horror as he made himself at home, strolling to peer into the sitting room, then onwards to the kitchen, into which he disappeared.

'Alessandro…' She galvanised herself into movement and hurried to the kitchen, to find him standing in the centre doing a full turn. It was a generous-sized kitchen which overlooked a small, private garden. It had been a persuading factor in her purchase of the house. She loved having a small amount of outdoor space.

'Very nice.'

'This is not appropriate!'

'Why not? It's hardly as though I'm a stranger. Are you going to make me a cup of coffee?'

Chase gritted her teeth as he sat down. The kitchen was large enough for a four-seater table and it had been one of the first things she had bought when she had moved in three years previously. She had fallen in love with the square, rough, wooden table with its perimeter of colourful, tiny mosaic tiles. She watched as he idly traced one long finger along some of the tiles and then she turned away to make them both some coffee.

'Is this your first house?' Alessandro queried when she had finally stopped busying herself doing nothing very much at the kitchen counter and sat down opposite him.

He hadn't laid eyes on her in three days but he had managed to spend a great deal of time thinking about her and he had stopped beating himself up for being weak. So what if she had become an annoying recurring vision in his head? Wasn't it totally understandable? He had been catapulted back to a past he had chosen to lock away. Naturally it would be playing on his mind, like an old, scratched record returned to a turntable. Naturally *she* would be playing on his mind, especially when she had remained just so damned easy on the eye.

'What do you mean?' Everything about Alessandro Moretti sitting at her kitchen table made her jumpy.

'Is this the family home?'

'I have no idea what you're talking about.'

'The dearly departed... Is this the marital home?'

'No, it's not.' She looked down. 'Shaun and I... We, er, had somewhere else when we were together... When he died I rented for a couple more years until I had enough equity to put in as a deposit on this place.'

Alessandro thought of the pair of them, young love-birds renting together, while she had batted her eyelashes at him and played him for a fool. He swallowed a mouthful of instant coffee and stood up, watching as she scrambled to her feet.

'Are you going to give me a tour of the place?'

'There isn't much to see. Two bedrooms upstairs; a bathroom. You've seen what's down here. Shall we think about going?'

Alessandro didn't answer. He strolled out of the kitchen, glancing upstairs before turning his attention to the sitting room. Why was she so jumpy? She had been as cool as a cucumber eight years ago when she had walked out on him, so why was she now behaving like a cat on a hot tin roof? Guilt? Hardly. A woman who could conduct an outside relationship while married would never be prone to guilt. Or remorse. Or regret.

Perversely, the jumpier she seemed to be, the more intrigued he became. He shoved one hand in his trouser pocket, feeling the coolness of his mobile phone.

'For a cool-headed lawyer,' he mused as he stared round the sitting room, 'you like bright colours. Anyone would be forgiven for thinking that the decor here suggests a completely different personality.' He swung round to look at her as she hovered in the doorway, neither in the room nor out of it. 'Someone fun...vibrant.' He paused a fraction of a second. 'Passionate...'

Chase flushed, and was annoyed with herself, because she knew that that was precisely the response he had been courting. He was back and he was intent on playing with her like a cat playing with a mouse, knowing that all the danger and all the power lay exclusively in his hands.

'And yet,' Alessandro drawled as he prowled through the room before gazing briefly out of the window which overlooked the little street outside, 'there's something missing.'

'What?' The question was obviously reluctantly spoken. As he began to walk towards her, she felt panic rise with sickening force to her throat. All at once she was overcome with a memory of how desperately she had wanted him all those years ago. Her eyes widened and her mouth parted on a softly indrawn breath.

Getting closer and closer to her, Alessandro thought he could *touch* the subtle change in the atmosphere between them. It had become highly charged and, for the first time in a very long time, he felt sizzlingly *alive*. Not one of the catwalk-model beauties he had slept with over the past few years had come close to rousing this level of forbidden excitement. The immediacy of his response shocked him, all the more so because he recognised that the last time he had felt like this was when he had been in the process of being duped by the very same woman standing in front of him now. Hatred and revulsion were clearly inadequate protection against whatever it was she had that was now pushing an erection to the fore.

The bloody woman had been elusive then, for reasons which he had later understood, and she was elusive now, this time for reasons he couldn't begin to understand.

'Are you afraid of me?' he demanded harshly and Chase roused herself from the heated torpor that had engulfed her to stare up at him.

'What makes you think that I'm afraid of you?' She tried to insert some vigour into her voice but she could hear the sound of it—thin, weedy and defensive, all the things she didn't want him to imagine she was for a second.

'The way you're standing in the doorway as though I might make a lunge for you at any minute!'

'I can't imagine you would do any such thing!'

Couldn't she? It was precisely what he wanted to do: behave like a caveman and take her, because she was tempting the hell out of him!

'I'm afraid of what you could do.' She backtracked quickly as her mind threatened to veer down unexpected, unwelcome paths. 'You've already shown that you'd be willing to punish Beth because you... Because of me.'

'And yet here I am now. Do you think I'm the sort of man who reneges on what he's said? I've told you that I intend to pay the full, agreed price. I'll pay it.' Not afraid of him? *Like hell.* She might not be afraid of him, but he was certainly making her feel uncomfortable. Uncomfortable enough to try and shimmy further away from him.

He extended one lean hand against the wall, effectively blocking any further scarpering towards the front door. He could smell her hair. If he lowered his head just a little, he would feel its softness against his face. Of their own accord, his eyes drifted to the prissy blouse and the even prissier navy-blue jacket. He was well aware that she was breathing quickly, her breasts rising and falling as she did her utmost to keep her eyes averted.

Just as quickly he pushed himself away, retreating from her space, and he watched narrowly as she relaxed and exhaled one long breath.

He wasn't going to lose control. He had lost control once with her and he wasn't about to become the sort of loser who made a habit of ignoring life's lessons and learning curves.

'I was going to say...' He led the way to the front door and paused as she slung her handbag over her shoulder and reached for the case on the ground. 'There's something missing from your house.' He opened the door for her and stood back, allowing her to brush past him. 'Photos. Where are the pictures of the young, loving couple, from before your husband died? I thought I might have seen the happy pair holding hands and gazing adoringly up at one another...'

Chase walked towards the waiting car, head held high, but underneath the composed exterior she felt the ugly prickle of discomfort.

'We didn't do the whole church thing.'

'Who said anything about a church?'

'Why are you asking me all these questions?' she burst out as soon as they were in the car. She had kept her voice low but she doubted the driver would have heard anything anyway. A smoked-glass partition separated the front of the car from the back. Presumably it was completely soundproof. The truly wealthy never took chances when it came to being overheard, not even in their own cars. Deals could be lost on the back of an overheard conversation.

Alessandro shifted his muscular body to face her. 'Why are you getting so hot under the collar?'

'I...I'm not. I...I don't like to be surrounded by memories. I think it's always important to move on. There are photos of me and Shaun, just not on show. Do you want to talk about the shelter? I...I've brought all the relevant information with me. We can go over it on the way.' Sitting next to him in the back seat of this car induced the feeling of walls closing in. She fumbled with the clasp of her briefcase and felt his hand close over hers.

'Leave it.'

Chase snatched her hand away. 'I thought you wanted to pick me up so that we could talk about this deal.'

'I'm more interested in the lack of photos. So, none of the husband. Presumably you have albums stashed away somewhere? But none of your family either. Why is that?'

Chase flushed. The adoring middle-class parents who

lived in the country. She was mortified at how easily the lie had come to her all those years ago, but then she had been a kid and a little harmless pretence had not seemed like a sin.

Who wanted a rich, handsome guy to know that you have no family? That your mother had died from a drugs overdose when you were four and from that point on you'd been shoved from foster home to foster home like an unwanted parcel trying to find its rightful owner. How wonderful it had been to create a fictitious family, living in a fictitious cul-de-sac, who did normal things like taking an interest in the homework you were set and coming along to cheer at sports days, even if you trailed in last.

She had loved every minute of her storytelling until it had occurred to her that she had fallen in love with a man who didn't really know a thing about her. The fact that she had been married was just one of the many facts she had kept hidden. By then, it had been too late to retract any of what she had said, and she hadn't wanted to. She'd been enjoying their furtive meetings too much. Okay, so she knew that they would never come to anything, but she still hadn't wanted them to end.

And now…

'My parents…er…moved to Australia a few years ago.' She hated doing this now but for the life of her she didn't know what to do. At least, she thought, sending her non-existent parents on a one-way ticket to the other end of the world would prohibit him from trying to search them out.

Although, why on earth would he do that? The answer came as quickly as the question had: revenge. Find her weak spots and exploit them because he hated her for what he imagined she had done to him. She felt sick when she thought of the number of ways he could destroy her if he set his mind to it and if he had sufficient information in his possession.

'Really?'

'It was…um…always a dream of theirs.'

'To leave their only child behind and disappear half-way across the world?'

'People do what they do,' she said vaguely. 'I mean, don't *you* ever want to disappear to the other end of the earth?' Although she was making sure to stare straight ahead, she could feel his probing eyes on her, and she had to resist the temptation to lick her lips nervously.

'I disappear there quite often, as it happens. But only on business.'

Chase could think of nothing worse than travelling the globe in the quest for more and more money and bigger and bigger deals. Stability, security and putting down roots had always been her number one priority. She had managed to begin the process, and she shuddered to think of him pulling up any of the roots she had meticulously put down over the past few years.

'I'm surprised that after all these years you haven't become tired of trying to make up for your parents' excesses.' It slipped out before she could think and Chase instantly regretted the momentary lapse. The last thing she wanted to do was establish any kind of shared familiarity. 'My apologies,' she said stiffly. 'I shouldn't have said that.'

The reminder of just how much she knew about him underscored his bitterness with a layer of ice. He had never understood how that had managed to happen, how he had found himself telling her things he had never told anyone in his life before.

But then, she had been different. He had never met anyone like her in his life before. Still and yet wryly funny; guarded and yet so open in the way she gazed at him; composed and brilliant at listening. Between the inane yakking of the students—who, at the end of the day, were only a few years younger than him, even though he had been light years removed from them in terms of experience—and the pseudo-bored sophistication of the people he mixed with in his working life, she had been an oasis of peace. And, yes, he had told her things. For a relationship that struggled even to call itself a 'relationship', he had confided and, hell, where exactly had it got him?

He clenched his jaw grimly. 'I'm really not interested in psychobabble,' he told her.

'That's fair,' Chase returned. 'But if I'm not allowed to talk about *your* history then I don't see why you should talk about *mine*.' For starters, the last thing she needed was detailed questions about her so-called parents and where exactly they lived in Australia. And how dared he imply that they somehow didn't care about her simply because they had fulfilled their lifelong dream of emigrating? She almost felt sorry for them...

She half-grinned at that and Alessandro's eyes narrowed. What was going through her head? He had a fierce desire to know.

'So the shelter...' He interrupted whatever pleasant thought had made her smile.

'The shelter...' Chase breathed an inward sigh of relief because this was a subject she was more than happy to talk about. He ceased being a threat as she began to describe life at Beth's House. She smiled at some of the anecdotes about the women who came and went. She told him about the plans Beth had had for upgrading the premises, and then assured him that he could see for himself what she was talking about as soon as he got there. She told him that he had a heart of stone for wanting to knock it down to build, of all things, a stupid mall for people who had more money than sense, but found it was impossible to generate an argument because he hadn't taken her to task for voicing her opinion.

As a professional, a lawyer in charge of the brief, voicing opinions was not within her remit but she hadn't been able to help herself.

By the time they made it to the shelter, her eyes were bright and there was colour in her cheeks. More to the point, her guard was down. Alessandro felt that he was watching the years falling away. He wasn't about to be sucked into believing that she was anything but the liar she undoubtedly was, but he was certainly enjoying the hectic flush in her cheeks and the lively animation on her face.

They made it to the shelter on time. He immediately understood its potential for investment.

The large Victorian house, clearly in need of vast sums of money for essential repair, sat squarely in the midst of several acres of land. For somewhere that was accessible by bus and overland rail, it was a gem waiting to be developed.

The car swung through iron gates that were opened for them only after they had cleared security and they drove up to the house which was fronted by a circular courtyard, in the centre of which stood a non-functioning fountain.

'Beth was left this property by her parents,' Chase told him. 'It's another reason why she's so reluctant to sell. It was her childhood home. She may have converted it into the shelter, but there are a truck load of memories inside.'

'Is this when you begin to repeat your mantra that I have no heart and that my only aim in life is to make money at other people's expense?'

'If the cap fits…' Chase muttered under her breath in yet another show of unprofessionalism that would have had her boss mopping his brow with despair.

Alessandro raised his eyebrows and she had the grace to blush before stepping out of the car into the sunshine.

Alessandro was more than happy to follow her lead. He had never been to a place like this before. They were greeted at the door by Beth, who was in her sixties, a woman with long, grey hair tied back in a ponytail and a warm, caring face. Whatever she felt for the big, bad developer who was moving in to sweep her inheritance out from under her feet, she kept it well hidden.

'Some of the girls who come to us are in a terrible way,' she confided as they toured the house which was laid out simply but effectively inside. 'Chase knows that.'

'And that would be because…?'

'Because I've taken an interest in the place from the very start,' Chase said quickly. 'This sort of thing appeals to me. As I told you, I was very tempted to go into Social Services or the police force, some place where I would be able to do good for the community.'

Alessandro personally thought that it was priceless that she could come over all pious and saintly in his presence but he kept silent. He made all the right noises as he was shown through the house and introduced to girls who looked unbearably young, many of whom had nowhere else to go and were either pregnant or with a child.

'I try and keep them busy,' Beth told him as they went from room to room. 'Most of them don't see the point of continuing their education and it's very difficult for a fifteen-year-old to go to classes when they have a baby to look after. Many of my dear friends are teachers and volunteer to hold classes for them. It's truly remarkable the goodness that exists within us.'

Alessandro's eyes met Chase's over the older woman's head and his lips twisted into a cynical smile. 'It's not a trait I see much of in my line of business,' he said.

'I'm sure,' Beth concurred with a sad shake of her head. 'Now, Chase tells me that you're a very busy man.'

'And yet,' Chase inserted blandly, 'he's managed to make time to come here and see what you're all about. Although, I guess that mostly has to do with him judging the potential for knocking down the house and developing the land as soon as the money changes hands.'

Alessandro was cynical enough to appreciate the underhand dig. No one could accuse her of giving up without a fight. Their eyes tangled and he gave a slight smile of amused understanding of where she was heading with that incendiary statement.

'I will personally see to it that your…operation is transferred to suitable premises,' he affirmed, raking fingers through his dark hair.

'Not the same. Is it, Beth?'

'I will certainly miss the old place,' Beth agreed. 'It may not seem much to you, Mr Moretti, but this is really the only house I've ever known. I've never married, never left the family house. You must think me a silly old woman, but I shall find it very difficult to move on. Well, in truth—and I haven't said this to you, Chase, and you must promise me that you won't breathe a word to anyone else—my thoughts are with retiring from the whole business once I move on. Of course, I shall make sure that some of the money I get from the sale goes towards another shelter—perhaps smaller than this—and Frank and Anne will run it.'

'Frank and Anne?' Alessandro made a point of avoiding the scathing criticism in Chase's eyes. He had absolutely nothing to feel bad about. He knew for a fact that there were vultures hovering over the place, waiting to pick it to pieces, and those vultures would not have parted with nearly as much cash as he was prepared to.

'My dear friends. They help me here. As for me, perhaps a retirement place by the coast… So, I expect you would like to see the land, Mr Moretti? There's a lot of it. My parents were both keen gardeners. Sadly, I haven't had the money to look after it the way it deserves, but if the place is to be redeveloped then I'm sure you won't find that a problem. Chase tells me you have grand plans for it to be an upmarket mall.'

Alessandro marvelled that 'an upmarket mall' could be made to sound like 'the tower of Babel', although when he looked at the older woman there was no bitterness on her face.

'It will bring a great deal of useful traffic to the community.'

So he made money. It was what he did. It was what he had always done. And he was still doing it. He frowned as he remembered Chase's barbed comment about his lifestyle.

He had enough money to retire for the rest of his life and still be able to afford what most people could only ever dream of. So was he trying to make up for his parents' excesses? He was angry and frustrated that he should even be thinking along these lines. His parents were long gone and he had barely known them. How could he have, when, from a toddler, he had been in the care of a succession of nannies who had all fallen by the wayside in favour of boarding school abroad?

His parents had both been products of ridiculously wealthy backgrounds and their marriage had provided them with a joint income that they had both happily and irresponsibly squandered. Untethered by any sense of duty, and riding high on the hippie mentality that had been sweeping through Italy at the time, they had zoned out on recreational drugs, held lavish parties, travelled to festivals all over the world and bought houses which they had optimistically called 'communes' where people could 'get in touch with themselves'. And then, to top it all off, they had seen fit to throw away yet more of their inheritance on a series of ill-advised schemes involving organic farming and the import of ethnic products, all of which had crashed and burned.

Alessandro, barely through with university, had had to grasp what remained of the various companies and haul them back into profit when his parents had died in a boating accident in the Caribbean. Which he had done—in record time and with astounding success.

So what if he had learnt from his parents that financial security was the most important thing in life? So what if nothing and no one had ever been allowed to interrupt that one, single, driving ambition?

A woman in whom he had once rashly confided things that should have been kept to himself was certainly not going to make him start questioning his ethos.

Beth was now chatting amicably about the wonderful advantages of the place being developed, which would bring much-needed jobs to the community. To Alessandro's finely tuned ears, it sounded like forced enthusiasm. It was clear that she hated the thought of leaving the house, and he couldn't help wondering what someone who had always been active in community life in London would do in the stultifying boredom of the seaside.

It was after midday by the time they were standing outside the house saying their goodbyes. His chauffeur had returned for them but Chase pointedly made no move in the direction of the car.

'I'll make my own way back,' she said politely.

'Get in.' Alessandro stood to one side and then sighed with exasperation as she continued to look at him in stubborn silence. 'It's baking hot out here,' he said, purposefully invading her space by standing too close to her. 'And that outfit isn't designed for warm weather.'

'I'll take my chances on avoiding sunstroke.'

'Which is something I would rather not have on my conscience.'

'You don't have a conscience!'

'And you do?'

Chase looked at him with simmering resentment. *He* didn't look all hot and bothered. *He* looked as fabulous, cool and composed as he always did. Plus, he had charmed his way into Beth's affections. She could tell. He hadn't come on too strong, he had pointed out all the benefits of selling the place but in a perfectly reasonable way that no one would have been able to dispute. He was just so... damned *persuasive*! She hated it. And she hated the way she had found herself staring at him surreptitiously, hated the way her imagination had started playing tricks on her, hated the way she had had to fight against being seduced by the dark, deep, velvety tones of his voice.

'You can drop me to the bus stop. It's about a mile from here.'

'Are you going back to your office? Perhaps I could go in, meet all these people you work with... Tell your boss what a great job you've done even though the shelter will be sold. At least you've got me to thank for a reasonably happy Beth.'

'She's not happy.' Chase slid into the back seat, barely appreciating the terrific air conditioning as she grappled with the horror of having him invade her work space as well as having invaded her house. 'And I'm going home, as a matter of fact. I have work I can do there.'

'I've noticed that you try and avoid looking at me as much as possible,' Alessandro said softly. 'Why is that?'

As challenges went, that was about as direct as they came. *Avoid looking at him?* She wanted to laugh at the irony because all she seemed to do was look at him—it was just that she was careful with her staring. She looked at him now and the silence seemed to go on for ever as he gazed right back at her. Her mouth had gone dry and, although she knew that she should be breaking this yawning silence with a suitably innocuous remark, her mind refused to play along.

When he reached out and trailed one finger along her lips, she gasped with shock. There was a sudden, ferocious roaring in her ears and she couldn't breathe. All the strategies she had adopted to keep him at arm's length, to make him know that there was nothing whatsoever between them now aside from a brief, dubious past that no longer meant a thing, disappeared like mist on a hot summer's day.

She was no longer the lawyer with her life under control and he was no longer public enemy number one, the guy who could ruin everything she had built for herself in one fell swoop. She was a woman and he was a man and she still, against all rhyme or reason, wanted him with every incomprehensible, yearning ounce of her being.

'What are you doing?' She finally found her voice and pulled back.

Alessandro smiled. If he had had any doubts that she was still attracted to him, then he had none now. 'Maybe you're right,' he murmured, obediently removing his hand and observing her neutrally. 'Your friend really doesn't want to leave her home. The memories…the experiences… I don't see a bungalow on the coast cutting it, do you?'

'No.' Chase glared at him suspiciously. Her lips were burning from where he had touched them but she refused to cool them with her fingers.

'So I have an interesting proposal to put to you. You'd like me to believe that you're all bleeding heart and caring for the defenceless. Well, how would you like to prove it?'

CHAPTER FOUR

CHASE DIDN'T ANSWER immediately. Alessandro slid back the partition and told the driver to deliver them to a well-known French restaurant. By the time that sank in, the car had already altered course.

'What the heck do you think you're doing?'

'We're going to discuss my proposal over food. It's lunchtime.'

'And I've told you that I need to get back to do some work! Besides, I can't imagine what sort of proposal you have for me that involves you kidnapping me!'

'I like your use of language. Colourful.'

Chase was still burning from where his finger had touched her lips. Her mouth tingled.

'What made your friend decide to go into the good Samaritan business?'

Chase looked at him with unbridled suspicion. He was leaning indolently against the door and she got the feeling that it was all the better to see her. Like the big, bad wolf in the fairy story. 'I don't know what good it will do for you to hear Beth's potted history.'

'I've never known anyone who erects so many obstacles to complicate a perfectly harmless conversation.'

'That's because everyone kowtows to you, I imagine,' Chase offered ungracefully. While he was supremely relaxed, legs slightly open, one arm along the back of the seat, the other hanging loosely over his thigh, she was as tense as a block of wood. Her legs were tightly pressed together. Her lips were tightly compressed. Her fingers were interlinked and white at the knuckles.

'Rich people seem to have that effect,' she continued, avoiding his speculative eyes. 'I've seen it. They like throwing their weight around and they take it for granted that everyone is going to agree with everything they say.'

'You're getting all hot and bothered over nothing,' Alessandro murmured with mild amusement. 'The food at this restaurant is second to none. Have you been there? No? Then you should be looking forward to the experience. So why don't you relax? Tell me about your friend.'

'You didn't seem that interested in her when you were downgrading the price of the place by a thousand pounds per minute.'

'That was before I met her.'

Every argument she engineered seemed to crash into a brick wall. He wasn't interested in arguing with her. She, on the other hand, felt driven to keep arguing because something inside her was telling her that, if she didn't, she might find herself in dangerously unchartered territory. She might start remembering how funny he could be, how thoughtful, how engaging.

'She obviously comes from a fairly wealthy background,' Alessandro murmured encouragingly. 'And yet the road she decided to travel down wasn't exactly the predictable one.'

When he had first laid eyes on Chase after eight years, he had been shocked. And hard on the heels of that shock had come rage and bitterness. It seemed that he had badly underestimated the effect she had had on him. He hadn't put her behind him after all. Had he succeeded in doing that, he would have felt nothing but indifference and contempt. So, yes, revenge had been an option but why make a third party suffer? Weren't there other ways of handling a situation that had landed in his lap?

Rage and bitterness were corrosive emotions and there was one very good way of permanently eliminating them. He smiled with slow, deliberate intent.

Chase took note of that smile and wondered what the heck was going on.

'She hasn't had a…normal upbringing,' she said reluctantly. 'I know this because I knew her before this whole business with the shelter cropped up. Actually, she came to me when she was approached with your company's interference because we were already friends.'

'Interference? I'll overlook your take on my generous offer to buy her out. How did you become friends? Oh no, don't tell me—you were drawn to her because of your "care in the community" approach to life.'

'I'm glad you think it's funny to want to help other people!'

'I don't. I think it's admirable. Like I said, I just find the sentiments hard to swallow when they're coming from you.'

'If I'm such an awful person, why are you taking me out to lunch? Why didn't you let me find my own way back? The sale's agreed. Your legal team could take it from here on in.'

'But then I would miss out on the pleasure of watching you.'

Chase flushed and wondered whether he was being serious or not. She told herself that she didn't care and squashed the unwanted sliver of satisfaction it gave her when she thought of him watching her and *enjoying* it. Suddenly, it felt safer to talk about Beth than to sit in silence, as he looked at her, and speculate on all sorts of things that threw her into confusion.

'Her parents were both really well off,' she blurted out,

licking her lips nervously and wishing he would just stop looking at her in that pensive, brooding way that made the hairs on the back of her neck stand on end. 'They were missionaries. Beth says that as though it's the most normal thing in the world.'

She began to relax and half-smiled as she remembered the conversation they had had years ago when she had first met her. 'I mean, they didn't want to convert anyone, but they wanted to help people in the third world. They rented out their house, which is now the shelter, and took themselves off to Africa where they spent their own money on various irrigation and building projects. In fact, there's a plaque dedicated to them in one of the little villages over there.'

'Good people.' Alessandro thought of his own feckless parents and marvelled at the different ways money could be spent.

'They returned to London to live when Beth was a child. I think they wanted her educated over here. Maybe they thought that they had done what they had set out to do. At any rate, they found that they couldn't just do nothing once they'd come back, so they did lots of volunteer work at various places. They were both in their fifties by then. They'd had Beth when they were quite old. Beth went to university and studied to become an engineer, but found herself drawn to helping others, and when her parents died and she inherited the house and land, the stocks and shares and stuff, she turned the house into a shelter and hasn't looked back.'

'So effectively it's really the only house she's ever lived in and the only work she's ever done.'

'Yes. So there you have it. I don't suppose you can really understand what makes someone like Beth tick.'

'Do me a favour and stop trying to pigeon-hole me because I happen to have a bit of money.'

'A bit of money? You're as rich as Croesus.' They were now in front of the restaurant and Chase stared down at her formal working suit in dismay. 'I don't feel comfortable dining in a place like this wearing a suit.'

'Don't wear the jacket and undo the top three buttons of the shirt.'

'I beg your pardon?' She looked at him, her cheeks bright red, and he grinned at her. A full-on charming grin that knocked her sideways. It was that same grin that had turned her life on its head eight years ago and had made her continue to see him even though everything in her had been screaming at her to stop.

'You heard me.' He stepped out of the car and leaned through to give his driver instructions; when he straightened, it was to see that the prissy jacket, at least, had been left behind in the car.

'What about the buttons?' he asked, with the same sexy grin that made her toes curl and her skin feel tight and prickly.

He didn't give her time to think about it. With their eyes still locked, he undid the offending buttons. The softness of her skin under the starchy top... The glimpse of a cleavage... His breath caught sharply in his throat, mimicking hers.

'Don't do that!' Chase clasped the top and stumbled back a few steps.

'Much better. After you?'

Chase barely took note of the restaurant as they were ushered inside. She had been to a few fancy places since she had started working at Fitzsimmons. Her inclination to stare in awe had thankfully subsided. Nor was her mind in full working order just at the moment, not when her body was still in a state of heightened response at that intimate gesture of his undoing those buttons as though...as though she was his; as though they were the lovers they never, actually, ever had been.

'You said you had a proposal to put to me,' was the first thing she said tightly as soon as they were seated.

Alessandro perused the menu and made a few helpful suggestions which Chase ignored.

'This isn't a social occasion,' she said, choosing the first thing off the menu and shaking her head when he tried to entice her into a glass of wine.

'But it could be,' he returned smoothly. 'Couldn't it?'

'What do you mean?'

'I mean that eight years ago you were a married woman, albeit without my knowledge. Now, you're not. Your husband is no longer around and, unless you have another one stashed up your sleeve somewhere…?'

Caught unawares, Chase laughed shortly. 'Marriage isn't an institution I'll be going near again. Been there, done that, got the tee-shirt.'

Alessandro maintained a steady smile but his jaw hardened. 'Still in mourning?' he asked softly.

'Too wrapped up with my career,' Chase answered steadily.

'You haven't answered my question, but no matter. It really doesn't make any difference to the proposal I have in mind.' So she was still wrapped up in the ex. Why else would she have been at pains to avoid his question? He harked back to his image of the man, good-looking in a thuggish sort of way, her type of guy.

And yet, wrapped up or not in the past, she was still affected by *him*. He knew that with some highly developed sixth sense. As affected by him as he was, unfortunately, affected by her. She was an itch that needed to be scratched and he intended to do just that. Scratch the itch, and he would get her out of his system once and for all.

'So what's your proposal?' Had she ordered crab

mousse? It seemed so, as one was placed in front of her. She tucked into it without appetite.

'Do you get as personally wrapped up with all your clients as you do with this particular one?' Alessandro watched as she toyed with the starter in front of her.

'I told you. I knew her before… She's been a friend for years.'

'She's in her sixties.'

'What does age have to do with anything?' Chase looked at him defensively. Yes, she knew where this was going. Why was a young girl in her twenties friends with a woman in her sixties? Of course, age was no barrier to friendship. Many young people had friends who were much older than they were. What was the big deal? But Beth was one of her few friends, one of the few people in whom she had confided to some extent.

'Nothing. It's laudable. Although…'

'Although what? I suppose you're going to tell me that my friends should all be young and frivolous? That I should be spending my free time going to clubs and drinking instead of hanging out with a woman old enough to be my mother?'

'Although…isn't there something that suggests you shouldn't be working for someone with whom you're personally involved? I wasn't going to lecture you on hanging out with anyone. You choose your own friends, Chase. Interesting, however, that you never seemed to have a lot of those when I knew you eight years ago.'

'I…' She stared at him and, as their eyes tangled, she had the strangest sensation that he could see what was going on in her head. 'How would you know what friends I had or didn't have? You were only around part of the time. We met occasionally. You didn't know what I did in my spare time.'

Alessandro sat back as their food was placed in front

of them. He was surprised to see that he had eaten his starter although he couldn't even remember what he had ordered. She could barely meet his eyes and, again, he had the strangest feeling that there was something going on which he couldn't quite see.

He cursed himself for even being curious. 'True,' he concurred. 'And yet I remember a couple of occasions when kids from your course came up to you. You barely acknowledged them. Once they asked you if you were going to a party and you turned white and got rid of them as soon as you could.' The memory came from nowhere, as though it had been lurking there, just waiting to be aired.

'I...I had a husband.'

Alessandro found that he didn't like thinking about her husband. In fact, the thought of that shaved head, the tattoos, set his teeth on edge.

'Who would have been the same age as you were. Practically a teenager.'

It struck him that that was one of the things that had drawn him to her, the fact that she hadn't acted like a typical teenager. She had been old beyond her years in ways he couldn't quite pin down.

'I've never been into clubs and partying.'

'Never?'

'Why the thousand and one questions, Alessandro?' Her cheeks were bright red. Once upon a time she had actually enjoyed going out. She must have been fourteen or fifteen at the time, unsupervised, hanging out with older kids because most of the kids her age had had some form of parental control.

Schoolwork had been a breeze. She'd never had much need to bury her head in books. Absorbing information had come naturally to her. Oh yes, she had had plenty of time to go to clubs and parties. She frowned and wondered now whether she actually had enjoyed those parties, the dancing, the dim lights...and the confused, angry feeling that she shouldn't be there, that there should be someone in her life who cared enough to try and stop her.

'We're here. Why don't you just tell me what you want to say?'

'How does saving your friend's house sound to you?'

'Saving her house? What are you talking about?' Chase barely noticed that the starters had been removed, to be replaced with yet more exquisite food which she couldn't remember ordering. Despite having said no, her wine glass had been filled, and with a small shrug she sipped some of the cold white wine which tasted delicious. 'Are you going to build your mall around it?'

'Somehow I don't think that people on a quest for designer shoes would feel comfortable having to circumnavigate a shelter for women in need of help, do you?'

Chase thought about that and laughed. It was the first truly genuine laugh he had heard from her since they had met again and, God, how well he remembered the sound of it. Even back then, she hadn't laughed a lot, and when she had it was the equivalent of the sun coming out from behind a cloud. It was exactly the same now and he looked at her with rampant male appreciation.

'I know.' She grinned and leaned towards him confidingly. 'But wouldn't it be a great ploy? They'd all feel so guilty that they would contribute bags of money just to clear their conscience before they went to the shop next door to buy the designer shoes! Beth would never have any financial problems in her life again!'

'It would certainly be a solution of sorts to her financial problems,' Alessandro concurred.

'But you don't mean that, do you?' Her laughter subsided. She nibbled at the edges of her food and decided not to bother trying to second-guess what he had brought her here for.

'Not quite what I had in mind but the image was worth it just to hear the sound of your laugh.'

'Then what?' She ignored the tingling those words produced inside her. 'Will it involve getting any lawyers in? I can't honestly make any far-reaching decisions without reference to my boss.'

'How will he feel when you tell him that you'd had no option but to sell the place to me?' Alessandro asked curiously and Chase gave it some thought.

'A favourable outcome would have been for our client to hang on to the premises. The truth, however, is that our clients don't earn the firm money. The big money comes from our corporate and international clients. Intellectual property lawyers, patent lawyers, even some family lawyers…they earn the big money. I'm just a little cog subsidised by the big-fee lawyers, and I'm there because Fitzsimmons is a morally ethical law firm that believes in putting back some of what they take.'

Alessandro wasn't interested in hearing a long speech on the moral values of Fitzsimmons. 'Wonderful,' he said neutrally. 'But this particular decision won't require involvement from anyone else in your firm.'

'Okay.'

'Nor is it illegal.' Alessandro read the suspicion in her eyes and looked at her with wry amusement. 'However, yes, it will involve the house remaining in your friend's possession. More than that, what if I told you that I would be prepared to pay off all her debts and inject sufficient cash to make sure she can keep the shelter going for a very long time to come?'

Chase gaped at him. For a few seconds, she honestly believed that she had misheard what he had said. Then she thoughtfully closed her knife and fork, wiped her mouth with her linen serviette and searched his face to see whether this was some way of making a fool of her.

'So Beth…' she said slowly, giving him ample time to cut her short and rubbish what she thought he had said, 'gets to keep the house, plus you pay off her debts, plus you put money into renovating and updating the place… am I getting it right?'

'That would be about the size of it.'

'And you would do this because…?' Brow furrowed, she suddenly smiled at him with genuine delight. 'I know why. You were impressed with what you found at the shelter, weren't you? I don't suppose you were expecting it to be as well run as it was. Beth spares no effort when it comes to doing good for those girls. It's hard to go there and not be moved by what you find. I'm so pleased, Alessandro.' She reached out impulsively and covered his hand with hers.

Alessandro looked at the shining glow on her face and was extremely pleased with himself for being the one to put it there.

'Can I call and tell her?' Chase asked excitedly. 'No, perhaps I'd better not do that.' She flashed him an apologetic smile. 'You'll have to forgive the lawyer in me, but we'll have to get this all signed on the dotted line. But, once she knows, she'll be over the moon. Between you and me, I don't honestly think she was looking forward to a quiet retirement by the seaside.'

'So you agree with me that this is a good idea?'

'Of course I do! I'd be a fool not to.' Even with her defences up, knowing how he felt about her after what she had done to him, she knew that there was a blazingly good streak in him. Those lectures he had given had been given for free, and he had taken considerable time out to individually help some of the students, had actually offered internships to a couple of them. He hadn't just been as sexy as hell, he had shown her a glimpse of humanity that she had never seen before and that, amongst other things, had roped her in and kept her tethered in a place she had known was desperately dangerous.

'Naturally, there's no such thing as a free lunch in life.' Alessandro shook his head ruefully, the very picture of a man who regrets that there wasn't. 'I wish I could say that I was the perfect philanthropist, but you have to understand that all this will cost me a small fortune.'

The smile died on her face. The bill was brought to them and she automatically reached for her bag but it had been settled before she could rummage out her wallet and pay her fair share. 'Of course it will,' she agreed coolly. 'And you'll want to be repaid for your largesse. Will your rates be competitive?'

'Shall we go?'

Chase could feel disappointment rising inside her as he waited for her to gather her things, standing aside so that she could precede him out of the restaurant. Once outside, she didn't bother with her stupid jacket. He had been right when he had remarked that it was impractical for the weather.

What had he been playing at? Stringing her along with all manner of empty promises only to yank them all back at the last minute? Didn't he realise that, if Beth had wanted to borrow money so that she could clear her debts and get the shelter really going, she would have gone to the bank? Of course, Chase thought uncomfortably, she *had* tried that some time ago but to no avail. She simply hadn't had the collateral to get a loan of the size she required, even though the bank manager had known her parents. Money was just not being lent, not to ventures that had nothing to gain. Had Alessandro checked that out himself and come to the conclusion that he could provide her with the money but jack up the interest rates?

'I really believed you for a minute,' she simmered, barely noticing that she was being ushered into the back seat of his car. 'I really thought that you had been so impressed by what you saw that you decided to do the right thing. I really thought that there was a part of you that was the same guy who gave internships to those girls years ago, and the same guy who put in extra time helping that little group of Asian students through their language barriers with some of their papers.'

'You remember. Those girls have been promoted several times. One left a year ago to have a baby and returned a few months ago to resume work. Two of the Chinese students work in my Hong Kong offices.'

'You kept in touch with them.' She fought against the pull of a connection that threatened her valued self-control. She severed the incipient connection. 'Where are we going?'

'To discuss my proposal further. Out of public earshot.'

'Beth can't afford to pay you back for a loan.' Back to business, but her mind was still straying dangerously close to memories of the man she had once been so irresistibly drawn to—the man she knew still existed even if those complex sides, revealed all those years ago, would never again get an airing in her presence.

'Whoever mentioned loans?'

'You're confusing me, Alessandro.'

'Ditto,' he murmured under his breath. He looked at her in silence, his searing attraction laced with a poignant familiarity that wasn't doing his libido any favours, until she shifted uncomfortably and took notice of her surroundings. They were away from the hustle and bustle.

'And you haven't said where we're going. This isn't the way back to my house.'

'Well spotted. It's the way to mine.'

'What?' Chase immediately felt her pulses begin to race. She didn't want to be here, in this car! Far less heading to his place, wherever that was! He had just pulled a

cheap trick, whatever he had said about his offer not being
a loan. He had really shown his true colours, aside from
which she knew that she should steer clear of him. But
the memory of how much she had craved to see where he
lived eight years ago slammed into her with the force of a
freight train. 'Let me out of this car *immediately.*'

'Calm down.'

'I'm *perfectly* calm.'

'You're as perfectly calm as a volcano on the point of
eruption. Relax. We'll be there in ten minutes.'

Chase felt ill at the thought of stepping foot into his private space. She had never thought that she would see him
again and, now that she had, she should be laying down
clear boundaries. Instead, the lines were blurring. He had
come to her house, seen the way she lived, formed his
opinions. Now she was going to his.

She watched with growing panic as the sleek, black
car manoeuvred through quiet streets, finally turning into
an avenue through imposing black wrought-iron gates.
The houses here were beyond spectacular. No superlative
could do justice to the pristine white-and-cream facades,
the ornate foliage, the lush greenery, the air of indecently
wealthy seclusion. The cars were all top of the range, high
end.

So this was where he lived. Never in her wildest, twenty-
year-old's dreams could she have come up with this.

'I'm not comfortable with this,' she said automatically
as his driver opened the passenger door for her.

'I wasn't comfortable conducting a private conversation in a public place.'

'There was nothing private about our conversation. It
was a business deal.' But she couldn't help staring at the
enormous house in front of her, the perfectly shaped shrubs
on either side of the black door, the highly polished brass
of the knocker. Nor could she help feeling, in some deep,

dark part of her, that their conversation had been threaded with undercurrents that were anything but businesslike.

'I love the way you constantly argue with me,' Alessandro remarked drily as he opened the front door and stood aside so that she brushed past him. 'It's refreshing. You did that eight years ago as well. And it was refreshing then.'

There had been times, countless times, when he had just wanted to scoop her to him and silence those feisty arguments with his mouth…just kiss them away. But he had been prepared to bide his time. He had been prepared to do way too much to attain the eventual goal of just having her. She had taught him the art of patience, damn fool that he had been.

Chase didn't say anything. She was too busy being impressed. It wasn't just the size but the pristine perfection: marble flooring, the colour of pale honey, was broken by silky rugs. The paintings on the walls varied in size but were recognisable—who on earth had paintings on their walls that were *recognisable*? The impressive staircase leading up gave onto a landing which was dominated by a massive stained-glass window that did magical things to the sunlight filtering through it.

She came back to planet Earth to find that Alessandro was watching her, hands in his pockets.

'You have a beautiful place,' she said politely.

Alessandro dutifully looked around him, as though taking stock of where he lived for the first time, then he shrugged. 'It works for me. Come through.'

'I honestly don't see why you couldn't have laid out your terms and conditions for this so-called "not a loan" at the restaurant.' But she followed as he led the way towards a kitchen that looked as though it had never been used. He didn't do cooking; she remembered him telling her that way back when.

'Have you *ever* used this kitchen?' she asked, perching on one of the top-of-the-range chrome and leather bar stools by the counter and watching as he attempted to make sense of the complicated coffee machine.

'You don't want coffee, do you?' he eventually asked, turning to glance at her over his shoulder.

'If I did, would you be able to figure out how that thing works?'

'Unlikely.'

'Tea would be nice.' She hadn't appreciated just how rich he was. These were the surroundings of a man to whom money was literally no object. She bristled when she thought of him holding her to ransom by reducing his offer for the shelter just because he could.

'I'm very good with a kettle and some tea bags.' He hunted them down, opening and closing cupboards. 'I come in here very rarely,' he offered by way of explanation. 'I have a housekeeper who makes sure it's stocked and a chef who does all my cooking on the occasions when I happen to be in.'

'Lucky you.'

There wasn't a single woman on the planet, Alessandro thought, who would have offered that sarcastic response when confronted with the reality of his wealth. 'You don't mean that.'

'You're right. I don't.' She took the cup of tea from him. The cup was fine-bone china, weirdly shaped, with an art deco design running down one side. When she thought of him trying and failing to work out how his high-tech appliances worked, she could feel a smile tugging the corners of her mouth, but there was no way that she would be seduced by any windows of vulnerability in him.

'Why do you have all these gadgets in here if you don't cook and barely use the kitchen?'

'I remain eternally optimistic.'

Chase wished he wouldn't do that, wouldn't undermine

her defences with his sense of humour. She didn't want to remember how he had always been able to make her laugh. She didn't want him to make her laugh now.

'Well, now we're here, maybe you could explain this business with the shelter?'

Alessandro looked at her. He wondered what it was about her that just seemed to capture his imagination and hold it to ransom.

'You have no idea what goes through me when I think of what you did eight years ago,' he murmured.

'You brought me here so that you could talk about that?' Chase fidgeted uncomfortably. She wanted to drag her disobedient eyes away from him but somehow she couldn't.

'But the past belongs in the past. What's the good dredging it up every two seconds? The best thing I could do right now is send you on your not-so-merry way, out of my life once and for all. Unfortunately, I find that there's something holding me back.'

'What?' It was a barely whispered response. She cleared her throat and did her utmost to remember that this was just an opponent whom she happened to have known a long time ago. It didn't work. She still found herself hanging onto his every word with shamefully bated breath, watching him watching her, and letting those deep, dark looks penetrate every fibre of her being. Dampness pooled shamefully between her legs, physical proof of something she was loath to admit, and her nipples tingled, sensitive and taut against her lacy bra. 'What's holding you back?' She shifted, felt her slippery wetness making her panties uncomfortable.

'You.' Alessandro allowed that one word to ferment in the lengthening silence between them until it was bursting with significance.

'I have no idea what you're talking about.'

'Of course you do,' he drawled smoothly. 'We can both

waste a little time while I indulge your desire to feign ignorance but what would be the point? We'll end up getting to the same place eventually. Despite what happened between us, despite the fact that my levels of respect for you are lamentably non-existent, I find that I'm still sexually attracted to you. And I wouldn't be telling you this now if I didn't know that it was a two-way street.

'And don't bother trying to deny it. I've seen the way you look at me when you think my attention is somewhere else and I've seen the way you respond whenever I get within a two-foot radius of you. We had it once and we have it again. It's a shame but...' He shrugged with graceful elegance.

'You're...you're mad...' Her words said one thing; her treacherous body however, was, singing a different refrain.

'Am I? I don't think so.'

Chase watched, mesmerised, as he slowly stood up and breached the short distance separating them to plant his hands on either side of her chair, locking her into place so that she could only raise her eyes upwards to stare at him. She could feel the pulse in her neck beating wildly, a physical giveaway that every word he was saying struck home.

'I'm the lawyer working for Beth; sure, we know each other...' The word faltered and died in her throat as he cupped her cheek with his hand and stroked it with his thumb.

Years ago, their chaste relationship had pulsated with unexplored passion and unspoken, untested lust. Now, as his hand remained on her cheek, she shuddered and resisted the urge to sink into the caress.

'Please, Alessandro, don't.'

'Your body is telling me something different.'

'I don't want to start any kind of relationship with you.'

'Relationship?' Alessandro queried huskily. 'Who's talking about a relationship? I could no more have a relationship with you than I could with a deadly snake. No, I'm not interested in a relationship. I'm interested in having sex with you, plain and simple. Just like you're interested in having sex with me. Don't you want to touch what you spent months staring at eight years ago? Don't you want to finish what you started? I do. A lot.'

Chase opened her mouth to tell him to get lost but nothing emerged. His cool, brilliant dark eyes held her in a trance even though she knew that every word that left that perfect mouth was offensive and insulting.

And yet…her imagination was going crazy. The fantasies she had had of him touching her all those years ago sprang from the box into which they had been firmly locked and attacked her on all fronts. She weakened at the thought of his fingers stroking the wetness between her legs, his mouth kissing the twin peaks of her breasts, nipping the tight buds of her nipples, suckling on them while he continued to stroke her dampness…

'So here's the deal.' Alessandro was finding it hard to contain his excitement at the prospect of netting the prey that had once escaped him and putting to bed, once and for all, feelings that had no place in his life. Her skin was like satin beneath his fingertips. 'You sleep with me for as long as I want you to and the shelter stays. Renovated, updated and modernised. Your friend's debts will be cleared.'

'You want to *pay* me for services rendered?'

'I want to take what you want to give. In return, you get the shelter. And please don't try and tell me that you don't want to touch me. You do.' His mouth met hers and Chase braced her hands on his shoulders, determined to push him away. But instead she was horrified to find that she was caressing him; that her mouth was returning his kiss with equal urgency; that she was sinking into him like a person starved of nourishment; that she was whimpering, little mewling sounds that shocked and excited her in equal measure and, worse, when he finally pulled back that the sudden space between them felt cold and unwelcome.

'I think I've proved my point.' There was a betraying unsteadiness in his voice. He might not like her or respect her but, God, did he want her. More than anything or anyone. 'Let's finish this business. A couple of weeks, tops, and you can disappear back to whatever life you have, having made your friend a very happy bunny.'

Chase had withdrawn and was rising to her feet, arms tight around her body.

'I'll never do that, Alessandro!'

Alessandro shrugged and tried to wrestle back his self-control, even though just watching her was affecting him in ways he could barely quantify. 'You have forty-eight hours to give me your answer then the deal is off the table.'

'I've already given you my answer!'

'Forty-eight hours…' he repeated, his eyes roving over her flushed face and her defiant yet tellingly shaken expression. 'And let's just wait and see if your answer remains the same after you've…thought things through.'

CHAPTER FIVE

BETH TELEPHONED THAT evening. She could barely contain her excitement. She might be able to hang on to the shelter!

'What do you mean?' Chase asked tentatively. She had spent the past few hours unable to get down to work. Alessandro's offer kept playing in her head over and over again, like a tape recording on a loop. She had stalked out of his house, her head held high, and he had made no attempt to stop her. She thought that that, in itself, displayed a level of arrogance that should really have had her turning her back on him for ever. She loathed arrogance.

Unfortunately, along with her determination not to be browbeaten into making a pact with the devil, there lurked the uncomfortable awareness that, devil or not, he roused something in her she didn't want but couldn't resist. He had kissed her and her whole world had felt as though it had been tilted on its side. It was the same something that had been there eight years ago; the same something that had made her behave in a way she had known she shouldn't. Sexual attraction: he had put his finger on it. Sexual attraction and more...

'I had a call from Mr Moretti.'

'Ah...' She drifted over to the sofa and sat down.

'He's a lot more compassionate than I originally gave him credit for. You know, when this whole business started, well, I just thought of him as a human bulldozer, not caring what or who got in his way.'

Chase smirked. 'What did he say?'

'That he's spoken to you and you've both come up with a plan to secure the future of the shelter; you're both trying to iron out the creases. Chase, my dear, I can't tell you how overjoyed I would be if this worked out. I've been dreading telling the girls that they'll have to go, plus the waiting list is so long of people who need us. Not to mention the seaside idea. Never could quite see myself retiring by the coast and having coffee mornings with all the other retirees.'

'I'm sure there's more to life by the coast than coffee mornings.' Her mind was in a whirl. She was also incensed. So much for the forty-eight hours after which her decision would be final! How could she have been foolish enough to believe that Alessandro wouldn't exert influence over a decision he wanted? 'Lots of people go down there to…er…sail…' she said vaguely.

'Can't think of anything worse. Drive me mad!'

'Did he mention what this idea of…ours happens to be?' Chase prodded gently.

'Not a word!' Beth hooted. 'Said it was something he wanted kept up his sleeve. Probably to do with tax!'

'Sorry?'

'Well, don't these awfully rich people enjoy tax breaks by giving money to charity? We *are* a registered charity…'

Chase sighed and decided to lay off the details of any such scheme. Despite a sharp brain and her degree in engineering, Beth's interest in all things financial was sketchy at best.

'Sometimes,' she said, noncommittal.

'At any rate, it all sounds very promising. I know what you're going to say, my dear! Don't count your chickens… But I get a good feeling from that young man. Did the minute I met him. Showed a real interest in everything we do here at the shelter.'

Alternatively, Chase thought, the man was a skilled actor with a golden tongue. Take your pick.

She spent another twenty minutes on the line as Beth waxed lyrical about Alessandro, and as soon as her friend was off the phone she hunted down the business card he had given her and telephoned him on his mobile.

'Well, that was a low trick!' was the first thing she said the minute she heard his voice on the other end.

At a little after nine, Alessandro had just finished wrapping up a two-hour conference call and was about to leave the office, which was deserted aside from him. In the act of reaching for his jacket, he flung it down on the leather sofa instead and relaxed to take her call. 'So Beth called you,' he drawled without an ounce of shame. 'I thought she might. She certainly was over the moon when I spoke to her. Charming woman.'

'You're a low-down, sneaky rat!'

Alessandro grinned. Whatever Chase's downsides, she was by far and away the most outspoken, feisty woman he had ever met in his entire life. It would probably be a tiresome trait in the long run, but just for the moment it was certainly invigorating.

'Now, now, now...is that any way to speak to your friend's knight in shining armour?'

Chase detected the wicked grin in his voice and gritted her teeth in frustration. 'What did you tell her?'

'Long conversation. I'll fill you in when we next meet.'

'How could you?'

'How could I what? Make that delightful woman one very happy lady?'

'Try and twist my arm into accepting your...your... No, I take that back; I understand perfectly how you did that!'

'It's comforting to know that you can read me like a

book. That way, there will be no mixed messages between us. Now, why don't you carry on working and I'll call you in the morning?'

'I haven't been able to do a scrap of work today!'

'Too busy thinking about me?'

Chase made an inarticulate sound of pure frustration and racked her brains for a clever riposte.

'Well, why don't you get some well-deserved beauty sleep and we'll talk in the morning…or later, if you'd like. After all, your forty-eight hour deadline won't yet be up. Don't worry. I'll be in touch.'

She was left clutching the phone which had gone dead because he had hung up on her. He'd barely heard her out! She felt that there was a lot more anger to be expressed. Unfortunately, without an adversary at which to direct her attack, she was left simmering and fuming on her own as she flounced down in front of the television, having abandoned all attempts at reviewing her caseload.

She was barely aware of what she was watching. It appeared to be a crime drama with an awful lot of victims and an extremely elusive murderer. She had fully zoned out of the story line when, at a little after ten, she heard the insistent buzz of the doorbell and was jerked into instant red alert.

Alessandro.

Surely he wouldn't have the cheek to show up at this hour at her house?

Of course he wouldn't. Why would a shark bother to stalk a minnow when it knew full well that the minnow would swim into its gaping jaw of its own free will?

Much more likely that it was Beth; as she slipped on her bedroom slippers and padded out to the front door, she was already trying to work out what she might say to begin killing her friend's already full-blown optimism.

She pulled open the door to Alessandro and her mouth fell open in surprise.

'Rule one,' he said, strolling past her to take up residence in the sitting room before she had had a chance to marshal her thoughts into order. 'When living in London, never open the door unless you know who's going to be standing on your doorstep.' He turned towards her, which instantly made her feel like a guest in her own home. 'I could have been anyone.'

'And, unfortunately for me, you're not!' She folded her arms and looked at him with gimlet-eyed stoniness. 'What are you doing here?'

'You said that you were finding it impossible to get down to work because you were thinking of me, so I thought I'd drop by.'

'I never said any such thing!' He was not in work clothes but in a pair of black jeans and a grey polo-necked shirt. He looked drop-dead gorgeous, which did nothing for her composure, because she felt far from drop-dead anything in her tatty old jogging bottoms and a tee-shirt that had lost its shape in the wash years ago. She also wasn't wearing a bra and she was conscious of her nipples poking against the cotton of the tee-shirt.

'I must have misunderstood. My apologies. But I'm here now, so maybe you could offer me a cup of coffee? Nothing stronger. I'm driving.'

'I wasn't about to offer you anything!'

'Don't you want to let off steam? You were breathing brimstone and fire down the line less than an hour ago.'

'Because you went behind my back and led Beth to believe that you were going to save her shelter—worse, led her to believe that the decision lies with *me*!'

'Oh, but it does, doesn't it?' He stared at her with a mixture of cool certainty and mild surprise that she should question the obvious.

'What on earth did you tell her?'

'That you and I were working on a plan to see whether the place could be saved and money invested.'

'Because you're such a good guy, right?'

'Let's not go down the tortuous route of moral ethics, Chase. However non-existent you think mine are, you're not exactly in a position to point fingers.'

Chase chewed her lip and glared impotently at him. 'I'll make you some coffee.' She shrugged and turned away. He was here now, in her house, smug and self-satisfied at the awkward position into which he had shoved her; sooner or later they would have to talk, so why not make it sooner? She couldn't see herself getting to sleep in a hurry.

She returned with two mugs of coffee to find him ensconced in one of the deep chairs, the very picture of a man totally relaxed in his surroundings.

'You gave me your word that I would have forty-eight hours.'

'And nothing's changed on that front,' Alessandro said smoothly. 'You still do. I've just thrown an extra something into the mix.'

'And that wasn't fair.'

'Between us, the gloves are off. You're as scheming as I am, so don't even bother to try and play the wounded party with me.' He had not been able to get her out of his head and, the more he thought about her, the more urgent his need to have her became. The sooner he had her, sated this voracious lust, the faster he would be rid of her. He couldn't wait.

Nudging the back of his mind was the uncomfortable truth that he was not a vengeful man by nature, that this sort of revenge was born from emotions which he had handed over to her eight years ago only to find them thrown back in his face. She had shown him his vulnerability and the force of his reactions now lay in that one, unmentioned reality. It was something he could hardly stand to admit even to himself and it lay there, buried like a pernicious weed, even when he had told himself over the years that he had had a narrow escape; that getting involved with a woman such as she had turned out to be would have been an unmitigated disaster.

'You think you know me,' Chase muttered bitterly, and Alessandro narrowed his eyes to look at her.

'By which you mean… Tell me.'

'Nothing,' she said in a harried undertone. 'This is an impossible situation.'

'No, it's not. It's the sound of the wheel turning full circle.'

'You don't like me, you don't respect me, so why on earth would you want to sleep with me? You must be able to snap your fingers and have a thousand women standing to attention and saluting. Why bother with the one who doesn't want to fall in line?'

Chase projected into the future. So she turned him down and the shelter became a shopping mall with her friend retreating to the seaside, where she would live out the rest of her days, bored, grumbling and dissatisfied. Furthermore, what would happen to their friendship? Alessandro had put her in an invidious position, for would her friend ever forgive her for being the one who failed to 'iron out the crease' that would have enabled her to hang on to what she loved?

She would never be able to tell Beth what that particular crease was and eventually the wonderful friendship they had would wither and die under the weight of Beth's misunderstanding and simmering resentment. How could it not?

'I've always considered myself a man to rise to the challenge,' Alessandro said coolly.

'And I'm your challenge.' There was no point moaning

about the unfairness of fate. He had seriously upped the ante by involving Beth and now she had to step up to the plate one way or another. He might well consider himself a guy who couldn't resist a challenge, but when had *she* ever been the sort of woman to back down? Her days of doing that had been put behind her.

And he talked about unfinished business… Wasn't it the same for her? Over the years, through everything that had happened, hadn't he been the burr under her skin? Hadn't she had broken nights dreaming of him? Hadn't she re-played scenarios in her head during which what they had had came to fruition?

More to the point, hadn't all those scenarios sprung back into instant life the second she had laid eyes on him again? Common sense had wrestled with what she considered her stupid weakness, because he was as out of bounds now as he had ever been, despite the fact that Shaun was no longer on the scene. But common sense was failing to win the battle. She knew she looked at him, wondered…

'Are you going to tell me that I'm not yours?' Alessandro asked softly. Two adults, he thought, who wanted each other and this time no hidden obstacle lurking in the way. On top of that, so much for her to get out of it. So where was the problem? He had never had the slightest curiosity to plumb the hidden depths of any woman, yet now he had a sudden, urgent desire to reach into her head and discover what was going on behind that beautiful, enigmatic facade. The thrill of the unexplored was heady and erotic and it took a surprising amount of will power to remain where he was, holding on to silence as a weapon of persuasion.

'It feels…odd. Just not right.'

'But you can't deny that what I'm saying makes sense. If we cut through all the redundant emotion, if we leave bitterness and the past aside, don't we still fancy the hell out of one another?'

Chase thought of his hands on her body, touching her. She had stayed far away from the opposite sex over the past eight years. Offers had been plentiful, some of them horribly insistent, but there was no way she was going to get involved with any man ever again.

So here she was, nearing thirty, unattached, with barely any social life to speak of. Wasn't it time for her to re-join the human race? And wouldn't she be able to do that once, as he had put it, business between them was finally finished? If she were brutally honest with herself, hadn't Alessandro been as much a reason for where she was now with her life, as Shaun had been? He had had such a dra-matic hold on her all those years ago and the way things had ended between them had scarred her to the extent that she had just simply withdrawn.

'It just feels so…cold and detached. So businesslike.' She rubbed her lightly perspiring hands along the soft cot-ton of her jogging pants.

'You're looking for flowers and chocolates and court-ship?' His mouth curled into a cynical smile. 'I believe I fell into that trap once before. I don't repeat my mistakes twice.'

Chase thought she could detect the rapid beating of her heart as he stared at her broodingly. She felt as though she had one foot raised over the edge of a precipice as she made her mind up as to whether to jump or not. Yet, she knew that that was a fallacy. She was older, wiser and tougher and, if this felt like a business arrangement, then it had to be said that business arrangements came with definite upsides. For starters, she would know all the parameters. She would not be hurt. She would be taking from him just as he would be taking from her and, when they walked away from each other, she would be freed from the strange half-emptiness of regret that had been her companion for the past eight years.

It was a tantalising thought.

As though she had opened a door to a gremlin, she was suddenly released from the constraints of having to fight the attraction that had been gnawing away at her. She *imagined*...and the images were so vivid that she felt faint.

'I can't think of anything I would want less than a courtship,' she informed him with as much cool detachment as she could muster. Certainly not flowers or chocolate. He had given her those once before. He must have realised, in the aftermath of her dumping him, that those tokens had hit the bin before she had had time to make it back to her flat. Thank goodness she had bluntly refused to accept anything else. At least he would never be able to add 'gold-digger' to all the other bitter insults he had heaped on her.

Watching her closely, Alessandro knew that he had won. She was going to be his. And yet, instead of the satisfaction of accomplishment, he was irked by the notion that she didn't want a courtship because she had already had a courtship from the one guy who had really counted in her life.

Who gave a damn about the ex-husband? The bald fact was that the man was no longer around and the one woman who had eluded him was going to be his. He was not now, and never would be, in competition with a ghost. When he was through with her, he would discard her and she could return to the photo albums she had stashed in a drawer somewhere. He didn't care. He would have got the one and only thing he wanted from her and for which, essentially, he was prepared to pay a high price, bearing in mind all the money that would need pumping into that shelter if it was to achieve habitable status.

'Is that because you've decided to limit yourself to one and that role was filled by your dearest, departed ex—or because you've had so many in the intervening years that you're sick of them?'

'I've been so busy in the past few years that I haven't had time for…for any kind of relationship.' How strange it felt to be sharing this kind of confidential information! Over time, she had become defined by her need for privacy. She knew that most of her colleagues her age thought she was weird. She knew they thought that, with her looks, she should be putting herself out there instead of working all the hours God made before scuttling off to a house to which none of them had ever been invited. She didn't care, and she had become so accustomed to self-containment that she now looked at Alessandro, wide-eyed, startled by her outburst.

'You mean…?' Curiosity kicked in with cursed force.

'There's actually nothing out of the ordinary about that. Relationships require time and I haven't had a lot of that while I've been trying to climb up the career ladder.' Chase knew how she sounded: tough, hard, cold. This wasn't the person she had ever set out to be but she wasn't going to apologise for the fact that her life hadn't been a round of parties, late nights and sex with random men.

'So ever since your husband died…?' he encouraged.

Chase tilted her chin defensively. 'I know how it must sound to someone like you.'

'Someone like me?'

'I expect you have an active sexual life. Lots of women. You're rich, you're good-looking, you're self-assured. You wouldn't have a clue how I could…hold off on relationships for quite a long time.'

'I managed it eight years ago. With you.' He shook his head, impatient with himself. And he did, actually, understand. Grief and mourning could do all sorts of things and have all manner of consequences. That said…

'It's not healthy,' he said brusquely.

Chase reddened. 'I haven't asked for your opinion,' she

said defensively. 'And the only reason I'm telling you this is because you might want to have a rethink.'

'Not following you.'

'I'm a little rusty in that particular area.' She gave a brittle, nonchalant laugh, but inwardly every part of her felt exposed, vulnerable and uncertain. What on earth was she doing? She wasn't like the women she imagined him being drawn to; she lacked the finesse and the experience. Did she want to risk the humiliation of having him look at her with amusement and disappointment just because she needed to know what she had missed all those years ago? Because, sure, the shelter would be a happy bonus, but she was already yielding for reasons that were far more complex than the desire to save her friend's shelter. Shelter or no shelter, she would never have allowed herself to be manipulated into doing something she didn't want to do.

Alessandro frowned. He had been quick to assert that his proposal was a non-negotiable arrangement designed to assuage the inconvenient need he had to sleep with her and thereby get her out of his system. He had been even quicker to inform her that he would not be investing it with any bells and whistles. It would be sex, no more or less. Yet, he found that he didn't care for the cool approach she was taking. Hell, she was still sitting a million miles away from him!

'I'll cope. Does that mean that you've made your mind up?'

'Perhaps you're right. Perhaps I've been curious. Maybe we do need to…eh…take what we have a step further.' Her heart was beating like a drum. 'But if I accept,' she continued firmly, because it was important for him to know that she wasn't making a decision based on blackmail or unfair persuasion, 'it's not to do with the shelter. Much as I love Beth, I would never do something I didn't want to because of her.'

'Right now, the only thing that matters is that we're going to be lovers.' He gave her a slashing, sexy smile and patted the space next to him on the sofa. 'So why don't you come and sit next to me and we can continue *bonding* with a little less physical distance between us?'

Chase thought she could actually hear her own painful breathing. Fear and apprehension at touching him, being close to him, warred with unbridled excitement. She had stepped off the side of the precipice and she had no idea what she had let herself in for but it was an adventure she needed to have. It was a situation over which she could only hope to exercise control and, for someone who had constructed walls of control all around her, it was a daunting prospect. But she had done daunting before. Many, many times. She could handle daunting.

'How long do you think this will take?'

'Come again?' Alessandro had never had to fight this hard for anyone. Sexual attraction had proved stronger than his very justifiable bitterness and dislike. He had had to swallow a lot and yet, having done that, having got her to the place he wanted, surely the going should get less tough?

'How long do you think it will take before we get past this...thing? A night? A couple of days?'

'How the hell should I know?' Alessandro raked his fingers through his hair and frowned at her. 'And why are we talking about timelines, anyway? All I want to do right now is touch you, so why don't we dispense with the conversation and get down to business?' He sprawled back, arms extended on the back of the sofa, legs loose and open.

He was the very essence of man at his most physical, Chase thought with a shiver, utterly and beautifully masculine; she licked her lips cautiously. She wanted this so badly. It felt as though it was something she had never stopped wanting. She tentatively closed the distance between them to sit like a wooden doll next to him.

'I feel I should tell you,' she whispered as Alessandro lazily removed one arm from the back of the sofa to trail it along her neck.

'You talk a lot,' he growled and then, almost from nowhere, plucked from thin air, 'You always did. As though you had too many words inside you that needed to get out.' He laughed softly, caught unaware by the memory. 'Do you remember the way you would mention a case file and then force me to have an opinion so that you could practise shooting it down in flames?'

Hell, what was he going on about? He angled his body round and pulled her towards him and it was like the promise of heaven. The undiluted thrill of having her in his arms was incomparable and he urgently sought her mouth, plundering it while his hands moved down to circle her waist. His erection was steel-hard and painful. More than anything else, he wanted to rip down those unattractive jogging bottoms, pull aside her panties and then just thrust into her, hard and fast, until he got explosive relief. There would be time enough to do the whole gentle foreplay stuff later.

Chase could feel the raw energy emanating from him in waves but that soft laugh, that nostalgic memory he had laid out bare for her without really thinking, was strangely seductive, strangely relaxing. Fingers that had been curled into his polo shirt suddenly splayed against his chest and she struggled back from him.

'Wait…'

'I'm not sure I can.' But he reluctantly drew back, his breathing ragged and uneven. She was stripped of her tough, outer shell, the consummate lawyer and assertive career woman. He glimpsed a uniquely feminine vulnerability that startled him, because she was the last woman on the planet he would ever have labelled *'vulnerable'.*

Once upon a time, sure, but then once upon a time he'd been an idiot.

'I'm not into playing games,' he drawled just in case she got it into her head that she could string him along for a second time. 'And, just in case you think that you might be able to pull off any "one step forward, two steps back" tactic, then forget it. This time round, you're dealing with a different person, Chase. My levels of tolerance when it comes to you are non-existent.'

'I know they are!' Whatever the backdrop to what they had had eight years ago, it all seemed so innocent now in retrospect. 'It's just…'

'Just *what*, Chase?'

'Never mind.' She wasn't looking for sweet nothings whispered in her ear nor was she looking for any shows of affection. She told herself that she was perfectly comfortable with an 'arrangement', yet as she reached to hook her fingers under the tee-shirt to pull it over her head, she knew that she was breathing too quickly, close to freezing up.

'Oh for goodness' sake,' Alessandro groaned and caught her hands in his. 'Why tell me that this is what you want if you have to squeeze your eyes tightly shut and give every impression of a woman who has to grin and bear it?'

'I *do* want it,' Chase insisted but she could hear the give-away wavering in her voice and she hated it.

'Then what's the problem?' He took in the hectic flush in her cheeks. What was going on here? Shouldn't this be straightforward—two consenting adults getting something out of their system? 'Tell me.'

'You're not really interested.'

'Let me be the one who decides that.' He nuzzled her ear and smiled as she quivered, because it tickled.

'I'm… I've…' She took a deep, steadying breath. 'I've never really been into sex,' she said in a rush. 'I know you can't bear me, and your tolerance levels are low, but I can't just fall on this sofa with you and have wild sex.'

'Never really been into sex?' Alessandro's voice held accusatory disbelief. 'You were a married woman,' he pointed out with ruthless directness. 'Married at what age—eighteen? Younger? Are you telling me that you were a gymslip wife who didn't enjoy sleeping with her husband?'

'I don't want to talk about Shaun,' Chase said quickly. *Or,* she mentally tacked on, *anything to do with my past, the past you think you know but don't.*

Alessandro looked at her in silence for a long time. She was flustered as hell but trying hard to put on a show of strength and assertiveness. Did he need all of this? It was just sex and, yet again, that surge of curiosity that was more insistent than the cold logic he wanted to impose. 'Why don't you want to talk about him?'

'Because…there's no point. I'll just say that things are never what you think they are.' Too much information. 'But it's been a long time for me…' she concluded hurriedly.

'You just want me to take it slowly, do you?'

Chase nodded.

'In that case, what about a show of good faith?' He shot her a slow smile. 'Taking it slow is one thing,' he murmured, playing with a strand of her hair whilst he tried to halt his runaway mind, which wanted to ask her what she had meant by her enigmatic remark about things never being what you thought they were. 'A standstill pace, on the other hand, just won't do. So why don't we both get naked and see what happens next?' He watched her carefully, wanting her more than anything, prepared to do the complex if that was what it took. 'If you're not comfortable down here, then you could always give me a tour of upstairs and we can end up in your bedroom. How does that sound?'

Chase nodded. 'You might be disappointed at what you see.' She tried to make her voice as normal as possible but her pulse was racing as they quietly padded upstairs. 'The whole of my upstairs could probably fit into your down-stairs cloakroom.'

He wanted a show of good faith and she couldn't blame him. She pushed open the doors to the small spare room, with its single futon, the desk at which she was accustomed to working until late into the night and the bathroom which was large and airy given the size of the house. They ended up in her bedroom.

Alessandro stood in the doorway and looked. The walls were a subdued cream but the four-poster bed was dressed and all romance. The prints on the walls were landscapes of deserted beaches. The dressing table, like the wardrobe, was old, doubtless bought at auction. He thought that he might be the first guy to step foot in this room and it gave him an unbelievable kick. Every single woman he had ever known had been keen to show him their bedrooms and the beds which promised inventive entertainment for as long as he wanted. Mood lighting had usually been a dominant theme. When he took in Chase's wary expres-sion, he could see ambivalence there.

'Your sanctuary.'

'Not any longer. You're in it.'

'By invitation.' His hand reached to the button on his trousers, but first he removed the shirt in one easy move-ment.

Chase practically fainted. He was the stuff daydreams were made of and she had had enough of those over the years. His body was burnished gold and honed to perfec-tion. When he moved, she could detect the ripple of muscle under skin. Her breathing picked up pace and her mouth went dry. Under her top, her bare breasts tingled, and she had the heady feeling that she wanted them touched, that she wanted her nipples played with.

'Your turn…' He liked the way her eyes skittered across his body as if helplessly drawn to stare at him. He remembered the way that used to do crazy things to him once and was uneasily aware that that should have changed—so why hadn't it? He found that he was holding his breath as her tee-shirt slowly rode up her belly, exposing her pale skin a slither at a time. She wasn't doing this because of undue pressure, yet there was an erotic hesitancy about her movements. The wealth of all her complexities crashed over him like a wave from which he had to fight to surface, to bring himself back in the moment.

He was a randy teenager all over again as he looked at her breasts, heavy and sexy and everything he had imagined. More. Her breasts were bigger than he had thought, tipped with perfect rosy-pink discs. She possessed a body that should never be constrained by a starchy lawyer's outfit. Her proportions were all feminine curves: bountiful breasts, a narrow waist and proper hips that swelled tantalisingly under the dreary track pants. He wanted nothing more than to stride over to her and feel her nakedness pressed against him.

With some sixth sense, though, he was aware of her skittishness. He didn't get it, but he could feel it. Any sudden moves and he got the feeling that she would take flight, even though she obviously wasn't embarrassed about her body, wasn't trying to be coy and hide her breasts behind her hands. He kept his eyes on her face as he removed his trousers and flung them to one side, still looking at her.

Chase felt her skin tighten at the glaring evidence of his arousal. His dark boxers could hardly contain it. She shakily reached to the elasticised waist of her joggers and stilled as he moved towards her.

'You look as though you want to run away,' he murmured. He swallowed hard because the tips of her breasts were almost brushing his chest and his hands itched to feel the weight of them. 'Believe it or not, this is taking it slow by my standards.'

'I believe you,' Chase said huskily. She touched his chest with one finger and felt his soft moan.

'Come to bed.' He stepped away from her. 'I'm not sure how long the slow plan can carry on for.'

When he turned his back to her, Chase knew that he was trying to hold himself back. She felt giddy with power. It was a wonderfully novel sensation and it afforded her a layer of strength she hadn't known she possessed. With Shaun, it had never been like this, never, not even in the very beginning. But she didn't want to think about her ex-husband. That was one very fast and very sure route to instant depression.

She slipped out of the jogging bottoms; his back was still turned when she crept into bed and under the covers.

'Now…' He wasn't used to taking sex slowly. He had never had to pace himself. He failed to consider that pacing himself with a woman for whom he harboured nothing more than a desire to even the score made no sense. 'Tell me…' he flipped onto his side so that they were lying under the covers, front to front, their bodies not touching but both of them vitally aware of their nudity under the duvet '…about the prints on your walls. And the four-poster bed…'

CHAPTER SIX

IF THERE WERE prizes for holding a man's interest, then Alessandro thought that Chase would be in line for all of them. He had planned on a straightforward conquest, aided and abetted by the trump card of saving the shelter. He would take her and, by taking her, he would rid himself of the allure of the inaccessible—which was the position to which she seemed to have been elevated over the years, apparently without him even having noticed. For him, the accessible had always had a short-lived appeal, especially when the quarry in question came with a truckload of dubious cargo.

And she had played him at his own game, had not been browbeaten but had laid her cards on the table. But then that hesitancy, that tentative admission that sex wasn't her thing… She had lain in his arms but he could feel her tension and he had backed off, even though his body had been on fire for her.

The rapacious, lying, deceitful, manipulative woman had shown a shrinking violet side to her that had got under his skin. Since when had he become the sort of man who was content to hold off, especially in a situation like this, with a woman scarcely worth his time and attention? He had held off with her once and look at where that had got him! But had he done what he should have done? Had he sneered at her attempts to play the shy maiden and ploughed forward? Hell, no! He had lain with her in his arms like the virgin she most certainly was not, had *talked*, and then he had left to return to his apartment and a freezing-cold shower.

Then he had gone abroad for two days, giving himself time to figure out why he was behaving so out of character and giving her time to wise up to the fact that what they had was a deal—and one he intended to cash, because her time limit for playing shy had been used up. He had returned late last night with two flights to Italy booked and the decidedly uncomfortable realisation that there might just be a need to shift gears slightly—to woo her, despite everything he had said about what they had not being a courtship. Somewhere along the line the whole 'time limit' speech had been shelved.

He just knew that when she came to him she would come of her own volition. She would jettison whatever the hell it was that was holding her back. In the space of a heartbeat, it had become a matter of pride—actually in the space of time it had taken for the notion of a break in Italy to take root, which had been fairly instantaneous.

If she was holding back because she hadn't managed to put the premature death of her husband behind her, then she needed to move on from that place and come to him willingly. There was no way he was going to sleep with any woman unless her thoughts were focused one hundred per cent on him and, if it took some seduction to get her to that place, then he would play along with it. The end result would be the same, wouldn't it? And he was an 'end result' kind of guy.

He had phoned her from abroad and announced the whole Italy idea with far more conviction than he had been feeling at the time, but she had taken little persuading as it turned out in the end. She was due some time off and she would take it. A little more enthusiasm would have been appreciated but he had met his match in her. She hadn't pandered to him eight years ago and she wasn't going to pander to him now, even though she knew him for the billionaire that he was.

Now, standing in front of the check-in desk at Heathrow surrounded by crowds, he scowled as he felt himself inevitably harden at the tantalising prospect of having her; of touching that flawless body; of sinking against those breasts, feeling them against his chest, against the palms of his big hands, pushing into his mouth. He had once lost his head over a mirage and now he would take what he felt was his due, take the promised fruit and kill the bitterness inside him that made such an unwelcome companion.

Through the crowds he spotted her weaving and looking around for him and he gave her a brief wave.

'You're ten minutes late. You should have let my driver collect you instead of coming by public transport.'

Chase looked up at his frowning face and was tempted to snap because, however much she wore her hard-won independence like a badge of honour, he obviously had a Neanderthal approach to women in general. But she bit back the retort because she could remember the way he had always taken command when she had known him: paying for whatever they had before she could offer to go halves; impatient with second-rate service; intolerant of anyone in his lectures who'd failed to try.

'I told you. I had some work to finish before I left.' Left for a week in the sun. She had no idea where that idea of Alessandro's had sprung from. She had fought against going, because she was all too aware that their relationship was destined to crash and burn, and the last thing she needed was a plethora of memories she would later have to work out of her system, but he had been insistent. Maybe being out of the country would infuse this weird closure of theirs with an unreality that would be easy to box away.

Italy, he had told her, was his home and, hell, why not. It was a nice time of year over there and he had just closed a massive deal. She could see his house. His casual tone of voice down the end of the line had told her that it wasn't a big deal. He would be going over there himself, she figured, with her or without her, but he would take her along because, as far as he was concerned, she had yet to fulfil her side of the bargain. Lying naked in his arms, tense as a plank of wood, didn't count.

Had they had sex, she was sure that he would not have suggested the Italy trip. Revenge lay behind his motivation and revenge was an emotion that could be sated very quickly. Certainly, a week of her would be enough. Did she deserve that? Maybe she did, in his eyes, and she would never disabuse him of the complicated story behind her lies because that would open up a whole new can of worms far worse than the one she was dealing with.

'Isn't that the old hoary line used by men?' Alessandro queried, moving towards the check-in girl at the first class desk. It occurred to him that he would have quite enjoyed having her at his beck and call and put that down to a caveman instinct he'd never known he possessed. Or maybe he only possessed it when the chase was still on, and only with her because she hadn't followed the pattern of the women he slept with.

'You're very chauvinistic, Alessandro. Women who have careers can't just jettison them the second something better comes along. As it is, I'll have a mountain of work to get down to when I get back. I shouldn't really be here at all, even if I *am* due time off.'

'Are you telling me that being with me is more compelling than your career?'

'I'm not saying anything of the sort!'

'You work too hard.'

'How else am I expected to get on?'

'What are you expecting to *get on* to?' They had checked in and were now heading through Passport Control, towards the first class lounge. Years ago he had considered the possibility of a private jet, if only to cut down on the inconvenience of a bustling airport, but had ditched the idea, because who needed to be responsible for such a vast personal carbon footprint when it could be avoided? Shame, though, because, had he had one, he could have introduced her to some creative ways of passing time twenty thousand miles up without an audience of prying eyes.

'I'd like to head up my own pro bono department. Maybe even branch out on my own and concentrate on that area. Bring in a few other employees…who knows?'

'And what about another prance up the aisle? Is that up there on the agenda? Surely your parents would want to hear the patter of little feet when you visit them in Australia? Or do visits to Australia get in the way of your career?'

Chase temporarily froze. The passing lie was not one on which she wanted to dwell. She wanted no reminders of her non-existent family. She knew that the last thing he would want to discuss would be her ex or her past treachery. His only goal was to get her into bed; her only goal was to put this murky, tangled, haunting past to rest. He was motivated by revenge, she by a need for closure. It was a straightforward situation. She needed no reminders of white lies that had been told and could not now be un-told.

How would he react were he to know that, not only had she once lied to him about her marital status, not only had she dumped him in a way that now made her cringe with guilt and shame even though she knew that it just couldn't have been helped at the time, but that her entire past was as substantial as gossamer?

'Australia is a long way away…' she muttered vaguely.

'Yes. I know. I've been there. You've never told me which part of Australia they live in. It's a big place.'

'You wouldn't have heard of it.' She could feel beads of perspiration break out all over her body. 'It's just a small town on the outskirts of…um…Melbourne. Look, I really don't want to talk about this. Discussing personal issues isn't what we're about, is it?' Never had she realised how being trapped in a lie could prove as painful as walking on a bed of burning coals.

'No,' Alessandro said shortly. 'It's not.' He looked at her blank eyes and tight smile and felt a surge of rage that the thing most women gave naturally to him—the desperate openness which they always seemed to hope could suck him into something permanent and committal—was the one thing Chase steadfastly refused to give. It angered him that he was even going down the road of quizzing her because it reflected a series of inner challenges that he knew were inappropriate. The challenge to get her into bed so that he could assuage the treachery he felt had been done to him had been replaced by the challenge to get her into bed willingly and *hot for him*; the challenge to wipe her ex out of her head when they finally had sex, the challenge to get into her head, to know what made her tick.

Where the hell did it end? Did he need her to remind him that the rules of the game precluded certain things?

'Call it making polite conversation,' he offered with cool politeness.

'I overreacted. It's just that…'

'No need to explain yourself. I'm basically not interested in your past. Like I said, small talk…'

Chase was silenced. Of course he was basically not interested in her past. He was basically not interested in *her*. He was utterly focused on one thing and one thing only. She nodded, nonchalantly indicating that she understood, that she shared the same sentiment.

When he began telling her about some of the complex legalities of the deal he had just pulled off, she let herself slide smoothly into career-woman mode, and then the conversation flowed faultlessly onto the subject of Beth and the shelter. It was a happy story and Chase felt herself once again relax. This was an odd situation but she could handle it, just as long as she didn't start feeling angst over stuff, just as long as she maintained the composed exterior that was so much part and parcel of her personality. She couldn't let herself forget that she wanted this as much as he did. They both had their demons to put to rest.

They landed at Cristoforo Colombo Airport at Genova Sestri to a brilliant day. The wall-to-wall blue skies, which had no longer been in evidence in London after their brief appearance, were here in full force. As soon as they stepped into the waiting limo, she could feel a heady holiday spirit fill her.

'It's been ages since I've been away,' she confided as she settled back to watch the stunning scenery gallop past from the back of the car. 'In fact…' she turned to him '…my only trip abroad in the past few years has been a snatched week at a spa resort in Greece.'

'In that case, I shall make it my mission to see that you enjoy every second of my country…when and if we have the time; bed can be remarkably compulsive with the right companion in it.' His dark eyes roved over her face, encompassing her luscious body, enjoying the delicate bloom of colour that tinged her cheeks.

This holiday would put an end to the game playing which he had sworn he wouldn't tolerate, yet had ended up indulging that one night which should have seen this uncontrollable passion slayed. As she had pointed out in a timely reminder, this wasn't about getting to know one another, this was about sex. Getting to know one another had been a pointless game which he had mistakenly played a long time ago, little knowing that he had been the only participant.

This time round, there'd be no more messing around and taking things at a snail's pace. He would move only as slowly as he felt necessary to get her where he wanted her—which was out of his system so that he could return to normality.

Vaguely annoyed at the contrary drift of his thoughts, he was aware of telling her about the Italian Riviera, on autopilot, pointing out the grandeur of the mountainous landscape in such close and unusual proximity to the sea, giving her a little bit of history about the place. His voice warmed as he described the vast olive grove plantations stretching across the hills, vast tracts of which had once been owned by his ancestors, only to disappear over the years, mismanaged and sold off in bits and pieces—the last by his parents, who had needed the money in their quest for eternal fun.

'You could always come back here…buy more olive groves. It's so beautiful; I can't see why you would want to live in London.' Not even in her wildest, escapist fantasies could she ever have dreamt up somewhere as beautiful as this. The landscape was bold and dramatic, the colours bright and vibrant. Everywhere was bursting with incredible, Technicolor beauty. Alessandro might have had irresponsible parents but it had to be said that, whatever he had gone through, he had gone through it in some style.

'I have a house here. It's where we're going.'

'But how often do you visit it?'

'As you'll be the first to agree, taking time out gets in the way of a career.'

Chase bristled at the implicit criticism in his remark. It reminded her that what they shared was simply a truce but, behind that truce, there was a lot he just didn't like about her. 'My career is important to me.'

'I've gathered.'

'You say that as though you disapprove of women who work.'

'On the contrary. Some of the highest positions in my company are occupied by women.'

'But you would never actually go out with a woman who had a career...'

Alessandro shot her a sidelong glance. The car was air-conditioned but he had chosen to have the windows opened and the breeze blew through her hair, tossing it across her face in unruly strands. She was no longer the high-powered lawyer with the pristine appearance. She was the girl he had once known and he railed against the pull of memories. 'There's little I find attractive about a woman who puts her career first.'

Chase rolled her eyes and sighed, because the breeze was too balmy and the scenery too exotic for arguing. 'That is because you're a dinosaur.' He had old-fashioned ideas. Years ago she had teased him that that was a back-lash from his parents' excesses but she had liked those old-fashioned ideas, never having come across them before.

'And I take it that under normal circumstances you wouldn't choose to go out with a dinosaur? Tell me about your husband.'

'I no longer have a husband,' Chase said shortly, rousing herself from bittersweet memories of their brief, shared dalliance.

'I realise that. What was he like?' He was curious. He found that he wanted to know. This wasn't polite conversation, although the casual tone of his voice gave nothing away.

The last thing Chase wanted to do was to talk about Shaun but she had a sneaking suspicion that, if she backed away from the subject, it would arouse his interest even further. 'We met when we were young. I was only fifteen. Just. We met at the local disco.'

'Cosy. And was it love at first sight?'

'We found that we had a lot in common.'

'Always a good start to a healthy relationship. Even at the ripe old age of fifteen. Just.' He found that he didn't care for the idea of them having a lot in common at whatever the hell age they had happened to meet. Nor had he intended to get wrapped up in pointless conversations about the thug who had been lurking behind the scenes when she had taken him for a ride and played him for a fool.

'So they say,' Chase murmured tonelessly.

'I take it he wasn't sharp enough to make it to university?'

'Shaun was plenty sharp.' She couldn't help the bitterness that had crept into her voice but she kept it at bay. Talking about Shaun would inevitably lead to all sorts of questions about the sort of world she had really come from. Chase found that she had moved on from the fear of him discovering the truth about her and eking out some kind of belated revenge by spilling the beans to her work colleagues. She honestly couldn't see him doing that.

No, what she feared—and she hated herself for this—was to have him walk away in disgust at the lies she had told, at the person she really was and the life she had really led. His pedigree was impeccable and although she knew that they would be the archetypal doomed lovers—in it for the wrong reasons but driven to fulfil their destiny—she still found that she wanted him to believe her to be the sassy, smart lawyer with the perfectly ordinary background when they parted company.

Wasn't that to be expected? What if she bumped into him at a later date? What if he met some of the partners in her law firm and started talking about her? If he knew the truth about her, then wasn't it likely that it would slip out in conversation? And, even if nothing did slip out, surely he would never be able to disguise the contempt in his voice at the mention of her name?

'Sharp as in…?'

She snapped out of her daydreaming to find his eyes narrowed on her. 'Streetwise; sharp as in streetwise.'

'And did your streetwise late husband have a job?' He thought back to the picture she had shown him all those years ago.

'He…worked in transport but he…he lost his job shortly before the accident. I'd bought him that motorbike. I'd been putting aside some money and I wanted to celebrate getting my first promotion…'

'So you celebrated by buying him a motorbike. Shouldn't *he* have been the one doing the buying to congratulate you? Or am I just thinking like a dinosaur again?'

'Alessandro, please, let's move on from this. I honestly don't want to talk about Shaun. Tell me more about here. It's amazing to think that there can be snow on mountaintops that are just a short distance from the Med…'

Alessandro heard the soft plea in her voice. 'Why did you give me a second look if you were so clearly head over heels in love with your husband?'

'I…I'm sorry. I made a mistake.'

'Which doesn't answer my question.' He raked his hand impatiently though his hair and sat back with his eyes closed for a few seconds. 'Scrap that. Not sure I could stomach whatever fairy stories you decide to come out with.'

'Alessandro…'

He inclined his head towards her and linked his fingers loosely in his lap. She had the face of an angel, the body of a siren and he was furious with himself for wanting to probe deeper. He pointed to a spot behind her as the car turned left. 'My house.'

Chase turned just in time to glimpse a sand-coloured

mansion rising up from the cliffs, overlooking the placid turquoise sea with a backdrop of woods of chestnut trees. She forgot everything and her mouth dropped open.

'I have two housekeepers who live in, make sure everything is ticking over. Occasionally, it's used by some of my employees, a little bonus if they do well. The promise of an all-expenses-paid long weekend here generates a lot of healthy competition, and it does no harm for the place to get an airing now and again.'

'It's huge. What about family members?'

'Oh, completely off-limits to them. My parents ensured their place in the pecking order as the black sheep of the family and I've inherited their generous legacy. I have little contact with my extended family.

'My parents were both only children, so there are strangely few people who bear a belated grudge towards me. I see a couple of slightly less distant relatives now and again when I'm in Milan; a few more work in some of my associated companies, my way of making amends for my parents' appallingly hedonistic behaviour which was, if all accounts are to be believed, ruinous to both family names.'

He edged towards her and pointed. 'You can't see it, but there's a winding path that leads down to a private cove at the bottom of the cliff face. Excellent bathing. Once upon a time, fishing used to be big here. Not so much any more. Tourism pays better, it would seem. The wealthy find the sight of yachts far more uplifting than the reality of fishing boats.'

'What a shame you don't get here often,' Chase said. When he was like this—charming, informative, his voice as deep and as dark as the most pure, rich, velvety chocolate—she could forget everything. She could lapse back to the past where dangerous, taboo emotions still held a certain innocence, a time when he didn't hate her. 'Don't you sometimes long to have someone to share this with?'

'Oh, but isn't that what I'm doing now?' Alessandro drawled. 'Admittedly, only for a few days, and with a woman who is destined never to return, but it'll do for the moment.'

He reached across, pulling her towards him. 'I've given my loyal housekeepers time off,' he murmured into her hair. 'It's hot here. I thought it might be nice for us to live as naturists for a few days. Why bother with clothes? I want to be able to touch you anywhere…at any time… And you'll discover that my house is perfect for ensuring one hundred per cent privacy. I'll make you thaw, my sweet; on that count, you can trust me…'

Chase was still smarting from the insistent stab of hurt his words had generated. *Destined never to return.*

They approached the sprawling villa through wrought-iron gates which had been flung open, revealing perfectly groomed lawns stretching out on either side of the gravel drive.

'How many people does it take to look after these gardens?' She shouldn't have been, but she was still shocked by the splendour.

'A small army,' Alessandro admitted drily. 'I'm single-handedly trying to do my bit to keep the economy going. There's a very private pool to the side of the house. I have vague memories of my parents throwing some extremely wild parties there.'

'I had no idea the house belonged to them.' Chase turned to look at him and their eyes tangled. Instantly, she could feel her breasts begin to ache in expectation of his caresses. With Shaun, she had become conditioned to viewing sex as something that had to be done. But when she had lain next to Alessandro her body had been fired up in a way that was new and, whilst they hadn't made love, it now thrummed at the prospect of being touched by him. It was a heady, exciting feeling and she was sure that it was all wrapped up in the culmination of what had begun all that time ago, what had never come to fruition.

'It was their pride and joy. The one thing they both hung on to.'

'And you kept it for sentimental reasons?'

'I never do anything for sentimental reasons. It's a good, appreciating asset.'

It was dreamy. If she had been able to conceive of a place like this, she might have been more elaborate in her teenage fantasies about perfect lifestyles instead of just settling for average. Then she decided that it was just as well, because how much more awkward would life have been now had her naïve, happily married parents in their two-up two-down been turned into minor landed gentry living in a small castle?

They were greeted by an elderly housekeeper and her husband who had stayed on to welcome Alessandro, tugging him into the kitchen so that they could show him the freezer full of food that had been prepared and the well-stocked larder. He managed to shoo them away after an hour and they departed wreathed in smiles.

'They've been with me for longer than I care to think. As you know, my parents were firm believers in handing over care of their offspring to hired help,' he told her as he played tour guide, taking her from room to room. He absently thought how many of those little details of his past she had been privy to, courtesy of that small window in his life during which his self-control had gone on holiday.

'I'm treating them to a well-deserved rest in a destination of their choosing, which as it turns out happens to be France, where their eldest is a dentist. I tried to persuade them into somewhere a little further afield but they weren't having it. Mauritius, apparently, is no competition for two hyper grandchildren.'

Chase's heart fluttered. This was how he had managed

to get under her skin. This was why she never wanted to have him learn the truth about her. This was why the thought of what he could do to balance the scales of justice should he want to avenge past wrongs was no longer the only consideration. Underneath his ruthlessly cold exterior were these flashes of genuine thoughtfulness that kept reminding her of why she had risked so much just talking to him eight years ago; that ambushed all her good intentions to keep her distance. Whenever he made her laugh, her defences slipped just a little bit more.

This was a dangerous game because she would end up being hurt. She would end up losing her hard-won self-control. She would end up with someone else having power over her, someone who didn't care about her, who wanted her for all the wrong reasons. Maybe she had already ended up there.

She had walked into this with her eyes wide open but now she felt as though she had walked straight into a trap, having stupidly failed to take account of its power for destruction.

The whole sex thing… Yes, she had wanted it, had *craved* it, but she had been scared because of past experience and he had respected her when she had turned into a block of ice in his arms. That consideration he had shown her, as it turned out, was just something else that had nibbled away at the edges of her defences so that what had once been a fortress, protecting her from the slings and arrows of emotional involvement with the human race, was beginning to resemble a broken down old castle open to all the elements.

She felt exposed in a way she never had in her life before. She felt as she had eight years ago: like a woman *falling in love*.

'You've stopped using rapturous superlatives to describe my house.'

Chase blinked and realised that he was several metres ahead of her because she had stopped dead in her tracks. Her brain had been so wrapped up contemplating the horror of falling for this guy again that it hadn't had any room left to give messages to her legs to keep moving.

'I think I may have run out of them.' She blinked and took in the raw sexuality of the man lounging in front of her with that killer half-smile on his lips.

'Where is this famous pool you've been bragging about?' Her voice was normal but her brain was malfunctioning.

'I never brag.' Again that smile that hurled her back in time. He took her hand to lead her through the house, out to the kitchen and towards the sea-facing side of the house, which took her breath away. 'Except in this one instance.'

He gestured to the open view as though he owned it and then relaxed back to look at her response. He had never given a damn what women thought of his opulent lifestyle and was indifferent to their gasps of awe whenever they stepped foot into his house in London. Yet he rather enjoyed the way her mouth fell open as she stepped out to stand next to him.

The house looked down to the sea that was turquoise and as still as a lake. The garden on this side was just a strip of green, broken by distinctive Italian palm trees and bordered by thick shrubbery. To one side a gate announced the winding stone steps, which Chase imagined led to the cove he had told her about.

This was her dream come true. She had somehow been catapulted into the prints she had hung on her walls. The romance which had not been part of the plan clung to her in a miasma, giving her all sorts of stupid illusions that somehow what they had might be the beginning of something real. It was time to start unravelling that piece of fiction.

'Are you sure it's completely deserted here?' She

squinted against the sun to look up at him, shielding her eyes with one hand.

Alessandro looked down at her. She was in a flimsy sleeveless dress which was far too baggy for his liking but which, on the upside, provided terrific fodder for his imagination. 'As a ghost town. Why?'

'Because I think we should explore that pool area you were bragging to me about... Oh yes, I forgot: you never brag...' Her hand fluttered provocatively to the small top button of the dress. 'It's so warm. I think I might need to strip off, have a dip in that pool of yours, the one—'

'I keep bragging to you about even though I never brag?' He laughed under his breath and felt the bulge in his pants as that part of his body which had been in charge of his brain ever since she had reappeared to smash into his ordered existence rose to immediate attention.

He linked his fingers through hers and began leading her across the lawn, swerving to the side of the house where exuberant flora, lemon trees, shrubs sprouting with brightly coloured flowers and hydrangea enclosed an exquisite infinity pool. The air was aromatic.

'I feel as though I've stepped into a travel brochure.'

Alessandro frowned. A nagging thought occurred to him. Had he seen those prints on the walls and brought her here so that he could deliver her those dreams of sun, sea and sand that had clearly never been realised? Had that been some weird, unconscious motivation behind his invitation to bring her to his house? He irritably swept aside a suspicion with which he was not comfortable.

'You said you were hot...?'

'So I did.' She would have liked to enjoy the scenery a bit more. Well, a lot more. But business was business, wasn't it? The longer this game between them carried on, the deeper her scars would be when they parted company, when he had got what he wanted. She undid the small buttons of the dress and it fell to the ground, pooling at her feet.

Alessandro remained where he was, looking at her with lazy, predatory satisfaction. 'Will this be a full striptease?'

'I want you, Alessandro...' *And I love you. I loved you once and I think it would be very easy to love you again.* She schooled her features to conceal the chaos of her thoughts. 'And I think we've both waited long enough...' She walked towards him, reaching behind her as she did so to unhook her bra, which she tossed onto one of the low, wooden sun loungers, never taking her eyes off his face.

Alessandro found that he could barely control his breathing. The moment was electric. His jaw clenched when she was finally standing in front of him and he had to steel himself against an unruly, premature overreaction as she slipped out of her panties so that she was now completely naked.

'The sun's pretty fierce...' He curved his hand around her waist, idly caressing it and pulling her against him at the same time. 'And you're fair. Any doctor would tell you that you need to lather yourself in sunblock...' He kissed her slowly, tugging her bottom lip with his teeth, gently tasting her mouth, taking his time as their tongues melded, even though it was agony trying to keep his libido in check.

'So what do you want to do about it?' She wrapped her arms around his neck and flung her head back with a sigh as his lips traced a path along the slender column of her neck. She was wet and ready for him. She reached to fumble with the button of his trousers and he stayed her hand.

'One good striptease deserves another,' he murmured in a sexy, shaky undertone that sent her blood pressure skyrocketing. 'But first...'

He sauntered towards what she now saw was a vine-covered pool house and emerged a couple of minutes later with towels and various creams. He dumped them on one of the vacant loungers and she watched, heart beating wildly, as he did what she had done only moments before.

His shirt was tossed to join hers and he kept his eyes on her as he walked slowly towards her. Every inch that brought him closer did crazier things to her nervous system. Her breath caught in her throat as he removed his trousers, then, when she felt that swooning was a real possibility, the final item of clothing joined the rest and he was as naked as she was, his proud, impressive erection proclaiming that he was as turned on as her.

When he was inches away from her, she reached down and firmly circled it with her hand.

'Three days ago you were as tense as a violin string...' He led her towards one of the loungers which was shaded by an overhanging tree and he neatly spread one of the towels on it.

Three days ago, she thought, *I had no idea that my body could feel like this; three days ago it started to come alive. I may have been apprehensive then at what I was feeling but I'm not apprehensive now...*

'I'm not now,' she said huskily.

'Then lie down. I'm going to put sun cream on you and it'll be the best foreplay you've ever experienced...'

CHAPTER SEVEN

'IT MIGHT BE a little cold,' Alessandro murmured. He had to make sure to keep his eyes away from her breasts, away from her flat stomach, away from the soft, downy hair that lightly covered the triangular apex between her thighs. He would save himself. 'I keep the pool house air-conditioned. Lie on your stomach…'

'You honestly don't need to bother with sun lotion. It's perfectly safe here in the shade.'

'Doctor's orders. Safety first is the main thing.' She was on her stomach and very slowly he began to explore every exquisite inch of her body, rubbing the sun cream into her, feeling the silky smoothness of her skin and, with each stroke of his hand on her body, getting more aroused.

He pressed his thumbs gently against each vertebra so that she was moaning softly and melting under his touch. He massaged her neck, then her sides, so that her mind went blank and she sighed and squirmed; then the rounded cheeks of her bottom and the length of her glorious legs which parted temptingly, inviting him to go further, but it was an invitation he wasn't going to take up until he was good and ready.

'This is… I never knew…' It was an inaudible sigh.

'Now, shift over. Lie on your back. We can't let an inch of you go unprotected, can we? I would never forgive myself if you were to get sunburned.'

Chase, cynical when it came to interpreting everything he said, wondered if he meant that he would never forgive himself should she be out of action while they were over here. Four days in paradise without the sex he had been anticipating wouldn't do, would it?

She nearly laughed hysterically when she thought that four days in paradise with him without sex would still be four days in paradise for her as opposed to a wasted trip.

'And stop frowning. Just relax. Enjoy.' Her face was first and then his long, supple fingers moved to her shoulders. He did his utmost not to look at her breasts, at the large, pink discs that were responding so enthusiastically to what his hands were doing. He was aware, though, that the tips had tightened into hard peaks as she became more and more turned on.

He watched, fascinated, at the slight flare of her nostrils as he began to lavish his attention on her breasts. 'You can't be too careful in this Italian sun…especially for someone with as little experience of hot weather as you.'

'Don't be silly, Alessandro. London gets hot.' Her eyes were shut tightly and her fists clenched in an effort at self-control as he continued to massage her breasts. It felt so good. 'Are you sure we're on our own here?' This as he bent to take one pouting nipple in his mouth and she moaned weakly as he suckled on it while spanning his hand across her rib cage.

'No one else would have permission to see this body,' he broke off to tell her. 'It's for my eyes only.' Then he returned to the matter at hand, moving to pay the same attention to her other nipple.

How long could he keep this up? Straddling her, he nudged her legs apart. Protection for the full thing, naturally. But he couldn't resist the feel of her moistness against him and he rubbed himself along her wet crease, an insistent, rhythmic movement that made her gasp out loud.

'How does this feel, baby?' he asked, his voice raw and unsteady and she whimpered a response that was answer enough. 'I'm not going to come in you. I just need to do this...'

But he had to stop when he knew that a few more seconds and he would push them both over the edge. The anticipation of having full-blown sex with her was filling his mind and sensitising every inch of his body. When she half-raised herself to take him in her hand, he gently pushed her back down. He had to control this. If he didn't, he would come right here, right now and that was something he didn't want to do. This time, he was going to feel the silky smoothness of being deep inside her.

He smoothed the cream over her inner thighs and breathed her in. The sweet, sexy smell of her filled his nostrils and he half-closed his eyes before dipping his head between her legs. The flat of his hands were on her thighs, pushing them apart, and he felt her tiny convulsion as his tongue made contact with her clitoris.

Chase's fingers tangled in his hair. Here, under the shade of a tree, the sun's heat was pleasantly diluted. The breeze was soft and balmy. Half-opening her eyes, she saw his dark head between her thighs and, framing him, the glory of the Italian scenery with its vista of blue ocean and in the distance the striking cliffs of the peninsula, lush green interspersed with picturesque hamlets, which were tiny dots seen from this far away.

She was living a dream. She was here, with Alessandro, making love to him, having him turn her on in ways that were unimaginable. Why shouldn't she stuff reality behind a door and enjoy what was on offer for its brief duration?

She smiled, moved against his mouth and smiled more when he raised his head and chastised her for moving too fast.

'More doctor's orders?' she teased breathlessly.

'You said it.'

It felt to her as though she had been building up to this moment for years, from the very first time she had had that first latte with him, a sneaky, stolen latte. She had nervously told herself that it would be a one-off, that she was in no position to have lattes with him or with anyone else, but then, as now, what she had told herself had had no bearing on what had actually transpired.

They had had the most sexually charged yet chaste relationship on the planet. Every touch had been accidental and every touch had left her craving more. She had dreamt about him back then and had been terrified that Shaun would somehow climb into her head and see her dreams. And he had continued to steal into her dreams like a silent intruder all through the years, long after she had picked up the pieces of her life and moved on.

So now she was ready.

'Alessandro…' she breathed huskily and he lifted his head to look at her.

'Alessandro what…?' The spoils of the victor. Triumph surged through him. This was what he had wanted: to hear her plead for him to enter her, to know that she could no longer hold out. The grieving widow shedding her black and getting back into mainstream life. With him.

'Tell me how much you want me,' he encouraged thickly. 'I want to hear you say it. No, hold that thought—but don't even begin to think that you can start cooling down.' There were condoms in his wallet. He couldn't fetch one fast enough. His erection was so hard that it was painful.

Cool down? Chase thought that she wouldn't have cooled down if a barrel of ice cubes had been thrown over her. She was on fire, burning for him. She looked at him hungrily, watching as he put on the condom, enjoying the way he was looking right back at her, his dark eyes bold and wicked.

'I'd better just check...' he murmured, straddling her on the super-sized lounger which could have been made for sex and—who knew?—possibly had been because it was as comfortable as a bed. 'Make sure you're still hot for me...' He slid his finger expertly over her throbbing centre and gave a slashing smile of satisfaction. 'Hot and wet.'

'I'm glad you approve.' She wound her arms around his neck and pulled him down to her. Her nipples rubbing against him were doing all sorts of delicious things to her body, adding to the overload of sensation. She sighed and arched up so that she could kiss him and simultaneously opened her legs. 'God, Alessandro, I want you so much right now...'

'Are you sure?'

Their eyes met and she knew that he was asking her if she was ready. Given half a chance, he was always more than prepared to tell her the depth of his bitterness towards her, to inform her that her place in his life was temporary, a passing virus of which he needed to rid his system. Yet, as now, when she could see old-fashioned consideration in his eyes which could flare up almost against his will, he could be just so damned three-dimensional.

'I'm sure.'

Alessandro thrust into her and never had anything felt so exquisite. She wrapped her legs around his waist and he levered her up, his hand on her bottom, so that she could receive him even better as he began moving, fast and hard and rhythmically. Her fingers were digging into his back, driving him on, and her head was thrown back, her eyes closed, her mouth slightly parted.

For a split second, he had a crazy desire to know whether she had ever felt like this with her husband. He certainly had never felt like this with any other woman but, then again, what other woman had he ever had under such extraordinary circumstances? His last girlfriend, a model whose appearance in his life had not outlived the three-month mark, had been a clone of all the other beauties he had dated in the past. Was it any wonder that this one was special? That *this* just felt so damned special?

Chase had died and gone to heaven. On one final thrust, she tipped over the edge as her orgasm ripped through her, sending her body into little convulsions and spontaneously bringing tears to her eyes which she fought to blink back. She felt his groan of fulfilment with every ounce of her being and never had she wanted more to tell him how she felt. Instead, she swept his hair back and smiled drowsily as he opened his eyes to look at her, at first unfocused, and then smiling back.

'That was…good…' she murmured as he slid onto his side to prop himself up on one elbow so that he could look at her.

'"Good" is not an adjective I've ever had much time for. It's along the same lines as "nice"…' He idly circled her nipple with his finger and watched as it responded with enthusiasm. 'How *good* was it?'

'Very, very good…'

'I'll settle for that. In fact, I'll enjoy trying to squeeze more superlatives out of you.' He dipped his head and closed his mouth over her nipple, which was still sensitive and throbbing in the aftermath of their love-making. He was utterly spent and yet he felt himself stir against her leg. 'Let's have a swim,' he suggested. 'And then some food. And then we can play it by ear; see what comes up…'

'Oh, very funny.' But she was laughing as they jumped into the pool. After four lengths, she was happy to take to the side and watch as he continued to slice through the water. She had learned to swim as an adult. Four years ago, she wouldn't have been able to jump into the deep end of this pool, never mind swim four lengths. He, on the other hand, had probably been swimming since he was a toddler, taught by a member of staff in one of the many pools he had probably enjoyed in various locations over the years.

The differences between them were so glaringly obvious, reminding her of the shelf life of what they had and of the shadowy undercurrents lurking just beneath the surface of their sexually charged relationship.

'Tired?'

'Swimming isn't one of my strong points,' she confessed. 'In fact...' what would this one simple admission hurt? '...I only learned to swim a few years ago.'

'You're kidding.'

'No, I'm not,' she said with a shrug.

'That must have been awkward on family holidays. I'm surprised your parents didn't sort that out.' He kissed her again, a little more hungrily this time, and pulled back with a grin of pure satisfaction. 'Besides, don't schools in England have arranged swimming lessons for kids? Something to do with the curriculum?'

'Some of them do,' Chase said vaguely. 'But, you know, I kind of had a phobia of water.'

'A little private tuition would have sorted that out, wouldn't it?' He swung himself neatly out of the pool and held out his hand to help her up. 'Better than Mummy and Daddy panicking every time their precious little darling got within a foot of the hotel pool. Hmm...nice...'

He enjoyed her wet body, running his hands along it, holding her close to him so that their bodies could rub together. 'No matter. Competitive swimming isn't on the agenda while we're here. I couldn't care less if you can only swim four lengths or four hundred.'

Chase opened her mouth, toyed with the idea of revealing a bit more about herself but then kept silent. This fantastic side to Alessandro was only in evidence for a reason.

Further proof of her lying would kill that reason dead because, even for the sake of finishing unfinished business, lust still had its outer limits. And without lust how much greater would be his anger in the cold light of day? She didn't want his anger and she certainly couldn't afford for that anger to be directed at punishing her through her work.

A sudden tidal wave of sheer misery immobilised her and it took almost more effort than she could muster to get herself back on track.

'Tell me what there is around here,' she eventually said, falling easily into step with him as he tossed her a towel and they began walking towards the house. 'All those gorgeous little villages... What do the locals do for a living? Do you know any of them? Personally, I mean?'

Exactly four days later, Chase understood what it must feel like to be in love with someone, living on cloud nine, where everything smelled differently and tasted differently and every single experience was a unique Kodak moment to be committed to memory and brought out at a later date.

She had seen him at his most relaxed. She felt that she could almost be forgiven for thinking that he really liked her and she guessed that, in a way, he did. He appreciated her quick mind; he appreciated her responsive body; he laughed when she tried to tell corny jokes.

Just so long as they both pretended that the past had never happened, everything was good between them. For her, it was so much deeper than anything he could possibly feel, but she refused to think like that. What was the point? She had made her bed and she would lie on it. She had accepted his proposal and only now and again did she think that, whilst she was falling deeper and harder for him, he was gradually working her out of his system.

Wrapped up in his arms at night, lying in a bed that was roughly the size of her spare bedroom, she had let her mind wander, analysed and re-analysed everything he'd said and every gesture he'd made. The one sure thing that sprang to mind was that, the more relaxed he was with her, the more he was putting her behind him.

It was an argument that made sense. When he had seen her again for the first time after eight years, his rage had been raw, out in the open, targeted and deadly. But that had changed. He would never, ever forgive her for what she had done to him, she knew that, but he was in the process of getting over it. Rage was becoming indifference and indifference was allowing him to stop treating her as public enemy number one.

She hated herself for trying to find alternative scenarios but they all led to the same dead end. Very soon, he would completely lose interest in why she had done what she had done eight years ago. He would simply stop giving a damn. He would no longer consider revenge because he would not care less. He would just use her and walk away without a backward glance.

The only consolation was that she had not dropped her guard. She had not let him see just how vulnerable she was, nor would she let him discover how successful he had been at claiming the revenge he had initially considered his due. Without him even realising it, he had indeed wreaked the ultimate revenge, because he would leave her broken and in pieces, whatever show of bravado she employed for his benefit.

And now here they were, last night, sitting across from each other at the kitchen table with an almost empty bottle of Chablis between them.

'So tell me again why you don't come here at least once a month, Alessandro.' Outside, another hot day had gradually morphed into a mild, starry night. They had spent most nights in the kitchen, which was huge, big enough for a ten-seater table at one end, and leading to a conservatory which doubled as an informal sitting area with comfy sofas and a plasma television. From here, they had an un-interrupted view of the sea down below, vast and silent, and the small back garden where they had spent much of their time by the swimming pool.

She felt lazy and replete after another excellent meal which had been prepared in advance by his housekeeper. They could have done their own cooking, and she had sug-gested it on day one, but he had killed that dead.

'Why waste time cooking?' he had questioned bluntly, 'When there are so many other things we could be occu-pied doing?' He had pulled her onto his lap and slipped his finger underneath her panties, leaving her in no doubt as to what those other things they could be occupied with were. Enjoying any form of domesticity was off the cards. That was not the reason why he had asked her on this holiday.

'You know why I don't come here once a month,' he re-plied wryly. 'It's the same reason *you* wouldn't come here once a month. Work wouldn't allow it.'

'But it's different for you. You're the big boss. You can do whatever you want. I can't.'

'Pull the other one, Chase. You're not a bimbo who would be content to while away her time walking bare-foot on a beach, no matter how powdery white the sand might be. You're one hundred per cent a career woman. You would be bored stiff in a job that allowed you to take time out every month to enjoy a holiday in the sunshine.'

He stood up, moved to the fridge to replenish the wine and remained there with his back against the counter, care-fully looking at her with his head to one side. She had caught the sun. Her skin was the colour of pale honey and from nowhere a smattering of freckles had appeared on the ridge of her nose.

'I recognised that the first time I laid eyes on you,' he continued casually. 'You weren't going to be distracted by anyone or anything. You barely seemed to notice what was going on around you.'

Chase fidgeted. Trips down memory lane never turned out well between them. However, his voice was mild and speculative, not in the least provocative. More proof that, whatever fireworks there might be on the physical level, on the emotional level he was breaking away. The medicine was working. Sex was finishing the unfinished business between them.

'I liked that,' he continued and she looked at him in surprise. 'You once asked me if I'd ever go out with a career woman and I gave you a negative answer.' He strolled towards her and resumed his seat at the kitchen table, tugging a free chair with his foot so that he could use it as an impromptu footrest. 'The truth is, you were the anomaly. Before you and after you, I've only gone out with...'

'Airheads? Bimbos?' Chase dropped into the brief silence. She smiled tightly. 'Women who are never ashamed to admit that their only ambition is to hunt down a rich guy and bag him even if it means a lifetime of doing exactly what he wants her to do?' The stuff of nightmares, she thought bitterly.

'There's absolutely nothing about a woman like that I can't handle, and you'd be surprised how easily they've slotted into my lifestyle.'

'Because they make sure to always tell you what you want to hear and do what you want them to do?'

'Some might say that a compliant woman is preferable to a liar.' He noted the swift surge of colour that flooded her cheeks. 'You *have* succeeded in persuading me, however, that there's something to be said for a woman with a brain.'

'I have?'

'You have,' Alessandro drawled. 'Don't get me wrong, Chase—agile though your mind is, and challenging though your conversation can be, you'll never be a contender for the vacancy—just in case your thoughts were heading in that direction.'

'They weren't!' Chase was mortified to think that he might have spotted some weakness in her armour that she hadn't been able to conceal. 'You're not dealing with an idiot, Alessandro. I know the rules of this game as well as you do.'

'I'm glad to hear it.'

'Why would you have thought any differently?' Just like that, his dark eyes had turned cool and assessing, reminding her that the so-called rules of this particular game were different for both of them, despite what she might say to the contrary. Reminding her, too, that his red-hot passion had changed nothing of what he fundamentally felt towards her.

'Look around you and tell me what you see.'

'We're in your kitchen.' Chase frowned, confused and flustered by the softly spoken question that seemed to have sprung from nowhere. 'I can just about make out the little garden at the back, and I can see where the pool is… Look, why are you asking me this?'

'What you see all around you is evidence of my wealth,' Alessandro inserted smoothly. He killed dead the passing twinge of hesitation at the thought that he might offend her. He reminded himself that no matter how good the sex was, and how much he might occasionally enjoy her rapier-sharp mind, she was still a woman whom he had met going by the name of Lyla; who had strung him along and lied to him; who had dumped him unceremoniously and who, certainly, he would never have clapped eyes on again had fate not decided to deliver her to his premises. At the end of the day, whether he offended her or not was immaterial.

'But,' he continued as she stared at him, perplexed, 'I

guess you were aware of the extent of my bank balance the minute you walked into my London place.'

'I don't see what your bank balance has to do with anything,' Chase said tautly.

'No? Let's just say that I wouldn't want you to start getting any misplaced ideas.'

'Misplaced ideas about what?' But she knew what he was talking about now. Well, it didn't take a genius to join the dots, did it? She should be enraged, but instead she was deeply hurt, cut to the quick.

'This is all about the sex—and it's great sex, I'll give you that. But don't think for a second that I've somehow forgotten the person you really are. I think this is a good point at which to remind you that you're a visitor in my life. You won't be getting your hands on any of this…' He gestured broadly to encompass the visible proof of his vast wealth.

He couldn't have thought of a more pointed way of humiliating her but she pinned a stiff smile to her face. She hoped she looked suitably amused and unimpressed. She hoped that whatever expression she was wearing revealed nothing of what she was actually feeling.

'Do you think I would actually *want* to be anything other than a…what did you call it, Alessandro?… *visitor* in your life?' Her heart contracted, squeezed tight with pain. 'You might have all…' she mimicked his gesture '…*this*. You might have the fabulous house on a fabulous coastline in a fabulously beautiful country, and you might have a house in London big enough to fit ten of mine, but I've never pursued money and I certainly would never, ever, set my sights on getting hold of someone else's by…'

'Fair means or foul?' He took his time standing up, flexing his muscles while watching her. Then he leant across to place his hands flat on the arms of her chair. 'I felt it a good idea to make sure we were both still singing off the same song sheet.'

'I could never be serious about someone as arrogant as you, Alessandro.'

'And yet you gave such a misleading impression eight years ago.'

'Will you ever forget that?'

'It's been imprinted on my mind with the force and clarity of a branding iron.'

So much for thinking that he was becoming indifferent, Chase was forced to concede. So much for thinking that revenge was a dish in which he might no longer be interested. 'You weren't arrogant then.' She met his stare levelly. She wasn't prepared for the feel of his mouth against hers as he crushed her lips in a driving, savage kiss that propelled her back into the chair.

Her hands automatically rose to push him away. How the hell could he think that she might be interested in having him touch her when he had just insulted her in the worst way possible? And yet her body responded, went up in flames like dry tinder waiting for the burning match. Reluctant hands softened to cup the nape of his neck.

In one easy movement, he scooped her off the chair and into his arms.

'Alessandro!'

He was heading up the stairs, towards the bedroom with its shuttered windows and thin, cream voile curtains, pale wood and wicker furniture.

'We've talked enough.'

'You called me a gold-digger! Do you…?' She was breathless as he kicked open the bedroom door. 'Do you honestly think that I…I get turned on being insulted?'

'I didn't call you a gold-digger. I warned you of the pitfalls of becoming one. And, no, you don't get turned on by being insulted. You just get turned on by me…' He unceremoniously dumped her on the bed and shot her a wickedly sexy smile as she scrambled into a sitting position to glare at him. 'I'm sick of talking.' He stripped off his black polo shirt and flung it to the floor. 'Get naked for me.'

Chase continued to glare but already her flustered mind was forgetting the hurt inflicted and keening towards the feel of his hands on her body. Still, she didn't rush to obey, but as he led the way, removing his shirt then his jeans, she could feel herself melting.

Their love-making was fast and urgent. She wanted to lose herself in it and forget the things he had told her, the coldness in his voice when he had reminded her of what their relationship really was all about. Did he honestly imagine that she was the type of woman who could look at someone else's possessions and work out how she could get her hands on them? Yes, of course he did. The distance between a liar and a gold-digger was very small.

She wanted to make love until she lost the hurt, and she did. She touched him, kissed him, dominating him in one move before yielding in another. She caught a glimpse of his back at one point and saw the marks of where her fingers had scored into his skin. He ordered her to talk dirty to him and she wondered how she did it so easily when she hadn't a clue what she was supposed to say. It was a complete release of all her inhibitions and it turned her on. It turned her on even more when he talked dirty back to her.

This was what it was all about—having sex. The most amazing, fulfilling sex she could ever imagine. It was all he wanted and, if it wasn't all *she* wanted, then that was something she would just have to live with.

Her orgasm was long and deep and filled every single part of her body. It dispelled all her dark thoughts. It made her feel as though she was soaring through space, out of reach of anything that might hurt her. She longed for it to last for ever. In fact, she closed her eyes and kept them firmly shut even after Alessandro rolled off her. He was breathing as unevenly as she was. She could picture every inch of his face, every line, the sweep of his dark lashes, his gleaming black eyes that could make her body go up in flames with a single glance. She had absorbed all the details and stored them in her head with the efficiency of a state-of-the-art computer housing data.

'Are you going to fall asleep on me?'

'I'm dozing.'

'Should I be flattered that I can send a woman to sleep?'

'Actually…' Chase opened her eyes reluctantly and propped herself on her side so that they were facing one another on the bed, front to front, her breasts brushing his chest. 'I was thinking…'

What would happen if she ever told him the truth about how she felt? Would she find it liberating? 'About work. How much I'll have to get done when I return. I may even go in tomorrow evening after we're back. Have I told you about the work that's due to start on the shelter? Beth keeps asking if I'm sure that the costs will be covered.' She ran her finger lightly along his shoulder blade, tracing muscle and sinew. 'She has a morbid fear of bailiffs banging on the front door because she hasn't been able to pay her creditors.'

Alessandro frowned. As pillow talk went, it left a lot to be desired, yet he realised that he should be feeling relieved. He had laid down his dictates and she hadn't blinked an eye. In fact, he need not have bothered. She had no interest in taking things between them beyond their natural course. Thank God. And, to prove how misguided he had been in imagining that she might get a little too wrapped up in *this,* here she was now, chatting about work. Did it get less romantic?

But who the hell wanted romance? 'I need a shower,' he said abruptly.

'Are you okay? I shouldn't have mentioned the shelter. I wouldn't want you to think that I don't trust you…' She sat up, slightly panicked by his sudden mood swing, and it occurred to her that this was something she would have to get accustomed to if she decided to stick it out. He didn't care about her. Why should it bother him if he was dismissive, if he decided to have a mood swing?

'You clearly have a way to go if you think that I would ever back down on my word, despite my assurances.' Alessandro eased himself off the bed. 'I can bring the flight forward if you have work issues. In fact, might not be a bad idea. I have a couple of major deals about to reach boiling point. I need to be back sooner rather than later. A few hours makes all the difference sometimes.'

Suddenly backed into a corner, Chase nodded brightly. 'I'll begin packing while you're in the shower.' She waited for him to relent, to tell her that they should stick to the original timetable; what did a few hours matter? He didn't.

And what happened with them when they returned? It was a question she was reluctant to ask.

It hovered at the back of her mind for the remainder of the night and through into the following morning. Flights had been rescheduled and still nothing was said and she refused to weaken. His mood had disappeared as fast as it had come. On the surface, everything was bright and breezy. When she looked back at the villa from the back of the limo as they were driving away, she felt a pang of intense sadness that she would never see it again.

He seemed to be lost in his own thoughts and she acknowledged that he was probably projecting ahead, thinking about those deals of his that wouldn't go away unless he was on the scene to sort them out.

The silence between them became oppressive but it was

only when they had touched down at Heathrow that she turned to him and said lightly, 'So, what happens next...?'

Alessandro had had no idea how tense he had been until she asked that question. He had been infuriated with himself for not much liking her air of casual insouciance. Did the woman give a damn one way or another? But now, his keen ears tuning in to a thread of nervousness in her voice, he was satisfied that she did, and that did wonders for his ego.

'I'll call you.' He curved a sure hand on her cheek and bent to place a hungry kiss on her lips.

Chase was ashamed of the enthusiasm with which she returned his kiss. If she could have, she would have dragged him off to the nearest hotel room and picked up where they had left off in Italy. Instead, she pulled away with a sigh. 'I've never had much time for those women who hang around waiting for the phone to ring.'

Alessandro laughed. Her kiss conveyed a thousand messages and all of them were good. 'I haven't had enough of you by a long shot. I'll call you tomorrow. Save you doing too much waiting by the phone...although, if you *do* find yourself waiting by the phone, then give my imagination something to go on. It would work if you waited there in your birthday suit...'

So what if she hadn't said anything? Would he have posed the question himself? Would he have wanted to know what happened next? Was this going to be her destiny for the foreseeable future—a day-to-day existence, only coming alive when Alessandro was around; not daring to breathe a word of how she really felt; living in fear of the phone calls stopping, grateful for whatever crumbs continued to drop her way? Was this what she had spent the past eight years working towards?

She took a taxi back to the house. She couldn't face the vagaries of the underground.

It was a little after two in the afternoon by the time she was paying the taxi driver. A thin, annoying drizzle had started, accompanied by a gusty wind, and as she fumbled in her handbag for her keys there was nothing on her mind other than getting inside the house and out of the rain.

She certainly wasn't expecting the man that stepped out of the shadows at the side of the house. When he spoke, all thoughts of the rain, getting inside and even of Alessandro flew out of her head. She gaped in horror as he smiled and pulled his hoodie down a little lower so that most of his face was in shadow.

'Long time no see, Chase. Been anywhere exciting…?'

CHAPTER EIGHT

CHASE WOKE WITH a start to the sound of her alarm going off. She had a few seconds of intense disorientation and then memories of the afternoon before broke through the barrier of forgetfulness and began pouring through her head. She had no idea how she had managed to get through what remained of the day, how she had managed finally to get to sleep.

She began getting ready for work on autopilot, showering, fetching her smart grey suit from the wardrobe, twinning it with a crisp white shirt. When half an hour later she looked at her reflection in the mirror, on the surface she was the same diligent, nicely dressed professional her colleagues would be expecting back at the office after a few days in the sun, with a companion or companions unknown.

Under the surface, she was barely functioning.

She had not expected to return to her house and find Brian Shepherd on her doorstep. In fact, she had not expected ever to have set eyes on Brian Shepherd again, but then didn't bad things have a habit of bouncing right back? Wasn't it true what they said, that you could run but you couldn't hide?

She had foolishly imagined Brian Shepherd to be nothing but a distant memory from the bad old days. 'Blue Boy' had been his nickname, because of his bright-blue eyes. He had been Shaun's closest friend growing up, the one who, from the age of ten, had shown him all the clever ways they could break and enter houses and all the tricks of the trade for getting their hands on valuable scrap metal. Six years older than Shaun, he had been his mentor until finally she and Shaun had moved to London, leaving behind Blue Boy for good. Fat chance, as it turned out.

And now he was back.

'Heard you were doing well for yourself,' he had said, inviting himself into her house and scanning it with the shrewd eyes of a born petty thief. 'Heard you found yourself a replacement for Shaunie.'

She had flinched every time he had reached out to touch one of her possessions but past experience had taught her that any sign of weakness would be a mistake with Brian Shepherd. She knew all about his temper.

There had been no need to ask him how he had found out about Alessandro. He had volunteered the information with relish: a friend of a friend of a friend had spotted them together on their little love-bird holiday in Italy. At the airport, of all places. Wasn't it a small world?

'Angie—Angie Carson. Remember her? Fat cow. Took a picture of the both of you. On her phone. Bet you never spotted her! Probably wouldn't have recognised her cos it's been a while, hasn't it? Anyone would think you were ashamed of all your old mates...'

He didn't remove his hoodie the entire time he was at the house, prowling through from room to room, touching and picking things up and turning them round in his hands, as though trying to figure out what they were worth.

Chase remained largely silent until, eventually, when she could stand it no longer, she asked him what he wanted, because of course he would want something.

Money. He was in a bit of a tight spot. Just enough to tide him over, and he knew she could lay her hands on some, because they'd driven off in a flash car and the luggage…

He gave a low, long whistle and eyed her up and down in a way that made her stomach lurch. Nice luggage. Expensive. Angie had been impressed. Snapped a few pics of that on her phone and all.

So, just a bit of money, spare change for a bloke who could zoom off in a chauffeur-driven limo with all that nice luggage in the boot. Angie had gone off with her mates but he was betting that, wherever that flash car had driven to, it wasn't going to be a one-star dump with dodgy air-conditioning.

So, what did she say? Did she think that she could spare an old friend a bit of loose change? Maybe, he said, he could persuade her. He knew where she worked…had done a little digging after those photos fat Angie had shown him…

Remember that club, the one that got busted by the coppers….? Course, she'd been underage at the time and she hadn't actually been doing drugs or anything—not like him and Shaunie and the rest of the gang. But those posh people at the law firm, they'd be really keen to know that she used to mix with a crowd who all had police records, wouldn't they? Might even get to thinking that *she* had a police record! Wouldn't that be funny? And, being honest, just the fact that she and he used to be mates would get them wondering, wouldn't it?

He had chuckled. 'You know what they say about the smelly stuff sticking…'

Her mobile rang now just as she was about to enter the office. Alessandro. She switched it off. There was no way that she could talk to him. Not just yet. But talk to him she would have to, because Brian Shepherd wasn't going to go away until he got his wretched money which, as it turned out, was hardly what she would have called 'loose change'.

It was certainly more than she had set aside, which was precious little after her mortgage repayments had been made and the bills paid.

Her life seemed to be unravelling at speed and she had to force herself not to succumb to the meltdown she knew was hovering just around the corner. She had weathered a lot of things and she would weather this as well. It would just take a little working out.

By the time she pushed through the doors to their offices, she had glumly decided what needed to be done.

Her first port of call was her boss's office.

Tony Grey was a short, round man in his fifties who would have been a dead ringer for Father Christmas were it not for the fact that he was almost entirely bald and his dark-grey eyes were way too astute for someone who spent all his time laughing and chuckling. In actual fact, Chase had never seen her boss laugh out loud, but he had always been fair and supportive. She would miss that.

She would have to hand in her notice. She had come to that conclusion as she had left her house. Brian Shepherd wouldn't just do what he threatened; he would go further if she didn't do as he asked. Hadn't he been banged up for nearly killing someone in a bar brawl when he was fourteen? What if he took it into his head to release his explosive temper on *her* if she didn't play ball? If he could nearly kill someone at the age of fourteen because they'd accidentally knocked into him without saying sorry, then he could certainly kill her if he wanted money from her and she refused to pay. She loathed the thought of having to yield in a situation like this but pride was no match for sheer common sense.

Well, on the bright side, she would find a company specialising more in the pro bono work she enjoyed and, even if Brian hunted her down there, he would be able to see for himself that it wasn't a money-making machine.

She still couldn't work out how he had discovered her whereabouts but there was no point wasting time trying to figure that out. With social-networking sites stretching their tentacles into every area of everyone's lives, it wouldn't have been beyond the wit of man for him to ferret her out the second he'd figured he could get money from her.

'My dear,' Tony said when she had explained that she would have to hand in her notice for personal reasons. 'Are you sure this is really what you want to do? You're on course to go far with this firm. Your dedication is second to none.'

But he assured her that, if he couldn't persuade her to change her mind, then of course he would provide her with glowing references. With just that sympathy and fairness which she would miss so much, he also agreed that she could leave as soon as she had tied up loose ends on the cases she was currently working on so that they could be handed over in good order.

She had no idea what he concluded her 'personal reasons' for leaving might be, but she suspected that health issues might be at the heart of it, and he was right in a way. She certainly wasn't feeling very well at the moment. Not when she considered the way her nicely controlled life had been turned upside down.

Alessandro... She thought that this might not be as similarly smooth sailing. She ignored a further two calls from him, only picking up his last just as she was about to leave the office on the dot of five. Clock watching had never been her style, but tying up loose ends was a dismal procedure. Nor was she up to chatting to all and sundry about her decision to leave.

'Where the hell have you been? I've phoned three times!'

'I'm sorry. I was...busy.' Just the sound of his voice

sent little ripples of awareness racing up and down her spine as she took the lift to the ground floor and emerged into yet another cool and overcast day to do battle with public transport.

'Busy doing what?'

'I, well, I've handed in my notice at Fitzsimmons.'

For a few seconds, Alessandro debated whether he had heard her correctly. But there was something in her voice, a tell-tale tremor that she couldn't quite conceal; a nuance which he felt that only he would have been able to pick up. Something was different, *wrong,* a little off-kilter.

He stood up, restlessly moving away from his desk towards the windows and absently looking down. 'You're kidding.'

'No, I'm not. Can we meet? I can…um…come to your office.'

'I can think of a better venue.'

'I'd rather your office, Alessandro.'

'What's going on?' he demanded bluntly. 'And please don't tell me *nothing.* You tell me you've handed in your notice, even though you've expressed nothing but satisfaction at your job there, and now…you want to meet me *in my office*?'

'Please.'

Alessandro sighed heavily and raked his fingers through his hair. He was getting a very bad vibe about whatever the hell was going on but he acquiesced. Whatever was happening, he would be able to get it out of her and things would return to normal. He was nothing if not wholly confident in his ability to take her mind off things.

'I'd rather not parade my personal life in front of my employees,' he drawled. 'And *you* may be scuttling out of the office because you've handed in your notice and lost momentum in your job, but my people are all still at their desks. If you can't wait until later and meet me somewhere private, then I can see you in forty-five minutes at that brasserie round the corner from my office. You know the one?'

She did. She made her way there slowly, forgoing the speed and ease of a black cab in favour of a laborious trip by public transport. It suited her mood.

How had life changed so fast in such a brief moment in time? As she neared the brasserie, she felt a sickening lurch of déjà vu. Eight years ago she had met Alessandro here with one thing and one thing only in her head—the need to get rid of him. She had walked towards a conversation she had known would break her in half and she was doing the same thing now. History was repeating itself. But it was so much worse this time, she would be taking so many more regrets with her when she was finished saying what she had to say.

Sitting at the back of the brasserie, nursing an extremely early glass of red wine, Alessandro had been waiting for ten minutes. He had been unable to get down to work after her phone call. He would never have imagined himself as one of those sensitive, intuitive sorts but something wasn't right and, however much he told himself that he could sort out whatever the hell it was that was eating her up, he was still vaguely uneasy.

And yet, why should he be? They had parted company the day before and everything had been just fine and dandy. There'd been no inconvenient intuition then. So, really, what could have materially changed since then?

He spotted her the second she walked through the door. For the briefest of moments he felt a sharp, inexplicable pang of nostalgia for the carefree girl in shorts and tee-shirts who had been his companion for the past few days. She was in full lawyer mode: prissy grey suit, even prissier white blouse, black pumps. He wondered how long he could wait before he ripped the whole lot off her and bedded her.

On cue, his erection pushed hard against the zip of his trousers and he shifted position uncomfortably to release some of the insistent ache in his groin.

He had not expected this crazy lust to be an ongoing situation after the countless times they had now slept together. He had assumed she would be more than just disposable: he would take what had once been denied him and then discard her without preamble. It wasn't working out quite as he had envisaged, but he shrugged that off. The unexpected could sometimes be a good thing and getting turned on by her on a semi-permanent basis was definitely not to be sneezed at, especially for him, a man whose tastes had become lamentably jaded over time.

He watched with masculine appreciation as she glanced around her. Already he was undressing her in his mind. Slowly. Revealing those generous pale breasts inch by succulent inch; exposing the pink nipples to take them one at a time in his mouth as they pouted temptingly up at him.

He pictured the prissy grey skirt hitting the ground, followed by whatever suitably functional underwear she happened to be wearing… He could almost taste the honeyed sweetness between her legs, hear her broken little whimpers of pleasure as his tongue found her sweet spot and worked it until the broken little whimpers became moans and cries of pleasure. The more horny he became, just sitting and watching her and letting his imagination run wild, the faster he knew he would have to sort out whatever was on her mind just so that he could get her back to his place. They might not even be able to make it to the bedroom.

He grinned as she spotted him and lazily attracted the waitress's attention without taking his eyes off Chase's face. Her looks were really quite startling. There was a sexiness to her, a perfection to her features, that made her naturally guarded expression all the more beguiling. He could see other men surreptitiously following her with their eyes as she weaved her way towards him.

'Alessandro…' Chase said weakly. She could feel her heart thumping like a sledgehammer inside her.

'So you've handed in your notice.' He broke off to order her a cappuccino. 'And you don't look very happy about it.'

'I…I…' She could barely string two words together. This was so much worse than she had envisaged. There was just no way that she could pretend to be cool, calm and collected. Her nerves were all over the place.

'Sit down. Tell me about it. Why?'

'I…I didn't have much of a choice,' she admitted truthfully. 'Personal reasons.'

'What personal reasons?'

'I'd rather not talk about it.'

'Are you ill?' He felt a sudden mixture of fear and irrational panic. 'Is that what this is all about?'

'No,' she said, waving a wistful goodbye to what could have been a fantastic excuse. As if lies hadn't landed her here in the first place. 'No, I'm not ill.'

'Then what? What personal reasons, and why don't you want to discuss them?' Alessandro scowled. Since when had he ever been interested in women's life stories? Mysteries dangling at the end of a line like bait to hook him in had always left him cold.

He eyed her narrowly as a new thought began to take shape in his head. 'If you're not ill,' he said slowly, 'and yet you've reluctantly had to hand in your notice, then there's only one explanation that springs to mind…'

Temporarily diverted, Chase looked at him in bafflement. 'Is there?'

'Someone's made a pass at you. Who is it?' His voice was low and controlled but he clenched his fists. The second he had a name, he would personally make it his business to make sure that the culprit paid.

'Made a pass at me?'

'Even wearing that starchy suit, you're still sexy as hell, Chase. And I won't be the only one who can see that. So, spill the beans. Tell me who it is. Your boss? One of your colleagues? What did he do? Did he touch you inappropriately? Try to feel you up?'

He imagined one of those rich kids thinking that he could have a go at the sexiest woman in the office and he was overwhelmed by an explosive rage. He had met enough twenty-something lawyers in his time to know that the majority of them thought that they were studs.

'No one touched me, Alessandro! And no one tried to *feel me up*! Do you think that I'm so feeble that I would allow anyone to get away with that? Do you think that I'm incapable of taking care of myself?' But his show of possessiveness touched her. She folded her hands on her lap to stop herself from reaching out and covering his hand with her own.

'Then what's going on?' Looking at her, it was clear that she could barely meet his eyes. She was fidgeting nervously with the handle of her coffee cup. Alessandro felt that he could do with the entire bottle of wine, never mind one careful glass. Instead he ordered a black coffee while he tried to sift through some plausible explanation for her behaviour in his mind. 'You're not…pregnant, are you?' It was a thought that only now occurred to him.

Chase glanced up at his face, suddenly ashen, and for a few moments anger replaced gnawing anxiety and dread. It was obvious from his expression that the mere suggestion of pregnancy had knocked him for six. 'And what if I *was*?' she queried boldly. 'What if I told you that there was a mini-Alessandro taking shape right now inside me?'

She fancied she could see the colour drain away from

his face as she allowed him time to absorb the full horror of that scenario. 'Don't worry, Alessandro. I'm not pregnant. I told you once that I'm not a complete idiot.'

For a few fleeting seconds, Alessandro had found himself ripped out of his comfort zone, staring down the barrel of a gun. She was having his baby. *His baby.* The gun barrel, strangely, was less of a threat than he might have imagined.

'Accidents happen,' he said grimly.

'Oh, Alessandro…' She sighed and sat back, head tilted up, eyes half-closed as the inescapable hurtled towards her with the deadly force of a bomb. 'I'm healthy, there's no mini-Alessandro on the way and no one's made a pass at me at work. And I wish there was some other way of saying this but there isn't…' She straightened and took a deep breath. 'I need to ask you something.'

'What?'

'I need to…borrow some money from you.'

Deathly silence greeted this request. Chase didn't dare look at Alessandro. What choice did she have? she wondered helplessly. Brian wasn't going to go away until he had his money and she simply didn't have it. If she got it, gave it to him and then convinced him that she had broken up with Alessandro, then he would go away. If she didn't, then she was, frankly, scared of what he might do. Scared of all the old horrors landing on her doorstep once again.

'Tell me I'm not hearing this.'

'I'm sorry and, naturally, I'll pay you back every penny of what I borrow. With interest.'

Alessandro laughed mirthlessly. 'So finally,' he said in a lethally soft voice, 'the real face of Chase Evans is revealed. I'm surprised you managed to keep it hidden for so long.' He felt as though he had been punched in the gut. This wasn't just anger; this was a level of hurt that he could barely acknowledge even to himself. He didn't know who

he loathed more—himself for having been conned a second time, or her for having been the one to do the conning.

'What do you need the money for?' He could scarcely
credit that he was willing to hear her out, willing to give
her an explanation that would allow him to make sense of
the situation. That window of willingness died the second
she looked at him and said steadily,

'I'm sorry. That's…none of your business.' The harshest
of words, yet they would provide the clean break.

'Right. So…when did you decide that you could screw
me for money?' he asked in the same ultra-controlled voice
that was far more intimidating than if he had stood up and
shouted at her. 'Was it when you came to my house? Or
was it when we went to Italy and you saw just how much
I had? Tell me. I'm curious.'

'You don't understand, Alessandro. I wouldn't be sitting here asking you for money if…if…I didn't have to.'

'And yet you refuse to tell me what you want the money
for.' He threw up his hands in rampant frustration as she
greeted this with stubborn silence. 'Are you in some sort
of debt? Hell, Chase, just be bloody straight with me!'

'I told you, it's none of your business. If you don't want
to lend me the money, then just say so.' Her heart was
breaking in two.

'And, just for the record, how much money do you fancy
you can bleed me for?'

She named the figure and watched as he threw his head
back and roared with laughter, except there was no humour
there. He was laughing with incredulity and his dark eyes
were as hard and cold as the frozen depths of a glacier.

'Well…?' Chase cleared her throat and valiantly met
his eyes.

'No explanations, no excuses, not even of the make-
believe variety… Sorry, not good enough.' He signalled
to the waitress for the bill. 'And consider this conversa-

tion over.' Hell, the woman could act. She was as white as a sheet and her hands were shaking—remarkable performance. He felt something painful twist inside him, an iron fist clenching on his intestines, and staunched it down.

'I think we can say that our unfinished business has been concluded. If you ever get it into your head to descend on me, either at my offices or at my house, I assure you I will have you forcibly removed either by the police or by my security personnel. Do you read me?'

Chase nodded. Had she expected him to part with cash just because she'd asked? Because she'd offered to pay him back? Was there some part of her that had hoped he might know her well enough by now to give her the benefit of the doubt? She couldn't tell him the truth. How could she? She was boxed in with no room to manoeuvre.

'I understand,' she said quietly.

'Question.' Alessandro was furious with himself for not walking away without a backward glance. He was even more furious with himself for the unwilling tug of compassion he was feeling for a woman who was nothing more or less than a gold-digger with great acting ability. And, underneath that maelstrom of emotion, he recognised the angry pain of disillusionment. 'If you're so desperate for money, why jack the job in?'

'I can't discuss that either.'

Alessandro stood up abruptly. 'Good luck finding your money,' he told her coldly. 'If anything needs to be discussed about the shelter, you might want another lawyer to handle it.'

'I've already begun tidying up all my ongoing case files. Someone else will be handling all the details with the shelter. I…I've been given permission to leave at the end of the week. I should be working out a month's notice but my boss—'

'Not really interested.'

Chase remained standing, watching his departing back. She told herself, bracingly, that it was always going to end—yet the hollowness filling her felt as destructive as a tsunami. If she wasn't a homeowner, if she had been one of the millions renting, she knew that she would have upped sticks and disappeared. No job, no Alessandro and a threat waiting for her when she returned: it took all her courage to gather herself and head back outside down to the underground.

Brian would be there. He had told her in a chummy voice laced with menace that he would be waiting when she returned, that he didn't mind just hanging out there, although if she wanted to hand her key over to him…

Chase shuddered.

Heading in the opposite direction back to his office, Alessandro angrily realised that the very last thing he was in the mood to do was work. He still had a conference call lined up for later that evening. He got on his mobile, spoke to his secretary and cancelled it.

Hell, could he have been *that* stupid that he had fallen for the walk up the garden path *yet again*? With tremendous effort, he side-lined the fury raging through him and tried to recall the details of their brief conversation in the brasserie.

She hadn't given him an answer when he had asked her why she had handed in her notice if she needed money. That, for one thing, made no sense. Whatever debts she had managed to incur, she wasn't so stupid that she could imagine settling them without a regular salary coming in. So had she been sacked? Had they discovered something? Had she been embezzling? It seemed a ludicrous idea, but hell, how was he to know when she had offered no explanation for her behaviour?

No, this was not going to happen again. He was emphatically *not* going to be left stranded with a bucket load of unanswered questions, as had happened last time round. Whether he ever laid eyes on her again or not was immaterial. He would pay her a little visit and would stay put until she answered all his questions to his satisfaction. Then, and only then, would he leave.

He called his driver to collect him. Rush-hour traffic meant that it took a ridiculously long time before his driver made it to the building, even though his car, parked outside his house, was only a matter of a couple miles away as the crow flew. It took even longer to navigate the stand-still traffic in central London.

His mobile buzzed continuously and he eventually switched it off. He was fully given over to trying to disentangle the conversation he had had with Chase. He felt like a man in possession of just sufficient pieces of a complex puzzle to rouse curiosity and yet lacking the essential ones that would solve the conundrum.

This, he told himself, was why he was sitting in the back of his car, drumming his fingers restlessly on the leather seat and frowning out of the back window. He had been presented with a complex puzzle and it was only human nature to try and figure it out, whatever the cost. Frankly, he would drag answers out of her if he had to.

It was considerably later than he had expected by the time the car swung into her small road. From outside, he could see that lights were on. 'You can leave,' he told his driver. 'I'll get a cab back to my house.' He slammed the door and watched as the Jag slowly disappeared around the corner.

If there was a small voice in his head telling him that his appearance on her doorstep made little sense, given the fact that she had never been destined to be a permanent feature in his life, he chose to ignore it. Finding answers seemed more important than debating the finer points.

He leaned his hand on the doorbell and kept it there for an inordinately long time. Where the hell was she? If the lights were on, then she was home. She had a thing about wasting electricity, just one of her many little quirks to which he had become accustomed. He scowled at the very fact that he was remembering that at this juncture.

Chase heard the insistent buzzing of the doorbell but it took her a second or two before she generated the enthusiasm to get the door. In the lounge, a fuming Brian was filling a bin bag with whatever he fancied he could take from her. There was nothing she could do about it; he was bigger and he had no conscience when it came to violence.

She'd have done anything to get rid of him, to have him out of her house. He told her to get rid of whoever was at the door.

'Too busy here for visitors, darling. Still a lot to get through before I leave!'

Chase pulled open the door and her mouth fell open in shock. Alessandro was the last person she had expected to find on her doorstep.

'You're not getting rid of me until you tell me what the hell is really going on with you!' were his opening words.

'Alessandro, you have to go.'

She was scared stiff; that much he could see. He pushed past her and halted as a man in his thirties sauntered out of the living room. In the space of mere seconds, Alessandro had processed the guy and reached his verdict. This was no smarmy, overpaid young lawyer. This was a thug and, whatever was going on, Chase was afraid.

'And you are…?' If there was going to be a fight, then he was more than up for it.

'Not about to tell you, mate. Hang on…thought you said you'd broken up with lover boy? Lying to me, were you? Don't like lies…'

Alessandro clenched his fists. Chase had backed away

and was stammering out some sort of explanation which he barely registered. No, this wasn't going to do. He had hold of the man's tee-shirt and felt roughly one hundred and forty pounds of packed muscle try to squirm away from him. Escape was never destined to be. He propelled the man back towards the sitting room. Out of the corner of his eye, he could see that the room had been decimated. A black bin bag was stuffed to overflowing on the ground. Another was half-full. Was this the 'spot of bother' she was in?

'You're going to tell me what's going on...' He addressed her but kept his eye on his frantically writhing captive. The man was a bully; Alessandro could spot the signs a mile away. The sort of loser who didn't mind throwing his weight around with anyone weaker than him but would run a mile if faced with stiff competition. Alessandro prided himself on being stiff competition. He listened intently while Chase babbled something about Brian wanting money...taking her stuff...

The missing pieces were beginning to fall into place. So the money had been a legitimate request. She hadn't been trying to con gold out of him. 'Here's what you're going to do, buddy.' His voice was low, soft and razor-sharp. 'You're going to unload that bin bag and return all the nice lady's possessions to her. Then you're going to apologise and, when you've finished apologising, you're going to leave quietly through that front door and never show your face here again. Do you read me loud and clear?

'And just in case...' He tightened his stranglehold so that the man was gasping to catch his breath. 'You get it into your head that you can ignore what I'm telling you, here's what will happen to you if you do. I'll employ someone to dredge up every scrap of dirt on you—and I'm betting that there's a lot—and then I'm going to make sure that you get put behind bars and the key is conveniently thrown away. And don't think I won't do it. I will. And I'll enjoy every second of it.'

He watched in silence, arms folded, as his orders were obeyed. Out of the bin bag came all the bits and pieces which, Alessandro knew, would have taken Chase years to accumulate. Some were worthless, some—such as her computer, her tablet, the plasma-screen television which she had laughingly told him had been an absolute indulgence because she really didn't watch much TV—weren't.

His apology was grudgingly given until Alessandro ordered him to try harder, to say it like he meant it...

He left as quietly as he had been ordered to do. Then there was just the two of them, standing in a room that looked as though a bomb had exploded in it.

'I'm sorry,' Chase mumbled. Yet she was so glad that he had come because now she felt utterly safe. She moved to begin picking up some of her possessions from the ground, stacking them neatly on the sofa, very conscious of Alessandro's eyes on her. 'Why did you come?' she asked.

'You need something stiff to drink.'

'I'm fine.'

'Do you have any brandy?'

'I'm fine.' She finally met his eyes and hesitantly perched on the edge of the chair with her hands on her knees. 'There's half a bottle of wine in the fridge,' she offered when he continued to look at her in silence. 'It's all I can do by way of drink, I'm afraid. I don't keep spirits in the house.' Shock was creeping over her. She didn't want alcohol but she had to admit that she felt a little better after she had swallowed a mouthful from the glass he placed in her shaking hand a minute later.

'I guess you want to know what all that was about,' she said wearily.

'Understatement of the decade, Chase.'

Chase stared down at her fingers. She'd been rescued

by a man who had only returned to the scene to find out what was going on because he was like that—would never have been able to accept a brush off without demanding answers.

She would have to explain how it was that she knew Brian, how he had happened to be in her house. She would have to come clean about her background and know that he would be filled with contempt. Contempt for a woman who had lied about a fundamental aspect of her life and maintained the lie all through the time she had been seeing him. But there still remained a part of her that she refused to reveal, because to reveal it would be to lower herself even more in his estimation.

'You'd better sit down and I'll tell you. And then…' She took a deep breath and exhaled slowly. 'You can leave and it'll finally be over between us.'

CHAPTER NINE

SHE WAS STILL in her work clothes, the same dreary grey suit, except she looked...*rumpled.*

'Did he lay a finger on you?' Alessandro asked suddenly. 'Did he touch you?' This was as far out of his comfort zone as he had ever been. Even with parents intent on squandering their inheritance—parents who had been shining examples of irresponsibility; who had opened the doors of their various houses to artists and poets and playwrights, most of whom had been pleasantly stoned most of the time—through all that, he had never come into contact with the seedier side of life. The side of life that threw up people like the thug who had just been thrown off the premises. Even with diminishing wealth, he had still lived a sheltered, privileged life.

'No. No, he didn't.' Chase could see the incredulity stamped on his beautiful face. He was shocked at what he had found, shocked that the woman he thought came from a solid, middle-class background could know someone like Brian Shepherd. 'Although it's not unheard of for Brian to lay into someone just for the hell of it, never mind if he thinks they've done something to him.'

'How the hell do you know that guy, Chase?' Alessandro frowned. 'When you said that you couldn't tell me why you needed the money, did you mean that you owed that creep money?'

'No, I did *not* owe that creep any money. He just…' She stood up, suddenly restless, but then immediately sat back down because her legs felt like jelly.

'What, then…?'

'If you would just sit down and stop *prowling*.'

Alessandro paused to look at her narrowly. 'If you didn't owe the guy money, then why would he have gathered half of your possessions and stuffed them into a bin bag?' He sat on the chair facing her. Their body language was identical, both sitting forward, arms resting loosely on their thighs although, whilst Alessandro's expression was one of intense curiosity, Chase's was more resigned and reflective.

'Brian and Shaun were friends,' she said quietly, not daring to meet his eyes, fearful of what she would see there. 'They were friends from before I met Shaun, childhood friends, even though Brian was older. They grew up on the same council estate.'

'Which calls into question the type of man you chose to marry.'

'When you're young, it's very easy to get drawn in to the wrong crowd.'

'I'm trying to picture your parents allowing you to get drawn in to the wrong crowd. Or didn't they have any say in the matter? Maybe they were too busy projecting to happy times ahead in Australia…?'

'There *is* no Australia.'

'Sorry, but I'm not following you.'

Chase nervously tucked a strand of hair behind her ears. She wondered what hand of fate it was that had returned Alessandro to her life, only to have her fall in love with him all over again. Instead of getting him out of her system by sleeping with him, by putting that unfulfilled fantasy to rest, she had managed to well and truly cement him into every nook, cranny and corner of her being.

'My parents don't live in Australia. In fact, I have no parents. I was a foster-home kid. I was shuffled from family to family, never staying anywhere for very long. I never knew my father. My mother died when I was very little from a drugs overdose. I pretty much brought myself up. So, you see, everything you think you know about me is a lie.'

Of all the things Alessandro had been prepared for, this was not one of them. 'Lyla…?'

'Was the name I chose when I met you. When I thought that I could create…make myself out to be…'

'You fabricated everything.'

'No. Not everything!'

Alessandro slammed his hand on the side of his chair and vaulted to his feet. He felt tight in his skin. He needed to move. Energy was pouring through him and he was at a loss as to how to contain it. This must be what it felt like to imagine your feet were planted on solid ground only to discover that you were trying to balance on quicksand.

'Everything about you has been a lie from beginning to end. God. Why?'

'I made stuff up. I was young! I met you and I wanted to make a good impression.'

'Not only were you married, not only did you choose to conceal that fact from me eight years ago, but you also chose to conceal everything else. So your husband was… what, exactly? And how did you manage to make it to university? Or maybe you weren't a student at all. Were you? Or was that another lie?'

'Of course I was!' Chase cried, half-rising to her feet in an attempt to halt the flow of his scathing criticism. She sat back down as quickly as she had stood up. What else might she have hoped for? That he might have been understanding? Sympathetic? Why would he be? To him, she was now a confirmed liar and, if she had lied about everything, all those significant details, then what else might she have lied about? Her emotions? Her responses? It felt as though she had built a relationship on a house of cards and, now the cards were all toppling down, she had no idea how to start catching them before they all fell to the floor.

'Really? What strands am I supposed to start believing now?'

'I *was* a student at university,' she said with feverish urgency. 'I never did a lot of studying…' At this she laughed bitterly. Studying, when she was growing up, had not been seen as something worth wasting time doing. They had all known where they were destined to end up: out of work and on the dole, or else in no-hope jobs earning just enough to scrape by with a little moonlighting on the side.

'But I discovered that I barely needed to. I had a good memory. Brilliant, in fact. I would show up at school after a couple of days doing nothing, playing truant, and somehow I'd still be ahead of everyone in the class. I'd skim through a text book and manage to have instant recall of pretty much everything I'd read…'

The handful of teachers who had noticed that remarkable ability had been her salvation. Because of them she hadn't become a quitter, although she had learned to study undercover. There had never been any mileage in standing out.

She looked at him and held his inscrutable gaze. 'I guess you must find all of this completely alien. I don't suppose you've ever known anyone from the wrong side of the tracks…'

The chasm between them had never seemed wider, now that she was revealing the truth about her background. Even if she had been the person she had once claimed to be, the middle-class girl with the normal parents, there would still have been a chasm between them. Of course, he would have been attracted to her because of how she looked. Sadly, physical attributes were not destined to last; she accepted that, in an ideal world, he would have dumped her sooner or later anyway. He had been born into privilege, whatever his disruptive background, and he would always have ended up looking to settle with a woman from a similar background.

Not only had she lied to him, but she had lied to herself for ever thinking otherwise. And she had. When she had met him again and when she had fallen in love with him again. When she had nurtured silly dreams of 'what if?'s…

'Coming from the wrong side of the tracks is one thing,' Alessandro said brusquely. 'Lying about it is quite another. Were you ever going to tell me the truth?' His sense of betrayal overshadowed every other emotion, including anger.

'What would have been the point?' Chase asked defiantly. 'As you pointed out…as *we* agreed…it's not as though we were ever going anywhere with this relationship. Why would I have spoiled things with lots of truths I know you wouldn't have wanted to hear?'

Alessandro's jaw hardened. He took in her beautiful, stubborn face and had a very vivid image of the teenager she must have been: wild, drifting, incredibly bright, incredibly good-looking. 'Shaun…' Just uttering her ex-husband's name left a sour taste in his mouth. 'Must have thought he had won the lottery the day he met you—clever kid who could be his passport out of whatever dead-end life he was looking forward to leading.'

Chase looked up at him with some surprise. 'I never thought about it that way,' she said truthfully. 'I…' Was that how he had seen her, whilst making her believe that it had been the other way around? That *she* had been the lucky one to have been noticed by *him*? 'I met him when I was fifteen. He was the leader of the pack, so to speak. Everyone looked up to him even though he was younger than nearly all the guys in the gang. He was fed up living on the outskirts of Leeds. He said he wanted more. He said that London was the place to be.'

'And of course, he encouraged you to sign up to university life he knew that it was the best way out for him.'

'I don't know how I managed to get through all my exams, and I did them all a year ahead of everyone else,' Chase confessed. 'Maths, further maths, economics, geography...' But she had. Her teachers had seen to it that she'd sat them all. They were the ones who had insisted on university, who had filled in all the applications on her behalf while she had been busy having fun and running wild.

She had landed herself a place at one of the top universities in the country and had been amazed that she had accomplished such a feat. Only in retrospect had she appreciated the energy behind the scenes that had got her there.

'So you went to university and you got married.'

'The other way around, actually. I got married. Yes. And I went to university. I never expected to meet someone like you. Or anyone, for that matter.'

'And yet you did. And, instead of being truthful, you thought that it would be a much better idea to concoct a fairy-tale story about yourself.'

Chase heard the undercurrent of contempt mixed with bewilderment in his voice and inwardly winced. She was not the person she had pretended to be and that mattered to a man like him, a man who occupied a stratosphere of wealth and power that few could even dream about.

She wanted to shout at him that he didn't have a clue, that he couldn't possibly understand, but shouting wasn't going to do. Losing control wasn't going to do. She would offer him the explanation he deserved to hear with detachment and lack of passion. She would demonstrate that she was already breaking away from him, just as he was with her. She would leave with her dignity intact, as much as it could be. She would save her tears for later.

'Yes.' She tilted her chin up and steeled herself to meet his eyes squarely and without apology. 'I was young. I just…gave in to the temptation to turn myself into someone I wasn't. I made up the background I always wanted for myself.'

Alessandro felt another unwelcome, piercing tug of compassion at the thought that a middle-class background could have constituted her dream life. Most girls would have dreamt up stories of money, overseas holidays and parents with fast cars. She, on the other hand, had dreamt of what most other young girls of her age would have grumbled about and considered normal and boring.

He squashed any notion of compassion as fast as it raised its inappropriate head. The bottom line was that she was a compulsive liar, not to be trusted, never to be believed. He had come to get some truths out of her and he was getting them—in shed-loads.

'Which brings us to that piece of rubbish who was filling bin bags with your possessions.'

Getting to the heart of the matter and the reason he had shown up on her doorstep, Chase thought. Because, the faster he could wash his hands of her and clear off, the better.

'When we went to Italy, one of the girls who used to hang out in our gang was at the airport. I didn't see her.' But then, she hadn't had eyes for anyone but the man silently judging her now.

'She took pictures of us on her phone and posted them on a social networking site. Brian saw them, clocked the Louis Vuitton luggage and the chauffeur-driven car and decided that he would turn up on my doorstep and squeeze me for money. I don't know how he got my address, but there are so many ways of finding people; I don't suppose he had much trouble. He may just have gone to the place we were renting before Shaun died, got in touch with the landlord and got the forwarding address I gave him all those years ago. Who knows? He threatened to tell the people at work about my background… It would have spelled the end of my career. And he might have done a lot more besides…'

It seemed ironic now that the life she had built for herself could have been undone by something as crazy as someone taking a picture of her with Alessandro at an airport. There was no point dwelling on what was fair or what was unfair, she thought. The only way was to move forward. She kept her voice as modulated and toneless as she could.

'He was waiting for me when I got back to my house from Italy.'

Alessandro felt rage wash over him, a perfectly normal reaction to the thought of any thug lying in wait for a helpless victim.

'He told me that he wanted money and…that's when I asked you. I didn't want to, and if you *had* lent me the money I would have paid you back every penny.'

'You mean from the proceeds of the job you jacked in? Why did you do that?'

'I thought it best to resign just in case… I've never brought my past to my work. What would happen if Brian decided to show up at Fitzsimmons…?'

'Catastrophe—because they too were victims of your lies. They believed what you told them about your background, just like I did, didn't they?'

'I've never discussed my private life with anyone,' Chase mumbled, feeling even more of a hopeless liar, even though her lies had been through omission of the absolute truth. 'I've kept myself to myself. I fought hard to get where I was.'

'If you had told me the truth, I might have been inclined to give you the money.'

Chase shrugged. 'He would have come back for more. He knew where to find me. It was stupid of me to even... Well, in moments of panic we sometimes do stupid things.'

'He won't be back.'

'I know. And...and I'm very grateful to you for scaring him away. You probably threatened him with the one thing he would have taken notice of.' She wanted to smile, because who would have thought that a billionaire businessman from a cushy background could have had sufficient forcefulness to intimidate someone like Brian Shepherd into running scared? 'Look, I know you probably hate me for all of this...'

'You mean the fact that you were prepared to perpetuate a piece of fiction about yourself?' Alessandro strolled to stand in front of her, legs planted apart, hands at his sides.

Chase looked up at him reluctantly.

'What other pieces of fiction did you perpetuate?' he asked softly. 'No. There's just one more thing I need to get straight in my head.'

'What's—what's that?' she stammered uncertainly. She watched as he slowly leant over her and she half-closed her eyes as she inhaled his familiar scent. It rushed to her head like incense.

'This...' His mouth crushed her in a savage, punishing kiss and Chase helplessly yielded. She arched back in the chair, pulling him towards her, tasting him hungrily. She knew she shouldn't. She knew that it should be impossible to feel this driving, craven lust for a man who felt nothing but scorn towards her, but she couldn't seem to help herself.

There was a refrain playing at the back of her head that was telling her that this was the last time she would feel his lips on hers.

He pulled her to her feet and somehow they found themselves on the sofa, still entwined with one another. She was breathing heavily and she didn't stop him when he began undoing the buttons on her shirt, very soon losing patience. She heard the pop as a couple were ripped off. She wanted him so badly that she was shaking. Pride or no pride, she felt that she *needed* this final joining of their bodies. Her hands scrabbled to open his shirt so that she could feel the breadth of his chest and she moaned when, eventually, her fingers were splayed against it.

Her nipples tingled against her lacy bra. He cupped her breast with his hand and then pushed it underneath the bra, shoving the bra up so that he could suck on her nipple, drawing the stem into his mouth and swirling his tongue against it until she was half-crying for more.

As he suckled, he nudged her legs apart and then his hand was there, not even bothering to pull down her undies but delving underneath them, finding her wetness and exploring every inch of it with his fingers.

He still hadn't taken off a stitch of his own clothes. She had managed to undo a few buttons on his shirt and had yanked it out from the waistband of his trousers. She feverishly tried to complete the task of undressing him but he wasn't helping. She couldn't get to the zip of his trousers, although she could feel the bulge of his erection.

She gave up as he continued driving his fingers against her, pausing in the rhythmic movement only to insert them into her, into that place where she knew she wanted his rock-hard shaft to be instead.

He reared up and yanked down his trousers and, with his hand tangled in her hair, he guided her to his erection and stifled a groan when she took him into her mouth.

Through half-opened eyes, he watched as she sucked and licked him. She knew just how to rouse him down there with her hands and her mouth and he let her.

She might be a liar; he might not be able to trust her as far as he could throw her—because who could ever trust

a woman who made a habit of fabricating her life story?—
but she certainly knew just which buttons to press.

He tugged her away from him and sank onto her. Her
breasts, with the bra pushed up above them, were full and
ripe and irresistible. With a groan of satisfaction, he covered them with his mouth, until the pouting buds were wet
and hard and he continued, giving her no respite, until she
was wriggling like an eel, desperate for more.

Her hair was all over the place and her cheeks were
flushed, her mouth slightly parted, showing her perfect,
pearly-white teeth. She had sunbathed in the nude by the
pool in Italy, and her body was a perfect honey colour.

How well he knew this body. How much of it he had
explored and committed to memory, from the freckle by
her nipple to the tiny mole on her upper arm.

He pulled down her panties, flattened his hand between
her legs and then stroked her down there, harder and faster,
until he could feel her orgasm building beneath his fingers.
He didn't stop and when she came he watched: watched
her eyes flutter; watched her breathing catch in her throat
for a few seconds; watched her whole body arch, stiffen
and finally slacken as the waves of pleasure finally subsided, leaving her limp.

'Alessandro…' She reached for him and he stayed her
hand, circling her wrist before releasing her and standing up.

For a few seconds, Chase was completely bewildered.
When he began to zip up his trousers, she clambered into
a sitting position and looked at him speechlessly.

'What are you doing?'

'What does it look like I'm doing?'

'We were making love.'

'I was proving to myself that the way you responded to
me wasn't yet another lie.'

'How could you say that?' She itched to pull him back

to her but he was already turning away, doing up his buttons and taking his time, as cool as a cucumber. 'I never, *never,* pretended with you. Not about that...'

Alessandro steeled himself. She had made him cry once. The memory of that rose uninvited like poison from the deepest recesses of his mind. He had given a lot to her and her betrayal then had rocked his foundations. Never again.

'So it would seem.' He turned around to look at her. She was utterly dishevelled and utterly bewitching. 'I came here to get answers from you and I got them, Chase. Now the time has come for me to tell you goodbye. It's been... I would say fun, but what I'd really mean is...it's been a learning curve. You can congratulate yourself on teaching me the dangers of taking people at face value.'

'Alessandro!'

'What?' In the process of heading for the door, he half-turned towards her. His eyes were flat, hard and cold. There was a tense silence that stretched between them to breaking point.

Chase found that she didn't know what to say. She just didn't want him to go. Not just yet. Her body was still burning from where he had touched her, where he had deliberately touched her, turning her on, bringing her to a shuddering orgasm just to prove to himself that the attraction she'd claimed to feel for him was real. It was humiliating, yet she still couldn't bear the thought of him walking away. How on earth had she let it go this far? How was it that the control she had spent eight years building, the ability to arrange her life just how she wanted it without reference to anyone else, had been washed away by a man who had always been unsuitable and inappropriate?

'Nothing.'

He looked at her for a few seconds, shrugged and then he was gone. Just like that.

Chase was left staring at the empty doorway. He was

gone and he would never be coming back. She disgusted him. Her awful life, her sleazy ex-friends…

And he'd had the nerve to look contemptuous because once upon a time she had given in to the temptation to make it all go away by pretending to be somebody else! She might not have known about his wealth back then, but she had known with some unerring sixth sense that he would not be the kind of guy who would find any woman who came from her background attractive or in any way suitable.

And of course, she *hadn't* been suitable. She had been married, for starters. But she had seized that window of forbidden, youthful pleasure and now, all this time later, she was paying heavily for it.

She spent two hours returning all the stuff Brian had hauled off shelves and from drawers back to their rightful places. She washed a lot of it. The thought of his hands on her things made her shudder with distaste.

She hoped that by occupying herself she might take her mind off Alessandro but, all the while, he was in her head as she remembered the things they had done together, the conversations they had had.

She shakily told herself that it was a good thing that they were finished. It had been destined to end and the sooner the better. How much worse would she have felt had they ended it in two months' time? Two months during which she would have just continued falling deeper and deeper in love with him! The longer they lasted, the more difficult it would have been to unpick and disentangle her chaotic emotions. She should be thankful!

And yet, thankful was the very last thing she felt. She felt devastated, tearful and…*ashamed.*

More than anything else, she was angry with him for making her feel that way. She was angry with him for being hard line; for not having an ounce of sympathy in him; for not even trying to see her point of view. She had known from the outset that his sole motivation for sleeping with her was to exact some sort of revenge, to have that wheel turn full circle, to take what he thought had been promised to him eight years ago. Yet, hadn't he got to know her *at all* during that period? Had she just been his lover and *nothing more*?

They hadn't been rolling around on a mattress all of the time. There had been so many instances when they had talked, when the past hadn't existed, just the present, just two people getting to know one another. Or so it had felt to her.

She hated him for wiping that all away as though none of it had existed. She hated him for finding it so easy to write her off as though she was worthless.

Over the next week, as she came closer and closer to her final day at Fitzsimmons, the frustration and anger continued to build inside her. If only she could have maintained the anger, she might have felt protected, but there were so many chinks through which she recalled small acts of thoughtfulness, his wonderful wit, his sharp intellect, his lazy, sexy smile. What they had had all those years ago had been unbearably intense and that intensity had given the times they had shared recently a deep level of communication that was almost intuitive. She missed that. She missed him.

She hadn't heard a word from him. He had truly disappeared from her life—although, by all accounts, he had been on the scene far more than anticipated at the shelter, where, from what Beth had blithely told her, he appeared suddenly to have taken a keen interest in all the renovations she had planned.

'He has so many good suggestions for how the money could be spent!' Beth had enthusiastically listed all the suggestions while Chase had listened in resentful silence. 'He's also been kind enough to put us in touch with contacts he has in the contracting business so that we can get the best possible deal!' Chase had muttered something under her breath which she hoped didn't sound like the unladylike oath it most certainly was.

Beth had no idea of the history she and Alessandro had shared. It would have been petty and small-minded not to have responded with a similar level of enthusiasm to the hard-nosed billionaire businessman who had previously threatened a hostile buy-out, only to morph into a saint with a positively never-ending supply of 'brilliant ideas' and 'amazingly useful contacts'.

On the Friday, exactly a week after he had walked out of her house, there was a little leaving drinks party for her at the office, to which far more people turned up than she had expected, bearing in mind she had not been the most sociable of the team out of work.

She would be sorely missed, her boss said in the little speech he gave to the assembled members of staff. Everyone raised their glasses of champagne. These were the people she had kept at arm's length, burying herself in her work and always feeling the unspoken differences between them. And yet, as various of her colleagues came over to talk to her, she could tell that they were genuinely delighted that she intended to pursue her pro bono work in a firm that was solely dedicated to doing that.

Numbers and email addresses were exchanged with various girls whom she had known on a purely superficial basis.

When she tentatively volunteered the information that she would find it tough financially because she had no family to help her out if she started going under, there were no gasps of horror. When she confessed to a couple of the girls that she loved pro bono work because, growing up on a council estate, she had seen misery first-hand and had always wanted to do something about it, they hadn't walked away, smirking. They had been interested.

By the end of the evening, she had drunk more than she had intended but had also made friends in unexpected places.

Had she made a mistake in erecting so many protective defence mechanisms around her that she had failed to let anyone in? Had her cool distance been a liability in the end, rather than an asset? Had her detachment, which had been put in place for all the right reasons, become a habit which had imprisoned her more firmly than the solid steel bars of a prison cell?

Her thoughts were muddled and all over the place when, at a little after nine, she hailed a black cab to take her back to her house. When she closed her eyes and rested her head back on the seat, she could see Alessandro, a vibrant image hovering in the deepest recesses of her mind.

She had told him bits and pieces of the truth. Was that sufficient? An enormous sense of lassitude washed over her when she thought about the rest of what had been left unsaid.

So, nothing would change. He would still despise her. He would still be repelled by the person he thought she had turned out to be, but wouldn't she feel better in herself? Wouldn't coming clean, laying all her cards on the table, leave her with a clear conscience when she walked away? And wouldn't a clear conscience be a far better companion when she lay down in her bed at night and allowed thoughts of him to proliferate in her head?

She had given away more of herself today with her colleagues than she had in all the years she had worked alongside them, and it had felt good.

She leant forward, told the cab driver to turn around and gave him Alessandro's address.

She had no idea whether he would be in or not. It was a Friday night and face it, he was once again a free, single and eligible guy who might very well have jumped back on the sexual merry-go-round.

The alcohol had given her Dutch courage. Even as the taxi pulled up outside his magnificent house, her nerves didn't start going into automatic meltdown. She had reached a point of realising that she had nothing left to lose.

Her hand only shook a little as she reached for the door-bell and pressed hard, the very same way he had pressed *her* doorbell when he had walked in on Brian depleting her house of all its worldly goods.

On his third whisky, Alessandro heard the distant peal of his doorbell and debated whether he should bother getting it or not. A package was due to be delivered by courier. Work related. Could he really be bothered?

His torpor exasperated him but it had dogged his every waking moment ever since he had walked out of her house. Try as he might, he hadn't been able to shake it. The confines of his opulent office had felt restricting. He had found himself avoiding it, not caring what his secretary thought, going to the shelter practically every day.

It was Friday night and, whilst his head told him that it was time to get back on the horse, to find a replacement for the woman with whom he should never have become entangled all over again, his feet had brought him right back to his house and towards the drinks cabinet. A bracing evening diet of whisky and soda had felt eminently more tempting than shallow conversation with the air-heads and bimbos who would circle him at the slightest given opportunity.

Of course, there was a limit to how long this crazy state of affairs could continue. Swearing softly under his breath, and with the glass of whisky still in his hand, he strolled to the front door and pulled it open. On his lips were a few select curses for whatever imbecile of a courier had had the temerity to keep his finger on the buzzer when he, Alessandro, was in the process of working his way down to the bottom of his glass, through which he hoped to see the world as an altogether rosier place.

'Alessandro. You're…' Any hint of incipient nerves flew through the window at the sight of an Alessandro who, for the first time ever, did not seem to be completely in control of all his faculties. 'Are you *drunk*?'

Alessandro leaned against the doorframe and swallowed back the remnants of whisky in his glass. 'What are you doing here at this hour? It's after nine. And I'm not drunk.'

The woman he had walked away from. He tried to think of all the pejorative adjectives that had sprung so easily to mind when he had last seen her. Before he had endured the most hellish week of his entire life. Where the hell had his bullish confidence gone about the fact that she was not worth his while? And where had she been anyway? He checked his watch and saw that it was actually a little before ten. Had she been out *partying*? A tidal wave of jealousy left him shaken.

'Living it up, Chase?' His mouth twisted as he focused on the much less prim and proper attire she was wearing, a fitted burgundy dress rather than her uniform of suits which was all he had ever seen her in for work.

'I know you're probably surprised to see me here. Shocked, even.' Although there was a glass in his hand and it was empty. Had he company? A woman? Chase refused to let that thought take shape and gain momentum.

Alessandro noticed that she had neatly avoided answering his question. He shouldn't even care. In fact, hadn't he made his mind up that he wanted nothing further to do with her? That he could never trust a woman who had lied to him? Hadn't he? 'What are you doing here? Thought you might pay a little social call? On your way back from wherever you've been out partying?'

So his mood hadn't changed. He was still hostile and contemptuous, still ready to attack. 'I haven't been *out partying*, Alessandro. I… It was my last day at work today. There was champagne at the office, that's all. I…I've come because there are some things I still need to say to you.'

So she had just been cooped up at the office. He felt some of his dark mood evaporate. She had more to say to him? Well, why not? The choice was either that or the rest of the whisky to keep him company. He turned on his heels, leaving the door open and Chase, after a few seconds' hesitation, followed him into the house.

CHAPTER TEN

SHE FOLLOWED HIM into the sitting room and immediately spotted the bottle of whisky, which was half-empty.

'How much of this stuff have you *drunk*?' she gasped in amazement.

'I think it's safe to say that my drinking habits are none of your business.' The burgundy dress lovingly clung to her body and outlined curves in all the right places. He could feel himself getting turned on and he scowled because the last thing he needed was his wilful body doing its own thing. He subsided on the sofa, legs apart, his body language aggressively, defensively masculine.

'So, what are you here for?' he demanded, following her with a glowering expression as she hesitated by the door. He watched broodingly as she took a deep breath and walked to one of the pale-cream leather chairs by the fireplace, a modern built-into-the-wall affair which she had variously claimed to have both loved and detested.

'I didn't ask,' Chase said in a thin voice. 'But is someone here with you?'

'Is someone here with me? Does it look like I have company?' He gestured to the empty room.

'You're drinking, Alessandro…' She nodded to the whisky bottle which bore witness to her statement. 'And since when do you drink on your own? Especially spirits. Didn't you once tell me that drinking spirits on your own was a sign of an alcoholic in the making? Didn't you tell me that your parents put you off giving in to vices like that in a big way? That they were a bigger warning against drinking, smoking and taking drugs than any lecture anyone could have given you?'

Alessandro's expression darkened. 'And since when are you my guilty conscience?' he demanded belligerently. He couldn't take his eyes off her. It felt as though he hadn't seen her in a hundred years and, whilst he knew that that certainly wasn't a healthy situation given the fact that she had been dispatched from his life, he still couldn't help himself, and that helplessness made him feel even more of a sad loser.

'I'm not.' Chase stared down at her entwined fingers in silence for a couple of seconds. Now that she was here, sitting in front of him, the nerves which had been absent on her trip over were gathering pace inside her. She had come to tell him how she felt but her moment of bravery was in danger of passing. She wasn't his guilty conscience. She was nothing to him. She was surprised that he hadn't slammed the door in her face, and she took some courage from the fact that he hadn't.

'I've…I've…managed to get a couple of leads on some promising jobs,' she heard herself saying, a propos nothing in particular. 'Out of London. One in Manchester. The other in Surrey. I guess I'll sell my place and move sticks. It'll be cheaper, anyway. I would probably be able to afford something bigger.'

'And you've come here to tell me this because…?'

'I haven't come here to tell you that. I just thought… Well…'

'Get to the point, Chase.' When he thought of her leaving London, he felt as though a band of pure ice had wrapped itself around his heart like the tenacious tendrils of creeping ivy.

She sprang to her feet and began walking restively around the room. It was a big room. The colours were pale and muted, from the colour of the walls to the soft leather furniture. It was modern and, when she had first seen it, she hadn't, been able to decide whether she liked it or not. Certainly, right at this very moment, it chilled her to the bone, but then wasn't that just her fear and trepidation taking its toll? The hard contours of his face spoke volumes for his lack of welcome. He might not have slammed the door in her face but he clearly didn't want her in his house. She felt that little thread of courage begin to seep slowly away.

'Do you remember that…that day, Alessandro?'

'Be specific. What day in particular are you talking about? The day you lied about the fact that you were a happily married woman, or the day you lied about the fact that the loving parents in Australia were a work of fiction…?'

Chase fought against the sneering coolness in his voice and sat back down, this time on the sofa with him, but at the furthest end of it.

'We met at that pub. Do you remember? The one by the park?'

He remembered. He could even remember what she had been wearing. It came to him with such vivid clarity that he almost thought that it had been lying in wait for eight years, just at the edges of his memory: a pair of very faded jeans, some plimsolls which had once been white but were scuffed way past their original colour and a light-blue jumper, the sleeves of which were long enough for her to tuck her hands inside them. Which she had done as she had delivered her blow.

'I told you about Shaun.'

'Believe me, I haven't forgotten that special moment in my life.'

'Please don't be sarcastic, Alessandro. This is really

hard for me. I just want you to listen, because you were right when you said that we had unfinished business between us. We did. And, for me at least, we still have until you hear me out. Or, rather, *I* still do….'

The palms of her hands felt sweaty and she smoothed them over the burgundy dress. 'Eight years ago, I fell in love with you.' She braved his silent stare and willed herself to continue. 'I was married and, believe me, I shouldn't have looked at you, far less spoken to you, but I did. You have no idea what you did for me. Being with you was like being free for the first time in my life. I finally understood what all those silly romance novels were all about.'

Alessandro frowned. This was hardly the direction he'd expected the conversation to go in. 'If you're hoping to pull on my heart strings, then you're barking up the wrong tree. I have perfect recall of your little speech to me. It involved you telling me that Shaun was the great love of your life, that it had been fun seeing me, but you were only in it for some help with work…hoped I didn't get the wrong idea. I'm recalling the moment you waved your wedding ring in my face and pulled out a photo of your loved one.'

'Yes.'

'So where are you going with this, exactly? Why have you come here to waste my time?' Another shot of whisky would have gone down a treat but he *did* remember what he had said to her about his parents teaching him the horrors of having no control, by example.

'I was an idiot when I married Shaun…' Chase stared absently into the distance. 'I was incredibly young and it seemed like an exciting thing to do. Or…or maybe not, thinking about it now. *Shaun* told me it would be an exciting thing to do and I went along with it because I had already figured out that it didn't pay to disagree with anything he said.'

'Watch out. You're in danger of wiping some of the shine from your blissfully joyous married life.'

'There was never any shine on it, and I wasn't blissfully married,' Chase told him abruptly. She refocused on his face to find him watching her carefully. When she thought about the horror that had been her married life with Shaun, she wanted to cry for those wasted years, but the self-control she had built up over the years stood her in good stead.

Alessandro found that he was holding his breath. 'Another lie, Chase?' But he wanted to hear what she had to say even though he told himself that he wasn't going to fall for anything she told him. Once bitten, twice shy.

'I haven't come here to try and make you believe me, Alessandro,' Chase said with quiet sincerity. 'I know you probably won't anyway. I know I've lied to you in the past and you'll never forgive me. You've made that crystal-clear. I'm here because I *need* to tell you everything. And, when I'm finished, I'll walk out that door and you'll never see me again.

'When I met you for the first time, I began something that was dangerous, although you weren't to know that. I've thought about what you said, about Shaun hitching his wagon to me because he knew that he would be able to go further with me shackled to his side. I think you were right, although at the time I didn't see it that way. By the time I made it to university, I'd lost the ability to think independently. My studies were the only thing keeping me going. We'd come to London and I had been taken away from my friends, from everything I knew, although I guess you would find "everything I knew" hardly worth knowing anyway. Shaun was in his element. I was married to him and he was in complete control, and he enjoyed making sure he exercised that control.'

'What are you telling me?'

'I'm telling you that I was an abused wife. The sort of pathetic woman you would find contemptible. The sort of woman who can really understand how all those women at Beth's shelter feel. Why do you imagine I have such empathy for them?'

'When you say abused…?'

'Physically, mentally, emotionally. Shaun was never fussy when it came to laying down laws. He used whatever methods suited him at the time.' She tilted her chin defiantly. She had come to say her piece and he could save his contempt for after she'd left. That was what her expression was telling him.

'He was very clever when it came to making sure he hurt me in ways that weren't visible. He let me out of his sight to attend lectures and tutorials but I was under orders to return home immediately, not to hang around and certainly never to cultivate any sort of friendship with any of the other students. I was just glad to be out of his presence. Anything was better than nothing and, besides, I thrived on the academic work. I found it all ridiculously easy.

'One of the first things I'm going to do when I leave London is to find the teachers who encouraged me and tell them how valuable their input was.' She made sure that he got the message that she wasn't looking for anything from him, that she was moving on, that she had her independence, whatever her story was.

'You say you were…in love with me. Why didn't you leave him?' *Because,* Alessandro thought, *I was certainly head over heels in love with you. I would have protected you.*

It was the first time he had ever really and truly given that notion house room and, now that he had, everything seemed to fall neatly into place. The manner in which she had departed from his life had altered his view of women and had, more profoundly, altered the sort of women he went out with. He had developed a healthy mistrust of anything that remotely smelled of commitment and had programmed every single relationship he'd had to fail by systematically dating women in whom he was destined to lose interest after very short periods of time. In the wake of losing his heart to a woman who had deceived him, he had simply pressed the self-destruct button inside him.

And then she had returned to his life under extraordinary circumstances. He had held her to ransom and told himself that he was exacting revenge. In fact, he had told himself a lot of things. The one single thing he had failed to tell himself—because he could see now that he just couldn't have brought himself to even think it—was that he still wanted her because, quite simply, he was still in love with her.

Chase sensed the infinitesimal shift in him. Was it too much to ask that he at least believed her?

'I couldn't,' she said, flushing. 'I've become very independent over the years. It's been so important for me to stand on my own two feet, to give nothing of myself to anyone, to make sure that no one had control over me. But back then there was no way that I had the inner strength to try and escape. He had sapped me of all my confidence. Anyway…'

She stared down at her fingers, drained from the confidences she was giving away. 'I haven't come here to make excuses, just to tell you things as they were. I met you and it was wonderful but Shaun found out. He got hold of my mobile phone; I had been stupid enough to have one of your text messages there. I had forgotten to delete it. It was arranging to meet for lunch. He went crazy. I can't tell you, but I was terrified for my life. He threatened to kill us both if I didn't end it and, to make sure I did what he said, he made me arrange the location we were supposed to meet. He told me exactly what I was to say to you, and he was sitting at the table behind us the whole time I gave you that little speech about being a happily married woman…'

'My God.'

'I could never have told you about how things really were and I still didn't want to when I saw you again because I was…ashamed. I knew how you'd react. I knew all your opinions of me as a strong career woman with a mind of her own would evaporate and I would be just a pathetic, abused woman, like all those women you didn't give a hoot about when you were going to buy the shelter and have them dispossessed.' She took a deep breath and made eye contact with him but what she saw there was far from contempt. The silence stretched between them until it was at breaking point.

'If we had met later…' she said in a low voice, half-talking to herself '…then things might have been different. Even if I'd still been with Shaun, I would have had more self-confidence. I would have had my degree, a good job; I would have had the courage to walk away from him, but at that point in my life it just wasn't there.'

'And then,' Alessandro said heavily, 'we met again and I hardly inspired the trust you needed to open up. I blackmailed you into sleeping with me…'

'I *wanted* to sleep with you,' Chase confirmed in a driven voice. 'I would never have let myself be blackmailed into doing anything. I said so at the time and I meant it. I'd learnt the hard way not to let anyone else have control over me. I *wanted* to sleep with you and I don't regret it.'

'And what happened to the…love?' Alessandro asked so quietly that she had to strain to hear him.

'I still love you, Alessandro,' she said proudly. 'And I don't regret that either. So, there you are.' She stood up and brushed her skirt to distract herself from speculating on what was going on in his head.

'Not so fast!'

Chase looked up at him in surprise. His command was imperious but there was a hesitancy underlying it that wormed its way past her common sense.

'I'm glad you came,' he said, flushing darkly and looking so suddenly vulnerable that she wanted to sidle a little closer to him, just to make sure that her eyes weren't playing tricks on her. She remained where she was, resisting the impulse. 'I'm glad you were honest with me. Yes, when we met again…'

Alessandro raked his fingers through his hair and shook his head with a rueful smile that did even more disastrous things to her common sense. 'It all came rushing back at me. I hadn't realised how much I remembered and I certainly didn't get why it was that I remembered so well. I just knew that I still…wanted you. Somewhere along the line, I figured out that I had never stopped wanting you. I couldn't make sense of it, couldn't understand how I could still want a woman who I felt had betrayed me in the worst possible way. Don't get me wrong; I understand why you wanted to keep your secrets to yourself, why you felt that they would be too dark for me to handle, but if only I had known…'

'Nothing would have changed, Alessandro. Nothing has changed now.'

'No, nothing's changed and everything's changed. You're the same person you always were, Chase, whatever you went through. What you mean to me will always be the same, just as it was all those years ago. You will always be the girl I fell in love with but was too damned stupid to own up to. I let pride rule my behaviour and only now… Well, I'm still in love with you.'

Chase wondered whether she had heard correctly or whether wishful thinking had taken complete control. Was it even possible to hear something you wanted to hear because you wanted it *so badly*? She found that she was holding her breath.

'Um…did you just say… Did you just tell me…?'

'That I'm in love with you? Yes, I did. And I'll tell you again if you'd move a little closer so that I don't have to shout across the width of the sofa.'

'It's not a big sofa,' Chase said faintly.

'Right now, with you sitting at the other end of it, it feels as wide as a canyon.'

She shuffled along and slipped into his arms with a soaring feeling of utter elation. 'What if I hadn't come tonight?'

'I would never have let you go. The past week has been the worst of my life. I've never hated my office more. I lost interest in deals, going to meetings, reading emails… I know more now about that shelter than I would ever have thought possible.'

'Beth said you'd been a frequent visitor.' She curled into him and heard the beating of his heart.

'It made me feel close to you,' he confessed shakily, 'Although I never faced up to that. I love you, Chase. I love you for the person you are now and I loved you for the person you were then. I can't live without you. I want you to be my wife. Will you marry me? Within the next hour?'

Chase lifted her head and laughed, her eyes glowing with happiness. 'Within the next hour might be stretching it,' she said softly. 'But, yes, I'll be your wife.'

'And never leave my side?'

'You're stuck with me for ever…' And never had the thought of being stuck with someone for ever sounded so good.

* * * * *

A GAME OF VOWS

MAISEY YATES

CHAPTER ONE

HANNAH WESTON swore as she tripped over the hem of her wedding dress, her focus diverted by the scrolling numbers on the screen of her smart phone. She'd said she wouldn't work today. She'd lied.

The exchange was closed today, but she had a lead and she needed to chase it up before she made her vows. She had clients depending on her. And he would never know.

She dropped into the limo, her eyes still trained on her phone as she gathered her dress up into a satin ball and pulled it inside, slamming the door behind her.

"Going to the chapel?"

Hannah froze, her blood turning to ice as the limo pulled away from the curb and headed into the San Francisco traffic. That voice. She knew that voice.

She couldn't look up, her eyes still set on her phone. She curled her fingers more tightly around the heavy fabric of her wedding gown, as she took a breath and raised her gaze, locking with the dark, intense eyes in the rearview mirror.

She knew those eyes, too. No one had eyes like him. They seemed to cut through you, possessing the ability to read your innermost secrets. Able to mock and flirt in a single glance. She still saw those eyes in her dreams. And sometimes her nightmares.

Eduardo Vega. One of the many skeletons in her closet. Except, he wasn't staying put.

"And I'm going to get married," she said tightly. She didn't get intimidated. She did the intimidating. Back in NY she'd had more guts than any man on the trading room floor. She'd had Wall Street by the balls. And now, she was a force to be reckoned with in the world of finance. She didn't do fear.

"Oh, I don't think so, Hannah. Not today. Unless you're interested in getting arrested for bigamy."

She sucked in a sharp breath. "I am not a bigamist."

"You aren't single."

"Yes, I am. The paperwork was…"

"Never filed. If you don't believe me, do some research on the matter."

Her stomach squeezed tight, the world tilting to the side. "What did you do, Eduardo?" His name tasted so strange on her tongue. But then, it had never been familiar. He was a stranger, essentially, her ex-husband. She had never known him, not really.

They had lived together, sort of. She'd inhabited the spare room in his luxury penthouse for six months. They hadn't shared meals, except on weekends when they'd gone to his parents' home. They hadn't shared a bed. Hadn't shared more than the odd hello when they were in his massive home. It was only in public that he'd ever really talked to her. That he'd ever touched her.

He had been quick, blessed with money, a strategic mind and a total lack of caring in regards to propriety. She'd never met a man like him. Before or since. Of course, she hadn't been blackmailed into marriage before or since, either.

"Me?" His eyes met hers in the mirror again, a smile curving his lips, a flash of white teeth against dark skin. "Nothing."

She laughed. "That's funny. I don't believe you. I signed the papers. I remember it very clearly."

"And you might have known they were never finalized if you had left a forwarding address for your mail. But that's not the way you do things, is it? Tell me, are you still running, Hannah?"

"What did you do?" she asked, refusing to let his last barb stick in its target. She didn't have to answer to Eduardo. She didn't have to answer to anyone. And she most definitely didn't have to run.

She met his eyes in the mirror and felt a sharp pang of emotion that mocked her previous thought. Why was this happening now? She was getting married in an hour. To Zack Parsons, the best man she'd ever known. He was respectful, and honorable. Distant. Able to help give her a career boost. He was everything she wanted, everything she needed.

"It's a complicated process," he said, his accent as charming as ever, even as his words made her blood boil. "Something perhaps...went amiss?"

"You bastard! You utter bastard!" She shut the web browser on her phone and pulled up the number pad, poised to dial.

"What are you doing, Hannah?"

"Calling...the police. The national guard."

"Your fiancé?"

Her stomach tightened down on itself. "No. Zack doesn't need to know...."

"You mean you didn't tell your lover about your husband? Not a great foundation for a marriage."

She couldn't call Zack. She couldn't let Eduardo anywhere near the wedding. It would topple everything she'd spent the past nine years building. She hated that he had the power to do that. Hated facing the truth that he'd had power over her from the moment she'd met him.

She gritted her teeth. "Neither is blackmail."

"We traded, *mi tesoro*. And you know it. Blackmail makes it sound sordid."

"It was. It continues to be."

"And your past is so clean you can't stand getting your hands dirty? We both know that's not true."

A very rude word hovered on the edge of her lips. But freaking out at Eduardo wasn't going to solve her problem. The very pressing problem that she needed to get to the hotel and take vows. "I'm going to ask you again, before I open the door and roll out into midday traffic and completely destroy this gown: What do you want? How do I give it to you? Will it make you go away?"

He shook his head. "I'm afraid not. I'm taking you back to my hotel. And I'm not going away."

Her lip curled. "Have you got a thing for women in wedding dresses? Because you got me into one quickly last time we met, and now you seem interested in me again...and here I am in a wedding dress."

"It's not the dress."

"Give me one good reason not to call the police and tell them I've been kidnapped."

"Hannah Mae Hackett."

Her real name sounded so unfamiliar now. Even more so coming from him instead of being spoken with a Southern twang. Even still, a lead weight settled in her stomach when he said it.

"Don't even say it," she bit out.

"You don't like your name? Well, I imagine not. You *did* change it."

"Legally. I am *legally* not that name anymore. My name is Hannah Weston now."

"And you *illegally* gained scholarships, and entrance, to the university in Barcelona by falsifying your school records."

She clenched her teeth, her pulse pounding hard. She was so very screwed. And he knew it. "This sounds like a conversation we had five years ago. If you recall, I already married you to keep you from spreading it around."

"Unfinished business."

"The only thing unfinished, apparently, is our divorce."

"Oh, no, there is so much more than that." He pulled the

limo against a curb in front of one of the famous boutique hotels in San Francisco. Marble, gold trimming and sharply dressed valets signaled the luxury of the place to everyone in the area. It was the sort of thing that had drawn her from the time she was young. The sort of thing she'd really started hungering for when she realized she had the power to change her circumstances.

Every time she checked into a hotel, as soon as the door was closed and she was isolated from the world, she would twirl in a circle and fall onto the bed, reveling in the softness. The cleanliness. The space and solitude. Even now that she had her own penthouse with thousand thread count sheets, she still did it.

The hotel wasn't evoking those kinds of feelings in her today. Not with Eduardo present.

The valet took the keys and Eduardo came to Hannah's door, opening it. "Wait…did you steal this?" she asked, looking at the limo.

As Eduardo bent down, Hannah fought the urge to shrink back. "I bought it from the chauffeur. Told him to go buy one that was newer. Nicer."

"And he didn't seem to care that he was supposed to pick me up?"

"Not when I gave him enough money for two new limousines. No."

"He was going to leave a bride stranded on her wedding day?"

Eduardo shrugged. "The world is filled with dishonest and self-serving people. You, my dear, should know all about that."

She snorted and rucked her dress up over her knees, climbing out of the car without touching Eduardo. She straightened and let her dress fall neatly into place. Then she tugged on her veil, fanning it over her shoulders. "Don't say it like you aren't one of the self-serving, my darling husband."

She looked at him fully. He was still everything he'd been five years ago. Tall, broad, arresting, a vision of perfect male beauty in his well-cut suit. His bronzed skin was highlighted perfectly by his white dress shirt; his dark hair reached the collar of his jacket.

He'd always made her feel like someone had put both hands on her shoulders and shaken her. He'd always had the power to disrupt the order of her life, to make her feel like she was dangerously close to losing the control she'd worked so hard to cultivate over the years.

It was the thing she'd always hated most about him. That he was so darned magnetic. That he always had the power to make her tremble when nothing else could.

It wasn't just that he was good-looking. There were a lot of good-looking men in the world, and she was too much in control of herself to let that affect her. It was the fact that he exuded a kind of power that she could never hope to achieve. And that he had power over her.

She breezed past him, ignoring the scent of his cologne and skin, ignoring the way it made her stomach tighten. She strode into the hotel lobby, well aware that she was making a spectacle and not caring at all. She breathed in deep. She needed focus. She needed to find out what he wanted so she could leave, as quickly as possible.

"Mrs. Vega, Mr. Vega." A woman that Hannah assumed was a manager, rounded the check-in desk with a wide, money-motivated grin on her face. "So lovely to have you here. Mr. Vega told me he would be bringing his bride when he came to stay this time. So romantic."

She had to bite back a tart curse.

Eduardo closed the distance between them and curled his arm around her waist. Her breath rushed from her body. For a moment, just one crazy moment, she wanted to lean against him. To draw closer to his masculine strength. But only for a moment.

"Very," he said.

"Is there liquor in the room?" she asked, wiggling away from him.

The manager, whose name tag identified her as Maria, frowned slightly. "There is champagne waiting for you."

"We'll need three," she said.

Maria's frown deepened. "I…"

"She's kidding," Eduardo said.

Hannah shook her head. "I've been hammered since I took my vows. I intend to spend the rest of the day that way."

"We'll just go upstairs."

"Send champagne," Hannah said as Eduardo attempted to drag her from the desk in what she imagined he thought was a loving, husbandly manner.

He ushered her into a gilded elevator, a smile pasted on his darkly handsome face until the door closed behind them.

"That was not cute, Hannah," he said.

She put her hand on her hip and gave him her sassiest smile. She didn't feel sassy, or in control, but she could fake it with the best of them. "Are you kidding me? I think I'm ready for my close-up. That was fine acting."

He shot her a bland look. "Your entire life has been acting. Don't expect accolades now."

Her smile faltered for a moment. "Look, I am on edge here."

"You aren't crying. No gnashing of teeth over leaving your fiancé at the altar."

She bit the inside of her cheek. "You don't know anything about my relationship with Zack, so don't pretend you do. I care about him. I don't want to leave him at the altar. I want you to come to your senses and give me the keys to your ill-gotten limo so I can drive myself to the hotel and marry him." The image of Zack, in that black, custom tux, standing in front of all of their friends and coworkers…it made her feel sick. She'd never, ever intended to put him through that kind of humiliation. The idea of it being reversed made her skin crawl.

"Whether I drive you there or not, your marriage won't be legal. I explained that already."

"They gave me a marriage license," she said, her voice sounding distant, echoey. Her hands were starting to shake. Why was she reacting this way? Why was she being so weak? Was she in shock?

"And we were married, and attempted to divorce out of your home country. Things get missed."

"How could something this important just get missed?" she said, exploding. "I don't believe for one second you... *forgot* to file the papers."

His smile turned dark. "Stranger things have happened, *tesoro*."

For the first time she noticed that he wasn't exactly the same. She'd thought his eyes the same, but she saw now they weren't. He used to sparkle. His brown eyes glittering with mischief. He'd been so amused at finding out her secret, that she wasn't who she'd claimed to be. He'd been even more amused at the thought of marrying an American girl to gall his father, when he'd mandated his son take a wife to gain leadership of their company. To prove he was a family man. It had been the best joke to him, to marry a college student with no money, no connections and no cooking skills.

The sparkle was gone now. Replaced with a kind of black glitter that seemed to suck the light from the room, that seemed to absorb any kind of brightness and kill it. It did something strange to her. Pulled at her like the sparkle never had.

"Like getting kidnapped on your wedding day?"

"Coerced away, perhaps. But don't tell me you haven't got pepper spray somewhere in your purse. You could have stopped me. You could have called the police. You could have called your Zack. You didn't. And you still aren't doing it.

You could turn and walk out of this room right now and get a cab. I wouldn't stop you. And you know that."

"But you *know*. You know everything. And I…"

"And it would ruin your reputation with your clients. No one wants to hear their financial adviser is a high school dropout who committed fraud to get her college degree."

"You're right, that kind of information does make client meetings awkward," she said, her voice flat, a sick feeling settling in her stomach.

"I imagine so. Just remember how awkward it made our meeting back when you were my intern."

"I think the real awkwardness came when you blackmailed me into marrying you."

"You keep using that word. Was it really blackmail?"

"According to Webster's Dictionary? Yes."

He shrugged. "Either way, had you not had something for me to hold over your head…it wouldn't have worked."

"You're so smug about it," she said, seething now. The clock on the nightstand read five minutes to her wedding and she was standing in an opulent hotel suite, in her wedding gown, with another man. "But you've had everything handed to you in your life, Eduardo. You work because your daddy gave you an office. I had to make my own destiny, and maybe…maybe the way I went about it was a little bit shady."

"The United States government calls it fraud. But *shady* is fine."

"You have no idea what it's like," she said.

"No, you're right. I can hardly speak around the silver spoon in my mouth. What would I know about hardship?" His lip curled, his expression hard, cynical. A new look for Eduardo.

"Your only hardship was that your father demanded you give up your life as a partying man whore and find a wife. So what did you do? You twisted my arm, because you thought a *gringa* wife, especially one who wasn't Catholic and couldn't cook, would be a funny way to follow your father's orders without actually following them. And I went along with it, because it was better than losing my job. Better than getting kicked out of university. Everything was a game to you, but to me, it was life."

"You're acting like I hurt you in some way, Hannah, but we both know that isn't true. I gave you your own room. Your own wing of the penthouse. I never intruded on you, never once took advantage of you. I kept to our agreement and released you from our bargain after six months, and you left. With all the money I promised you," he said. "You keep forgetting the money I gave you."

She clenched her teeth. "Because I didn't spend it." She hadn't been able to. Leaving him, or more to the point, his family and the city that had started to feel like home, had felt too awful. And she'd felt, for the first time, every inch the dishonorable person she was. "If you want your ten thousand dollars, it's in a bank account. And frankly, it's pennies as far as I'm concerned at this point."

"Oh, yes, you are very successful now, aren't you?"

She didn't feel it at the moment. "Yes. I am."

Eduardo advanced toward her. "You are good with finances, investments."

"Financial planning, strategies, picking stocks. You name it, I'm good at it."

"That's what I want from you."

"What? Financial advice?"

"Not exactly." He looked out the window, his expression inscrutable. "My father died two years ago."

An image of the hard, formidable, amazing man that Eduardo had been blessed enough to call his father swam before her eyes. Miguel Vega had been demanding. A taskmaster. A leader. He had cared. About his business, about his children. About his oldest son, who wasn't taking life seriously enough. Cared enough to back him into a corner and force him to marry. It was a heavy-handed version of caring, but it was more than Hannah had ever gotten from her own father.

Eventually, that man, his wife, Eduardo's sister, had come to mean something to her. She'd loved them.

"I'm so sorry," she said, her voice muted now, a strange kind of grief filling her heart. Not that Miguel would have missed or cared about her. And she didn't deserve it. She'd lied to him. And as far as he was concerned, she'd left his son.

"As am I," Eduardo said. "But he left me in charge of Vega Communications."

"And things aren't going well?"

"Not exactly." A muscle in his jaw ticked. "No, not exactly."

"Do you need me to look at your books? Because I can do that after I marry Zack."

He shook his head, his dark eyes blazing. "That can't happen, *tesoro.*"

"But it can," she said, desperation filling her again. It was past bridal-march time. She could just picture the hotel, all decked out in pink ribbon and tulle. Her beautiful pink wedding cake. It was her dream wedding, the dream she'd had since she was a little girl. Not some traditional wedding in a cathedral, conducted entirely in Latin. A wedding that was a show for the groom's family. A wedding that had nothing to do with her.

It was a wedding with a groom who didn't love her, but at least liked her. A groom who didn't find the idea of taking vows with her to be a joke. He at least wanted her around. Being wanted on a personal level was new for her. She liked the way it felt.

"Sorry, Hannah. I need you to come back to Spain with me." He looked out the window. "It's time I brought my wife back home."

"No is the same in both of our languages, so there should

be nothing lost in translation when I say no." Hannah took a step back; her calf connected with the soft edge of the mattress, her dress rustling with the motion.

"Sorry, but this isn't a negotiation. Either you come with me now, or I march you down the aisle at the hotel myself, and you can explain, in front of your guests, and your groom, exactly why you can't marry him today. How you were about to involve him in an illegal marriage."

"Not on purpose! I would never have done this to him if I would have known."

"Once the extent of your past history is revealed, he may not believe you. Or, even if he did, he may not want you." His lips curved up into a smile, his eyes absent of any humor. And that was when she had the very stark, frightening impression that she was looking at a stranger.

He was nothing like the Eduardo she'd once known. She didn't know how she'd missed it. How it hadn't been obvious from the moment she'd seen his eyes in the rearview mirror. Yes, he had the same perfectly curved lips, the same sharply angled jaw. The same bullheaded stubbornness. But he no longer had that carefree air he'd always conducted himself with. There were lines by his eyes, bracketing his mouth. A mouth that looked like it had forgotten how to smile.

Maybe the death of his father had taken a serious toll on him. But she didn't care. She couldn't afford to care. She had to look out for herself, just as she'd been doing all of her life. No one else would. No one else ever had.

"Bastard," she spat.

"You're getting repetitive," he said dryly.

"So what? You expect me to come back to Spain and just… be your wife?"

"Not exactly. I expect you to come back and continue to act as my wife in name only while you help me fix the issues I'm having with Vega Communications."

"Why?"

"Because I don't need anyone to know there are issues. Not my competitors, I don't need them smelling blood in the water. Not my mother, she has no need to worry. My sister… I don't want to worry her, either. No one can know." There was an edge to his voice, evidence of fraying control. She could work with that. She could definitely work with that.

The pieces started falling into place in her mind. "So you think it can look like a reconciliation five years in the making. Your wife is suddenly back in Barcelona and hanging on your arm. Rather than letting anyone in on the fact that you needed to bring in outside consultation to help straighten up your finances?"

"That's the sum of it," he ground out.

It made sense now. All fine and good for him to sweep in like a marauder and demand her cooperation. But all that sweeping was hiding very real problems.

And those problems meant she had a lot more power than she'd thought she'd possessed thirty seconds earlier.

Her lips curved into a smile, the heated adrenaline she always felt when presented with a battle spreading through her chest, her limbs. "You need me. Say it."

"Hannah…"

"No. If I'm going to even consider doing this, you admit it. To me, and to yourself. You never would back then, but now…now I'm not a scared college student trying to hold on to my position at school." She met his eyes without flinching. "Admit that you need me."

"You were never a scared college student," he bit out. "You were an angry one. Angry you'd been caught out and desperate to do anything to keep it secret."

"Well, now you're sounding a little desperate." She crossed her arms beneath her breasts and cocked her hip to the side. "So, at least say please."

His lip curled into a sneer, a muscle in his jaw ticking. He was weighing his options. "Please."

She tilted her chin up and smiled, the sort of smile she knew would make his blood boil. "Good boy."

The feral light in his eyes let her know that she'd just about gone too far. She didn't care. He couldn't screw up her day any more than he already had.

He didn't move for a beat. She could see him, calculating, making decisions. For a moment she thought he might reach out and grab her. Take her in his arms and...strike her? Certainly not. No matter what Eduardo was, he wasn't a monster. Kiss her?

That he might do. The thought made her stomach tighten, made her heart beat faster.

She saw him visibly relax. "A lot of confidence and attitude coming from a woman who could face criminal charges if the right words were spoken into the wrong ears."

She put her hands on her hips. "But you showed your hand, darling," she said, turning his use of endearments back at him. "I may be over a barrel, but you're tied to me. If I go over the cliff, you're coming, too. I might be stuck, but you're just as stuck. So, let's be civil, you and I, huh?"

"Let's not forget who stands to lose the most," he said, his voice hard.

She examined his face, the hard lines etched into it. Brackets around his mouth, creases in his forehead. Lines that had appeared sometime in the past five years, for they hadn't been there back when she'd first met him. "I have a feeling you might have a bit more to lose than you're letting on."

"What about you? At the least you stand to lose clients, your reputation. At the most?"

He didn't have to finish the sentence. It was possible she could lose...so much. Everything. That she could face criminal charges. That she could find herself with her degree revoked. That she could find herself back in Arkansas in a single-wide mobile home that had a lawn with more pink plastic flamingos than it had grass.

She couldn't go back to that. To that endless, blank hell that had no end. No beginning. No defining moments. Just an eternity of uncomfortable monotony that most people she'd lived around had tried to dull with the haze of alcohol or the high of drugs.

No. She wasn't taking any chances on returning to that life. Not ever.

"Your point is taken," she said. "Anyway…I can't go and marry Zack now, no matter what, can I?"

"Not unless you want to extend your list of criminal activity."

"I didn't hurt anyone, Eduardo," she said stiffly.

Eduardo surveyed the slim, cool blonde standing in front of him, arms crossed over the ornate bodice of her wedding dress. His wife. Hannah. One of the images in his mind that had remained bright and clear, no matter how thick the fog was surrounding other details, other memories.

His vision of her as a skinny college student with a sharp mind and more guts than any person he'd ever met, had stayed with him. And when he'd realized just how much of a struggle things were becoming with Vega Communications, it had been her image he'd seen in his mind. And he'd known that he had to get his wife back.

His wife. The wife who had never truly been his wife beyond her signature on the marriage certificate. But she was a link. To his past. To the man he'd been. To those images that were splintered now, like gazing into a shattered mirror. He had wondered if seeing her could magically put him back there. If she could make the mirror whole. Reverse things, somehow.

Foolish, perhaps. But he couldn't get her out of his mind, and there had to be a reason. Had to be a reason she was so clear, when other things simply weren't.

Thankfully, he'd managed to get his timing just right. And

in his new world, one of migraines and half-remembered conversations, good timing was a rarity he savored.

"Does that make falsifying school records all right, then?" he said, watching her gray-blue eyes turn a bit more gray. A bit more stormy, as she narrowed them in his direction.

He personally didn't care what she'd done to get into university. Back then, he'd selected her to be his intern based on her impeccable performance in college, and not on anything else. Clearly she'd been up to the task, and in his mind, that was all that mattered.

But he'd use every bit of leverage he had now, and he wouldn't let his conscience prick him over it. Hannah knew all about doing what had to be done. And that's what he was doing now.

"I don't suppose it does," she said tightly. "But I don't dwell on that. I gave myself a do-over in life, and I've never once regretted it. I've never once looked back. I messed up when I was too young to understand what that might mean to my future, and when I did realize it…when it was too late…"

"You acted. Disregarding the traditional ideas of right and wrong, disregarding who it might hurt. And that's what I'm doing now. So I hope you'll forgive me," he said, aware that no sincerity was evident in his voice. He felt none.

She was testing him, needling him, trying to make him angry. It had worked, but it wouldn't divert his focus. She was his focus.

"So you think that makes it okay?" Her full lips turned down.

"I'm not overly concerned with questions of morality at the moment. I need to drag Vega back up to where it belongs."

"How is it you've managed to let it get so bad?" she said, again, not hesitating to throw her own barbs out.

There was no way in hell he was talking about his shortcomings. Not now. Maybe not ever. It wasn't her concern.

"We all have strengths," he said tightly. "It's the budget I'm having an issue with. Investments. Taxes. I am not an expert."

"Hire someone."

"I did. He didn't do his job."

"Basically, you didn't notice that he was screwing up?"

The thought of it, of trying to keep track of that, plus the day-to-day running of Vega, made his head swim, made his temples pound. His breath shortened, became harder to take in. Panic was a metallic taste on his tongue.

Would he ever feel normal? Or was this normal now? Such a disturbing thought. One he didn't have time to dwell on.

"I didn't have time," he gritted.

"Too busy sleeping around?" she asked.

"Different heiress every night," he said, almost laughing out loud at his own lie.

"Better than toying with the domestic staff, I suppose. Or blackmailing interns into marriage."

"Ours was a special case," he said.

"Oh, yes, indeed. I suppose that's why I feel suffused with a warm glow of specialness."

He chuckled, gratified when Hannah looked stymied by the reaction. She wanted to make him angry. He wouldn't allow it. One of the gifts of his head injury, one of the few. It had cooled his passions, and while that had been inconvenient in some ways, in others, it had proven valuable. He was no longer hotheaded. Usually. No longer impulsive. According to some, he was no longer fun. But he didn't know how to fix that. He found he didn't care anymore. Another gift.

"Well, it is your big day. Shouldn't a bride feel special?"

She uttered a truly foul word and sat on the edge of the bed, the white skirt of her dress billowing out around her. Like an angry, fallen, snow angel. "Low."

"Do you love this man? The one you were meant to marry today?" He found that did trouble his conscience, even if it was only a bit of trouble.

She shook her head slowly. "No."

He shook his head. "Using someone else?"

"Hardly using him. Zack doesn't love me, either. Neither of us have time for some all-consuming passionate affair. But we *like* each other. I like him. I don't like the idea of him being stood up. I don't like the idea of humiliating him."

"More humiliating, I think, if he finds out his almost-wife has been lying to him. About so many things."

She looked down at her fingernails. "Zack has his secrets. He doesn't think anyone realizes it…but he has them. I can tell. And I know better than to ask about them."

"And that means…"

"He would have accepted that I had mine. We didn't share everything."

"I doubt he intended to share you with another husband."

"Well, it's not going to happen now." A brief expression of vulnerability, sadness, crossed Hannah's features. And as quickly as he'd glimpsed it, it disappeared. Clearly, she had some amount of feeling for her lover, no matter what she said.

"Plans change." As he knew all too well.

"I have to call…someone," she said, her heart twisting.

"It's too late to salvage the day."

"I'm aware," she snapped. "Just…give me a minute."

She pulled her phone from her purse.

"Who are you calling?"

"My assistant. She's in the office minding things since I'm away. Shelby?" Her tone turned authoritative.

She paused for a moment, her cheeks turning a dull pink. "I know. I can't…I can't go through with it. It's complicated. And I can't get to the hotel." She gave him a pointed look. "Can you drive over and…and tell Zack?"

"Tell him what?" Eduardo heard her assistant's shriek from where he was standing.

"That I'm sorry. That I wish I had been brave enough to do

it differently but I can't. I know it's rush hour and it's going to take forever, but please?" Hannah paused again.

"Thank you. I...I have to go." She hit the end call button and rounded on him. "I hope you're pleased with yourself." He wasn't, not then. But this wasn't about how he felt. This was about what had to be done. This was about trying to fix Vega. Trying to fix himself.

"Not really. But I promise you in the end you will be."

"I doubt that."

"Once everything is resolved I will give you permission to speak of your part in the resurrection of my family's company."

He hadn't intended on giving her that much. The offer shocked him. He wasn't usually spontaneous anymore.

"Really?" she asked, her expression guarded, but the interest in her eyes too keen for her to conceal entirely.

"Really. I promise, in the end, I'll divorce you and you can crow your achievements. What I don't want is anyone undercutting the business while it's vulnerable. But afterward, say whatever you like, drag me through the mud, talk about my inadequacies. It's only pride," he said. Pride he'd had to give up a long time ago. He clung to what he could, but it was limited.

"You'll really divorce me this time? Forgive me for not trusting you."

"If you don't move around like a gypsy, then you should get papers letting you know when everything is final." The first aborted divorce hadn't been intentional. Another side effect of the accident that had changed everything. But, this side effect happened to be a very fortunate one indeed.

"Fine. We have a deal." Hannah extended her slender hand and he grasped it in his. She was so petite, so fine-boned. It gave the illusion of delicacy when he knew full well she possessed none. She was steel beneath that pale skin.

A smile curved his lips, satisfaction burning in his chest. "Good girl."

CHAPTER TWO

"You made me buy my own ticket." Hannah stood in the doorway of Eduardo's penthouse, exhausted and wrinkled from travel, still angry at the way everything had transpired. She'd had short notice, and limited options. She'd had to fly economy.

An infuriating smile curved Eduardo's lips. "I did. But I knew you could afford it."

"Doesn't chivalry dictate you buy your blackmailed wife's plane ticket?" Hannah dropped her suitcase next to her feet and crossed her arms. The most shocking thing about Eduardo's appearance had been his departure, with a demand that she meet him in Barcelona in twenty-four hours. And she could get there herself.

It had been a blow to her pride, and he knew it. Because she'd been forced to get herself to Spain. She'd been the one to board the plane. If he'd tied her up and thrown her into cargo she could have pretended he'd truly forced her. That she was a slave to him, rather than to the mistakes of her past and her intense need to keep them secret.

But there was nothing more important than her image. Than the success she'd earned. Than never, ever going back to that dark place she'd come from.

Because of that, she was a slave to Eduardo, and a coward where Zack was concerned. More than a day since their almost-wedding and she hadn't called him. Of course, he hadn't called her, which spoke volumes about the quality and nature of their relationship.

"I checked and there was no specific entry in the handbook about the most chivalrous way to force one's estranged bride to come and do their bidding."

"What's the point of even having a handbook, then?" She let out a long breath and looked pointedly at the doorway Eduardo was blocking with his broad frame. "Aren't you going to invite me into our home?"

"Of course," he said.

They'd shared the penthouse for six months five years ago. They'd been the most bizarre six months of her life. Sharing a home with a man who hardly acknowledged her presence, unless he needed her for a gala or to make a show of togetherness at a family dinner.

It was a six months she'd done a very good job of scrubbing from her mind. Like every other inconvenient detail in her past, it had been chucked into her mental closet, the door locked tight. It was where every juicy secret belonged. Behind closed, difficult-to-access doors.

But now it was all coming back. Her fourth year in Spain, when she'd been accepted into a coveted internship at Vega Communications. Everything had been going so well. She'd started making connections, learning how things worked at a massive corporation.

Then one day, the boss's son had called her into his office and closed the door.

Then he'd told her he'd done a little digging and found out her real name. That she wasn't Hannah Weston from Manhattan, but that she was Hannah Hackett from Arkansas. That she hadn't graduated top of her class, but that she had no diploma at all.

And then, with supreme, enraging arrogance he had leaned back in his chair; hands behind his head; humor, mocking, glittering in his eyes, and he'd told her that her secret would be safe.

If she would marry him.

That sickening, surreal moment when she'd agreed, because there was nothing in the world that could compel her to lose the ground she'd gained.

Eduardo stepped aside and she breezed past him, leaving her suitcase for him to handle. Things were rearranged. His furniture new, but still black and sleek. The appliances in his kitchen were new, too, as was the dining set.

But the view was the same. Cathedral spires rising above gray brick buildings, touching the clear sky. She'd always loved the city.

She'd hated Eduardo for forcing her into marriage. Had hated herself nearly as much for being vulnerable to him, for needing to keep her secrets so badly.

And then she'd moved into his home, and she'd started to think the forced marriage wasn't so bad after all. It was so expansive, plush, and refined. Like nothing she'd ever experienced.

Secretly, shamefully, she'd loved it. As long as she could ignore the big Spaniard that lived there, too, everything was wonderful. Comfortable.

She'd made it into school, but she was still living on a meager budget. And Eduardo had shown her luxury she'd never seen before. She'd thought she'd known. She hadn't. Her imagination hadn't even scratched the surface of what true wealth meant. Not until she'd met the Vega family.

It had given her something to aspire to.

"Everything looks…great." Surreal. She'd never gone back to a place before. When she left, she left. Her childhood home, Spain, her place in New York.

"Updated a bit. But your room is still available."

"Haven't had any other temporary wives in my absence?"

"No, unlike some people I think having more than one spouse at a time is a bit too ambitious."

"Yes, well, you know it wasn't my intention to have more than one," she bit out, a sour feeling settling in her stomach. "Zack was decent, you know." She eyed the open door, and her suitcase, still occupying their position in the hall. "He was one of the few truly good people I've ever met. I hate that I did this to him."

"Have you been in contact?"

"No."

"Perhaps you should…?"

She clenched her teeth. "I don't know if that's such a good idea. Anyway, he hasn't called me, and he didn't come by my house, so, maybe he doesn't care." That actually hurt a little.

"If he thinks you're missing, he may send out a search party. I didn't think you wanted to publicize our marriage. Or rather, why you ran out on your wedding. It doesn't matter either way to me."

She swore and took her phone from her purse. "Fine. But Shelby did go and speak to him." She bit her lip and looked down at the screen. Still no calls from him, and she'd been sort of hoping there would have at least been one. There was a text from Shelby.

"And have you heard from him?"

"No." Strange. But she couldn't really imagine Zack playing the part of desperate, jilted groom. Decent he was, but the man had pride. She opened the text from Shelby and her heart plummeted. "Zack wasn't at the hotel when she arrived."

"So he still hasn't heard from you at all."

She clutched the phone tightly against her chest. Eduardo was watching her far too closely. She needed a moment. Just a moment.

"Why don't you bring my bags in?" she asked.

Dark eyes narrowed, but he walked over to the entry and pulled her bags just inside the door, shutting it behind him.

She bit her lip and looked back down at her phone.

"Scared?" he asked.

"No," she muttered. She opened up the message screen and typed in Zack's name, her fingers hovering over the letters on the touch screen as she watched the cursor blink. She really didn't know what to say to him. "Nothing about this in the chivalry handbook?" she asked.

Eduardo crossed his arms over his broad chest and leaned against the back of the couch. "I think we both have to accept that we're on the wrong side of honor at this point in time."

"Good thing I never gave honor much thought," she said.

Except she was now. Or at least giving thought to what a mess she'd made out of Zack's life. She growled low in her chest and shot Eduardo one last evil glare.

I'm so sorry about the wedding, Zack.

She let her thumb hover over the send button and then hit it on a groan.

"What did you tell him?"

"Nothing really yet." She pulled up another text window.

I met someone else. I— She paused for a moment and looked at Eduardo. If she'd been speaking, she would have gagged on the next word. —love him.

She closed her eyes and hit Send. Let him think that emotion had been in charge. She and Zack were both so cynical about love…he might even find it funny. That had been the foundation of their relationship really. Zack had wanted a wife, the stability marriage would bring. But he wanted a wife who wouldn't bother him about his long working hours, and who didn't want children. Or love.

They'd been so well suited.

"There. I hope you're happy. I just ruined things with my best bet for a happy ending."

"You said you didn't love him," Eduardo said.

"I know. But I like him. I respect him. How often do you get that in a marriage?"

"I don't know. I've only ever had separate bedrooms and blackmail in my marriage. What excuse did you give him?"

"I told him how much I loved you, dearest," she bit out.

He chuckled. "You always were an accomplished little liar."

"Well, I don't feel good about this one."

"You felt good about the others?"

She truly didn't know the answer. "I...I never thought about how I felt about it. Just about whether or not it was necessary. Anyway, I don't lie as a matter of course."

"You just lie about really big things infrequently?"

"Every job application has started with questions about college. Didn't I get near-perfect grades at university? Didn't I have a prestigious internship at Vega Communications? No lies. No one wants to know about high school, not once you've been through university."

"And your fiancé?"

"Never asked many questions. He liked what he knew about me." And neither of them knew all that much. Something she was realizing now that she was being haunted by her past. She and Zack had never even slept together. Not for lack of attraction. She'd been quite attracted to him, impossible not to be, but until things were legal and permanent between them she'd felt the need to hang on to that bit of control.

It was so much easier to deny her sex drive than to end up back where she'd been nine years ago. Being that girl, that was unacceptable. She never would be again.

"Lies by omission are still lies, *querida*."

"Then we're all liars."

"Now, that's true enough."

"Show me to my room," she said, affecting her commanding, imperious tone. The one she had gotten so good at over the years. "I'm tired."

A slow smile curved his lips and she fought the urge to punch him.

"Of course, darling."

This time, he picked up her bags without incident and she followed him into her room. Her room. Her throat tightened. Her first experience with homecoming. Why should it mean anything? He had replaced the bedding. A new dark-colored comforter, new sable throw pillows, new satin curtains on the windows to match. The solid desk she'd loved to work at was still in its corner. Unmoved. There was no dust on it, but then, Eduardo had always had a great housekeeper.

"This is…perfect," she said.

"I'm glad you still like it. I remember you being…giddy over it back when we were first married."

"It was the nicest room I'd ever been in," she said, opting to give him some honesty, a rare thing from her. "The sheets were…heaven."

"The sheets?"

She cleared her throat. "I have a thing for high-quality sheets. And you definitely have them here."

"Well, now you get to live here again. And reap the benefits of the sheets."

She arched a brow. "My fiancé was a billionaire, you know."

"Yes, I know. I would expect you to find nothing less," he said.

"I'm not sure how I feel about your assessment of my character, Eduardo. You express no shock over Zack's financial status, or over the fact that we weren't in love."

"You're mercenary. I know it…you know it. It's not shocking."

She *was* mercenary. If being mercenary meant she did what she had to to ensure her own success. Her own survival. She'd needed to be. To move up from the life she'd been born into. To overcome the devastating consequences of her youthful actions. And she'd never lost a wink of sleep over it. But for some reason, the fact that it was so obvious to Eduardo was a little bit unsettling.

"Is it mercenary to try and improve the quality of your life?" she asked.

"It depends on the route you take."

"And the resources available to you are a major factor in deciding which route to take," she said.

"I'm not judging you, Hannah, believe it or not."

She planted her hands on her hips. "No, you're just using me."

"As you said, you do what you must to improve the quality of your life." His expression was strange, tense. Dark.

She looked away. "I have to do something."

"What is that?"

She looked down at her left hand, at the massive, sparkly engagement ring Zack had given her a few months earlier. She tugged it off her finger, a strange sensation moving through her like a strong wind. Sadness. Regret. Relief.

"I have to send this to Zack." She held it up and realized her hands were shaking. She couldn't keep it. Not for another second. Because mercenary she might be. But she wasn't a thief. She wouldn't take from Zack. Wouldn't do any more damage than she'd already done.

"I can have someone do that for you. Do you know where he is?"

"Thailand," she said, without missing a beat. "We were supposed to honeymoon there."

"And you think he went?" he asked, dark eyebrows raised.

She smiled. "Zack had business in Thailand, so yes, I think he went. No, I know he went. He's not the kind of man to let a little thing like an interrupted marriage keep him from accomplishing his goals."

Eduardo studied her, dark eyes intense. "Perhaps he was perfect for you."

"Yeah, well, I'm trying not to dwell on that." She held the ring out and Eduardo opened his hand. She dropped it into his palm. "I have the address of the place we were meant to stay at."

"*Bien.* I'll call a courier and have it rushed." He closed his hand around the ring, the glittering gem disappearing. All she could think of was that he held her future in his hand. The future that might have been. The one that was not eclipsed by Eduardo.

She looked up, their eyes clashing. Her throat tightened, halting her breath.

"Good," she said, barely able to force out the words. She turned to the desk and saw a pad and pen slotted into the wooden slats built into it for organization. It was where she'd kept them when she'd lived here. She bent and scribbled the address for the house she should be in now, with Zack.

Her fingers felt stiff and cold around the pen. She straightened and handed him the note. "There. That should do it."

"I'm surprised you don't want to keep the ring."

"Why? I didn't keep the one you gave me, either."

"We had a prior agreement. I get the feeling you didn't have an agreement like that with him."

"Separate beds, separate lives, unless a public appearance is needed? No. We were meant to be married for real." She swallowed hard. "And all things considered, I don't feel right keeping his ring. I was the one who wronged him."

"Careful, Hannah, I might start thinking you grew a conscience in our time apart."

"I've always had one," she said. "It's been inconvenient sometimes."

"Not too inconvenient."

"Oh, what would you know about a conscience, Eduardo?"

"Very little. Only that it occasionally takes the form of a cricket."

A reluctant laugh escaped her lips. "That sounds about

right. So…if you could mail my ring to him, that would be great."

"I'll call now." He turned and walked out of the room, leaving her alone.

She sat on the edge of the bed, her emotions a blank. She wasn't sure what she was supposed to feel. Why she suddenly felt more relieved than upset about leaving Zack behind. Marriage to him would have been good.

And yet, when she thought of the honeymoon, when she thought of sharing his bed…she couldn't make the man in her vision Zack.

The man she saw was darker, more intense. The man she saw was Eduardo. His hands on her skin, his lips on her throat…

She flopped backward and covered her face with her hands. "Stop it," she admonished herself. She rolled onto her side and grabbed a pillow, hugging it tightly to her chest. She hadn't done that since high school. Comforting then, even when the world was crumbling around her, and just as comforting now.

Eduardo had always been handsome. He'd always appealed to her. That was nothing new. But she'd never once been tempted to act on any kind of attraction while they'd lived together. It hadn't been part of her plan. And she didn't deviate from her plans. Plans, control, being the one in charge of her life, that was everything. The most important thing.

Not Eduardo's handsome face and sexy physique.

"Feeling all right?" Eduardo asked from the doorway.

She snapped back into a sitting position, pillow still locked tightly against her breasts. "Fine."

Eduardo couldn't hold back the smile that tugged at the corner of his lips. Hannah Weston, flopped on her bed like a teenage girl. A show of softness, a show of humanity, he hadn't expected from an ice queen like her. Like her reaction when he mentioned her fiancé. Like when she'd given back the other man's ring.

It suited him to think of Hannah as being above human emotion. It always had. He needed her. He didn't know all the reasons why, but he did. And that meant it was easier to believe that she would simply go with the option that benefited her most and feel no regret over leaving the inferior choice behind.

But that wasn't how she was behaving. And it gave him a strange twinge in his chest that seemed completely foreign.

Hannah stood up from the bed and put the pillow gingerly back in its place. She cleared her throat and straightened. She looked…soft for a moment. Different than he'd ever seen her before. She was beautiful, no question, more so now than she'd been as a too-thin college student.

She was still thin, but her angles had softened into curves, her cheekbones less sharp, her breasts small but round.

Instantly, an image of him pushing her on the bed, tugging her shirt up, filled his mind. He could take those breasts into his hands…suck her nipple between his lips, his teeth…

A rush of blood roared through his body, south of his belt. How long had it been since that had happened? Since he'd been aroused by an actual woman. In solitude, with a fantasy, he could certainly find release. But with a woman? One he had to somehow seduce and charm when he had no more seduction and charm left in him? That had been beyond him for quite some time.

"I can see that. You epitomize 'fine.'"

"I'm ready to find out what your game plan is, Vega," she said, crossing her arms beneath those small, gorgeous breasts.

"My game plan?"

"Yes. I don't like not knowing the score. I want to know exactly what you have planned and why."

"Tomorrow, I plan to take you to the office, to let you look at things and get a feel for the state of the company."

"All right. What else?"

He felt the need to goad her. To shake her icy composure. As she was shaking his. He took a step forward, extended his hand and brushed his knuckles over her cheek. Her skin was like a rose petal, soft and delicate. "Well, tonight, my darling bride, we dine out." Her eyes darkened, blush-pink lips parting. She was not unaffected by him. His body celebrated the victory even as his mind reminded him that this had no place in their arrangement. "I intend to show all of Barcelona that Señora Vega has returned to her husband."

CHAPTER THREE

GLAMOROUS events and upscale restaurants had become typical in Hannah's world over the past five years. But going with Eduardo wasn't.

The car ride to La Playa had been awkward. She'd dressed impeccably for the evening, as she always did, her blond hair twisted into a bun, her lips and dress a deep berry color, perfect for her complexion.

Eduardo was perfectly pressed as always in a dark suit he'd left unbuttoned and a white shirt with an unfastened collar.

All of that was as it should be. The thing that bothered her was the tension between them. It wasn't just anger, and heaven knew she should feel a whole lot of anger, but there was something else. Something darker and infinitely more powerful.

Something that had changed. It was directly linked to the change in Eduardo, the dark, enticing intensity that lived in him now. The thing she couldn't define.

The thing that made her shake inside.

Eduardo maneuvered the car up the curb and killed the engine. She opened the door and was out and halfway around the car when she nearly ran into him. Her heart stalled, her breath rushing out of her.

"I would have opened your door for you," he said.

She inhaled sharply, trying to collect herself. "And I didn't need you to."

"You're my wife, *querida,* here to reconcile with me. Don't you think I would show you some chivalry?"

"Again with the chivalry. I thought you and I established that honor wasn't our strong point."

"But it will be as far as the press is concerned. Or, more to the point, our relationship needs to seem like a strength." He leaned forward and brushed his knuckles gently over her cheekbone, just as he'd done back in the penthouse.

And just as it had done back at the penthouse, her blood pressure spiked, her heartbeat raging out of control.

She'd had a connection with Zack, and certainly physical attraction. They hadn't slept together, but they'd kissed. Quite a bit. Enough to know that they had chemistry. Now the idea of what she'd shared with Zack being chemistry seemed like a joke.

It had been easy to kiss Zack and say good-night. To walk away. His lips on hers only made her lips burn.

A look from Eduardo made her burn. Everywhere.

She'd lived with him before, though, and nothing had happened between them. There was no reason to think she couldn't keep a handle on it this time.

She turned her face away from him, the night air hitting her cheek, feeling especially cold with the loss of his skin against hers.

He cupped her chin with his thumb and forefinger, turning her face so that she had to look at him. "You can't act like my touch offends you."

"I'm not," she said, holding her breath as she took a step closer to him, as she slid her hand down his arm and laced her fingers with his. "See?"

She was sure he could hear her heart pounding, was certain he knew just how he was affecting her. Except…he wasn't gloating. He wasn't poised to give her a witty comeback, or make fun of her.

"You seem so different," she said, following him to where

the valet was standing. He ignored her statement and gave his keys to the young man in the black vest, speaking to him in Spanish, his focus determinedly off Hannah, even while he held on to her hand.

He tightened his grip on her as they walked on the cobblestones, to the front of the restaurant. It was an old building, brick, the exterior showing the age and character of Barcelona. But inside, it had been transformed. Sleek, sophisticated and smelling nearly as strongly of money as it did of paella, it was exactly the kind of place she'd imagined Eduardo would like.

It was exactly the kind of place *she* liked.

A man dressed all in black was waiting at the front. His face lit with recognition when Eduardo walked in. "Señor Vega, a table for you and your guest?"

"Sí," he said. "This is Señora Vega, my wife. She's come back to Barcelona. I'm very…pleased to see her." He turned to the side, brushing her hair off her face. Heat sparked, from there down through her body. She tried to keep smiling.

The man cocked his head to the side, clearly pleased to be let in on such exclusive news. *"Bienvenido a Barcelona, señora.* We're glad to have you back."

She could feel Eduardo's gaze on her, feel his hold tighten on her waist. She forced her smile wider. "I'm very glad to be back."

"Bien. Right this way."

He led them to a table in the back of the room, white and glossy, with bright red bench seats on either side of it. There was a stark white curtain shielding part of the seating area from view, giving air of seclusion and luxury.

Eduardo spoke to their host in Spanish for a moment before the other man left and Eduardo swept the curtain aside, holding it open for her. She looked at him, the smile still glued on her face. "Thank you."

Back when they'd been married, they might have gone to a

place like this late on a Saturday night. And everyone inside
would know Eduardo. Would clamor for his attention. And
she would play her part, smiling and nodding while mentally
trying to decide what appetizer to get.

There was none of that tonight. If people had looked at
them, it had been subtle. And no one spoke to Eduardo. No
one stopped to ask about business. Or where the next big party
was. Or which nightclub was opening soon.

She looked behind them and saw that people were staring. Trying to be covert, but not doing a good job. Their expressions weren't welcoming. They looked... They looked
either afraid or like they were looking at a car crash and she
couldn't figure out why.

"You play your part very well," Eduardo said, not paying
any attention to the other diners, "but then, you always did."

"I know," she said. She played every part well. A girl
from the Southern United States with bad grades, a thick-
as-molasses accent and a total lack of sophistication had to
work hard to fit in with the university crowd in Barcelona.
But she'd done it.

She'd dropped most of her accent, studied twice as hard
as anyone else, and perfected an expression of boredom that
carried her through posh events and busy cities without ever
looking like the country mouse she was.

It was only when she was alone that she gave herself freedom to luxuriate in comfortable sheets and room service,
and all of the other things her new life had opened up to her.

"And you're never modest, which, I confess, I quite like,"
he said. "Why should you be? You've achieved a great a deal.
And you've done it on your own."

"Is this the part where you try and make friends with
me?" she asked.

He laughed, a sort of strained, forced sound, nothing like
the laugh he'd once had. It had been joyous, easy. Now he
sounded out of practice. "Don't be silly, why would I do that?"

"No reason, I suppose. You never did try to be my friend. Just my fake husband."

"Your real husband," he corrected. "Ours just hasn't been a traditional marriage."

"Uh, no. Starting with you calling me into your office one day and telling me you knew all my secrets and that, unless I wanted them spilled, I would do just as you asked me."

A waiter came by and Eduardo ordered a *pre fixe* meal. Hannah read the description in the gilded menu and her stomach cramped with hunger. She was thin—she always had been—but it had more to do with her metabolism than watching her diet. Food was very important to her.

When the waiter had gone, she studied Eduardo's face again. "Why did you do that? Why did you think it would be so…funny to marry me?"

He shook his head. "Very hard to say at this point in time. Everything was a joke to me. And I felt manipulated. I resented my father's heavy hand in my life and I thought I would play his game against him."

"And you used me."

He met her eyes, unflinching. "I did."

"Why?"

He looked down, a strange expression on his face. "Because I could. Because I was Eduardo Vega. Everything, and everyone, in my life existed to please me. My father wanted to see me be a man. He wanted to see me assume control. Find a wife, a family to care for. To give of myself instead of just take. I thought him a foolish, backward old man."

"So you married someone you knew he would find unsuitable."

"I did." He looked up at her. "I would not do so now."

She studied him more closely, the hardened lines on his face, the weariness in his eyes. "You seem different," she said, finally voicing it.

"How so?" he asked.

"Older."

"I am older."

"But more than five years older," she said, looking at the lines around his mouth. Mostly though, it was the endless darkness in his eyes.

"You flatter me."

"You know I would never flatter you, Eduardo. I would never flatter anyone."

A strange expression crossed his face. "No, you wouldn't. But I suppose, ironically, that proves you an honest person in your way."

"I suppose." She looked down at the table. "Has your father's death been hard on you?"

"Of course. And for my mother it has been…nearly unendurable. She has loved him, only him, since she was a teenager. She's heartbroken."

Hannah frowned, picturing Carmela Vega. She had been such a sweet, solid presence. She'd invited Eduardo and Hannah to dinner every Sunday night during their marriage. She'd forced Hannah to know them. To love them.

More people that Hannah had hurt in order to protect herself.

"I'm very sorry about that."

"As am I." He hesitated a moment. "I am doing my best to take care of things. To take care of her. There is something you should know. Something you *will* know if you're going to spend any amount of time around me."

Anticipation, trepidation, crept over her. He sounded grave, intense, two things Eduardo had never been when she'd known him. "And that is?" she asked, trying to keep her tone casual.

Eduardo wished the waiter had poured them wine. He would have a word with the manager about the server after their meal.

Before he could answer Hannah's question, their waiter

appeared, with wine and mussels in clarified butter. He set them on the table and Eduardo picked up the glass, taking a long drink.

When the waiter left again, he set it on the table, his focus back on Hannah, his resolve strengthened.

"I was involved in an accident, very soon after you left."

"An accident?"

"At my family's stables. I was jumping my horse in a course I had ridden hundreds of times. The horse came to a jump he'd done before, but he balked. I was thrown." That much, he had been told by others later. It was strange how vividly he remembered the moments leading up to the accident. The smell of the dirt, grass and the sweat of the horses. He could remember mounting his horse and coaxing him into a trot, then a canter. He could remember nothing after that. Nothing for days and days after. They were gone. "I wasn't wearing a helmet. My head hit the edge of the jump, then the ground." The regret of that burned in him still. It had been a simple thing, a commonplace activity, and it had changed his life forever. "It's funny, because you see, I did forget to file the divorce papers."

Hannah looked pale, her cheeks the color of wax, her lips holding barely a blush of rose. For the first time since he'd known her, she looked truly shaken. "It doesn't sound funny."

"You can laugh at it, *querida*. I don't mind."

"I do. I mind, Eduardo. How badly were you hurt?"

He shook his head. "Badly enough. There has been…damage." He hated to speak of it. Hated to voice the lasting problems the accident had caused. It made them seem real. Final. He didn't want them. Five years later and he couldn't believe he was trapped with a mind that betrayed him as his did.

"I have issues with my memory," he said. "My attention span. Frequent migraines. And I have had some changes in my personality. At least I've been told so. It's hard for me to truly…remember or understand the man I was before."

He looked at her face, stricken, pained. Strange to see her that way. She had always been as cool and steady as a block of ice. Even when he'd called her into his office all those years ago to tell her he'd discovered she'd faked her paperwork to get into college, she'd been stoic. Angry, but poised.

With a calm that women twice her age couldn't have affected, she'd agreed to his foolish marriage scheme. It seemed foolish to him now, anyway. He'd been such a stupid boy, full of his own importance, laughing at life.

Yes, he certainly had changed.

Even now, sitting across from Hannah, as he had done that day he'd coerced her into marriage, he couldn't understand the man that he'd been. Couldn't understand why it had been so amusing. Why he had felt entitled to drag her into his game.

He had been convinced that being near her would…

"I noticed," she said, her voice soft.

"I suppose you did." He lifted his wineglass to his lips again, trying to ignore the defeat that came when the crisp flavor hit his tongue. Wine didn't even make him feel the same. It used to make him feel lighter, a bit happier. Now it just made him tired. "It is of no consequence. With the changes came no desire for me to change back." It wasn't true, not entirely, but he was hardly going to give her reason to pity him. He could take a great many things, but not pity.

"Is this why you're having problems with Vega?" she asked.

"Essentially." The word burned. "I had someone hired to…" He chose his words carefully. He disliked the word *help* almost as much as he disliked saying he couldn't do something. Of course, the verbal avoidance game was empty, because it didn't change reality. "To oversee the duties of managing finances and budgets. Someone else to do taxes. Neither did an adequate job, and now I find myself with some issues to work out, and no one that I trust to handle it."

"And you trust me?" Her tone was incredulous, blue eyes round.

"I don't know that I trust you, but I do know your deepest and darkest secrets. In the absence of trust, I consider it a fairly hefty insurance policy."

She took another sip of her wine. "There are some things about you that are still the same," she said.

"What things?" he asked, desperate to know.

For a moment, she felt like the lifeline he'd built her up to be. No one else seemed to see anything in him from before. They saw him as either diminished in some way, or frightening. His mother and sister, loving as ever, seemed to pity him. He felt smothered in it.

"You're still incredibly amused by what you perceive to be your own brilliance."

Unbidden, a laugh escaped his lips. "If a man can't find amusement with himself, life could become boring."

"A double entendre?" She arched her brow.

"No, I'm afraid not. Further evidence of the changes in me, I suppose." And yet with Hannah, sometimes he felt normal. Something akin to what and who he had been. It felt good to exchange banter, to have her face him, an almost-friendly adversary. For the moment.

"You're also still a stubborn, arrogant autocrat." She seemed almost determined to prove to herself that he was the same.

"As ever."

"And your father's business? Vega Communications? Is it all still a joke to you?"

"Is that what you thought? That it was a joke to me?"

She looked down. "You taking me as a wife was certainly a joke. A joke you used to convince him to pass Vega into your hands then."

"Evidence that nothing about Vega Communications was ever a joke to me."

"Because providing mobile phone service to an ever-increasing number of countries is your passion?"

"Because it's my birthright. It's part of my family legacy." And because if he failed at that, he had nothing to strive for. "Like you, I did very well at university. I earned a degree... I earned my position. Yes, I had connections, but you managed to get into Vega as an intern. You've managed to make your own connections. Why be disdainful simply because my course was more set than yours?"

She looked thoughtful as she took a mussel on the half shell between her thumb and forefinger. "I was disdainful because I never thought you cared about it. Or even wanted it. Not really."

"I expected it. I suppose, given that it seemed a certainty, I lacked the blatant desperation you possessed."

She put the mussel between her lips and sucked out the flesh. It wasn't a sexy action. Not really. And yet, when she did it, it was oddly compelling. It was because her lips managed to look sensual, inviting and soft, all while her eyes told him she'd happily bite his tongue if he dared follow the impulse that originated south of his belt.

"Desperation?" she asked, taking the white linen napkin from her lap and dabbing the side of her mouth. "Drive, maybe."

"If it makes you feel better."

"It does. Humor me."

He inclined his head. "If you wish. Anyway, I may sympathize with you a bit more now. I have to fix this. Vega is my family. My life."

The glee she'd seemed to take from her initial thought of his being desperate had diminished. "You used to like other things better."

"I did."

"Parties. Loose women."

"I was faithful to you during our marriage." A statement

more true than she realized. But the fallout from the head injury had been extensive. He'd lost his passion for everything. Had lost friends. He'd had a hunger for life once. For fun and pleasure, for laughter.

He had nothing more than a white-knuckled grip on existence now. A human, biological need to keep breathing. And with that, came the need to save Vega.

It gave him a reason to go on, anyway, and that was, at this point in his life, more valuable than passion.

"Prince Charming in the flesh," she said lightly.

The waiter returned and set a fish course before them, Spanish rice and spiced greens on the side. Hannah wasted no time in helping herself. She had always liked eating. He'd been fascinated by it. When they would go to his family's house for dinner, she'd always eaten as much as he did, if not more. Still, she'd always looked thin. Hungry. But he'd suspected, even then, that her hunger wasn't for food.

She'd been hungry for money. Status. Success.

She still was. It was why she was here with him. Why he'd been able to demand she return to Spain.

"Not entirely," he said, his tone heavier than he intended it to be.

"So tell me then," she said, blue eyes glittering with mischief. "Will you be faithful to me during our reconciliation?" Her lips closed around her fork and his gut tightened.

"That all depends, Hannah," he said, words forming before thought, his body leading the proceedings.

"On?"

"On whether or not you intend to share my bed this time."

Hannah nearly choked on her rice. "What?"

Eduardo leaned back in his chair, a dark glint in his eye, a lean, hungry look to his features. "You heard me, *querida.* Will I need to seek my amusement elsewhere? Or will you share my bed?"

"I am not sleeping with you," she said, the very idea of the invasion, the intimacy, the loss of utter and complete control, making her feel shivery and panicky. Hot.

"Then I suppose the answer to the question is not your concern."

"No," she bit out.

She didn't truly care who he slept with. She'd been trying to goad him, nothing else. They did that. They always had. Verbal sparring had been the only level they'd ever truly connected on.

They shared a love of arguing, which, in some ways, made them the perfect married couple for the public. For all she knew of married couples.

"At least we're on the same page," he said, returning his focus to his dinner.

What did that mean? That he didn't want her? That made her…mad. And it shouldn't. She shouldn't care. Men, attraction, sex, none of it fit into her life. She'd been about to make room for Zack, and of course she'd intended to sleep with him eventually. But she'd been in control of it, no question. She'd been able to wait, and so had he. She and Zack were both all about control, about keeping things in order, in their neat little boxes.

Eduardo would never fit into a box. She would never be able to shove him to one side of her life and ignore him unless she wanted to open him up and indulge. Nope. That wasn't possible. He was too much. Too…present. He was impossible to simply ignore.

She didn't want to sleep with him anyway. She'd denied her sex drive, rightly, necessarily, for the past nine years. Sure, she'd been about to end the dry spell with marriage. But it hadn't been the attractor to marrying Zack. It had never been that important. It wasn't all-consuming.

It wouldn't be with Eduardo, either. She could keep on ignoring it, no question. And Eduardo wouldn't change that.

So his lack of desire for her shouldn't matter. Her ego was just feeling bruised.

"Good thing. So," she said, "what's your plan for tomorrow? Just waltzing into the office and announcing we're reconciling?"

A smile curved his lips. An unsettling, dark smile that made her stomach tighten and her heart pound. "Why don't we just see what happens?"

CHAPTER FOUR

Why don't we just see what happens?

Even getting out of the car the next morning, business armor in the form of a sleek-fitting pair of slacks and a dark blue button-up shirt, she heard his words playing through her head. They'd sounded like a double entendre. Like he'd disregarded the previous portion of the conversation where she'd said she wouldn't sleep with him.

Smug-ass Spaniard.

She tightened her hold on her laptop bag and chanced a glance at him out of the corner of her eye. He was looking sexier than he ever had, at least to her, in a navy suit, his dark hair left slightly disheveled, as if theirs was a reconciliation made in the bedroom.

He paused in front of the heavy glass door of the tall, modern building and held it open for her, his dark eyes never leaving hers.

She made eye contact as she walked in. She wasn't about to let him intimidate her. Nope. Not going to happen.

Her gaze was steely. She was sure of it. And his was... amused. It was the first time she'd seen him amused, really amused, in a way that reminded her of the old Eduardo, since he'd hijacked a limo and disrupted her wedding.

A leaden weight dropped into her stomach. A sudden reminder of why he'd changed.

She tossed her hair and continued into the building. She

knew it well. She'd interned there for months and then she'd become the boss's daughter-in-law. She'd learned about the way a big business ran here, had faced down Eduardo for the first time.

Another strange wave of homecoming melancholy washed over her. She tried to clear her tightened throat.

"*Buenos días,* Paola." Eduardo greeted the woman sitting behind the reception desk.

"*Buenos días, Señor Vega.*" She looked up for the first time, her eyes rounding when she saw Hannah. "Hannah," she said.

Hannah's heart beat against her breastbone. She remembered her? She'd never wondered much if people remembered her. She'd never been back to a place to find out.

"Hi, Paola." She'd always like Paola. The other woman had always been nice to her, not laughing at her mangled Spanish, always offering her a smile when she'd come in for work after classes.

She wondered what Paola had thought when she'd suddenly "abandoned" Eduardo and their six-month union.

"You're...back?" she asked, her focus darting from Eduardo and back to Hannah.

"Yes," Eduardo said, turning to her, his expression soft, the hard glint in his eye telling her the expression was a lie. "She is." He lifted his hand and brushed his finger lightly over her cheek.

A shiver wound through her, tightening her stomach, her lungs, her nipples. She'd tried to forget this part of being near him. Had tried, and failed, so many times to forget what it had felt like on their wedding day when his lips had touched hers.

To forget that he brought out a beast in her. One that was normally asleep, or at least dormant, kept mollified by the occasional fantasy and gratuitous amounts of cop shows with men in tight uniforms.

This was different than those contained, allowed moments

of desire. This was different even than the attraction she'd felt for him back when they'd first married. This wasn't something she had a grasp on; it was nothing she could control or shut off.

The wedding kiss, and feelings it had created in her, had lingered. But she'd been able to keep it where it belonged. Stored for her convenient use late at night, never invading her body or thoughts during the day. Never when it wasn't appropriate.

It was invading now.

She swallowed hard and worked at composing her face. She wasn't going to break; she wasn't going to show nerves. Or arousal. "That's right," she said. "I am."

Then, just to prove to him that he wasn't the only one who could play the game, she leaned in, pausing for a moment as his scent hit her. Sandalwood and skin. She couldn't remember ever noticing the way he smelled before. It was foreign. Sexy. Piquing her curiosity, her need to draw closer.

So she did, because that had been her intent. Not for any other reason. Her eyes met his as her lips connected with his cheek. Smooth still, clean, a hint of aftershave lingering. She closed her eyes, just for a moment, and let the feel of him beneath her lips fully wash over.

Then she pulled back, quickly, her head swimming, her heart pounding.

"Yes, I'm back," she said, blowing out a breath and smiling at Paola, trying to ignore the intense quivering in her stomach.

"Good," she said. "Very good. We're glad to have you."

"As am I," Eduardo said, his eyes never leaving Hannah. "Come, *querida,* I want to show you some of the changes I've made."

She offered Paola another smile and a stilted nod before following Eduardo into the first elevator on the right. She let out a breath when the platinum doors closed.

"Very convincing," Eduardo said, a strange smile curving his lips. It was almost predatory.

"I know, right?" she snapped. "I'm a great actress, remember?"

"Why didn't you just head to Hollywood instead of pursuing a career in finance? You wouldn't have had to fake school transcripts."

She cleared her throat and tightened her hold on her bag. "Too much chance involved. I don't do chance. I do certainty. Control. Something I could work hard enough to achieve. Luck has never really been on my side—" she swept a hand up and down in Eduardo's direction "—obviously. So I didn't figure I should make a plan that included lucking into anything."

"Are you saying our association has been unlucky for you?"

She gritted her teeth, thinking of the letter of recommendation that had happened to find the firm she'd wanted so badly to get a job at in New York. A letter from the HR department at Vega. "Not entirely, but you have to admit, getting kidnapped on your wedding day isn't good luck."

He chuckled as the elevator stopped. "Now, that depends."

The doors slid open and he stepped out; she followed. "On what?"

"On how you feel about the person you're marrying."

The floor was quiet, essentially vacant. The highest offices in the building were reserved for the big dogs of the company, and at this point, Eduardo was the biggest dog.

He opened the door to what had been his father's office, and Hannah's throat constricted. More emotion. She wasn't used to it. She didn't like it, either.

"You don't have to open doors for me, you know," she said, sweeping into the room. "I know you aren't a gentleman."

He arched a brow and closed the door behind them. "I'm hardly trying to convince you otherwise."

"Obviously."

"All right, Hannah," he said, moving to his desk, his demeanor changing. He sat down and hit a few keys on his keyboard, waking up the flat-screen monitor. "This is what we're looking at."

"What's this?"

"Financial records for the past few years."

"I need to sit," she said.

He stood from the computer chair and she slid past him, trying to ignore the little jolt of pleasure she felt when she brushed against him. "So, what exactly do you think is going on?"

He blew out a breath. "Certain things in particular are problematic for me. Remembering numbers and dates are among them. But it wouldn't be as big of an issue had I not hired someone to handle it that didn't do his job."

"On purpose or…criminally?" she asked, opening the report for the previous years' finances.

"I'm not entirely certain."

"Well, incompetence should be criminal," she said, skimming the numbers. "And please hold all comments on how I should be an expert on the matter. I am in here saving your butt, after all."

"You are so very charming, Hannah."

She gritted her teeth and leaned in closer to the computer screen, trying to close him out of her range of focus. "Yeah, well, had I gone to charm school I probably would have failed there just as spectacularly as I flunked out of high school."

"Why did you fail high school? Because we both know you're capable of doing the work."

Her stomach dipped and she tried to will away the gut-tearing pain that always came with this set of memories. Tried to put herself firmly in the present, as Hannah Weston. Not as the Hannah she had been. "I didn't try."

"That doesn't sound like you, either."

"Yeah, well, making stupid financial decisions doesn't sound like you, and yet here we are."

She chanced a look at his face. His expression was hard, his lips set into a grim line. She'd gone too far again. She knew that. But she wasn't opening the door on her past. She just wasn't. She couldn't.

He gripped the arms of the chair and turned her so that she was facing him. "Stupid? Stupid decisions? Is that what you call them?"

"I was making a point." She slid the chair back and stood. The idea was to bring her up to his level. But since her eyes only met his chest, the only point it served to make was that, even in three-inch heels, she was a whole lot smaller than he was.

"Then you won't mind if I make one of my own." He wrapped his arm around her waist and tugged her against him, her breasts coming into contact with his chest. He raised his hand, brushing his shaking thumb over her lip, the gesture shockingly gentle given the heat and anger visible in his eyes.

The rage in him was palpable, satisfying in a way. She'd brought him to the brink with her words. His muscles trembled as he held her. She waited. For his lips to crash down on hers. Rough and painful. The way it often was with men when they lacked control or were just too turned on to think straight. The way it most certainly would be with him so angry.

But there was no crash.

He dipped his head, his lips a breath from hers. The breath fled her body, all her focus diverting to him. He was so close. So tempting. She found her face tilting so that her mouth could meet his, found herself giving in. Giving up.

His lips were hot, firm. And suddenly, he wasn't holding her to him anymore. She'd melted against him. His tongue slid against the seam of her mouth and she opened, heat flooding her, making her core tighten, her breasts feel heavy. He wrapped his other arm around her and she lifted her hands, pressing them on his hard chest.

He angled his head, deepening the kiss, tightening his hold on her. She whimpered and freed her hands, sighing when her breasts met his chest. She wrapped her arms around his neck, threading her fingers through his hair, holding him to her.

He devoured her, and she returned the favor. Never, not in their six months of marriage, had they kissed like this. Nothing more than proprietary pecks for public displays. A slightly more intimate kiss on their wedding day, since they'd had an audience.

But this was just them. Alone. And there was no control. No thought. She hadn't even tried to maintain her hold on either, she'd simply released them, and drowned in his kiss.

Then, just as suddenly as he'd embraced her, he released her, his eyes dark black pits that seemed to draw her in and repel her at the same time. And she realized she didn't have half the hold over him as he did over her.

"The point I was making," he bit out, his tone rough, strained, "is that you might not like me, and you might want to think that I'm somehow stupid, but we both know that I have the power here."

She took in a shaking breath. "You…bastard."

"Don't forget it. I'm not a boy you can manipulate. I'm not the foolish idiot I once was who might have been distracted by a pretty face." He turned away from her, heading out the door. "Let me know what you find."

She didn't answer. She couldn't. As soon as he exited the office she pounded her fist on the desk, letting the sting alleviate the burn of humiliation that had taken over.

She wouldn't let him make a fool of her like that. Never again.

Eduardo drew a shaking hand over his face. He had not meant to do that. He had not meant to touch her, or kiss her. He hadn't meant to lose control.

Rage had been a feral beast inside of him, pushing him,

driving him. Rage, and then, the hot surge of lust that had tipped him over the edge.

His body burned. He'd been so close to pushing her on the surface of the desk and…

He laughed into the empty room and gave thanks for the mostly private floor.

He hadn't touched a woman in five years. Five years of celibacy that he hadn't minded in the least. Now it seemed to be crushing him, five years all added together and suddenly very, very apparent.

It was more than that, though. It was this thing in him that he didn't know. This strain of unpredictability that he couldn't control or anticipate.

He didn't understand the man he'd been. He didn't know, or like, the man he was.

This wasn't how it was supposed to work. She wasn't supposed to appeal to the new, darker side of him. She was supposed to remind him of that light, easy time. Was supposed to bring those feelings back.

Beyond that, he did need her to help straighten out the company's finances, and he could not afford to be distracted. He had to see this through, and he could not afford a distraction. He couldn't afford to divert his focus any more than it already was. He had no control over the effects of his injury. No control over the forgetfulness or the migraines. But he would damn well control his body's reaction to her.

He gritted his teeth and walked back into the office. Hannah jumped and turned.

"Knock for heaven's sake," she growled, turning back to the screen.

"It's my office."

"Well…you left."

"And now I am back."

"Yes, you are," she said, her shoulders rolled forward, her expression intense, focused on the screen. She let out a short breath. "It's not that bad." She turned the chair so that she was facing him, a guarded expression on her face.

"You don't think?"

"No. The fees you incurred for late taxes...I can't help you with that. That was the work of a very sucky employee and I'm glad he's been fired. The rest is manageable. I could recommend some investment and savings strategies and, actually, you're missing a few tax breaks you could take advantage of while making sure your employees get better benefits."

"You make it sound...easy."

"It is," she said. "When it's your area of expertise. Can you explain to me exactly what isn't working for you? I need to know so I can help you get a system in place."

He hated that word. *Help.* He had thought nothing of it before his accident. But then, he hadn't needed it. He was supposed to be the one who provided help, the one people went to. He was the man of the Vega family. He wasn't supposed to need so much.

"Numbers and dates get reversed when I read them. And I have a very hard time remembering them. And my attention span has...shortened. It's hard to sit down and read something for a long time. Harder to retain it."

"Do they think it will ever change?"

He shrugged, like it didn't matter. "Probably not, but it's impossible to know, really."

"You're okay with it?"

A chuckle escaped his lips, not because he felt there was anything funny, but because it seemed the only response he was capable of for a moment. "Would you be okay if you woke up with a brain that wasn't yours? That's how I feel. All the time."

She looked down, her complexion pale. "I've been trying to be someone else for the past nine or ten years. I might not mind."

"Trust me, *querida,* you would. But, either way, I cannot

change what is. So I only concern myself with what can be changed."

She planted both hands on his desk and pushed herself into a standing position. She seemed to have forgotten the kiss, her expression as icy and composed as ever. He still shook inside.

"What I would like to do, is work on implementing a system that will be easier for you to track. Then I want to make sure you find some good, trustworthy financial managers. Not until everything is corrected, you understand."

"You always did think quickly on your feet. Or in an office chair."

Her lips curved into a smile. A real smile, not a smirk or a forced expression. "This is what I do. I'm good at it."

"You always have been. That's why I came to you."

"That and the leverage."

"A man can't go into battle unarmed."

A flicker of heat sparked in her eyes and he knew that she was replaying the kiss. So, she wasn't unaffected. She hadn't brushed it off. But she was right, she was an accomplished actress. She'd gotten even better, even harder to read since the beginning of their sham marriage. He had worried about her breaking character then. Even now, with the little spark visible in the depths of her eyes, he doubted anyone else would see anything beyond the cool, composed beauty she seemed to project. It would keep most people from looking deeper.

She was a petite blonde, well dressed, perfectly coiffed. She had a look that could easily become generic, and might be to some. It was her eyes that showed how different she was. That showed her intelligence, her steel.

She cleared her throat, tilted her chin up. "Well, I doubt anyone would accuse you of that."

"I'm flattered by the assessment."

"Don't be, or I'll have to punch you in the ego again."

"I see, so you're trying to knock me down a couple of pegs in an attempt to gain the upper hand. It won't work. I'm happily absent an ego, in many ways. Social status means little to me. I haven't tried to impress friends or women in so many years I can hardly remember why I ever bothered in the first place. Though, the forgetting could also be a side effect of my head injury."

She shifted, her lips bunching together.

"You don't like it when I joke about my accident?" he asked.

She shrugged. "It's your trauma, man. Deal with it however you want."

"I've dealt with it," he said, his words coming out harsher than intended. Lies. "I've dealt with my father's death, with trying to ensure my mother and sister are happy, well taken care of. And now, I'm dealing with fixing what has fallen into disrepair here at the company."

"And I'm here to help you do it." She arched her pale eyebrows. "Under sufferance, you understand, but I am here. And I am helping."

For some reason, his entire body didn't seize in response to the use of the word.

"You are."

CHAPTER FIVE

HANNAH leaned against the railing on the penthouse terrace and looked down at the city. The sky was dark, stars piercing holes in the blackness, and below, Barcelona was lit. Cars still crowded the road, people headed to restaurants and clubs.

She breathed in deep—warm air filling her lungs. She smelled salt, the sea, but it wasn't the same as it was in San Francisco or New York. Here it seemed spicier, richer. It always had. It had always called to her in a different way. Begged her to strip off her control and let herself go free.

And she had always denied it.

"Having trouble sleeping?"

She turned, her heart catching when she saw Eduardo leaning in the doorway. He'd traded in his work attire for casual black pants and a tight T-shirt that hugged his muscular physique almost as tightly as she'd hugged him earlier in his office.

Don't think about that.

She wouldn't. Not again. That was over. Done. No more kissing. Not in private anyway.

"I'm still a little off. Jet lag and all."

"Tell me, Hannah."

Her throat tightened, strange, irrational fear assaulting her. "Tell you what?"

"Tell me what you've been doing with yourself these past five years."

She almost sighed in relief. Five years she could do. "Working. I was in New York for about three years, working on Wall Street, of all things, then I relocated to San Francisco. I started to get a good client base at the firm I was with, doing personal financial management and investments. I hit a bit of a wall, though, because male bosses, coworkers and clients always seemed to think single meant available. So when I met Zack a year ago, it seemed perfect. I could get married, and I could do my job without so much sexual harassment."

"And that's the only reason you were going to marry him? I hate to be the one to tell you, but men who are inclined to behave that way sexually harass women with wedding rings, too."

"Sure they do, but Zack is influential. Wealthy. It would be a brave man who attempted to poach on his territory."

Eduardo chuckled, dark and enticing. "Like me?"

"Yes. Brave or stupid."

His eyes locked with hers. "Do you remember what happened last time you used that word?"

Heat and regret assaulted her. Heat from the memory of the kiss, regret because she'd insulted him. She wished she felt more regret in regards to the actual kissing.

"I won't do it again."

"Good." He walked to the railing, resting his forearms on the metal surface. He was barefoot. Strange that she noticed. He seemed slightly more human than usual in that moment. "Were you going to have a family with him? Children?"

A shiver started in her stomach, working its way through her. "No. No children."

"You don't want them?"

"No. Never. What would I do with a baby, anyway?" She laughed, as though it were the most ridiculous thing in the world. And she fought hard against the tight, clenching pain in her womb. Against the memories.

"Raise it, I suppose. But then, wearing a baby in a sling

while you're cursing and trading stocks is maybe not that practical."

She swallowed the bile that was rising in her throat. "You want children?"

"No," he said. Just no. Good. She didn't want to talk about her aversion to children, either. Didn't want to open up that box. It held so much fear, and regret and guilt. She just couldn't look in it at the moment. She did her best to never, ever look in it. To never remember.

"Not practical for people like us," she said. She and Zack had had a very similar conversation once. And in his response she'd sensed the same dark grief that she felt hovering around the edges of his answers. Another reason she'd never pressed him for his secrets. She was certain they shared something too similar, too painful. She knew it was why he'd never pressed for hers.

"Of course not."

"We were going to be partners. Help each other out. It's good to have a partner in life."

"I suppose so," he said slowly. "But that isn't how I want to live."

"No?"

"No. I would rather be able to do things independently. If I ever had a wife...I would have wanted to take care of her."

"Not every woman wants to be taken care of." But for a moment she wondered what it would be like. To have someone shoulder some of the pain. To have someone who knew every secret. Who shared every fear. Someone who would cover her, shield her.

A silly thought. She didn't want that. She was the only person she could trust. The only person she could depend on.

"It's how I think things should be done. That's how my parents did things. They were happy."

"How is your mom?"

"Grieving. Still. She spent more than thirty years with my father. His death has been hard for her."

"I'm sorry. Your parents were… They're the only place I've ever seen love, let's put it that way."

"The only place? What about your parents?"

What was the harm in giving him a little? He knew more about her than anyone else. "I don't know. I don't think they ever married. When I was three my mom left me at my dad's single-wide and never came back. She had all my stuff tied up in a little plastic bag. Anyway, he didn't know what to do with a kid. He…he tried I guess. But he was kind of a mess."

He frowned. "Your mother left you?"

"Not every family is perfect. But I don't dwell on it."

"You don't even acknowledge it."

"I lived in this dirty, dusty mobile home. The park it was in had a dirt road and when trucks would drive by, the dirt was like a cloud. It settled on everything. Everything was always dirty. I actually felt lucky to only have one parent. There was no fighting in my house. I could always hear the neighbors screaming at each other. My father never yelled. He just barely ever said hi, either."

She could stay out all night and he'd hardly ever raise an eyebrow when she'd come in at breakfast. She could still see him, sitting in his chair with a bowl of cereal in his lap and a beer already in his hand.

"How were the sheets?" he asked.

"I didn't have any. Just a mattress on the floor and a blanket. We didn't have a washer and dryer so…I used to hitchhike to the Laundromat sometimes so I could clean my blankets and clothes."

She shook her head. "I mean…would you want to talk about that? Who wants that life?"

He frowned. "No one. Is that why you erased your past?"

She swallowed. "One of the many whys. But let's not even get into that." It was one thing to talk about her parents, such as they were. To talk about the things that had been out of her control. The poverty, the neglect. She could handle that.

But she'd made her own mistakes. Those were the ones that stayed closest to her, like a layer over her skin, protective and confining at the same time, impossible to remove. A part of her she wished away every day, and one she depended on to move forward.

"Fine by me." He looked out at the view. "Tell me, Hannah, what is it like to walk away from everything?" His tone was husky, sincere. Surprising.

"I… It's like walking out of prison," she said. "Like I imagine it might be, anyway. You spend all this time in a place you know isn't right, and yet, you have to stay. Until one day, you just walk out into the sunlight. You'd never go back, even though going forward is frightening. Because there's so much possibility when before that…there was nothing."

"How did you end up in Spain? Why Spain?"

Admitting she'd sort of put her finger on the globe in a random place would seem silly. As silly as the fact that she'd chosen her new last name from an upscale department store she'd seen on TV. But that was the truth. She'd been so desperate then, to shed who she was, to try and be someone else. To make something else of herself. "I wanted to get very far away. I wanted out of the country because…"

"It would be easier for you to get away with false transcripts."

"Yes. Of course they were very good, and I had changed my name legally by that point." She didn't know why she was telling him all of this. Only that with him determinedly keeping his focus on the street below, the darkness surrounding them, it seemed easy.

"And where did you get the money for it?"

The fifteen thousand dollars she never wanted to talk about. Fifteen thousand dollars she did her best to *never* think about. It had bought documents; it had supplied her with her plane ticket and passport, ID that carried her new name.

A gift. The money had been a gift, not payment, because how could a price be put on what she'd given? At least, that was what they'd told her. The Johnsons, from somewhere in New Hampshire. The couple she'd given her baby to. Oh, they'd paid all the legal adoption fees, and her hospital bill, but in the end, they'd wanted to do more. To get her on her feet. Provide her with a new start so she didn't end up back in the same place.

They had. They truly had. She should be grateful. She was.

But thinking about it was like drawing her skin off slowly. It still made her feel raw, freshly wounded and bleeding. Still made her ache with guilt. Guilt over everything. That it had ever happened. That she'd made the choice she had. And then there was the guilt that came along with the occasional, sharp sweep of relief that she'd chosen to give the baby up. That she hadn't kept him. That she hadn't spent their lives repeating the cycle her parents had been a part of.

"From a friend," she said. It was a lie. But it was the kind of lie she was used to. The kind of lie that kept all the events from her past glossed over. The kind that kept it hidden away. Kept it from being drawn out into the light and tearing her apart.

"Good friend."

"Oh, yeah. Great friend." She cleared her throat and blinked hard. "And you, Eduardo, what's it like to have a place you can call yours? What's it like to feel at home?" She wished she hadn't asked. It was too revealing. The ache in her voice was so obvious, at least to her own ears.

"I have never thought very much about it, or rather, I never had. Not before. I always took it as my due. Vega was to be mine, my position in both society and my family always sure and set. Now that I know what it's like to feel like a stranger to myself? Well, now I wish I would have appreciated the ease a bit more."

Silence fell between them and she closed her eyes, listening to the traffic below, music coming from somewhere nearby.

"Did we just have a moment?" she asked.

"A what?"

"A moment. Like, a human moment where we talked without fighting or snarking or trying to put each other down."

"I think we did. But we need never speak of it again."

She opened her eyes and looked into his. Even in the dim light, she could see a glimmer of mischief there, something like the old Eduardo.

"It's a deal," she said.

For one moment, her mind went blank of everything. Everything but his face, and what it had been like to be in his arms earlier. What it had been like to kiss him. And in that moment, she couldn't remember why kissing him wasn't a great idea. But just for that one moment.

Then that blank simplicity got crowded out by reality, by the reason why she couldn't kiss him. Not now, not ever.

She wasn't building a life here with him. When this was over, she had to go back home. To her clients, to her job. Assuming Zack wasn't having her blacklisted.

"I'm tired now," she lied. She didn't think she would ever be able to sleep right while she was here. While she knew he was right across the penthouse from her, sleeping. Possibly naked. It hadn't bothered her five years ago. She didn't know what had changed in her since then.

That was a lie. She did know. Eduardo had changed. And there was something about him now that called to her.

She really had to get a grip on herself. And the weak, mushy emotion she seemed to be tempted to wallow in the past few days. She didn't have time, she didn't need to, she didn't want to.

She was Hannah Weston. She was her own invention, her own woman. And she could do this.

"Good night, Eduardo," she said, bringing a little steel back into her tone. "See you at the office tomorrow."

CHAPTER SIX

"Your wife is back and you didn't tell your mother?"

Eduardo turned to face Hannah, who was sitting at his desk, holding his phone more tightly to his ear as his mother's voice rang through loudly.

"*Lo siento, Mama.* It happened very suddenly. I have been working at…making amends." Bringing his mother into the charade wasn't ideal, but he would do what had to be done. He'd been avoiding her for weeks. That period of avoidance had clearly ended.

"You've been making amends? For what, Eduardo? She was the one who left you without a word. After six months of marriage. Divorced." She said the word like it was something truly foul.

"Ah, yes, but we were not divorced. We never have been. Hannah and I are as married today as we were that day in the cathedral."

Hannah's focus snapped up from the computer, her blue eyes trained on him, her expression hard. *"What?"* she mouthed.

He covered the mouthpiece on the phone. *"My mother,"* he mouthed back to her.

Then her lips formed a soundless version of a truly filthy word. He chuckled and uncovered the phone.

"We will come to see you this weekend. In fact, let's make it a long weekend at the *rancho*. Bring Selena, of course."

Hannah threw her hands in the air, her eyes round. He offered her a half smile and she put her hands on her throat like she was choking herself, then pointed at him. He suppressed a laugh and listened to his mother's response.

"See you then," he said, cutting off any last protests. She would be there. She would never disappoint him.

"What did you do that for?" Hannah exploded.

"Because, it's what I would do if we were really reconciling, which means it's what we should do in order to make it look like we're reconciling. *Entiende?*"

"No. *No entiendo.* I don't understand at all. Why bother bringing your mom and Selena into this? It's not…fair."

"To them or to you?"

"Either one," she said. "Look, I liked your family—a lot—when I was here. They were really good to me and I hated lying to them. I don't want to do it again."

"You're sparing my mother from the possibility of losing Vega. I think she'll forgive you."

"I'll be honest with you, Eduardo. I don't think you're in danger of losing Vega. Things aren't quite as good as they were a few years ago, but that's true for a lot of companies. And anyway, your personal assets are quite healthy. Once you get your financial manager in place—"

"But if I don't figure out a system…"

"We will," she said, moving into a standing position and grasping her hands behind her back, arching forward, stretching, a short little kitten sound escaping as she did. His body kicked into gear, a hard and serious reminder of the power she seemed to command over him.

Her breasts were perfect. Small and round. He ached to have them in his palms. In his mouth.

"We had better," he bit out, averting his eyes. He had to get a grip. He had other things to worry about, things much more important than his neglected sex drive.

"I'm confident that we can figure something out," she said,

rounding the desk, her hips dipping with each step. She was still angry. Her hips moved more when she was angry, her lips pulled tight. "Now," she breathed out, "do we really have to spend the weekend with your family?"

"Yes. My mother will not let it go…you know it as well as I do. And I think it would do us both good to get out of the city."

"It's only been a few weeks. And anyway, I like the city, so I feel no such need."

"Ah, but you do." He started to circle her. Her head swiveled as far as it possibly could as she tried to track his movement. He put his hands on her shoulders, savoring the heat of her body coming through her thin top. "You're very tense." He moved his thumb into her muscle and discovered that tense was an understatement.

"Ow," she groused.

"You will feel better in a moment." He moved his thumb on the other side, digging deeper. She arched back, whimpering.

"It doesn't feel better yet."

"Your muscles are like rocks. It doesn't help that you hunch at the computer."

"Shut up, I do not hunch."

"You do." He worked both of her shoulders until he felt some of the tightness ease, until she stopped fidgeting and started melting into his touch. He swept her blond hair to the side and slid his thumb up the back of her neck. This time, the sound she made was decidedly pleased, and more than a little bit sexy.

"Yes, just like that," she said, arching into his touch, instead of trying to escape it.

"I do like to hear you say that," he said. He tilted his head to the side and pressed a kiss just beneath her earlobe. She stiffened, then pulled away from him.

"I'm still mad at you," she said, turning to face him, her eyes looking a little glazed, her cheeks flushed.

"That's okay. It doesn't mean you can't kiss me. You were mad at me last time, too."

She drew her plump lower lip between her teeth and shook her head. "Nope. Not kissing you."

"Why not?"

"Because it's not what we're here to do."

She was right. He knew it. And until he'd touched her again, he'd firmly believed it. There was too much at stake for him in so many ways. And yet he couldn't find it in him to suppress the desire. "That's true. But mixing a little pleasure in with business doesn't have to be detrimental."

"Maybe not, but it usually is."

"Speaking from experience."

"No, I'm way too smart for that. I keep business and personal very, very separate. And you, my dear, are business. Always have been."

She was lying. He extended his hand and drew his finger along the curve of her cheek, felt her tremble beneath his touch. Now *she* knew she was lying, too.

"We'll finish up work for the day, and when we get back to the penthouse, we'll get ready to drive to the *rancho* first thing in the morning."

Eduardo owned a Jeep, which surprised her almost as much as his insistence they make the drive out of Barcelona and into the countryside with the top down.

But the air was warm and the scenery was beautiful, so she wasn't going to complain. Even though her hair was whipping around so violently she nearly swallowed a chunk of it. She tugged the strands from her lips and shook her head, hoping to get it somewhat back into place.

"I don't think I ever came out here with you…before, I mean," she said, competing with the wind and the engine.

"No. This is new. I bought it after my accident. I liked

going to a place where I could think. Somewhere away from the city and…people."

"You have horses?"

He nodded, his eyes never leaving the road. "Yes. I don't ride them."

"You don't?"

"No."

"I assume you have staff that do?"

"Of course. And you know Selena is really into horses."

"I remember. She must be…not a teenager anymore." She remembered Eduardo's younger sister, all long skinny limbs, round eyes and glossy hair. She'd been fifteen when Hannah had seen her last, but she would be twenty now. A woman, not a girl.

"No, she's not."

"Strange because it doesn't feel like it's been that long since… Well, in some ways. There are times when it feels like this was part of another lifetime. And like I'm in an alternate dimension now."

"It's very possible, I suppose. Maybe I'm in one, too, and I'll wake up with a throbbing headache and my memory fully restored."

"Click your heels together and say 'there's no place like home.'"

"Qué?"

"Dorothy. *The Wizard of Oz.* You don't know that movie? Everyone knows that movie."

He shook his head. "I've seen it. I…didn't remember the reference."

An uneasy silence fell between them, her stomach tightening as the meaning of his statement settled in. "If I clicked my heels together," she said, "and said that, I wonder where I would end up? Maybe in the middle of nowhere."

"You don't have a home?"

"Right now I have an apartment in San Francisco. But is

it home? I don't know about that." She looked down at her hands. "Sometimes I think it would be a blessing to have a little memory loss."

"Was it that bad?"

Unbidden, she thought about what it had felt like to have her baby move inside of her. Of the moment he'd been delivered. Of having to turn away as the nurse carried him from the room so that she wouldn't have time to memorize his tiny, perfect face.

She had it memorized anyway. One moment was enough. And not enough.

She tried to breathe past the tightness in her chest. "Some things really are that bad."

"I've forgotten a great many things that didn't matter. But I don't know they don't matter. And that's the worst part. You're not sure if you've forgotten something trivial, or vital. A lot of the time I'm unsure if I've forgotten anything at all. I could neglect an important document and never once have that nagging feeling you count on having to keep you on track."

She redirected her thoughts, pulling the door closed on her memories, on her emotions, locking it tight. "Have you set up alerts?"

"What kind?"

"You could have them on your phone, your computer. We could sync them up so you could be reminded at different times of the day that certain things need doing."

"I don't forget everything," he said, his tone rough.

"I know that. But you don't always know what will slip your mind, do you? So you have to be willing to put down your pride for a little bit and cover your bases. This isn't about hanging on to your manly image."

"The hell it's not," he grumbled.

"Eduardo." She sighed. "Get over yourself."

"Why would I want to do that? I am so wonderful." He tossed her a smile and for a moment, the heaviness in her lightened. For the rest of the trip, they kept the topics neutral, choosing to avoid anything real or personal.

When they pulled off the main road and onto a winding, single-lane paved road that wound up the mountain, Hannah tried not to show any nerves.

"You're bothered by heights?" he asked.

"Oh, only a little," she said. She hated to show fear, of any kind. Especially a silly fear of heights. "I mean, if another car came around the corner our only options are the side of the mountain and plummeting to our doom."

"I promise to keep the plummeting to a minimum."

"Appreciated," she said tightly.

She breathed a sigh of relief when the road curved in, away from the drop and through a thick grove of trees. It was cool, green and lush, shaded from the heat of the day.

The trees thinned and faded until they were surrounded by green fields, stretching to the mountains on one side, and to the edge of a cliff on the other, overlooking the brilliant, jewel-bright sea.

Large iron gates secluded the property from the rest of the world. Eduardo used an application on his phone to enter in the code and the gates swung open.

"I use letters in my security code," he said as they drove on. "They're easier for me to remember. I'm not sure why."

"I'm not, either. I would have to do some reading on the subject."

The house was set back into the property, nearer to the sea, bold floor-to-ceiling windows reflecting the sun. It was an angular, modern house with traditional white stucco and a red ceramic tile roof. A mix of the old and new, very like its owner.

"This is beautiful," she said. "Quiet, too."

"Away from the noise," he said. "For a while I badly needed that. Things are better now than they were."

"I'm glad to hear that."

"I still prefer to be here. Alone."

"That's very unlike you. You used to drag me to parties all the time. Parties with music so loud we rarely had to talk to anyone. And if I didn't go, you went by yourself."

"I used to like that sort of thing. I don't now." He pressed another button on his phone and a door to the large garage opened, and he pulled the car inside.

"Very techie," she said.

"It makes my life easier."

"And I'm sure we can come up with even more ways to make it easier on you. Why haven't you seen anyone about this before?"

His body tensed. "I saw doctors."

"I know, but have you ever gone to programmers or anything with a list of your specific issues? I'm almost certain there are some simple…"

"No. I'm not spreading this around for the world to see. I'll not be made to look like a fool. Or stupid," he said, his dark gaze pointed on hers. He looked down at his hands. "Tell me something, Hannah."

"What?"

"Why did I like going to all those parties?"

"What?" she asked.

"Why did I like them? The idea of going to parties…now it seems like it would be loud and…confusing. I can't imagine what it was that made me like them before and sometimes I think if I could just remember…then I could make myself feel it again."

Hannah's stomach tightened. "Eduardo…I…" She took a breath. "You liked to be around people. To have them see you. You always commanded the room and you…thrived on that."

He rested his head on the back of the seat. "I still can't…" He let out a long breath. "I can't feel it now."

He killed the engine and slammed the driver's-side door shut, skipping the chivalry and walking straight into the house alone. She unbuckled and followed him out of the Jeep and into the house.

Yet again, the luxury available to the Vega family floored her. She was no slouch, and she made a darn decent income, but this was beyond the everyday version of luxury.

Sweeping vistas of the sea, intensely green fields and mountains, marble floors and a grand, curving staircase. Light poured in, light everywhere, making it feel like she was still outdoors, bringing the natural beauty into the man-made extravagance.

She pulled her lips tight, doing her very best not to look impressed. "Eduardo…I'm going to get lost in this palace without a guide." She was determined to change the subject. Determined to ignore the pain in her chest. His pain.

He came into the entryway, his expression neutral. So she wasn't the only one trying to play a game, trying to hide her feelings. "I will happily give you the tour." There was a glimmer in his eyes, one she didn't like at all. She had a feeling he was about to do something to make her angry, since that seemed to be the only thing that made him laugh these days.

"What?" she asked, following him up the curving staircase. "And shouldn't I go get my bags?"

"I don't know what you mean, and one of my staff will have your bags delivered to the room later."

"You know what I mean. You look amused, and that never bodes well for me. And *the* room?"

"Yes. The room. Our room."

So that was the cause of the glitter. "Our room? I do hope you're having a malfunction with your English, darling."

"No malfunction, I speak English as well as you do. But we're selling a reconciliation here, and we can hardly sleep across the hall from each other."

She sputtered. "You…you…"

"Relax, *querida,* I'm giving us rooms that connect to each other. I'm not so base as to try and force you to share a bed with me. Still, we will have to be careful that it's not suspected you aren't sleeping with me."

She made a face at him. "You did that just to make me mad."

"I have to confess, it is one of my few joys in life. To watch the color rise in your cheeks." He paused at the top of the stairs and turned to face her, his eyes dark, assessing. Far too assessing. "I love to watch you lose control."

"I did not lose control. You couldn't make me lose control," she said, realizing she sounded childish and very much on the edge of control. Unable to stop it.

He chuckled and turned away from her. "If you say so."

"I do," she muttered, crossing her arms beneath her breasts and trailing behind him, down the expansive half floor, open to the living area below. There were two dark double doors at the end of the hall, and he opened them to an impressive luxury suite.

"I trust you will find this suitable. This is, of course, my room. And that is the door to yours." He indicated a door on the far end of the room. She passed him, her eyes resting longingly on the massive king-size bed piled high with silk pillows, and went to the other door.

She turned the knob and opened it, revealing a smaller, but no less impressive suite.

The bed wasn't as grand, the linen white with pink ribbon edging the bottom of the bedspread, and tied around the throw pillows, making them look like little gifts.

The walls were white, the floors a pale marble, decorated with fuzzy-looking pink carpets.

"It's so pink," she breathed, hating in some ways how perfect it was.

"It's not quite as edgy as you are, I confess."

She turned and saw Eduardo leaning in the door. A giggle bubbled in her throat when she realized that he'd probably imagined she would hate it. But he hadn't seen her very,

very pink wedding cake, or the pink bows she'd selected to go on all of the chairs. He'd never seen her pink dishes in her kitchen, or the pink bed set in her room.

"I happen to love pink," she said, smiling sweetly. "My room when I was a teenager was very..." Dirty. Dark. Depressing. "It wasn't to my taste and I used to dream of decorating my own place as feminine and frilly and bright as I liked. So as soon as I could, I did. It's something I've never grown out of, alas."

One dark brow shot up. "I never would have guessed that about you."

"No, I doubt anyone would. But my life is not an open book."

"I have noticed that."

"Now you know my deep, dark secret. Beneath my ass-kicking facade, I have a thing for ruffles." She liked that she'd caught him off guard. It was a small thing, but she took more than a little pleasure in it.

He shook his head. "Now that is interesting."

"I live to interest."

"I seriously doubt that."

"You're right. I don't care enough about what people think." That wasn't true, either. She wished it was. "What's the thread count on the sheets?"

"I can't remember *The Wizard of Oz.* You think I'll remember that?"

The corner of her mouth tugged up in a reluctant half smile. "Fine, I'll read the tags when you leave."

"I think my mother and Selena will be here soon. If you'd like to dress for dinner."

"Is there something wrong with the way I'm dressed?"

"Do you own anything that's not designed to fit into a boardroom environment?"

"Pink pajamas."

"And now that no longer surprises me, but you can't wear that for dinner, either."

"Yes, I have some other clothes."

"Good. Then I'll have your things sent up." He turned away, then stopped. "Hannah, try to relax. You can think of this as a vacation."

CHAPTER SEVEN

"I DON'T take vacations."

Eduardo turned at the sound of Hannah's voice.

She was at the foot of the stairs, wrapped tightly in a black, knee-length dress, her blond hair loose for once, cascading over her shoulders in an elegant wave. She shifted, her expression tight, painted red lips pulled into a pucker.

"Why does that not surprise me?"

"I hear you don't take them anymore, either."

He shook his head. "I've no inclination to. I often work from here."

"Is it easier? Less distraction?"

He nodded slowly. He'd never really thought of it in those terms. He'd just thought he liked the quiet now, when before he'd thrived in the frenetic pace of the city. He'd enjoyed staying up late and getting up for work the next day. Had liked being surrounded by constant motion and high energy.

He didn't now. He liked solace. Privacy. Order. When there was no order his brain was utter chaos. He'd realized and adjusted for that early on.

"I suppose so. Plus, it's nice to avoid the stares. I'm the accident people can't help but gawk at, after all. Rich playboy, victim of a horrible, unfortunate incident. The public very often enjoy seeing people brought down."

"I don't see you as being brought down. Things are just different, that's all."

Her words, spoken from tight lips, with stilted, stubborn confidence, did something to him. To his chest. His heart. It was strange. Hannah wasn't looking at him with pity, far from it. She seemed to disdain him, but she also believed in him. Not out of obligation or caring, but because she simply did.

It was more valuable in some ways than the confidence shown him by his mother and sister. More valuable than he cared to acknowledge.

Are you so weak you need validation from a woman who would happily spit on you?

No. He wasn't. He was Eduardo Vega, and someday, all of him would remember that. And what that meant.

He heard an engine, tires on gravel. "They're here. Time to play loving couple."

"And dodge verbal barbs," Hannah grumbled, moving to stand next to him. She kept a thin line of space between their bodies. She didn't want to touch him, and that bothered him.

Because she needed to, needed to be comfortable with him if they were to look like a reconciling couple.

He slid his arm around her waist and she stiffened for a moment before relaxing beneath his touch. "They still think our marriage was real, and they need to think it's real now. Remember, we are deliriously happy to be back together."

"We should write that down," she whispered. "It keeps slipping my mind."

"We can't both start forgetting things, Hannah. We'll be in serious trouble if neither one of us can remember what's going on."

He felt her frame jolt with shocked laughter.

"That's better," he said.

Hannah steeled herself for the invasion of Eduardo's family. It wasn't going to be easy, and why should it be? She'd lied to them. So had Eduardo. They both deserved a little contempt. Of course, she was the only one who would get any.

The door opened and Carmela walked in, followed by

Selena. Both women were dressed in a flamboyant yet so-phisticated manner, complete with gloves that extended to their elbows and hats with wide brims.

"*Hola,* Eduardo," Selena said, striding forward. Eduardo released Hannah and leaned forward, embracing his sister.

When they parted, Selena eyed Hannah as if unsure of how to receive her or what to say. Hannah very much felt the same unease.

Carmela hung back.

"Hello," Hannah said, calling on all of her nerve, wondering why it was hard. Why she cared. Normally, she could turn off fear, and embrace control. Could put on an easy, charming persona that made everyone feel at ease. Just like she could turn into a pit bull in business negotiations. She swallowed. "It's good to see you again. I'm…pleased to be back. Pleased to be here with Eduardo and…both of you."

Carmela nodded stiffly. "If he is happy to have you, then so are we. No more must be said on the subject. There will be no anger. Come, I am hungry." She led the way into the dining area and Selena followed. Eduardo held back, and Hannah followed his lead.

"If she says she's not going to be angry, she won't be. You can unclench."

Hannah let out a breath. "I'm sorry, I feel like a jerk. I can't believe you're making me do this to your family. Again. How do you look in the mirror?"

For a moment, Eduardo's expression was unguarded, his dark eyes stripped of their shields. It was an expression of cold, deep fear. It was one she could relate to. The kind of fear that lived deep in her, waiting to wrap its icy hands around her throat at the first opportunity. The kind she ran from every day.

"It helps that I hardly recognize the man looking back at me," he said, his voice rough. "I am doing what I must. I cannot fail."

And she knew then, that this wasn't about the media, but

about him. About proving he was still who he used to be, even though it was so clear he wasn't. The question he'd asked her in the car swam through her mind, made her stomach twist. His desire to understand who he'd been, to try and take himself back there.

To make himself something else.

But it echoed in her. She knew it. Understood it. Lived it every day. The need to be more than who she was. Although, while she was terrified she'd someday morph back into who she'd been, he was afraid he would never be the same.

"I will make sure you don't," she said, the vow coming from deep inside of her, from a core of emotion she hadn't realized she still possessed.

He nodded once, wrapped his arm around her waist and guided her into the dining room.

Hannah sank slowly into the warm water of the in-ground hot tub, her knotted muscles protesting the attempt at forced release.

She was stressed. Stressed was a normal state for her so she was rarely aware of it, but she darn well was now. Dinner with Eduardo's family had been difficult. Going to their room, knowing there would be much speculation had been even worse. Which was why, at eleven o'clock, she'd given up any hope of sleeping, even in her princess bed, and had dug in her bags until she'd produced her black, one-piece swimsuit.

She did need a vacation. But not here. Not with Eduardo. Not for the first time, she wondered about Zack. It was weird how much she didn't miss him. She was starting to be thankful, really thankful, they hadn't gotten married.

Still, she felt bad. She draped her arm over the edge of the hot tub and grabbed her phone, which was close by, as always. She fired off a quick message to him before she could think better of it.

It only took a few minutes for a message to ping back.

Fine. I'm with Clara.

Clara was Zack's best friend and business partner. Hannah had been, on a couple of occasions, slightly jealous of the other woman. She'd had a piece of Zack Hannah had never been able to tap into. A piece of him she hadn't wanted to try and tap into, truth be told. Well, he'd taken Clara on their honeymoon, which was proof of how special she was to him.

Maybe…maybe it had turned into something more? She wasn't usually a squishy romantic, but it really helped to think of Zack finding someone else. Someone better.

Are you having a good time?

It was inane and stupid to ask, but she did care.
His reply came a moment later.

Better than I imagined.

She found herself smiling.

I hope you're happy. Happier than you would have been with me.

She hesitated before hitting Send, then took a breath and pressed it.
A reply pinged back.

You be happy, too.

She laughed.

Okay.

She hit Send one last time and put the phone down. Happy. What was that anyway? She'd always thought of it as something she'd reach the farther away she got from Arkansas. The further away she got from the moment the nurses had whisked her baby from the room and handed him to another woman. That the more she made, the more status she gained, the closer it would bring her there. None of it ever seemed to be enough, though. She never seemed closer to happy.

"Do you ever sleep?"

Hannah turned to see Eduardo standing there, dressed in black swim shorts, his chest bare. She almost swallowed her tongue. He was the single most beautiful man she'd ever seen. Well-defined pecs, covered with a fine dusting of dark hair. His abs…she had the completely unbidden thought that it would be heaven to run her fingers over the ripple of muscle. Not just her fingers. Maybe her tongue, too.

Gah! Where had that come from?

"I don't sleep much," she said. Her thighs trembled a little bit when he took a step toward her and she realized, stupidly late, that he was probably planning on getting into the hot tub with her.

"Neither do I." He rounded the hot tub and descended the steps, the water covering his muscular thighs, lean hips, up to his belly button. Not that she was watching with rapt attention. No.

She edged away, trying to put some distance between them, trying to do it subtly. "Yeah, well, I'm always on red alert. Thinking about all the things I have to do at work, stuff like that."

"About your ex-fiancé?"

"Uh, funny you should mention him. I just texted him. He took another woman on our honeymoon so hopefully he's doing all right."

"That doesn't bother you?"

"I actually know her. She's a friend of his, so it could be platonic. But if not…well, I sort of hope it's not. I want him to be happy."

"And the idea of your ex-lover with another woman doesn't…doesn't make you angry?"

Hannah cleared her throat. "Zack was never my lover."

To his credit, Eduardo's face remained unreadable. "I find that hard to believe."

"Yeah, I figured you would. That was why I never corrected you before. Frankly, I don't really care what you think of it, but it is true."

"Why is that?"

"Why weren't we lovers?"

"Yes."

"We weren't in love. I didn't want him to use me. So I figured if we waited on that until after the wedding…no danger." It wasn't entirely true, but she was hardly giving him the whole truth about her sex life. It wasn't his business anyway.

"I don't believe that, Hannah. You don't seem like the sort of woman who could be used. You're far too hard and savvy for that."

She shrugged, her shoulders rising from the warm water, the night air biting them. "All right then, why do you suppose I didn't sleep with him?"

"You like control too much. So making him wait gave you control."

She rolled her eyes and leaned her head back. "You make it sound like I was leading him around by the—" She popped her head back up and met Eduardo's mocking gaze. "I wasn't. That wasn't why. But yeah, maybe control a little bit. Just not like you mean it."

"I understand control, Hannah, wanting it, going to great lengths to keep it. You hardly have to justify yourself to me."

"I feel like I do when you look at me like that. It's your superpower. I never justify myself to anyone. But with you, I do, a little bit."

"Too bad it's a superpower that's of no use to me."

"Thanks," she said, smiling at him. A big fake smile.

He sighed and sat down, draping his arms over the back of the hot tub. She was across the tub from him and she still felt hotter. Felt like she was way too close to him.

"So," she said. "Did your mom say terrible things about me in those few minutes you hung back in the dining room with her?"

"No. She said she wants me to be happy. Just like she said in front of you."

Hannah sighed. "She's a better person than I am. I would hate me."

"If someone did that to your son?"

Hannah's heart dropped into her stomach. "I...I'll never know. I don't have a son. I don't want children." It sounded slightly panicked, and not the least bit cool. But she didn't want to think about it. Didn't want to get anywhere near the topic.

"So you've said."

"Yes, well, I'm saying again." And now she sounded defensive.

"Who hurt you, Hannah?" he asked, pushing off from the wall and walking to the middle of the tub. His chest gleamed in the light from the house, bronzed and muscular. He looked like the angel of death, trying to confront her with the thing she feared most.

"I already told you. My parents sucked."

"But that's not it, I think."

He drew closer, knelt down in front of her, his eyes level with hers. "What happened?"

She couldn't stand it. The concern on his face, in his tone. Couldn't deal with the slow ache it caused in her heart. "Why the hell do you care? You won't remember it twenty minutes after I tell you."

His hand shot out, gripping the back of the hot tub; his eyes blazed with heat. Anger, certainly, and something else. The anger she could handle; it was the else that scared her.

He lifted his other hand, cupped her chin. "Why do you do that?"

"Do what?" she asked, jerking her face away.

"Why do you lash out? Is it when I get too close?"

"What? What does that mean?"

"You can be so pleasant, I've seen it. And then you can put all your shields up and go on attack. I think it's when I start to get close to the truth. And it scares you."

Yes, it scared her to her soul. She wanted to deny it, and she couldn't, because she was trembling inside. But being angry was so much easier than being afraid. And pushing someone away was so much easier when she was being mean.

She pressed her back against the wall, trying to put some more distance between them. "Maybe I'm just not a nice person. Did you ever consider that?"

"I don't think that's the case. I've been accused of being a terrible, boring bastard the past few years. But I don't think that's your problem."

"Maybe you just aren't very good at reading people."

He shook his head. "An interesting gift, or rather, strange side effect, of my injury. I do not surround myself with so much noise, so it seems I have more time, more of an ability to look closely at the people who are around me. You aren't mean, Hannah. You're afraid. The question is, what are you afraid of?"

Her heart was pounding, her body hyperaware of his nearness. She took a breath and pushed off from the wall, standing so that he was slightly beneath her. She put her hand on the back of his neck.

"I'm not afraid of anything," she said, lying. Boldly. Her hands were shaking, her body was shaking. But she couldn't let him win. Couldn't let him see any weakness. Couldn't let him see her.

He took his hand off the wall and put it on the small of

her back, his fingers rough, hot against her skin. Steam rose between them and stirred when she breathed out.

"Is that so?" he asked.

In response she dipped her head, brushing his lips with hers. A hard zip of attraction punched her, deep in her core. He wrapped his other arm around her, his hand splayed between her shoulder blades. She wrapped her arms around his neck and leaned down, deepening the kiss as much as she could in her position.

Her brain was screaming that she was making a mistake. Walking into danger.

Her body was complaining that she wasn't walking fast enough.

She'd been out to prove a point, but everything, the previous conversation, the reason behind her action, was shrouded in the mist that curled between them, that seemed to have wrapped itself around her mind, shielding her in a blessed haze where all that mattered was the feel of his hard body against hers, the feel of his mouth covering hers.

He lowered his hand slowly, cupping the curve of her butt, down to her thigh, tugging gently. She followed his lead, lowering herself so she was straddling his legs, the hard ridge of his arousal apparent, thick and tempting between them.

He pulled her hard against him and she let her head fall back as he kissed her neck, her collarbone. His mouth so hot on her wet skin, warming her where the night air had left her cold.

"Oh, yes," she said, rocking against him, seeking out the pleasure she knew he could provide. Pleasure she knew would far surpass any sexual experience she'd had before.

She tightened her hold on him, claimed his mouth again, her tongue delving deep, his returning the favor, exploring, creating a delicious friction that made her internal muscles tighten.

She could lose herself in him. In this. Close out everything and embrace the passion. The moment. The need to have him deep inside of her, thrusting hard and deep, mirroring the action of his tongue.

She wanted to surrender. To her feelings. Her body's needs. To him.

She wanted to give him her control.

Panic hit her, hard in the breast and she pushed at his chest, trying to free herself from his embrace. He slowly released his hold on her, his expression confused, hazy. She stumbled back, splashing water up around them, and climbed up the side of the hot tub, not bothering to get around him by using the stairs.

"No, this isn't happening," she said, panic clawing at her. Mocking her. Reminding her that she wasn't brave, that she wasn't different. That if she let go, all of the trappings, everything she'd built for herself, would fall away and reveal who she really was. The stupid girl, needy girl. Ready to give it all up so someone would just pay attention to her for a minute. For a few hours. So that she could have someone look at her like she mattered. Forget what she wanted. Forget self-esteem, self-respect. Control.

"I think it is. It has," he said. "It seems to keep happening."

She shook her head. "No. I'm not sleeping with you."

"Oh, so what was that then? Another effort on your part to keep a man controlled? To lead him around by his balls?"

"If you didn't think with them, it wouldn't work so well," she shot back, dying inside. She felt like her defenses were crumbling, like all of her armor was melting from the heat of Eduardo's touch. And she couldn't allow that.

"Perhaps I was wrong, Hannah. Perhaps I was looking for more where more did not exist."

"I told you." She turned and grabbed a towel from one of the lounge chairs, wrapping it around her body. A physical barrier in the absence of a much-needed emotional one.

"You did. Understand this, though—unlike your ex, I will not be a part of your games. You will not play with me."

"You just let me." She turned on her heel and walked out of the courtyard, leaving a trail of wet footprints behind her.

She climbed up the stairs, towel clutched tightly to her chest. She opened the door to her room and closed it firmly behind her, leaning against it. Then she put her hand over her mouth and muffled a sob.

She slid down to her knees, her body shaking as she gave in to tears for the first time in more years than she could count.

Eduardo knocked on the door that connected his room to Hannah's. He had a feeling he would regret checking on her. He shouldn't care what she was feeling. She'd played him. She'd tried to use her body to control him; she'd insulted him.

And yet, he found he still didn't believe it was her. Still didn't believe she was being genuine. She had been afraid. Not just when he'd asked her about her past, she'd been afraid when they'd kissed. Of the passion that had flared up between them.

He felt wild. He didn't feel like himself, whoever the hell that was. And looking at Hannah, touching Hannah, didn't take him back. It took him somewhere else entirely. He had no idea what to do with that.

He knew what he wanted. And for now, wanting something, needing, that was enough.

She didn't answer. He let out a growl and opened the door without waiting for a response.

He saw her, sitting against the wall, her knees drawn up to her chest, her head down. She looked like a broken doll.

"Hannah?" he asked, a pang hitting him hard in the chest.

She raised her head, and he saw tears shining on her cheeks, illuminated by the moonlight. She wiped her cheek with her arm. "Go away."

He took a step toward her. He didn't know what it was tha

compelled him when it came to this woman. He didn't know why she felt so imbedded in him, and yet, she did. A part of him he couldn't escape, a part he couldn't forget.

He hadn't wanted to pursue anyone since his accident. He'd had no focused sexual desire.

But Hannah, tough as nails Hannah, who liked pink, who was sitting on the floor now, wet, still in her bathing suit, all her armor stripped, looking like she would shatter if he touched her, she drew him.

She had fascinated him back when they'd first met. A scrappy, low-class, determined girl who had clawed her way up from nothing, just to get an education. To try and change her life. But the fascination had changed. It was different now. Deeper. As though she'd burrowed beneath his skin.

"Are you all right?" he asked.

She pushed up from the floor and stood. He expected her to yell at him. To insult him. Because he'd caught her feeling vulnerable, and that was what she did when he spotted a crack in her armor.

Instead she just straightened, blond hair flicking over her shoulders like a silvery wave, her chin tilted upward. She was like a proud queen, one who would never acknowledge what he'd just witnessed. She would pretend to be above it, above him, if she had to, in order to protect herself. To keep herself securely locked in her ivory tower.

"Of course."

She would never take sympathy from him, and he didn't like seeing her broken. "You owe me an apology, Hannah," he said, changing tactics, hardening his tone.

She tipped her chin up. "For?"

A smile curved his lips, heat pooling in his gut as he stepped toward her. "You insulted me. Good manners dictate you tell me you're sorry."

"But I'm not."

It was a bad idea to push her. It had been a bad idea to

come to her room in the first place. "Perhaps I can change your mind."

She took a step toward him. "I doubt it."

"I don't."

Hannah sucked in a deep breath, tried to erect a barrier between herself and the dark sensuality radiating from Eduardo.

She hated how she shook when she was near him. How much her body ached for his. She hadn't had sex in nine years. Pathetic, but true. All because of fear. All because she was afraid that if she ever let herself lose control, she would find out that she had never changed. It was why she lashed out at him, it was why she ran from him.

She hated fear. Hated how much of it lived inside of her. She'd bought into her own lie of strength. Had done for years. She'd found someone who hadn't challenged her, who hadn't tapped into any sort of deep sexuality, who hadn't worked at uncovering her secrets, and she'd been able to pretend. Pretend that nothing had ever happened to her, that she had never been Hannah Mae Hackett. High school dropout, pregnant teenager, fraud.

With Eduardo, she couldn't pretend.

With Eduardo she couldn't hide the fear, not from him, not from herself. He stripped her with one look. And his touch...

It had to stop. She wouldn't be afraid. She could still have control, even in this. She had to.

She took another step toward him and put her hand on his face. He reached up, wrapped his fingers around her wrist. "Do not test me, Hannah, not again. I am not playing games. If you kiss me, you had better intend to follow through."

"Or what?"

He chuckled. "I would never hurt you. Would never force myself on you. But I will never allow you to touch me again, either. I do not play. If you turn back now, nothing will happen between us."

"I don't intend to turn back," she said.

"Then why did you earlier?"

"Because this is a very, very bad idea. I thought I would turn back while I still could." Now if she turned back she would be doing it because of fear, and she would know that was why. But if she kissed him… She could do it now. While she had him off guard. While she was in command.

He turned her hand and pressed a kiss to the underside of her wrist, his dark eyes never leaving hers.

"Why don't you kiss me?" she asked.

"Why don't you apologize?"

A laugh escaped, nervous. Strange sounding. "I might feel more sorry if you just give me what I ask for."

He hesitated for a moment, dark eyes glittering. Then he dipped his head, his mouth claiming her quickly, fiercely. She didn't want anything intruding, no thoughts, no emotions; she only wanted what he made her feel. The intense ache that he brought to her core, the desire to have him, over her, in her.

She ran her hands down his bare chest, relishing the feel of his muscles beneath her palms. She'd never touched a man who looked like him, had never been with a real man, truly. Fumbling teenage boys who didn't know what foreplay meant hardly counted as comprehensive sexual experiences.

They hadn't been the complete sensual playground that Eduardo was. He was so masculine, so perfectly formed.

She felt her breath getting short, choppy, and she slowed it, taking a few steadying breaths to help reset the rhythm. To keep herself from losing her mind.

She had the control here. He wanted her; she could see the hunger in his lean face. She held the power.

He moved his hands up her waist, kissing her deeply, thoroughly, his thumbs skimming the undersides of her breasts. She moaned into his mouth and an answering sound of pleasure reverberated in his chest.

He slid his hands higher, cupping her, teasing her nipples. A shot of pure, liquid heat poured into her core. She put her hands on his butt and drew him tighter against her, his erection pressing hard against her hip.

He gripped one of the straps on her swimsuit and tugged it down, dropping a kiss onto her shoulder, peeling the Lycra away from her skin, exposing her breast. "Oh, yes. So beautiful," he said, his voice rough, pained.

He lowered his head, his tongue caressing her nipple, circling it before he sucked it deeply into his mouth. She raised one hand quickly, fisting his hair, holding him to her. He lowered her other strap, baring her other breast. He moved his attention there, lavishing it with the same, very thorough attentions.

She closed her eyes, the sheer intensity of the desire rocketing through her making it impossible to move. Impossible to breathe. Impossible to do anything but stand there and just let him have his way with her body.

When he gripped her swimsuit and pulled it down the rest of the way, a flash of panic hit her. But it was dark. He wouldn't be able to see. Wouldn't notice the silvery lines that trailed over her stomach.

Even if he did, it didn't mean he would know what they were.

He sucked harder on her breast while he teased the other one with his thumb and that last conscious thought fled.

He raised his head and kissed her mouth again, his hair-roughened chest providing the stimulation now.

"Yes, yes," she repeated, over and over, mindlessly as he backed her to the bed and lowered her onto the soft surface.

Dimly, she remembered that she was supposed to take control, that this was about proving that she wasn't afraid, that she could master her need for him, and hold him in the palm of her hand.

The only part that registered was the last one.

She reached down between them and touched at the apex

of his thighs with her hand, moving her palm over the hard ridge of his shaft.

A little tremor of fear shot through her. Fear of pain. It had been a long time. And it had never been with a man like him.

"I… Do you have condoms?" she asked, a trickle of panic hitting her. She shook it off. She wasn't going to let fear have anything in her anymore. Wouldn't let it have anything in this.

He swore. "Just a moment."

He rose from the bed and walked out of the room. She scooted to the center of the mattress, reclining against the pillows. Some of the arousal fog cleared without him there, touching her and kissing her.

It was too late to turn back now. If she did, it would be because of fear, and she wasn't going to let fear have a foothold anymore.

But she was taking the control back. She wasn't letting him turn her into a mindless pleasure zombie. That was her job.

He returned a few moments later, a box in hand. "It was in the bathroom. What conscientious staff I have."

"You didn't know if they were in there?"

"I have not needed them." He set the box down on the nightstand and tore it open, taking out a condom packet. And then she forgot to ask him why he hadn't needed them.

He handed the condom to her and she got up onto her knees, scooting to the edge of the bed. She swallowed hard and hooked her fingers in the waistband of his swim trunks, the damp fabric clinging to his body and she dragged it downward.

When she'd gotten the shorts off, she took him into her hand, reveling in the hot, silky skin, the hardness of him. She squeezed him lightly and he groaned, the sound deep and satisfying.

"You are certainly no ordinary man," she said. He let his head fall back, a raw groan coming from deep inside of him.

"That's right, Eduardo," she whispered. "Let me." A straight shot of power coursed through her, making her feel fearless.

She lowered her head and flicked the tip of her tongue over his shaft, her stomach tightening with desire as his hand came up to her head, his fingers tangling in her hair. She explored him with her tongue and he tightened his hold on her, halting her movements.

"I can't," he rasped. "I'm too close."

She lifted her head, satisfied that she was in his power. That she was going to do this her way.

She tore open the packet and rolled the condom onto him, then straightened and wrapped her arms around his neck, kissing him, drawing him down onto her.

"Not yet," he said, lowering his head again, kissing her breasts, her ribs, her stomach. Her breath caught when he lingered at the tender skin beneath her belly button. Then he parted her thighs gently, his tongue hot and unexpected against her core.

She arched off the bed, scrambling for something to hold on to, finding his shoulders and clinging tight. "Eduardo…"

His breath was hot on her sensitive skin, his lips hovering just above her. "Now tell me you're sorry, Hannah." Another light touch of his tongue sent a flash of brief pleasure through her.

She put one hand over her face, her cheeks burning, her body begging for release.

"Tell me, Hannah." He kissed her inner thigh and her body shook.

"No."

The tip of his tongue blazed a trail from where he'd kissed her, straight to her clitoris. Just a tease. Nothing more. "Do you want to come or not?"

"You…bastard," she panted.

He chuckled. "That doesn't sound like an apology."

"It wasn't."

He moved his hand between her thighs, his thumb sliding over her slick flesh. She gripped both his shoulders, hard, her teeth locked together. Her hips moved in rhythm with his touch. His fleeting, too-light touch.

"Touch me, dammit," she said.

"Not until you tell me you're sorry."

Her muscles were shaking, her body begging her tongue to simply say the words. She needed release. She needed him. To hell with control. "I'm sorry."

He gave her a wicked grin, then lowered his head, his tongue working magic on her as he slid one finger inside her tight body.

"Oh, yes," she breathed. It had been worth it. No amount of pride was valuable enough to hold on to, and miss this.

He lavished attention on her, fully, completely, with his mouth and hands. Something started tightening inside of her. Tension she was afraid might break her.

A second finger joined the first and the tension in her broke, shattering through her like a million glittering stars. There was no thought; there was nothing but the blinding intensity of her release.

When she returned to earth, he was there, poised above her, dark eyes intent on hers. He pushed her hair off her damp forehead, his hand shaking. Evidence that he didn't have the control he'd appeared to have. "Now," he said.

He put his hand on her thigh and lifted it so her leg hooked over his hip. The thick head of his erection pressed against her body and she arched into him. He slid in easily, filling her, stretching her in the best way.

She gripped his shoulders, her nails digging into his skin. He began to move, his thrusts hard, controlled and perfect. She moved against him, met his every move. Each time their bodies connected a sharp, white-hot sensation of pleasure struck her. She didn't think it was possible to be so turned on so quickly again.

But she was. She was craving release, needing more of the heady rush he'd always given her.

His breath was hot on her neck, quick and harsh. She turned her head and kissed his cheek, and he turned, catching her mouth, a shudder rolling through his body as she slid her tongue against his.

"*Dios,* yes," he ground out.

The controlled nature of his thrusts frayed; his movements turning choppy, desperate, keeping time with the manic need that was rolling through her, demanding release again.

He thrust into her one last time, his muscles going stiff, his entire body freezing as he found his release on a feral groan. She flexed against him and her own orgasm washed over her, waves of pleasure coursing through her as her body tightened around his. He was so deep in her, so connected with her, and in that moment, it was all that mattered.

He collapsed onto his forearms, his breathing harsh, his muscles trembling. Then he separated from her body and gathered her close to him, her backside curving into his body, his hand resting on her stomach.

They didn't speak for a long moment; the only sounds in the room were their broken, uneven breaths. He curled a lock of her hair around his finger, the touch comforting, almost as intimate as sex in a strange way.

Her brain felt foggy. Events from only moments ago running together, reduced to points of aching need and sweeping, powerful release. Sometime soon, she might feel humiliation at the fact that she'd given him so much, so quickly.

But not now.

"I didn't forget how to do it," he said finally, still out of breath.

She laughed. "What does that mean?"

"You are the first woman I've been with since my accident. I suppose I've been true to our marriage vows all this time," he said, a strange note in his voice.

It was her instinct to try and ruin the moment. To break the spell of closeness that seemed woven around them. But she couldn't. She didn't want to. She just wanted a moment. Then tomorrow, she could go back to holding him at a distance. Things could go back to the way they'd been. Mystery solved. Sexual tension broken.

But now, just now, she wouldn't ruin it.

"So have I," she said softly.

"You have what?" he asked.

"Been true to our marriage vows. I haven't…I haven't been with anyone since our wedding."

"And you didn't even know we were still married," he said.

"No. But I imagine both of us had reasons other than that for staying out of physical relationships." A stupid thing to say, because she didn't want to get into her reasons.

"There's never been time." He paused. "Or desire. I haven't truly wanted anyone since it happened. I've been too busy licking my wounds."

"And tonight you licked me," she said, injecting some completely inappropriate levity, trying to draw the topic away from where it was.

He laughed and rolled her beneath him, kissing her lips. "I have to go take care of things."

He got out of bed and she watched him walk to the bathroom. Watched the masculine, perfect shape of his backside. He was gorgeous, no question.

He returned a moment later, his expression stormy. "We have a problem."

CHAPTER EIGHT

"WHAT?" Hannah tugged the covers up over her breasts and even with the current issue hammering away in his head, he felt a pang of regret.

"The condom broke." Something that had never happened to him before. He knew it was possible, but what the hell was the point of them if they were so fragile? "Are you on birth control?"

She hesitated. "No?"

"What's that supposed to mean? Why did you say it like you don't know?"

"I…I do know. I'm not. I mean…I didn't need to be. I mean…but things happen. These things do. The odds are so low. And I mean, a little leak will hardly…"

"Release millions of sperm?"

She cringed. "Well, okay, when you put it that way. But…"

"But it's enough to cause an accident."

Her expression turned dark. "I know how all that works, but thank you for educating me."

"I'm being realistic. We may have a situation."

"We won't," she bit out. "No one is that unlucky."

Anger boiled in his stomach. Of course it would be unlucky to be pregnant; it would be unlucky for both of them. But it struck a blow to his pride. All he could think was that she wouldn't want to be shackled to a *stupid* man for the rest of her life.

"Well," he said, his tone soft, deadly, "if you are so unlucky as to be carrying my child, be sure to let me know."

"I'll deliver the message by rock through your office window," she spat.

"Appreciated." He turned toward his room, his broad back filling the door. She'd pushed him away again. But she had to. She really had to.

It was the only way she could protect herself.

"Don't think you're going to force an apology out of me this time," she said.

He froze, his shoulders rising slightly before he turned, his eyebrows drawn together. "Don't play like I forced you, Hannah, when we both know you were begging."

She curled her fingers around the bedding. "Go away, Eduardo."

"Running again?" She opened her mouth and he cut her off. "Oh, yes, Hannah, you're running, even if you are staying in your bed. You have to do it by making a bitchy comment or whatever you think it will take to push me, or anyone else in your life, away. You don't fool me. You aren't hiding your fear from me. I will leave, only because I have no desire to spend another moment in your company tonight. But understand, you're not pushing me away if I don't want to be pushed."

He turned and walked out, shutting the door firmly behind him.

Hannah sat in the middle of the big bed, naked, physically and emotionally. She picked up one of the silken pink pillows and threw it in the direction of the closed door. It was safer to be angry than to cry again. She wasn't going to cry. She wasn't going to think about the torn condom. What that might mean.

She wasn't going to think about how it had felt to have him inside of her. Connected with her.

She really wasn't going to think about how it had been

the first time she'd felt close to someone in her entire life. And she wasn't going to think about how much she wanted to do it again.

When Hannah appeared at breakfast she didn't look much like a corporate barracuda who spat venom at unwitting victims with little warning. She looked nervous. Her blond hair was tousled and there were dark circles under her eyes. Her skinny-cut black pants and fitted, black short-sleeved shirt enhanced the thinness of her frame, and the paleness of her skin.

Eduardo leaned back in his chair and raised his coffee mug to his lips. His mother and sisters both nodded in greeting.

"Morning," Hannah said, not making eye contact with him as she took her seat at the table.

"Good morning," he said, setting his mug down on the table, taking no satisfaction in the shudder of her shoulders when his mug clattered against the glass tabletop. "Did you sleep well?"

She forced a smile. "Not really. You hogged the covers all night."

"My apologies, *querida*."

"None needed. Some coffee might be nice, though."

His mother reached out and rang a bell that sat at the center of the table. Eduardo cringed. He hated that thing. He was far too modern-minded to ring for his servants. But Carmela Vega insisted. She was old money and old class. Although, perhaps that had little to do with it, because he could easily imagine Hannah ringing for servants.

"Thank you," Hannah said to his mother.

"De nada."

Rafael came in and Hannah ordered her coffee to her specifications. She really did look exhausted. Pity he hadn't been able to keep her up all night in the way he'd like to have kept her up all night. But the fact that he'd irritated the sleep out of her was a close second as far as his personal satisfaction went.

"What are your plans for the day, Mama?" he asked.

"I thought Selena and I might go down to the shops."

Only his mother would leave Barcelona and shop in a small, seaside town. "That sounds like fun."

Selena turned her attention to Hannah. "You can join us, if you like, Hannah."

Hannah looked like a large-eyed woodland creature caught in the pull of headlights. "I...I..."

"Hannah and I have work today." He didn't want to let her out of his sight for the day. She might run. "She's helping me implement some new systems at Vega. Hannah is something of a financial genius."

"Is that right?" Carmela asked, eyebrows raised.

"I've been busy the past five years," Hannah said, her tone soft. She was so subdued. It was very unlike her and he found he didn't care for it.

"Yes, well, that is commendable," his mother said. "We'll leave you two."

"*Adiós,* Eduardo. Bye, Hannah," Selena said, standing with her mother and exiting the room.

"Your mother hates me," Hannah said when the women disappeared.

He shrugged. "Maybe."

Rafael returned with a fresh cup of coffee and a half-filled French press. *"Gracias,"* Hannah said, taking a sip of her already-prepared coffee. Rafael left again and Hannah set her mug down. "I would rather if she didn't hate me, but I suppose it doesn't do any good for her to like me since I'm leaving again...whenever. As soon as we get these systems in place and you feel comfortable."

"I suppose not." He found his body rebelled at the idea of her leaving. He felt possessive of her now. Stupid because before his accident he'd slept with any number of women and he'd never felt possessive of them. Quite the opposite, he'd felt ready to bolt out of bed, call them a cab and see they were safely delivered home so that he could sleep. Alone.

He frowned. The memories pricked his conscience and he realized that he didn't like the way he'd treated women then. He wondered if that had to do with the accident, with the changes in him, or just being older.

Interesting, since he normally envied the man he'd once been to a certain extent. But not in that area. He'd been a playboy, happily seeking release with any willing woman. Now the emptiness of that echoed in him.

With Hannah it had been more. More than release. More than amusement. It had been something serious, something that made him feel different in the bright light of day. He was angry with her, for the way she'd acted after, and still, he felt a connection with her that hadn't been there before.

As if, when he'd parted from her last night, he'd left a piece of himself behind.

"What is the work plan for the day?" she asked, her expression projecting extreme annoyance and boredom at the same time.

"Bring your coffee up to my office."

She stood and waited for him, then followed him out of the room and up the curving staircase, down to the end of the hall. His home office faced the sea, large expansive windows letting in plenty of natural light. And all easily covered with blinds that dropped at the push of a button. Just in case he got hit with a particularly bad migraine.

Fortunately, he felt fine. Which meant the only headache he would have to contend with was Hannah.

"Did you have anything more to show me?" she asked.

"No. I was hoping you would start presenting some solutions."

She shifted her weight to the balls of her feet. She looked like she was ready to sprint away if need be. "Actually, I do have some solutions. Well, thoughts mainly."

"Do you?"

"Yes. You prefer to work here now?"

"It's noisy in the office. I don't care for it."

"Right, which is why you have your floor essentially vacant," she said slowly.

"Yes. I can't handle the noise of all the people talking all the time. Even without people working on the floor, the interruptions, the traffic, it can start to…"

"It wears on you."

An understatement. The lowest moment in his memory was of throwing a mug at the wall in front of his secretary when she'd come in talking and he'd been in the throes of a migraine. It hadn't been aimed at her, and it hadn't come anywhere near her, but the blinding pain and anger…the fact he'd had no control over it in that moment. That he'd frightened her. It lived with him.

She'd quit soon after and he couldn't blame her.

"I find things easier here," he said, looking at his hands.

Hannah frowned. "Did you have trouble working around people before?"

"I just don't like noise," he said.

"What about it?"

He looked out at the sea, frowning. He'd been through some of this with a doctor years ago, and had since given up. He didn't like talking about how nothing had changed. There was no point. "It makes my head hurt."

"Anything else?"

"And I get irritable."

"Yeah, I've noticed," she said dryly. "What else?"

"I can't concentrate," he bit out.

"And numbers, finances, they give you the most trouble."

"I can't…I can't hang on to a thought about it for long enough to make decisions."

"And it's high pressure," she said, pushing.

"Yes."

"I think it might have less to do with you having trouble understanding the financial side of things and more to do with you having a harder time focusing on things that stress you out."

An uncomfortable tightness invaded his stomach. "It does not stress me out. I just… The answers are there in my brain but I can't seem to make a fast decision. I can't find the answer in time. Or at all." And the more he thought about it, the less able he was to reach out and grasp onto a thought firmly. It slipped away from him, hiding deep in the dark corners of his brain that seemed unknowable to him now.

"It does stress you out. Why haven't you talked to a doctor about this? I'm sure…"

"I don't need to talk to a doctor," he said, something exploding inside of him. "Not again. I don't need to go and sit there, and outline the same problems and have some old man look at me with pity in his eyes as he tells me, again, that they may never go away. That I will never be the man I was. That I won't have all the answers, or a witty joke on hand. That I will never be able to take the reins of Vega as I should have been able to, because I will never be able to make snap decisions, or keep meticulous records."

He planted his hands on his desk and leaned in so that his face was a breath from hers. "I can't concentrate long enough to fill out a damn report. How am I supposed to keep track of intricate financial details? Do you know the answer?" He pushed off and straightened, running his hand through his hair. "Do you?" he asked again, his voice sounding rougher this time, desperate. He loathed it. Despised himself in that moment. He was shaking. With anger. Fear.

"I…I just don't know," she said softly. "But we can figure it out."

He swallowed hard, his chest seizing up tight. "Or maybe I should just concede to the fact that I can't."

She stood and slapped her palms down on his desk before

rounding to the front, her blue eyes blazing. "No. That's... that's just wrong, Eduardo. You can do this. You aren't stupid. What I said...that was wrong, too. And I'll apologize for that willingly, with no...coercion." Her face turned pink when she said that last part. "It's just a matter of figuring out loopholes. Shortcuts."

Anger burned in him. At her. At the world. "I shouldn't need them," he growled.

"But we all do sometimes," she said, her tone rising with his.

"Maybe you do, Hannah Weston, but I don't. I am Eduardo Vega, son of one of the greatest business minds that ever lived, and I sure as hell should not need a shortcut."

"Then it's your pride keeping you from succeeding. Not your injury. Keep that in mind if you start losing a handle on things again. I can't help you if you won't accept help."

"I am accepting help," he shouted, well beyond his limits now. Beyond the point of sublimating his rage. "Why do you think I asked you here?"

Hannah came closer, not cowed by his outburst. "You didn't ask me here. You all but forced me and you know it. And you aren't accepting help. Did you think I would come in, take a look at things, make some investments and leave you?"

"Yes," he said, realizing as he spoke the word that it was true.

"Just leave you without solving the problem?"

"Yes," he said again. Because he hadn't wanted to admit there was a real problem. A reset. He'd been after a reset. To get everything back to a golden point so he could move forward, steering the ship, on course again.

That he would see Hannah, and remember who he was. Not just remember, but feel those same feelings. That amusement, that desire and ability to simply flip his middle finger at the world, enjoying his position of success, feeling invincible. Untouchable.

Far from that, he felt like he was drowning, reaching blindly for a hand. Hannah's hand. Praying she would be able to hold him above water.

Such weakness. Such horrifying, unendurable weakness.

"That can't happen, Eduardo," she said.

"Why not?" he asked, drained now, the anger, the fight, leaving him in a rush. Leaving him defeated.

He looked so bleak. Hannah had never seen that expression on his face before. Had never seen him look so tired. And in spite of the fact that she'd been determined to hang on to anger where he was concerned, she found in that moment she couldn't.

It had been easy to fight him, to rage at him while he was raging at her. But she saw beneath it now. Saw it for what it was.

"Because things have changed. You've changed." She wasn't telling him anything he didn't know. But she wondered if she was the first person, other than doctors, who'd been brave enough to tell the almighty Eduardo Vega the real and absolute truth he didn't want to hear. "And all you can do is work with what you have. Not what you wish you had, not what you once had, but what you have, here and now."

He shook his head. "I don't want to." It didn't sound petulant like it might have, it simply sounded dry. Resigned.

"Eduardo, you were always fun in your way. A bit of an ass, I mean, enough of one that you blackmailed me into marrying you as a way to goad your father. But you were easygoing, outgoing. And you never would have taken the responsibility of running Vega seriously. You used to kill me with your smug smile and your dismissal of your duties. Everything was a game to you. And now…now it's not. Now I believe you have it in you to do it. So yeah, maybe there are some other issues, but you can work around those. We can work around those."

He let out a slow, shaking breath. "So I am forced to confront the fact that I would never have chosen to live up to my full potential before, and now that I would…now that I would, my potential is greatly diminished."

"That's not it at all." Her stomach tightened, that fierce feeling of empathy, of connection, she'd felt with him that day his mother had arrived at the house intensified. Until that moment she hadn't felt closer to him since they'd slept together. If anything, she'd felt like any connection they might have had had been severed. But now it was back, and it was stronger.

He laughed. "It's not? Enlighten me then, Hannah."

"It will only be that if you insist on beating your head against a brick wall you could walk around if you weren't so stubborn. If you weren't letting your pride have control."

He raised his head, dark eyes glittering. "Pride is the one thing I still have."

She shook her head. "It's not. Trust me."

"It's myself I don't trust," he said, his eyes blank. "I don't know my own mind."

"Then learn it. When you're ready." She walked past him and out the door of the office. She was feeling…too much. Feeling in general. Tomorrow they would go back to Barcelona. She could get back to the business of seeing him as business. She could forget that this weekend ever happened.

She had to.

CHAPTER NINE

EDUARDO drew a hand over his face, fighting the anger, the frustration that was mounting inside of him. Then he gave up, giving it free rein as he pushed every piece of paper off his desk in a broad sweep and watched them all flutter to the floor.

He took a sharp breath, trying to gain a hold on himself. Trying to satisfy the dark, uncontrollable feelings that were firing through his veins. He put his head down and pushed his fingers through his hair, trying, desperately to think of what he'd just read.

Nothing. There was nothing. A void. A blank void that the information had fallen into and no matter how hard he tried, he couldn't get it back.

He let out a growl of frustration and picked his paperweight up from his desk, hurling it at the wall. Not even that helped. Nothing helped.

He pushed back from his desk and put his hands on his head as he paced.

The door to his office opened and Hannah walked in, the corners of her lips turned down. "Are you okay?"

Something in him shifted when he saw Hannah. It had been three weeks since they'd been back from his ranch. Three weeks of living together like strangers. Of pretending they'd never touched each other. That he'd never been inside her.

It was slowly driving him crazy. The financial reports from his retail stores were finishing the job. Quickly.

"Do I look okay?" he asked, moving his hand in a broad stroke in front of him, indicating the papers on the floor.

"No," she said, closing the door behind her. "What's up?"

"I can't do it, Hannah." The words burned his throat. "I can't remember. I can't…"

"Hey, take a breath."

"I did take a breath," he said through clenched teeth. "Then I realized it didn't fix anything so I destroyed my office instead."

"Productive."

In spite of himself, he snorted a laugh. "I thought so. Just as productive as me attempting to comprehend anything in these reports."

"Eduardo…"

He turned away from her, from the pained expression in her eyes and looked out at the city. "Do you have any idea how…frustrating it is, to have such a lack of control. To… I can't make it work. I can't make my mind what it was. I can't make it what I want." A dagger of pain pierced his temple and he winced.

"Maybe you should take a break."

He turned back to her. "I don't have time for a break."

"Then maybe ask for help instead of being so stubborn!"

The anger drained from him, as sudden and as uncontrollable as it had come on. And now he just felt exhausted. Down to his bones. "Help me, Hannah."

Something in her expression softened. If she tried to touch him…if she said she was sorry…he couldn't handle that.

Then, just as suddenly as the softness had appeared, it was replaced by her mask of hard efficiency. A mask he needed her to wear.

"What do you need help with?"

"In general. Help. All the help you can give me. I can't

focus on this." He indicated the papers again. "I can't retain it. I can barely read it. The words just keep…moving. I don't know why. Today it's like everything is moving too fast. I can't…"

She bent and gathered up the papers, glancing at the page numbers and, with a speed that made him vaguely jealous, put them in order.

"Close your eyes." He frowned. "Do it," she said.

He complied and felt a rush of calm go through him. All of the light and busy surroundings shut out, and he felt like he could think a bit better.

She started reading. Out loud. To him. Like he was a child who needed a bedtime story. About the amount of returns over the Christmas shopping season.

He straightened in his chair, his eyes popping open. "I'm not a child."

"I know. I'm not treating you like one. What I'm curious to know is how it is for you to listen to things rather than read them. Some people are auditory learners rather than visual."

"I never had a problem with visual…"

"Before. I know. But that was before."

"How do you know so much about this?"

"About learning? I had to teach myself how to learn when I decided I wanted to go to college. So, I researched every studying trick imaginable. Every way I could think of to do well on tests. I had to take an entrance exam, you know? And I only went to two years of high school. I had to study more than anyone else going into those tests, and I wasn't a natural intellectual. But I needed to be. So I learned to be."

"What kinds of things did you do?"

"Well, sometimes I would record my notes, and then play them back in headphones before going to sleep. I would write things out dozens of times. Drink coffee while I was study-ing, and again while I was taking the test. Taste is a really powerful memory trigger it turns out. Anyway, I don't see why we can't try to apply the principles to you."

A strange feeling moved through him. Respect? Yes, respect for Hannah. Intense and strong. And with that, the feelings of attraction he'd been working so hard to repress over the past few weeks.

Every time he'd passed her as she went into her office on his otherwise secluded floor. Every time he passed her in the hall in his home. Every time he closed his eyes at night and thought of her, so near, and yet so unobtainable.

"You are very clever, Hannah. Smart."

"No less for needing to use those tricks?"

"More so, perhaps. You found ways to make it work for you."

"And that's what you'll do, Eduardo." She lifted the stack of papers again. "Now, close your eyes."

This time he let her read and he found he had an easier time grasping meaning. Holding on to details that had passed through his mind before like water through a sieve. And when she quizzed him at the end, he could remember most of what he'd heard. Not all, but much more than he would have remembered had he read through it, and in much less time.

Now, when he spoke to his managers he wouldn't sound completely ignorant. Would sound more like a man who was equipped to hold his position.

"Better," he said, rising from his chair and rounding the desk.

"Yes," she agreed, a smile on her beautiful face. Was she happy for him? Or was it her own success that had her beaming from ear to ear in such an uncharacteristic way? "Now this is an easy one. You just need phone calls. They can fax you the reports so you can have them on file, but you can get a verbal briefing on the phone."

"You are truly a genius, Hannah," he said. And impulsively, he leaned forward and kissed her on the cheek. "Thank you."

She put her hand up to her cheek, her eyes round. "You're welcome."

He realized it was the first time he'd touched her since their night together. Unbidden, images of her hands on his body, his mouth on her breasts, came into his mind. He'd been without sex for five years until recently, largely of his own accord, and now three weeks without seemed a hellish eternity.

"Hannah…"

She backed away. "No. Not… I'm glad that that's helping. I want to keep helping. I'm really close to being able to give you some nice projected stats on how well we could do if we bought out Bach Wireless. But…no."

He hadn't realized that the hunger inside of him had been projected so clearly. And of course she'd said no. Of course she had. She should. Being with her had been like being thrown into a fire. It had been all-consuming, a flame that would ravage and devour everything in its path. He didn't have the kind of time needed to devote to something like that.

He had to focus on Vega. He had to keep things moving forward. They both needed to be fully engaged in business for that. Not fully engaged in bedroom games.

"Back to work then," he said.

She nodded curtly and walked out of the room. He tried to ignore the ache that started in his groin and seemed to spread to his entire body. Hannah was off-limits. If he said it enough times, he might start to believe it.

She was late. She was late, late, late. And her shady, private detour was making her late for work, and not just for her period. She wanted to crawl under the potted plant in the lobby of Vega Communications and cry. But she didn't have time.

She had to go pee on a stick, see one line instead of two, and get to work.

Eduardo was already in his office on the top floor. She walked past, trying to keep her steps quick but quiet, trying to keep from disturbing him as she made her way to the private bathroom at the end of the floor. She closed herself in and locked it, unwrapping the box that contained the test with shaking fingers.

The test itself was wrapped in some sort of heinous, indestructible foil. Keys. She did have the keys from home in her purse. She grabbed one and jabbed at the packaging until she worked the slim, innocuous-looking white test free.

Actually taking the test was easy. It was the wait that was hard.

She'd never imagined she'd be back in this position again. Except, instead of huddling in a cramped, filthy bathroom in her childhood home, shaking and on the verge of vomiting, she was huddled in a gorgeous, spotlessly clean bathroom on the highest floor of one of the world's largest and most prestigious companies. Shaking and on the verge of vomiting.

She paced while she waited. And counted. And closed her eyes. And considered throwing up.

"Just one," she whispered. "Just one line." She opened her eyes slowly and looked down at the white test lying on the white counter. All that stark white made it impossible to miss the two glaring pink lines that had bled into the test.

And then she did throw up.

"Hannah?" The door behind her shook as Eduardo knocked on it heavily. "Are you okay? Are you sick?"

"Yes," she called back. She shifted so that she was sitting inelegantly by the toilet, a cold sweat had broken out across her forehead, down her back.

"You're okay or you're sick?"

"I'm sick," she called back.

"Do you need help?"

"No." She pulled into a sitting position and took the test

off the counter, wrapping it four times over in toilet paper before throwing it into the garbage.

Why was this happening to her? Why was she being punished for sex? Was she just extremely fertile? Or extremely unlucky.

Everything started hitting her. The test she'd taken at sixteen. All the options she'd weighed then. Going to the clinic. Leaving the clinic, on a dead run, unable to go through with ending the pregnancy. Going to the adoption agency. The first time she'd felt the baby move. How strange, miraculous and heartbreaking it had been.

Labor and delivery. That brief flash of pink, wrinkled skin. Her baby squalling as he was taken from the room and to his parents.

He wasn't her baby. He belonged to Steve and Carol Johnson. He was their son. But he still felt like part of her. Part of her she couldn't get back. Part of her she'd had to give up. And with him, she gave up so much more.

And then she'd made a promise. That she would do everything to be the best she could be. That she wouldn't waste her life. Through extreme pain, physically and emotionally, she'd been given a wake-up call and she had vowed she would make the absolute most of it.

And she had. She'd done it. She'd made a success of herself. She'd let go of the girl she'd been. At least she thought she had. She didn't feel like it now. She just felt scared.

She couldn't do it again. She couldn't. It would break her.

Loss, a deep, unending sense of loss filled her and she put her hands on her stomach to try and stop the pain from spreading.

"Hannah? Do I have to break the door in?"

She shook off the pain, tried to find her strength. Tried to find Hannah Weston, so she wouldn't drown in Hannah Hackett. "You'll do yourself another head injury, Ed, so maybe don't."

"Hannah," he growled.

She turned on the sink and ran cold water over her hands, dragging them over her face, not caring if she smeared her makeup. Then she jerked the door open and came face-to-face with Eduardo. She had no idea what to say to him.

"Hi."

"You look terrible," he said.

"Thanks"

"You're pale," he said. "And you look like…well, you look sick."

"I am," she snapped.

"Do you need anything?"

A time machine. So she could go back to four weeks earlier when she'd decided having sex with him would be a way to regain control. It hadn't worked. Not in the least. And it certainly wasn't worth the consequence.

"I don't think there's anything you could do for me at the moment. Let's go in your office."

One thing she wasn't, was a coward. She wasn't going to hide it from him. It was implausible at best. So she would tell him. But she didn't know what she would tell him. She was the world's worst candidate to be a mother. But she honestly didn't know if she could go through giving up another child.

But she wasn't sure if she could be a mother, either. She knew nothing about it. She'd never had one. She didn't know if she had a nurturing bone in her body. She was insensitive. She swore. She was a workaholic. She had a criminal history.

The list went on.

"Sit down," she said.

"Hannah, what is it?"

"You remember how we had sex?"

One of his dark eyebrows shot up. "Yes, I seem to remember something about that."

"Right, well…also, remember the condom broke."

"I do remember," he said, his tone turning heavy, wooden.

"Well, I…we…that is…you…"

"You're pregnant."

"Well, when you say it like that you make it sound like it's all my fault. But you know I didn't get that way on my own."

"Hannah, I am well aware of how it happened and I am not fobbing the blame off onto you, so stop panicking for a second," he growled.

"Stop? Stop panicking? Eduardo, I have barely started panicking. There is an entire repertoire of panic for me to work through before I can even begin to wind down the panicking."

"There's no need to panic."

"Why is there no need to panic?"

"Because we're more than capable of handling this situation."

"Are we?" she asked, her throat almost completely constricted. "Do you have any idea… I mean. Do you? And what will we do with a baby, Eduardo, what? Will you strap him to your chest and bring him to work? You can't concentrate as it is. And me…what? I'm going to put on an apron and turn into Susie Homemaker?"

"We'll get nannies," he said.

"What kind of life is that for a child?"

"A life. There doesn't seem to be an alternative."

"Adoption," she said. The word sounded flat and cold in the room.

"I'm not giving away my child."

His words hurt. They cut her deep, tapped into a wound still raw and bleeding, covered, but never healed. "That's not what adoption is. It's giving your child the best chance possible. That's what it is. Wouldn't…wouldn't I have been better off? If my mother had given me up instead of neglecting me for three years of my life and then dropping me off with a father who didn't want me?" She couldn't voice the rest. Couldn't say anything about how this had happened before. It all just stuck in her throat. Painful. Horrendous. "Do you understand what it's like? To live with someone who just doesn't give a damn about what you do? Who doesn't even worry about you if you stay out all night? I was doing everything you should be afraid your child is out doing. Drinking, and having sex and he never… He didn't care. So tell me, Eduardo, what kind of life was that? Why should a child, anyone, ever live where they aren't wanted?"

"Are you saying you don't want the baby?"

"No. That's not it…that's not…"

"We could take care of a child, Hannah. It's different. We both have money."

"Money isn't enough."

"It's a start, at least."

She took a shaky breath. "Nothing has to be decided now," she said finally. "It's early. There's no need to—" she laughed "—well, to panic."

Eduardo felt like he'd been hit in the chest. He couldn't breathe. He could hardly think. Hannah was pregnant. The only time he'd ever thought about children had been in terms of preventing them. He'd vaguely assumed, prior to his injury, that he would settle down for real one day and in that scenario, there had been a hazy assumption of children, but he'd never truly thought about it in a real sense.

And since his accident…well, he'd avoided women. Avoided all kinds of relationships. The thought of having a child when everything was so much harder than it had once been… Hannah was right in many ways. He wasn't sure he could handle being a father and running Vega. He could scarcely run Vega, and Hannah knew it better than most.

Knew what sorts of limitations she was dealing with when it came to the father of her baby.

"Right," he said, as if having decided that maybe they could just put it out of their minds for a while, but he doubted he would think of anything else. He wasn't sure how he ever could.

"Right," she said, looking as unconvinced as he felt.

"Let's go back to the *rancho*," he said. He needed solitude. Quiet. He needed to not be here, in this place that reminded him of his shortcomings.

"What? When?"

"This weekend," he said. "I don't think I can...concentrate here. There's too much. This...makes it too much."

"Right," she said. "I just need my phone glued to me because I have to get that deal nailed down."

"I understand. We'll bring work with us." But the room felt like it was closing in on him, the whole city, just outside the windows, felt like it was folding on top of him. His mind was cluttered and he couldn't figure out how to sift through it. Especially not with the pounding that was starting in his head. With the way the light was starting to feel, like a knife going in through his eyes.

"We leave tomorrow."

Hannah nodded, for once without any kind of sassy comeback. "Okay."

CHAPTER TEN

"ARE you all right staying in here?"

Hannah looked around the frilly pink-and-white room. The room she and Eduardo had made love in. The room they'd conceived the baby in.

"As fine here as I would be anywhere," she said, her head spinning, a strange, heavy numbness invading her chest and spreading outward. She was so tired. Exhaustion seeped into her bones.

"I want to be close to you."

"I'm not going to do anything desperate, Eduardo."

"I know."

Except he didn't know. And that was fair enough, because she'd never really let him know her. He'd seen her naked and he still didn't know her. No one did. Not really. She wasn't sure she did anymore. Wasn't sure what she wanted. Wasn't sure if she could clear the next hurdle that had been placed in front of her.

Just the thought of what the next few months would bring, of what it would mean to watch her baby be carried from the room again, never holding him, never touching him, made her feel cold. Made her feel like the life was draining from her.

What if you kept him?

For a moment she imagined it. Holding her baby at her breast, looking into eyes that were dark like his father's. Having someone to love. Someone who would love her.

Her stomach seized, tears threatening to fall.

"I'm fine," she said, mostly for her own benefit. But she knew she was lying.

"Do you want to lie down for a while?"

"I'm not symptomatic yet."

"When does that usually start?"

"Six weeks or so," she said.

He frowned. "Do all women just…know this stuff? You don't seem like you would."

Shoot. Yes, she would have to tell him sometime. It wasn't like it would matter. Except it did. It was her pain. It had never been anyone else's.

"You'd be surprised," she said. "I am a little tired. I think I'll take a nap. We'll talk later?"

He nodded curtly. "If you feel up to it, I'd like to walk down to the beach with you."

"That would be great."

She ushered him out of the room and rested her back against the closed door. Her old life was crashing head-on into her new one, and she wasn't sure anymore where one ended and the other began.

It was her worst nightmare unfolding in front of her. And she wasn't sure there was anything she could do to stop it.

She woke up feeling sleepier than she had when she'd lain down. Her head was swimming, and it was dark outside. So she'd missed her walk. It was okay, though; she hadn't really felt up to talking to Eduardo. Not now. Not when she'd have to be honest with him.

A tear rolled down her face and back into her hair and she didn't bother to wipe it away. Eduardo was the only person she'd felt close to in so long, and even they were in opposition half the time.

Maybe she wasn't meant to be close to people. It was pretty obvious she didn't really know how to be. Even with Zack there had been calculated distance. They hadn't shared themselves. They'd met where they were at in life and moved forward, never digging deep, never really getting to know each other. And she'd been happy with that.

Eduardo pushed her; he made her angry. Made her feel passion and lose control. It didn't make her all that happy, and it had led to a pretty big mistake. But she did feel more genuine when she was with him. More herself.

She wasn't sure if that was a good thing or not.

She pulled her knees up to her chest and rolled to her side. She felt like she was breaking apart. For once she couldn't outthink a situation. Couldn't control it or change it. It was what it was. She was pregnant. With Eduardo's baby.

She sat up and wiped the tears from her cheeks. She needed to get her mind off it. She needed to be near Eduardo, and she couldn't fathom why. But it didn't matter why. She hurt everywhere. She felt like she was being scraped raw inside.

And she was so tired of being alone. She was always alone.

With shaking limbs she stood from the bed and padded across the room, to the door that separated her room from Eduardo's, walking into his room without knocking.

For a moment, she didn't see him. It was dark in his room, and he wasn't in the bed. Then she saw him, slumped in his chair, his hands gripping the armrests.

"Hi," she said, her voice sounding huskier than she intended it to.

He shifted. "Hannah? Are you feeling all right?"

"As well as can be expected. Yourself?"

"I had a migraine. I'm better now."

"Have you been drinking?"

"No. That makes it worse. Why?"

"Just...it's good to know. I...I really need you," she whispered.

"What?"

"I can't be alone. And I'm cold. I need you to make me

feel…make me feel again." She battled against the tears that were threatening to fall, threatening to choke her. "Make me warm."

He stood quickly and wrapped his arm around her waist, pulling her up against him. "Hannah…"

"I just want to stop thinking. For a minute. I just want to feel. You make me feel so good. When you touch me…" She swallowed hard. "I'm asking you for help now, Eduardo."

"Oh, Hannah."

He picked her up, holding her close to his chest, and she wrapped her arms around his neck. She'd never given a lot of thought to her feelings on over-the-top masculine displays of strength. Turned out, she liked them.

She placed her palms flat over his chest, over the hard muscles, maddeningly concealed by his thin T-shirt. She lowered her hands and found the hem of the shirt, sliding her fingertips up his hot, hair-roughened skin.

He groaned and set her down on the bed, tugging the shirt over his head. She could see the outline of his body, moonlight gleaming from the hard ridges of his chest and abs, his jeans low cut, delicious lines pointing right down to his erection.

And that was all she was going to think about. Just him.

"You're really sexy," she breathed.

He chuckled, his hands on his belt buckle. "So are you. Trade."

She tugged her shirt over her head and lay back, waiting for the rest of Eduardo to be revealed.

He shook his head. "Not enough."

"Grr." She got up on her knees and torqued her arms around, unhooking her bra and sending it sailing. "Better?"

The heat glittering in his dark eyes sent an answering fire down to her belly. And farther down.

A smile curved his lips. "Much better."

He worked his belt through the loops and tugged it free.

Then shrugged off his pants and underwear in one deft motion.

"Come here," she said.

"Your wish is my command."

He joined her on the bed, his bare shaft hot against her stomach. "Oh, yes," she whispered, the edges of her mind getting fuzzy with arousal. This was what she needed.

He unbuttoned her jeans and tugged them down her legs, then quickly took her underwear down with them. He teased her with his fingers, his thumb sliding over her clitoris.

She arched into him, clawing at his back, letting her mind go blank of everything but the white-hot pleasure that was pouring through her.

Then he bracketed her face with his hands, kissing her. Deep. Long. Passionate. She clung to him, letting the kiss intensify, learning his rhythm, relearning her own.

This was less intimate than the way he'd touched her a moment ago, but also, somehow, infinitely more so. When he finally released her mouth to trail kisses down her neck, she was shaking, more turned on than she'd ever been in her life. On the verge of tears.

She forked her fingers through his hair, craving deeper contact, craving more.

He kissed her belly, heading lower.

"No," she breathed. "No time."

She needed him inside of her. As deep as he could be, as close as he could be. She hadn't needed anyone in longer than she could remember. She'd never been able to afford to.

"I need you," she said. Meaning it, with every fiber of her being. He continued down, a low chuckle escaping his lips. "No," she said. "This isn't…a game or anything. I need you."

He raised his head, moving back up her body, his dark eyes intense, locked with hers. He pushed her hair back from her face, then kissed her lightly on her lips. She parted her thighs and felt him at the entrance of her body.

"Yes," she whispered.

He slid slowly inside of her. With every inch she felt some of her emptiness fade, and when he was inside her completely, as close to her as two people could be, she felt like she understood sex in a new way entirely.

Sex had never been intimate for her. And she hadn't been after intimacy tonight. Back in high school she'd been after oblivion, a moment of happiness, of closeness even. But not true, deep intimacy.

But she felt it now. As if Eduardo had become a part of her. As if she would leave his bed changed.

He moved inside of her, every stroke perfection, driving her closer to the edge of bliss. Every thrust bringing him closer to her.

His pace increased and she locked her legs around his hips, moving with him; she arched back, her release crashing over her like a wave. He gripped the sheet by her head and shuddered out his own orgasm a moment later.

She lay against his chest, her heart pounding hard, her head swimming. She wanted to speak; she couldn't. A moment later she realized she was shaking. And crying, tears falling on his bare skin.

"I…" she started.

But there was nothing to say. She was overwhelmed. She was pregnant with this man's baby. This man who held her so tightly. Who made her feel close to someone for the first time ever.

No one had ever loved her. And she had never thought of it before. But now…now, in his arms, she wished so much that it could be different. That she could be different. That she could be loved.

He kept his arms wrapped tightly around her and held her close. She kept shaking and he reached down to grab the covers, drawing them up over both of them.

"Sleep now, *querida*. We'll talk more tomorrow."

She nodded wordlessly, unable to speak around the lump in her throat.

She curled up against him, inhaled the scent of him, so uniquely Eduardo. Then she closed her eyes and tried to fall asleep. Trying to fight off all of the demons that were threatening to tear her apart.

Eduardo woke up as the first rays of sun began to filter through the expansive windows of the room. He'd forgotten to close the blinds because his headache had hit after dark.

He rolled over to look at Hannah and his heart seized.

She was so beautiful. And achingly vulnerable. He didn't know how he'd missed it for so long. He'd imagined her invincible, a fair target to bring into his sphere. She could handle herself, after all, and he would never leave her empty-handed.

But he could see now that he'd been wrong. Very wrong.

He thought about what she'd said the day before. About him barely being able to run his business, much less run it with a baby around to distract him. She was right. And yet, when he thought back to his own childhood, the way his father had been, stern and distant, but steady and so very present, he couldn't imagine being anything less for his own child.

He had the resources to care for a son or daughter. And his mother would be thrilled.

And if you can't do it? If the crying gives you migraines and lack of sleep makes it impossible for you to concentrate? If it gets so bad you can't see? What will you do then?

He would figure it out. He had no other choice. They could get nannies, the best available. He would have to. But he could make it work.

He knew it now, with certainty. It had been too hard to process in his office, beneath the bright fluorescent lights. But now, in the gray light of dawn, with Hannah warm and naked by his side, it did seem clear.

He'd wanted to decide what to do about the baby before

anything else happened between them…but when she'd come to him, so vulnerable, so achingly sad, he hadn't been able to deny her. Especially as her misery seemed to be a reflection of his own.

She'd asked him to make her warm. She'd made him warm.

He moved his hand down to Hannah's stomach and his heart pounded faster. Harder.

"Are you awake?" he whispered.

Hannah's eyes opened slowly. "Oh…"

"You sound disappointed," he said.

She rolled over and buried her face in her pillow. "I slept with you again."

"I remember."

She rolled over again. "It wasn't a good idea. It…confuses things."

"Can things be any more confusing?"

"Oh, I don't know, but this can't possibly help clear it up."

"Okay, that's probably true." He moved into a sitting position, unconcerned with the fact that he was still naked. Hannah averted her eyes, clearly of a different opinion, clutching the sheets to her chest. "I'd like to talk to you. About the baby."

"I…" She bit her lip. "Now?"

"Why don't you go shower. I'll shower. We'll have breakfast. Then I'd like to walk with you for a while. On the beach."

She nodded slowly. "I can do that."

"Good." He leaned in and kissed her forehead, the move not planned. And he found he didn't regret it.

He got out of bed and walked toward his bathroom, taking a small amount of satisfaction in Hannah's muffled squeak, likely brought on by his continued nudity. He turned and saw her scrambling out of bed with the sheet still wrapped tightly around her body.

"You might as well let it drop, Hannah. I've seen it all."

Something in her expression changed, a sad smile lifting the corner of her lips. "Not in daylight. I'll see you in a bit."

She turned, still covered, and walked out of the room.

Hannah was done showering before Eduardo, and had a few moments down in the breakfast area by herself. She nibbled on a bowl of fruit for a while, then asked one of Eduardo's staff if she could get some bacon. Bacon sounded good. It wasn't a pregnant craving, she was pretty sure it was too soon for that. She was just feeling horrible and trying to comfort herself with food.

She nibbled on the bacon while she thought about how today would play out. Yet again, it seemed impossible to plan.

She would have to tell Eduardo. There was really no way around it. Because she had to explain to him where she was coming from.

He appeared a few moments later, dressed in shorts and sandals, ready for a casual walk on the beach. She only had one pair of jeans, so she was going to have to settle for rolling them up past her ankles.

"I'm not really hungry," he said. "Are you ready?"

She picked up another bacon strip. "Yeah." She stood and took a deep breath, following him out the back door of the house. There was a little path that cut through the meadow and led down the hillside, tall grass rising up, making the walkway feel enclosed. Private.

The ground softened and turned from dirt to sand, the chilly, salty air stinging her cheeks. They were quiet until they reached the shore.

"How are you feeling now, Hannah?"

"Now that I've had a full twenty-four hours to process it?" she asked.

"Yes."

"Not great."

"Tell me," he said, still walking. Heading toward a grove

of trees that was at the far end of the beach. "Do you still want to give the baby up?"

Her throat tightened. "It's not a matter of want, Eduardo. It's about…about doing what's best for the baby. I wasn't very nice yesterday, to you, when I said that about caring for a baby and the company, but my point is still solid. I'm married to my work, and you're willing to do anything for your job. So when exactly are we going to find the time to raise a child? And with me in the U.S. and you here in Spain…"

"So, be here."

"Me? Move to Spain?"

"You've lived here before. You liked it."

She'd more than liked it. She loved Spain. In so many ways it felt like her home. "Yes," she said slowly, "but I have a job back in San Francisco, assuming they haven't cleaned out my desk."

"You've left plenty of jobs."

"That's not really the issue."

"Then what is?"

The truth hovered on the edge of her lips, but she couldn't quite bring herself to say it, not just yet.

"My father was very much committed to his business," Eduardo said. "He was still a good father."

"You were angry with him half the time."

"I know. Because I was young and stupid and entitled. And if there's one change I am thankful for in myself, it's that my fall seems to have knocked some of the jackass out of me."

She laughed. "Some, maybe. But you still have plenty."

They reached the little cluster of trees and they walked beneath them. Hannah looked up at the green leaves, a spiderweb of sunlight breaching the foliage.

"Do you know how all-consuming a baby will be?" she asked, her stomach churning.

"I'm not sure that I do. But no parent really does until they have one of their own."

It had been years since she'd thought of that long-ago baby as her son. She couldn't. Couldn't let herself have that connection to him. Because she knew better than most that it took more than blood to be a parent. For her son, his parents were the people who had raised him. Who had stayed up nights with him. She had simply carried him.

If only that were enough to abolish the connection she felt.

"I'm afraid," she whispered, tears clogging her throat.

"Of course you are, Hannah. Childbirth is…an unknown experience. Pregnancy is certainly…"

"No." She shook her head, trying to ignore the pain that was crawling through her veins. "I know all about being pregnant. About what it's like to feel your baby move inside you for the first time… It's…it's a miracle, Eduardo." She felt a tear slide down her cheek. "Labor is as awful as they say. But in the end there's this perfect little…life. And it's so worth it. All of it. The morning sickness, the stretch marks. The pain."

"Hannah," he said, his tone flat, cold.

"I was sixteen when I got pregnant," she said. She'd never voiced the words out loud before. Had never confided in anyone. "And I knew there was no way I could take care of a baby." Another tear fell and she didn't wipe it away.

"I gave him up. Because it was the right thing to do. But… but I'm not sure I can go through it again. I don't think I could give this one up, even if I should. And I'm afraid…I'm afraid that if I do keep this baby, I'll really understand what I gave up then."

CHAPTER ELEVEN

HANNAH felt emotion coming in thick, unendurable waves. She could drown in it, in the pain, the misery. The starkness of the truth. It was so very ugly, and yet, it was a part of her.

"Hannah that must have been…"

"There are days when I'm so glad that I did it. Because I was this poor, high school dropout with no future and what could I offer him? Nothing. Nothing but more of the same. More poverty. More…neglect maybe while I tried to work and earn enough money to keep us in whatever filthy apartment I could afford. Was I going to take him back to the single-wide I shared with my dad? Expose him to secondhand smoke and mice and bugs and everything else we had to contend with?" She looked down. "But some people make it. I just…I knew I wasn't strong enough. I knew I didn't know how."

"What about the father?"

She shook her head, a faint feeling of embarrassment creeping over her, joining the misery. "I didn't really know him. He was this senior guy I hooked up with at a party. He wasn't my boyfriend. Obviously, I was very irresponsible. It wasn't the first time I'd done something like that, classic acting-out behaviors. I'm kind of a shameful stereotype. No attention from Dad so…anyway, you get the idea. He went away to college. I called about the baby but he…he didn't call back."

"He didn't call you back?"

"We were both young and stupid. He had college to look forward to. A way out of the hellhole we lived in and probably the last thing he wanted was to deal with having a kid back home. It doesn't excuse him but...I'm not mad at him for it. I...did it by myself."

"And after that, that was when you changed your name?"

She nodded, ready to tell now. "I needed to be someone different. I don't know how else to explain it. I just...I couldn't be...that girl anymore. The Johnsons, the adoptive parents, they paid for my prenatal care and my hospital bill, but they also had the agency send me a monetary gift. Something to help me start over. I felt like I had a choice in that moment. To go back to the place I'd always called home. Back to my old friends, who were still wasting any potential they might have had by partying it away. Back to a father who never seemed to notice what was happening with my life. Or I could try and take the fresh start. In that moment, everything seemed... new. For the first time, I felt like I could be anything. Do anything. I changed my name and figured out what I would have to do to get into college. Found the right people to help me forge the transcripts. And then I bought a plane ticket to Barcelona. And then I hit the ground running."

"And you've been running ever since."

She nodded. "I have been." She looked out at the sea, the white-capped waves rolling into the shore. "But I can't run from this."

"Neither can I. It's not in me. This is reality and we have to face it. But I'm certain we can make it work."

"I'm afraid that...it's going to bring it all back. I've spent so many years trying to let go. And it's a process. Like I said, some days I'm thankful. I'm glad for the stable life I'm sure he's had. Glad he's been able to grow up in comfort. Glad I was able to...to make something better of myself. But..."

"Come here." He sat down at the base of one of the trees and leaned against the smooth bark.

Hannah moved to where he was and sat. There was space between them; neither of them looked at each other. "Things are different now, Hannah. We can make this work. We'll do it together."

She put her hand on her stomach. "Can we?"

He put his hand over hers and a spark shot through her. "We will. We'll do it, because you're the strongest woman I've ever met. And I'm...not as much as I used to be but... But in some ways..."

"In some ways better," she said. Thinking of the Eduardo he had been. The laughing, mocking man who had taken nothing seriously.

"Yes, that, too."

She shivered. "I'm afraid of screwing a kid up. Like my parents did to me."

"I don't blame you."

"But your parents love you. You know how it's supposed to be."

He nodded slowly. "Yes. My parents do love me. They, especially my father, were never overly demonstrative, but I always knew that he had my best interests at heart. He made sure we were all cared for. Provided for. He was the pillar of my family. Still, I plagued him. I married an American girl he didn't approve of."

"Not at first," she said, remembering how things had been in the end. How Eduardo's father had told her she had one of the finest minds he'd ever encountered. That she could achieve great things if she kept going. "But in the end...well, before I left you and made him hate me again...he treated me better than almost anyone else in my life. I'll always be grateful to him for his confidence in me."

"You know what you were missing growing up, Hannah, and I truly believe you'll know what needs to be given to your child."

She broke free of him, moving into a standing position.

One thing was certain, she wasn't going to be able to think clearly while he was touching her.

"I hope you're right."

"Every parent starting out is afraid of whether or not they'll be good enough. So I hear."

"What if it affects your work?"

"It won't. I'll make sure that everything is taken care of. If things slip a bit, then they slip."

"But it's not what you want."

"Of course not. It's never been what I wanted. That's why I went to such great lengths to bring you back." A stark reminder that it had been her brains he wanted, not her body. Not that that was a bad thing. Really, it was flattering. Positive even. "I'm completely certain we can put the proper systems in place to ensure that nothing bad happens with the company."

She was glad he was feeling certain about something. She was feeling…dull. Achy. On edge. Far too close to having her past and future collide. To losing the detachment she'd made with that long-ago self.

"I remember his face," she said, not sure why she'd allowed the words to escape.

"Your child?"

She nodded. "He was a boy. They said that when he was born. And they lifted him up and I thought I could turn away quickly enough. That I wouldn't have to see him. That I could pretend it hadn't been real at all. But it was. He was." She blinked hard, trying to keep from dissolving completely. "I'll never forget his face."

"Perhaps you shouldn't."

She shook her head. "I don't want to anymore. But I did for a long time. I wished I could make it go away. Wished I didn't…ache for him. Like something was missing from inside of me."

"Is it like that? Still?"

She swallowed. "In some ways. But…I just…I have to let him go, don't I? I'm not his mother. Not really. I don't even know what they named him. I never held him or kissed him. I didn't watch him take his first steps. Or see him go to school for the first time. I never put a bandage on his scraped knees or…or…" She couldn't breathe. It took her a moment to realize it was because she was sobbing. Great gasps of air that came from deep inside of her and made her feel like she was breaking in two.

She sat down, on her knees in the sand, moisture seeping through the thick denim fabric of her pants. Her throat was burning, raw and painful, like she'd been screaming. But she hadn't been. She'd never allowed herself to let go so much. This was the first time she'd truly cried in years, not just tears, but with every piece of herself. This was the first time she'd cried for her son.

The first time she'd let herself fully realize what she'd lost.

Dimly she was aware of Eduardo hovering near her. He knelt down beside her, not touching her, and she was glad. Because if he did she would melt into him completely.

Finally, the storm passed, almost as quickly as it had hit. She shifted so that she was sitting on her backside, knees drawn up to her chest.

"I never told him I loved him," she said.

"He was a baby, Hannah," Eduardo said, his voice rusty.

"I know but…I don't even think I really let myself feel it." She looked up at him. "I did, though. I do."

"I know," he said.

Eduardo felt like his heart was going to hammer out of his chest. Fear. It was pure fear that had him shaking and on edge. He didn't know what to do with such raw emotion, didn't feel like he had the strength to handle it. What Hannah had been through…it was beyond him. What she had lost…it was so much greater than anything he had lost.

And yet, she knew, and he did, too, that she'd had very little choice.

He moved closer to her, unsure if he should touch her, take her in his arms, or not.

"Hannah, look at all you've accomplished in your life. You made the right choice. For both of you. So you could both live better."

"I know," she said, her voice firm. "I do know. But…just because a choice is right doesn't mean it won't hurt like hell."

"No, that is true."

"It hurts so much to love like this," she said softly. "To love a child. You're never the same again."

Another pang of fear hit him hard. "That's okay."

"You really think so?"

"I have to. No matter what, we've made a baby." She winced. "Sorry, cheesy choice of wording perhaps, but no matter what…there will…most likely be a baby. And we either face giving him up or keeping him. I think…I think we should keep him." The idea terrified him in many ways, but not more than feeling the sort of grief that came from Hannah in palpable waves.

Hannah wrapped her arms around herself like she was cold. "I…I think…"

"We'll do this, Hannah. Together. I'll be with you."

Her pale blue eyes, looking brighter thanks to the red rims they'd acquired during her crying jag, locked with his. "I trust you."

And he knew that that was probably the deepest compliment he had ever received. From Hannah or anyone.

He tried to block out the weight of it. The responsibility he might not be able to live up to. He winced against the pain in his head.

He would do it. He didn't have a choice.

Eduardo lifted his head from the floor. How was it possible for the medicine cabinet to be so far away? After the beach, his headache had steadily gotten worse until every fragment of light, every sound had become excruciating.

And he'd put off going for his medication. Put off acknowledging it because he didn't want Hannah to know.

His vision blurred and another stab of pain went through his head, through his body. Nausea rolled through him and he laid his head back down against the hard tile. He prayed that somehow the cold would work like an ice pack. That it would provide some relief. Enough that he could stand up and get his pills at least.

A fresh wave of pain hit him and he groaned, curling up, trying to shield himself from further attacks. It was impossible. He knew it, but it didn't stop him from trying.

If he could just stand up.

"Eduardo?"

Hannah's voice cut through the door. Cut through his skull. He wanted to tell her to go away, but just imagining the pain that would cause brought the acidic taste of bile to the back of his throat.

"Eduardo?" She was closer now, her voice sharper.

He growled against the floor, planting his hand in front of him, trying to push himself up. He was rewarded with another knife through his skull, so strong it put black spots in his vision.

"Go away, Hannah," he said. A rough sound escaped his lips as another shot of pain cracked through him. It hit him like a wall, the force of it enough to black out his sight entirely. He couldn't see anything. Couldn't move. Couldn't have found his way to the medicine cabinet now even if standing were a possibility.

"Are you okay? You're scaring me."

He pressed his forehead back down on the tile. He took a deep breath, steeling himself for the agony he was about to put himself in. But she couldn't see him. Not like this. On the floor, immobilized, sweating, shaking. Blind.

No. She couldn't see this.

"Go away, Hannah!" he roared, the shock of his own voice lancing him with intense physical torment that started at his head and worked through the rest of him. His face, his cheeks, were wet. From sweat or from unforgivable weakness, he didn't know.

"Eduardo, I am about to open the door. Sorry, but I am. You're freaking me out now."

She pushed the door open and he stretched his hand out, trying to stop it, but he was too weak to lift his arm. He was too weak in every way.

"Oh…are you…are you okay?" Hannah was down beside him, her voice too close, her hand on his face.

He shook his head, trying to find it in him to speak again. She was here. And he needed his pills. "Medicine cabinet," he said.

He heard her stand, the noises she made while rummaging through the medicine cabinet drumming in his head. He heard the water running and Hannah was kneeling beside him again.

Hannah looked down at Eduardo, panic racing through her. He'd mentioned migraines and she hoped that was all this was. Though…there was nothing minor about it, even if the symptoms weren't fatal.

She shifted so that she was sitting on her bottom behind Eduardo's head. Then she gripped him beneath his arms and tugged him up so that his head was resting on her thigh. His face was damp, with sweat and tears and her heart burned for him. His eyes were unfocused, open and staring.

She hated that she was seeing it. Not for her, but for him. Because she knew that this was flaying his pride, killing a part of him that was so essential to him.

She picked up the cup of water she'd set on the floor and tried to angle his head. She opened her hand and he opened his mouth as she put the pills on his tongue. She put the water glass to his lips and tilted it slowly. He swallowed the pills and his eyes fluttered closed, his head falling back to her lap.

She set the glass down and leaned back against the tub, her hands on his chest, feeling the steady beat of his heart beneath her hands. Every so often his muscles would tense, his face contorting, and her heart would burn.

The tile started to feel really hard, and the tub wasn't any better against her back, but she kept sitting there. Kept holding him.

There was nothing, not a sore butt or aching back, that was going to move her. Because Eduardo was hers. She tightened her hold on him and took a sharp, halting breath. She didn't know what that meant, she only knew that he was. That of all the people in the world, he was the only person who seemed to understand her. The only person who seemed to want to try.

Eduardo mattered. Her heart started beating faster as the realization worked its way through her. He mattered more than work. More than her personal success or her image. *He* mattered.

The beautiful, broken man in her arms was worth caring about. And she could. She did. No, he wasn't slick, urbane Eduardo from five years ago, but she didn't need him to be. That man hadn't called to her. That man hadn't reached her heart.

She moved her hand to his forehead and smoothed the lines there, trying to rub out his concerns. Trying to ease his pain.

Her heart tightened.

Maybe she could do it. Maybe they could do it.

One thing she knew for certain, as she sat there with her body aching, Eduardo in her arms, was that some people were worth caring for, worth working for. Eduardo was worth it. Their baby was worth it.

A sharp sense of longing, of tenderness, hit in her in the chest. She closed her eyes, letting a tear fall down her cheek. She lowered her head and rested her forehead on his.

She didn't know anything about marriage. Or about children. Or being a mother. But he made her want to try.

"Hannah?" When Eduardo woke up, it was dark. At least he hoped it was dark. His vision had gone before during migraines, but it never lasted long. He hoped it never did.

The fact that Hannah had seen him at his weakest...it galled him. And yet, he had needed her. That didn't make it feel any better.

"I'm right here," she said. She sounded tired, like she'd been sleeping.

It took him a moment to realize that he was in bed, and that she was sitting a few feet away.

"How did you manage to get me into bed?"

"Ah, gee, Eduardo, I've gotten you into bed a couple of times. I can't say it was all that hard."

"Hannah," he said, moving into a sitting position, every muscle in his body screaming at him, "I'm serious." His eyes started to adjust to the dim room, and he could see her, in his chair, her legs tucked up under her.

"Truthfully? You walked with me...you were just really out of it. And anyway, it's not that far."

"I don't want you to have to deal with things like this...."

"How often does this happen?" she asked.

"Migraines? Once every week or so. Migraines like that? It's been months since I've had to deal with anything on that level. They've gotten further apart but..."

"All this stress."

He shook his head. "Not necessarily."

"I've been thinking."

"You never stop thinking, *querida*."

"Granted. But I've been thinking specifically about our baby. And about our future."

He swallowed. "What about it?"

"We're already married."

"A fact we're both well aware of as it caused you grief a few weeks ago."

She nodded curtly. "Yes, but now I'm thinking it's advantageous."

"How do you mean?"

"We're having a baby."

"So many things manage to slip my mind, Hannah, and yet that one has not."

She laughed, a small, nervous sound. He wasn't used to Hannah sounding nervous. "I know…I— Do you want to talk later? I mean…that was a bad… It was bad. If you don't feel up to talking, I understand."

"Talk, Hannah."

"Okay. I think we should stay married. I think we should be a family."

"A…family? What do you think makes a family, Hannah? Marriage?"

She hopped out of the chair and started pacing. "I don't know, Eduardo. I…I don't really. I've never had a family. But on that note, I can tell you what doesn't make a family. A mother who never comes to see you. A father who can't be bothered to say four words to you on a daily basis. Do you know, he never did one thing for me? He bought frozen dinners and I heated them up for both of us. The school bus made sure I got to school. No one went to my parent-teacher conferences. I…" She took a breath. "I was seven when one of my friends said something about my hair not being brushed before I went to school. She started doing it for me on the bus. So, that's what family isn't. I'd really like to try and make a real family."

His heart hurt, for Hannah. The woman she was now, the little girl she'd been. He wanted to hold her close. Erase every bad thing that had ever happened to her. He wanted to care for her.

And then he remembered the events of the past few hours.

Remembered the fact that Hannah had just spent the afternoon caring for him.

He couldn't give her what she needed, what she deserved.

"Hannah, do you really understand what you just saw? When that happens…I can't move. I can't see. You want to try and make your perfect vision of family with me?"

"You're the one who wanted to try this. And I do, too," she said, conviction infusing her tone. "You said we'd do this together. I want to make this work. And the great thing is, we don't have to do anything. We're already married. We already talked about me coming to live in Barcelona. Really… really, it's perfect."

"And us, Hannah?" His whole body tightened when he thought of the other benefits of Hannah being his wife.

"I…"

Hannah felt like her insides had frozen. Of course sex would come into it. The sex between them was great. No question. And she wanted it, there was no question there, either. And if they were going to be married…well, it was only logical.

Then she thought back to that moment on the floor of the bathroom, when she'd held him in her arms. When she'd felt like he was part of her.

Just the thought of what it would be like to kiss him now, to be skin to skin with him now, when she felt so emotionally raw and stripped bare, when her defenses were gone, frightened her down to her soul.

"I can't think about it right now," she said. "That's just to say…I have to process one thing at a time. You and I will have…all the time ever to figure each other out."

Although, she was afraid she would need that much time just to sort herself out.

"That seems fair," he said, his voice rough.

"So…will you stay married to me?"

"Yes, Hannah," he said.

"Great. Good. That's…great. And good. Do you need anything?"

"No. Just sleep."

"Good, I'll leave you to that, then."

Hannah walked out of Eduardo's room and closed the door behind her. And only then did she realize she'd been holding her breath. She was going to have to get it together. She couldn't risk letting herself fall for him. She'd never believed in love, or at least she'd never believed that she could love anyone. That they could love her.

And she couldn't afford it. Couldn't afford to depend on him like that. To need him so much.

She thought back to that moment of fierce, pure possessiveness she'd felt, kneeling on the bathroom floor with him. That he was hers.

She tried to swallow past the lump in her throat. She would deal with the emotion stuff later. For now, she just had to focus on the positives. She was having a baby; she and Eduardo were doing the best thing possible for their baby. She had a plan.

She inhaled and exhaled slowly. Yes, she had a plan. And when she made plans, she kept them. A plan always fixed things.

Suddenly everything felt much more doable.

CHAPTER TWELVE

HANNAH hit the send button on her email and whimpered inwardly. She'd resigned from her job in San Francisco. Not the first job she'd resigned from. But she'd liked the job. She'd contacted a removal company about clearing out her apartment the day before, and had her now-ex-assistant working on listing the furniture and home for sale.

She was used to leaving, but it still felt strange. Sad.

The door to her new and now-more-permanent office at Vega opened and Eduardo entered on a loud and virulent curse.

"Why are you swearing? I'm the one that just resigned from my job." They'd been back in Barcelona for the whole week and they'd kept things very civilized and organized between them.

There was no mention of resuming a physical relationship. No mention of the future. And no mention of the migraine. She could handle that. Was using the time to try and heal, to try and rebuild her walls. To get a grip on the soft gooeyness that seemed to be overtaking her.

They had their system in place, her in her room, he in his, and they came to work together. And, it had even been decided she would be the new financial manager at Vega.

So, all in all, a good week. Even if she did feel confused and lonely. And a little nauseous.

"There's a…charity dinner tonight and I forgot about it. I

had it in my calendar but then I forgot to sync the calendar and so it didn't end up on my phone."

"Tonight?"

"Yes, after work."

"Well, that's not so bad. Go put on a tux and mingle for a couple of hours. It won't kill you."

"I'm not fun."

"You're not…boring."

"You have to come with me."

"No thanks."

"Hannah Vega, you have to come with me, because you are my wife. And my company and the success of it, is very important to you. Which means, the appearance of stability in my life should be very important to you. This is your son's or daughter's legacy, after all."

"Don't be a bear, Eduardo."

"I don't know another way to be. I told you, I'm not fun."

Her cheeks heated as she thought of some of the ways she'd had fun with Eduardo. Oh, no, she was not going there. No, no, no. "You'll be fine. We'll be fine. Not sure I'm up to going out, looking saucy and conspicuously avoiding drinking the champagne, but hey, why not?"

His expression lightened suddenly, concern filling his dark eyes. "I'm sorry, I didn't consider you might not be feeling up to it. I…forgot."

"Don't worry about it. I'm more worried about you. You're up to it?"

His expression darkened. "I'm fine."

"Good. Just tell me what color to wear, and I'll be ready by…when do you need?"

"Eight."

"Eight. I'm good at these kinds of things."

"I know you are," he said, his eyebrows drawing together a bit.

She wanted to go and touch him, comfort him. She wasn't

all that great at comforting people, not historically anyway, but she wanted to. Although, she wasn't sure what was allowed in the neutral zone that was their relationship. They weren't any closer than they'd been a week ago. They hadn't fought more, either. She actually missed fighting with him. Missed the spike of passion that had been between them in some form from the moment they'd met.

She missed the sex even more.

"So, just reap the benefits then and stop looking like the world is crumbling all around you." She stood up and took her purse off the hook behind her desk. "So, what color do you need me to wear?"

"Why?"

"I need to go shopping."

Something in his expression changed, darkened. Went back to how it had been before. And she liked it. "Wear red," he said.

She looked him up and down, heat firing in her blood. "Yeah. Maybe."

She swept past him and walked out of the office.

Eduardo was in hell. He was with the hottest woman in the room, in any room on the planet, he was certain, and yet, she was off-limits to him. Because she needed time to think about where things would go between them. Hell, he needed time. They weren't in a position to have a fun, heated affair. They were married. They were going to be parents.

It wasn't that he couldn't touch her. He had to touch her. She was his wife, and they were playing the reconciliation game. He realized that in many ways they were now playing it for life. No one was to suspect they weren't the loving couple they appeared to be. That he slept alone, with a hard-on that wouldn't quit.

Everyone had to see a committed, devoted couple. The press, most especially, had to see a committed, devoted couple.

But with Hannah dressed in a slinky red dress, with only one strap that gathered at her shoulder like a bow and made her look like a particularly tempting present, her curves hugged close and displayed perfectly by the close fit of the gown, the game was torture. And a simple touch wasn't enough.

"That dress makes quite the statement," he said, his eyes on the elegant curve of her neck. She was scanning the room, looking for the most influential people. At least, he imagined that's what she was doing. She had that way about her. Like she was always on alert. Always on show.

"That was the idea. And it matches your tie." She turned to face him, feathering her fingertips over the silk fabric of his necktie.

"I doubt anyone has noticed my tie."

"It's impossible not to notice a hot man in a great suit," she said, blue eyes raking over him, the appreciation in them open and undisguised. "So trust me, you've been noticed."

"To what do I owe the compliment?"

"Just honesty." Her smile widened and she took a step forward, bringing him with her as she intercepted an older man with a date some twenty years his junior.

They made casual conversation with him, Hannah enquiring after the man's grown children, asking him about his business. Eduardo followed her lead and managed to engage both the man and his date, whom he introduced as Laura, in a steady conversation for a few moments before they both moved on.

When they left, he frowned and leaned in to Hannah. "Why didn't he introduce himself?"

Hannah looked at him, her eyes wide. "That was Carlo Caretti."

He knew the name, and worse, he had the sinking feeling he'd met the man. On more than one occasion. In fact, several occasions. "He's placed some very large orders with

Vega for exclusive mobile phones for Caretti International," he said, everything slotting into place.

"Yes. He's a very big client for you. Has been for years."

"I haven't seen him since…"

"I know. It's fine. You covered fine."

He set his glass of champagne down. Hannah wasn't drinking; she couldn't drink. So he shouldn't, either. Which reminded him that he'd forgotten to ask how she felt.

"How are you?"

She waved her hand. "I'm fine."

"Not tired?"

"No. I like parties. Well, parties like this." She laughed. "Sort of over the whole high school undercover kegger."

"Been to a few, have you?"

She tossed him a look. "My former self? Yes. She enjoyed them. They made her forget how sad she was. Hannah Weston? No, she doesn't like them much."

Her admission hit him hard. More aching sadness for the strong, beautiful woman he called his wife. "What about Hannah Vega?"

"I haven't changed my name."

He frowned. "Will you?"

She blinked rapidly. "I…I hadn't really thought about it."

Another couple stopped and chatted with them for a while and thankfully, he'd never met them so he didn't feel stupid when they left. "I really didn't know them, right?" he asked, checking with Hannah.

She shook her head. "I don't think so. If you did, I don't know why, so they can't be that important. Ack, that sounds mean."

"Well, that's how you see things isn't it? In terms of business value."

She frowned. "Generally. I'm not sure I like it."

"I don't mind it."

"I don't see everything that way," she said, and he knew she meant the baby.

"I know you don't."

She bit her lip and nodded slowly. He wrapped his arm tightly around her waist and led her deeper into the opulent ballroom. People were milling around, looking at the artwork on the wall, placing written bids that were much higher than any of the work was worth. But proceeds went to a children's hospital charity and that meant generosity was high, and very few people actually cared what it was they were bidding on.

Hannah stopped in front of a painting of a woman. The woman was on a busy street, in a crowd. She was facing a different direction to everyone else, and there was space around her, while all the other people in the picture nearly blurred together into an indistinguishable mass.

"She's special," he said. She certainly stood out. She reminded him of Hannah. A woman who could never simply blend.

"She looks lonely to me," Hannah said.

He turned to look at her. She was staring at the painting, her attention rapt. "No one is touching her. No one's going with her."

"But she stands out," he said.

"By herself."

He extended his hand and brushed his thumb across her cheek. She turned to face him, eyes wide. "She's not alone."

She blinked. "I…I want to bid on this one." She took a slip of paper from the podium and wrote down a number she hid from him, then dropped the folded white square into the box.

"I think I'll place a bid, too." He got his own slip of paper and wrote his own bid on it. He was certain he would beat her. And then he would give it to her.

"You look confident there, Eduardo."

"I am," he said, dropping his bid into the box. "I think I'll win."

"Do you?"

"I do."

"A wager then."

"A wager?"

"Mmm-hmm. If I win, I get a favor. If you win, you get a favor."

"A favor?"

"A foot rub, a half day at work. Something. Be imaginative."

"I don't know if I'm imaginative."

"I'm sure you can be," she said.

"All right then, I take your bet."

She extended her hand and he shook it, then he leaned down and pressed his lips to her knuckles. Heat shot through him, down to his gut, gripping him tight with fiery fingers.

"Good," she said, her tone light, breathless. "When do they announce the winners?"

He checked his watch and the sign on the podium. "Bidding is closed in five minutes and it looks like they'll take about thirty minutes to announce the winners."

"Then we have some mingling time."

He could have groaned at that, but he kept his mind busy thinking of just what he would ask of her when he got his favor. A kiss maybe. More. The image of her lips on his body, on his shaft, as she'd done the first night they were together haunted him, intoxicated him.

They'd been strictly hands-off for the past week, and for good reason. And it was likely she hadn't intended the favor to be sexual, but damned if he could think of anything else.

He would ask for something else when he won. But for now he would let his mind wander.

The announcement was five minutes late, and in that space of five minutes he was more aware of the time than he'd been in his recent memory.

The man who was orchestrating the evening started reading off the auction winners and directing them to go to the back of the room to write their checks.

"Lot number fourteen goes to Hannah Vega," he said, barely taking a breath before moving on to fifteen.

Hannah shot him a triumphant smile. "I win." She breezed away from him, going to write her check and claim her spoils, he imagined. He followed after her.

"What did you bid?"

"A lot," she said, smiling sweetly.

"Why?"

"I can. I have a lot of money, Eduardo. But you know that."

"I know it, but I didn't know you were the type."

"I very much am. I give a lot to charity. And I really liked the painting."

"It looked like it made you sad."

She shrugged. "I connected with it. I'm going to hang it in our house."

"How much was your bid?" he repeated.

She gave him a figure that made his brows raise. They reached the back table and she dashed off a check and handed it to the woman manning the station.

"Would you like it delivered, Señora Vega?"

Hannah nodded. "I would, thank you." She bent and scribbled his address on a piece of paper. "To this address, please."

Eduardo took his own checkbook out and wrote a check for double what Hannah had bid on the painting. "I would like to add a contribution," he said, setting it on the table.

She lifted a brow but didn't say anything until they walked away. "Big man," she said.

"It's for a good cause, Hannah."

"Yes, but you mainly did it to show me up."

He shrugged. "I don't want people thinking you had to be the one to bid and pay."

"Does it matter?"

"Of course it does. I'm your husband, I'm supposed to take care of you."

She raised a brow and pursed her lips. "Oh, really. Well, all right then. I'm just glad you donated."

"Are you ready to go?"

She nodded. "If you are."

"I was ready to leave before we got here."

She laughed and took hold of his arm, giving little finger waves to everyone they passed by. "Don't look like such a storm cloud."

He forced a smile. "Better?" he asked.

"Much better," she said through her teeth.

They took a car back to his penthouse and she didn't make a mention of her favor the whole ride there. She was uncharacteristically quiet. Hannah was not known for her quiet.

When they got inside she leaned against the door, staring off into space, chewing her bottom lip.

"You must be tired," he said.

"A bit."

"Me, too. I'm going to head to bed. I'll see you in the morning, Hannah." After tonight, with her in that dress, with all of the touching and teasing that had happened at the charity event, it took every ounce of his strength to keep from going and kissing her.

"Wait," she said, just as he turned his back.

"What is it?" He turned to her, his heart pounding heavily.

"You still owe me a favor."

CHAPTER THIRTEEN

HANNAH felt like she was going to shake apart. At least, the shaking seemed to be happening from the inside out. There was small consolation in the fact that when she pushed off from the door and took a step toward him, her limbs didn't tremble.

"You're not getting out of it so easily," she said.

"Granting you your favor?"

She nodded, still not quite sure how she was going to execute the next part of her plan. Not quite sure when it had become her plan. She was hazy on the whole thing. But sometime between putting the huge figure down on her auction sheet and getting in the car with Eduardo, his heat so close to her she felt like she was burning up, she'd decided that her favor was going to involve getting him back into her arms. Back into her bed.

To what end? Oh, that she wasn't sure about.

About the only thing she was sure about was how much she wanted him. And she was ready to act on it.

"First things first, how much did you have to drink tonight?" she asked.

He lifted his chin, one dark brow lifted. "Why?"

"I'm stone-cold sober, a side effect of pregnancy, and I refuse to take advantage of a drunk man."

"I'm as sober as you are."

She nodded. "Excellent." She sounded so calm. Her voice

was odd to her own ears because it simply didn't match the
jittery, fearful excitement that was rolling through her body.
She looked around the penthouse, trying to plan her next
move, trying to figure out what to ask him to do.

She closed her eyes and shook her head. She wasn't planning it. She was just going with what she wanted.

The idea of Eduardo as her personal playground was fairly
enticing. The idea of getting just what she wanted from him.
No-holds-barred access. She was on board with that.

She walked toward him, her heart pounding hard. "Take
off your tie."

He raised his hand to the red knot at the base of his throat
and paused. "Is that the favor? Because I was going to do this
up in my room anyway."

"No. My favor comes in stages."

"Is that allowed?"

She smiled, a flush of warmth suffusing her. "Maybe not.
But I'm up for a little rule breaking. How about you?"

He didn't move and for a moment, she was afraid he would
say that he wasn't in the mood to break any rules. That they
needed to keep things bland and passive and safe between
them.

Then he started working the knot on the tie, the bit of red
silk sliding down the front of his black jacket and pooling on
the floor. He stood, waiting. For another command.

"Jacket," she said.

He obeyed.

"Now your shirt."

She watched, her heart in her throat as he undid the buttons at his cuffs, then worked the buttons at the front of the
shirt, consigning it to the floor, as well. She was happy for
the chance to look at him with the light on, to really take in
the sight of his body. The sculpted, well-defined muscles, his
broad masculine frame.

Just looking at him made her breasts ache, her nipples

tighten. She'd never wanted like this. Never before him, never in the years during their separation. She knew she never would again.

He put his hands on his belt and her eyes fell to the very clear outline of his erection. She sucked in a sharp breath. "Not yet."

He removed his hands. His eyes glittering in challenge. He was enjoying the game, she could tell. But she was also willing to bet he was waiting for the right moment to reverse it.

The thought sparked a flicker of heat low in her belly.

"Go sit on the couch."

He turned and walked toward the couch and she followed, her eyes on his backside.

"Checking me out?" he asked, sitting on the smooth leather couch, draping his arms across the back of it.

"Absolutely. And now I'm trying to decide what to do with you next."

She put her hands behind her back and gripped the tab of her zipper, lowering it slightly. The strap of her dress slipped, dropped so that the top fell dangerously low, draped over her breast, coming close to revealing the gossamer red bra she had beneath it.

Eduardo's face tensed, his hands curling into fists. He didn't move.

She arched and tugged the zipper down farther, letting the dress fall to her waist.

She heard his breath release in a sharp hiss.

"More?" she asked.

"You're the boss," he said, teeth gritted.

She smiled and brought the zipper down the rest of the way, letting the dress slide down her hips and pool at her feet. Showing him her thigh-high stockings and matching lace bra and panty set.

She walked over to the couch and sat next to him, his heat

warming her, the hunger in his gaze erasing any unease she might feel.

She put her hands on his chest and ran her fingertips over his finely sculpted muscles. And she didn't want to play games anymore.

"You're the sexiest man I've ever seen," she said, dipping her head and running her tongue over his nipple. He reached up and forked his fingers through her hair, holding her to him.

She pressed a kiss to his stomach, tight and flat, utter perfection. "I'm the luckiest woman alive, no question."

He laughed hoarsely. "I don't know about that, but I must be the luckiest man."

She put her hands on his belt buckle. "I've been told my mouth gets me into trouble."

"I would love to see that for myself," he said, voice tight.

She smiled and worked at his belt, then the closure of his pants. He helped her pull them off and then he was naked in front of her. She gripped his erection, squeezing, watching his head fall back, reveling in how labored his breathing became.

She leaned in and tasted him, gratified by the harsh sound of pleasure that escaped his lips. She pleasured him that way until he was shaking, until a fine sheen of sweat covered his olive skin.

"Hannah," he said roughly, "not yet, Hannah. Please."

She lifted her head and pressed a kiss to his stomach. "Not yet?"

"Not like that. I thought I owed you the favor?"

She laughed. "I didn't do anything I didn't want." She straightened and leaned in, kissing him on the lips, deep, passionate, pouring everything into it.

When they broke apart, they were both breathing hard. He held her chin between his thumb and forefinger, his dark eyes burning into hers. She felt a response in her chest, a strange tightness that made it hard to breathe. She wanted to cry, and laugh at the same time.

Instead, she kissed him again and he pulled her into his lap, his hands roaming over her curves, mouth and fingers teasing, tormenting, bringing her to the edge and then easing her back, building and retreating, the most perfect torture she could imagine.

She planted her hands on his shoulders, pressing herself tight up against him, his erection teasing her right where she was wet and ready for him.

He pressed a kiss to her collarbone, trailed a line with his tongue down to where the flimsy lace bra met the rounded curve of her breasts.

At the same time, he pushed his finger beneath the lacy edge of her panties and slid the tip of it over her clitoris, the strokes sending white heat through her, ramping up her arousal. She whimpered, tucked her head against his neck, kissing him there.

"I can't wait anymore," she said, her voice shaking. Gone was the control, the steadiness. She didn't have any of it now. She was too filled with her need for him to think, or seem cool. To wait to get the rest of her clothes off, her shoes off.

He tugged her panties to the side and pushed up inside of her. She gasped and arched against him as he filled her. The race to the peak was furious and fast. Eduardo gripped her hips pulling her down onto him as he thrust into her, his movements hard, lacking in finesse, utterly perfect.

She didn't want his control, because she didn't have any. She didn't want evidence of practiced sexual technique. She didn't want anything but him, out of control and just as dizzy with need for her as she was for him. She moved against him, tension drawing tight as a bowstring inside of her until it snapped, releasing her, letting her fall over the edge into bliss, her pleasure washing over her, leaving her spent, consumed in the aftermath.

He thrust up into her one last time, his fingers biting into her flesh, her name a harsh groan on his lips as he found his release.

He rested his head against hers, his breath harsh and hot, fanning over her cheek. Her arms wrapped around his neck, he lifted his hand, pushing her hair, which had come completely unpinned, from her face. His hands were shaking.

She leaned in and rested her head on his shoulder and he held her. While she held him. She never wanted to move. She just wanted to rest with him. She realized that the lights were on, bright and revealing. That she'd just lost her composure in his arms, utterly and completely, and that she wasn't embarrassed at all.

She'd been so afraid of a moment like this. Of being without her trappings. Without her makeup, and sleek hair. Without that suit of armor she kept on at all times. Keeping herself under tight control so that she would never, ever become that wild, stupid girl she'd been when she was growing up.

But she suddenly realized that she wasn't that girl anymore. She'd changed. She wasn't just stomping her down, or covering her up. But she had been holding down the real Hannah Weston. Choking the life out of her because she was so afraid.

So afraid of what? Of being hurt. Of caring.

Of loving.

And now, here she was, with the one man who knew her secrets, caring. Caring so much she felt as if it was pouring from her like blood. But she didn't feel as if it was running out, didn't feel as if it was leaving her weak.

She felt stronger than she had in a long time. Maybe stronger than she ever had. And she wasn't dressed for a business meeting; she wasn't giving someone the steely eye. She was mostly naked, curled up against Eduardo, on the edge of tears.

"Do you need me to move?" she asked, inhaling deeply, the scent of him filling her, making her chest feel like it was expanding.

"No," he said, tightening his hold on her.

"Mmm…good." She kissed his neck again. "I suppose things have the potential to get complicated now. But, on the plus side, the sex between us is very good."

He laughed, shaking beneath her, the low rumble sending a little thrill of pleasure through her. "You could say that."

"That will work, though. This will work."

"Hannah, you think too much. And at the moment, I can't think at all."

"Okay, I'll stop thinking." She shifted to the side and he put his hand on her stomach. She looked down at where his palm was, spread over her pale skin.

They looked up, eyes clashing, her heart squeezed.

"When I look at your face I keep expecting to see the girl I first met five years ago," he said. "In fact, I was counting on it."

"What do you mean?"

"I thought that by bringing you back…I thought if I had you back in my house, in my office, in my life, I might remember what made me blackmail you into marrying me in the first place. The height of my entitlement. An act that so epitomized who I used to be. I thought if I could understand it, feel it again…"

"You were trying to go back," she said.

"Yes. But it didn't work, Hannah. Because I don't see you the same way now. Everything then…everything I was… it was about how it could benefit me. How people could be used to make my life more comfortable. More entertaining. I looked at you and saw a chance to play a game. Now I look and I see you. The real you."

Hannah blinked, trying to stop her eyes from stinging. "I think you're the only one who ever has."

He lifted his hand and looked down at her stomach, a faint frown visible on his face. He traced one faded, white line with the tip of his finger.

"Stretch marks," she said, for once not feeling cagey or weird about the past. "I got them pretty bad with…with him."

"Signs of your strength," he said, his voice rough.

"Or my weakness."

"Never that, Hannah. You are the strongest woman I've ever known. Everyone makes mistakes, but it takes someone truly great to go on and succeed in spite of them."

"I always think I succeeded because of them," she said, voicing a thought she'd never spoken out loud before. "Because getting pregnant the first time forced me to look at myself. To realize I was no better than my parents, who I despised so much. That I was just as irresponsible. That I would repeat the cycle unless I did something to break out of it."

"You did."

She nodded slowly. "Yes." More than that though, she felt like she'd only just really broken out. Yes, she'd gone and gotten an education. And yes, she'd gone and made money. But until this very moment, she doubted that she'd ever really cared for anyone. She doubted she'd ever loved.

She looked up at Eduardo again. She did now. She loved him.

"I…" She found she couldn't speak.

"I think it's time we took this to bed," he said. "And you can lose the shoes." He reached down and disposed of her spiky black heels. "The rest I'll be happy to take care of for you."

He lifted her up and she held on to him tight, unable to take her eyes off him, unable to stop turning over the immense, tender feeling that was spreading from her chest through the rest of her body.

She loved Eduardo. Love was different than she'd imagined.

It was better.

Two weeks passed and every night, Eduardo had Hannah in his bed. Every day, he tried to go to work and concentrate on what he was supposed to do. Sometimes he was more successful than others. He wasn't sure how much of it to blame on his new, unimproved brain and how much to blame on Hannah herself.

She was soft as silk, pale and perfect. The image of her, the thought of how her skin felt beneath his fingertips, seemed to invade his mind constantly. The taste of her, the overwhelming sensation of right when he slid inside of her wet heat.

Even now, as they waited at the exclusive doctor's office, his thoughts were on what was beneath the yellow silk dress she was wearing. Well, his thoughts were bouncing back and forth between that, and the health of their baby.

She was getting things confirmed today and it was enough to have him on edge. The pregnancy had been unintentional, but as they walked into the plush office he felt everything in him seize up and the realization of how important the baby had become to him hit him fully.

The nurse left them in the room and Hannah slipped out of her clothes, tugging a white linen hospital gown on over her body before lying back on the bed.

"Feeling good?" he asked, moving to stand by her head.

"Yeah," she said, her eyes wide. She looked nervous. The sight made his heart wrench up tight. He wasn't used to Hannah being nervous. Lately she'd been…softer. Not in an emotional wreck kind of way, but in a way that made her seem more real. More human. A way that made him want to protect her, shield her from the world. A way that made him want to hold her close and never let her go.

The doctor came in a few moments later and explained the Doppler machine to him before lifting Hannah's hospital gown and squirting a bit of clear gel onto her flat stomach.

"I see this isn't your first pregnancy, Hannah," Dr. Cordoba said.

Hannah shook her head. "No."

"Everything healthy with the last one?"

"Yes," Hannah said, her voice strong. Eduardo wanted to hug her. Kiss her. Tell her how brave she was.

"Good. Very good to know." The woman put the Doppler on Hannah's stomach, moved it lower. It made a kind of strange, white noise sound, changing slightly as she adjusted position.

His eyes were glued to Hannah's, even more specifically, to the little crease between her eyebrows. And then the sound changed to a fast, whooshing sound and the look on her face changed, a smile spreading her lips.

"That's it," she said, reaching for his hand.

He just stood and listened to the sound of his baby's heart filling the room. Listened to it all become real. To every intention of nannies and detachment vanishing, evaporating like smoke.

He felt like he was in a cloud, lost to reality, for the rest of the appointment. Everything was on track. She should come back next month. They'd do a sonogram to get measurements and confirm dates.

They walked out of the doctor's office and back out to the car, and he was thankful that today he'd used a driver. His head was too full to even consider driving at the moment.

He opened Hannah's door for her and settled in beside her. She leaned over and wrapped her arms around him, a sweet smile on her lips. "He's okay," she said. "I'm so glad I...I think part of me was afraid that..."

He wrapped his arm around her, even as fear flooded his chest. "You don't have to be afraid, Hannah."

"I know. Can we...can we stop by a courier's office?"

"Of course, what do you need?"

"I need..." She pulled her purse onto her lap and took a white envelope out, handing it to him. "I want to send this. I... Would you read it?"

He opened up the envelope and took out a handwritten letter. He swallowed hard when he started reading, a lump settling in his throat that stayed with him through the entire letter.

It was to her son. A letter telling him about her circumstances. Telling him that she thought of him. That she hoped he was well. That she loved him.

"It's going to the adoption agency," she said. "That way if he ever wonders about me, he can go look at it but...but if he doesn't...then...I don't want to interrupt his life."

"I think it's perfect, Hannah," he said, his chest feeling tight.

"It's everything I felt like I needed to say. Everything I thought he might want to know. Mostly, I needed him to know that he wasn't unwanted. And that...that he has an extra person in the world who loves him and thinks about him."

He kissed her head. "Two."

"Two?"

"I'll think of him now. Always."

She smiled. "Thank you."

He nodded and brought her close to his body, ignoring the rush of fear that was burning through him. Reading Hannah's letter to a child she barely knew, seeing how much she loved him, even now, made him understand something that he hadn't wanted to understand.

A child would change things. It would change him.

And then there was Hannah. And somewhere, in all of that, was Vega. He was the man who was supposed to take care of all of that.

He closed his eyes and gritted his teeth, fighting hard against the migraine that was threatening to take him over again.

CHAPTER FOURTEEN

"EDUARDO, do you have the quarterly reports in from the retail stores?"

Hannah walked into his office looking every inch the cool businesswoman she was. Different, too. Her face glowed with…happiness.

She was a force of it. He couldn't ignore her, and he didn't want to.

He looked back at his computer screen and closed the window on the internet browser. He'd been looking at colleges. For their son or daughter who was a tiny embryo at that very moment.

He blinked and redirected his focus. "What?"

"The quarterly reports. I need them. Finances. Dollar signs. The thing you pay me for. I just need you to forward them to me. Last week. But unless you have a blue police box capable of time travel, I'll let it go."

"What?"

"Never mind. Do you have the reports or not?"

"I…somewhere. Hold on. They have to be in my in-box somewhere." She was watching him, her blue eyes trained on him. He waited to see impatience, and there was none. She was simply waiting. "Sorry, I'm not right on top of it, Hannah, I know you would be."

She waved a hand. "It's fine. I already did everything else

I had to do today. Anyway, I missed you, so it's nice to come and visit for a while."

She walked over to the desk, her delicate fingers resting on the wood, tracing idly over the designs in the grain. He gritted his teeth and tried to refocus his attention. He swore and slammed his hand down by his keyboard. Hannah jumped.

"I can't find them."

"Do a search."

Of course. He knew that. His mind was moving too slowly, and Hannah was too large in it. He couldn't focus. "Dammit, Hannah, do you mind not hovering?"

She frowned and he could have stabbed his own hand with a pen. "I'm sorry," he said, his voice rough.

"Are you having a hard time? Just let me find it for you."

"It's an email search. I can handle it." He typed in quarterly reports and it brought them up. Suddenly it was like the fog had cleared. He forwarded them to Hannah. "There, you have them now."

"Thank you."

"I'll see you when I'm through here."

She nodded, her lips turned down now. "Okay. See you."

She turned and walked out of his office and he leaned back in his chair, drawing his hand down his face. He was sweating. Why had that been so hard? Why had he forgotten the reports in the first place?

It was the distractions. All the time. All he could think about were Hannah and the baby. And when he wasn't thinking about them, he seemed to want to be thinking about them. So he found excuses to go to Hannah's office, he used Google to look up colleges and real estate listings in the city limits that weren't sky-high penthouses.

He'd thought he could do this. He had to do it. If he didn't, what legacy was there for his son or daughter? It mattered now, even more that he hang on to Vega. It wasn't about personal pride, it was about inheritance. About his child's right to not have their fool of a father destroy what could have been theirs.

Yes, he had a private fortune, but it was much less valuable than what he had here. The potential with Vega Communications was untapped. He knew it could be more. He'd always intended to make it more when his father was running it, and he knew it now. But if he continued to do stupid things like forgetting to forward financial reports, none of it would happen.

Hannah would have to remind him. Hold his hand. She was his wife, and he was meant to care for her. But he wasn't doing his job. He was failing her. He would fail her, continually. Until death did them part. He had tied her to him, to a deficient man, when she was exceptional, brave and bright, brilliant beyond any he'd ever known.

He was sure that when he'd intercepted her on her wedding day she'd wished him to hell a thousand times. But for the first time, he wished himself there.

Eduardo was still tense when they got back to the penthouse. Tense didn't even begin to cover it. She was almost afraid to say anything for fear he would explode. Not that she couldn't handle him. But she was getting the increasingly worrying feeling that he wasn't happy. And that bothered her.

Because she was happy. Going to bed with him every night, waking up with him every morning. It was more than she'd ever imagined marriage to be. What he made her feel when he touched her was divine, but more than that was the connection between them.

She'd been skin to skin with men, boys really, before. She'd had lovers, if they could be called that. But she'd picked up and left them when they were through and felt…nothing. It had frightened her sometimes. When she was with them, she'd gotten the thrill, but it hadn't lingered, and they had never lingered in her mind, and certainly never her heart.

But Eduardo...he felt like he was a part of her. And she knew, knew for a fact, it had nothing to do with carrying his baby. She'd felt no mystical pull to the boy who'd gotten her pregnant the first time. No sense that she had a piece of him with her.

No, Eduardo was utterly unique and so was the connection she felt to him. It was deeper than sex. In fact, it had existed before the sex.

When the door closed behind them, he didn't speak, he just pulled her into his arms. His kiss was rough and demanding, his hands roaming over her curves, tugging at her shirt, her skirt. She pushed his jacket down his arms and onto the floor, devouring his mouth, conducting an exploration of her own.

They left a trail of clothes on their way to his bedroom. His movements were urgent, his mouth hard and hungry.

"There are ways I can care for you that no other man can," he said, his voice rough as he laid her down onto the bed. "There are things I can do." He put his hand down between her thighs and slid his fingers over the damp folds of her flesh. "Things I can make you feel, that no other man can make you feel."

She could only nod as he slid one finger inside of her.

"You want me?" he asked.

She nodded, her breath coming out on a sob. "Of course."

"Say it."

She opened her eyes, met with his intense, dark gaze. "I want you, Eduardo Vega. My husband."

A smile curved his mouth and he lowered his head, sucking hard on her nipple before continuing down, his mouth hot and demanding on her body, making her feel restless, so turned on she couldn't think or breathe.

When his mouth covered the heart of her she couldn't do anything but ride the wave of pleasure that threatened to carry her away.

Eduardo was drowning in her scent, her taste. His body

was on fire, his heart threatening to beat from his chest. He felt her tense beneath him, felt her body tighten as she found her release.

He pressed a kiss to her stomach and put his hand under her bottom, lifting her so that he could enter her in one smooth thrust. She arched against him, a hoarse cry escaping her lips that he captured with his own.

She was so tight and hot around him, her legs pinning him against her body, her small breasts, tight nipples, pressing into his chest. She tightened around his shaft and he just about lost it then and there. But he was going to make her come one more time.

He thrust hard into her and she tightened her hold on him, pressed wet kisses to his neck, whispering in his ear. How sexy he was. How good he felt.

And his blood roared in his ears, all thoughts of control and finesse lost in the rising tide of pleasure and urgency that was flooding him.

His orgasm overtook him like wildfire, impossible to stop, impossible to redirect, consuming everything in its path. He let out a short, sharp sound of pleasure as he spilled himself inside of her and he was aware, dimly, of Hannah shuddering out her own release.

He rested his head on her breasts, waited for his heart rate to return to normal. Waited for thoughts to start trickling through his brain.

All he had now was an intense emotion that seemed to be filling his chest. That seemed to be taking over.

He turned his face, inhaled her scent, let it fill him. She stroked his face, her hands soft, her touch soothing him down deep.

And he realized that no matter how many orgasms he'd given her, no matter how many he gave her over a lifetime, it wasn't proof that he was caring for her. Even now he was starving for her, for what she could give him. To have her arms around him, to have her hold him close.

And when the time came for another migraine, when he was curled up on the floor, unable to see, barely able to breathe, she would be the one who would have to hold him.

He would be a dead weight to her. To all she'd worked for. One more thing to hold Hannah back in life.

He would be damned if he did that to her. Of course, it was entirely possible he already was.

"You look extra broody this morning," Hannah said, walking into the kitchen and seeing Eduardo sitting at the table, his expression dark.

He lifted his cup of coffee to his lips and offered her a bored look.

"That's all you've got for me? At least say something rude," she said, rifling through the fridge for a bottle of milk. She liked that it was only the two of them living in the penthouse. He had staff that came in while they were gone, but otherwise it was just the two of them.

"Hannah, we need to talk."

She straightened then shut the fridge, the milk bottle clutched tightly in her hand. "What about?"

"About this arrangement."

"What about it?" She turned and opened one of the cabinets, reaching for a bowl, ignoring the unease that was making her stomach tighten.

"It's not working."

She dropped the cereal bowl she'd just grasped onto the counter and it clattered loudly against the hard surface, thankfully not shattering. "What?" She grabbed the bowl and stopped it from shivering against the tile. "I mean wh-what about it isn't working? The amazing, soul-shaking sex? The relative harmony in which we live?"

"It's not that. It's… You were right. I'm not doing a good

job of balancing domestic life with Vega and it has to change. It's going to get even harder when the baby's born."

"But…Eduardo…"

"I think it would be best if we kept things as simple as possible. Perhaps…perhaps it would be best if we didn't try to force a marriage between us. I've been looking for houses outside the city, but still close. A place more suitable to raising children. I would be happy to install you there with the child and a nanny. I could stay here during the work week."

"What? That doesn't make any sense, it doesn't… I mean… How can we…be a family if you don't even live with us?"

He stood up, slammed his palm down on the table, his expression thunderous. "I am not the man you should cast in your little sitcom, Hannah. I cannot give you whatever your vision is of what a perfect family should look like."

She gripped the edge of the counter, her heart pounding as she listened to him. Was that what she was doing? Was she trying to project her idea of perfection onto him? To force an idea that possibly wasn't real? Had that been what all of it was? Her trying to build a new fantasy?

The sharp pain in her heart told her no. That her feelings were real.

"You think you know the way the world works, Hannah," he continued, his voice a low growl. "You named yourself after a retail store because you thought it was fancy. You think black-and-white television shows are an example of how real life should work. That we can put a picket fence around the yard and get a dog and you can have all the things you've always fantasized about. You play so sophisticated, but in so many ways you're naive. A little girl playing dress-up."

"Is that what you think?" she said, her voice soft, anger rising up inside of her. Unreasonable, and unstoppable. And with it, pain, pain that she felt down so deep she wasn't sure she would ever find the bottom of it. "I'm going to let you have it now, Eduardo Vega, but this isn't just me spouting pithy one-liners to keep you from getting close. This is me being honest. I gave myself to you, and that wasn't pretend. That wasn't something I didn't understand, and you damn well gave yourself to me. So, now what? You're scared? You're freaked out because you forgot to hit Send on an email and now you're letting it get in your head."

"That's not all," he said, his voice fierce. "You know how bad it gets. You've seen."

"Yes, you had a migraine. A horrible one. You have them... I get it. But if I can handle it, then it's not up to you to say that I can't. You're making up excuses, and blaming things, blaming me, blaming you, for the fact that you're just scared because whatever this is between us...it's big. And you're scared of it."

"I'm going to get ready for work now, Hannah. You can call my driver and he'll take you later."

"Are you running?" she asked.

He whirled around to face her, his expression dark, dangerous. "I'm not running. I'm being reasonable. What did you think this would be?" he asked, his voice raw. "You're right. I can barely concentrate on the duties I already have. I don't have it in me, not the energy or the desire to be a husband to you. I can't...I can't take care of you."

Pain washed through Hannah, acute and sharp. "You don't...want to be my husband?"

"No, Hannah," he said, something in his tone jagged. Torn. "Okay."

"What?"

She shook her head. "Fine. Okay. Then I don't want you to be my husband. I'm not going to force it. It's funny...I was ready to marry Zack even though...even though he didn't know me. He didn't even especially want me. I mean...we weren't really lighting things on fire with our passion, you know? But that was okay with him. It's not okay with you and I only just realized that."

"What do you mean?"

"I won't be a duty to you. I want you to divorce me. And you be the best father you can be for our child. But I'm not going to be that wife you have to keep because you feel some sense of duty."

"All or nothing then."

"Yes." It broke her to say it, because there was a piece of her, that girl who was searching for permanent, for stable, who wanted desperately to cling to whatever he could give. Who wanted to marry the facade and forget the rest.

But the new Hannah, the one Eduardo had brought out, uncovered after so many years, she wanted more. She wanted it all. Not just duty, but love. Real love, not just a few hours of mindless pleasure every night. She wanted to share more than his bed. She wanted to share his heart. His life.

"Then it has to be nothing."

He turned and walked out of the room and she stood, watching the spot where he'd been, adjusting to him not being there.

When he got home from work, Hannah was gone. Not just gone for the moment, but gone. Her things were gone. The sweet sense of comfort he felt when he came home now was gone with her.

His head wasn't clearer. It pounded. Ached. Along with his entire body.

But then, he'd known that would be the case. Everything he'd said to her was utter bull. He went to his bar and poured himself a shot of tequila. Perfect for doling out the punishment he so richly deserved. If he imbibed enough tonight he wouldn't be able to move in the morning. Maybe it would even trigger another migraine. All the better. It would cover up the real reason he was curled up on the floor writhing in pain.

He carried the glass into his room with him and slammed it on his bedside table.

He'd blamed her. He'd told her she didn't know what she was getting into, and it was true. That he couldn't be everything for her, and that was true, too.

But he'd lied when he'd said he didn't want to be her husband.

He did. More than anything, he wanted to be by her side all of his life. But how could he do that when he wasn't everything a husband should be? His father had been so strong and capable; he'd cared for them all. He'd made sure his mother was beneath his protection, always. And he, Eduardo, was so...so weak.

He had feet of clay and he feared one day they would crumble beneath him.

He lay down in his bed and put his hand over his eyes, trying to dull the ache in his chest, trying to staunch the sudden flood of emotions that was washing through him like an endless river of pain.

Yes, he would have his child. He was thankful for that. He would be the best father he could be. But he wouldn't force Hannah to be with him. She would thank him later.

Dios, but he wanted her. If only this could somehow be enough. If only caring for her would make him worthy of her. After all she'd been through, the disgusting living conditions and neglect...

She deserved more. A champion. For someone to come in and make her life easier, not harder. She deserved a man who could be a strong father to their child. A man who could be a capable husband. A strong businessman who didn't make mistakes.

He wanted to howl at the irony. He'd had it. Back when he'd first married her, he'd had that capability. To be the man she deserved. And he hadn't cared. He hadn't tried. And now he was hampered, hampered by an altered mind, and now that he cared desperately about being everything for her, about loving her as she deserved, he couldn't.

He reached out and fumbled for his tequila but couldn't quite grasp the glass. He shoved it off the nightstand and lay back, embracing the pounding migraine that was starting behind his eyes and stabbing deeper with each passing moment.

He focused on it. Reveled in it.

Because it took the edge off the unendurable pain in his heart.

CHAPTER FIFTEEN

AFTER spending the day locked in his penthouse, he'd called his driver and made plans to go to the ranch the next day. He wasn't in the right frame of mind to drive up to the house. His head was pounding and he felt slow and thick.

Then he'd called around and found out Hannah was staying at a luxury hotel. He hoped they had sheets with a suitable thread count.

The thought made his eyes sting.

They would work it out to the point where they would see each other. He would buy her a house, get everything set for the baby. That would be worse in some ways. Seeing her, being so close, and not being able to have her.

Because of his own weakness. His own fault.

He wanted to peel his head open and pull his brain out. Fix it, get a new one. He hated it. Hated the feeling that he was trapped. Limited.

Hated being without her even more than that, because he felt like he was missing something of himself.

Because something had changed since Hannah had come back into his life. He didn't want to be the man he'd been anymore. That man had been a fool. Arrogant. Selfish. He no longer missed him, no longer wished he could be him.

An empty realization since the man he was now couldn't give her what she needed, either.

He exited the penthouse and got into the black town car

that was idling against the curb. He rested his head against the back of the seat and concentrated on the pounding in his head.

The car pulled away from the street and out into the flow of traffic. It didn't take long to get out of the city and he felt the pain in his head lessen, even as the one in his chest got worse.

He looked up for the first time, his eyes clashing with the blue eyes of the driver, reflected by the rearview mirror.

"Have I been kidnapped?" he asked, his voice sounding hollow, shocked, even to his own ears.

"*Kidnapped* is a harsh word," she said. "I prefer to think of it as being commandeered."

"Is it any different?"

"A bit."

His stomach tightened down. "What is it you want, *querida?*"

"Me? A fair hearing. You don't just get to decide how things are going to be. Or did you not get the memo that marriage is a partnership?"

"I believe I decided we wouldn't have a marriage."

"Yes, well, I don't agree. And if I recall, when I tried to marry someone else, you very much didn't agree, either. You told me we were married and that was my tough luck. So guess what, Eduardo? We're married. Tough luck. That means we talk this through and you don't just mandate."

"What did you do with my driver?" he asked.

"I paid him off. I'm very wealthy, you know. And persuasive."

"Hannah…"

"Back to the subject at hand, though." She maneuvered the car off the rural road, into a little alcove and put it in Park, killing the engine.

She unbuckled and got out, coming around to his side of the car and opening the door.

"As I was saying, you don't get to make all of the decisions in this relationship. I want some say, too." She lowered herself to her knees in front of him. "I'm really hard to live with sometimes. I'm stubborn, and I can be materialistic, and selfish. Until recently I was afraid to care for anyone, afraid to feel anything, because I couldn't control feelings. But not anymore. And it's because of you that I'm not afraid now."

His mouth dried. "How did I…how did I make you not afraid?"

"Because you have accepted me. No matter where I was at. No matter what I said. You didn't let me push you away. You didn't make me feel ashamed for what I'd done, for my fears. You were just…there. No one, not in my whole life, has ever simply accepted me. Has ever stood by and supported me. But you have. You've done that."

"But…Hannah…I can't…I can't take care of you. I can't be everything that a husband should be to you. I'm… I make mistakes."

"Yeah, so do I. Remember the fraud?"

"You did what you had to do."

"I'm not perfect. And neither are you, but that's okay. I love you, Eduardo. And when everything else in this world fails, that's what will remain. It's what will matter."

He lowered his head, pain seizing his chest. "You can't love me."

"Let me tell you something, Señor Vega. I try to control and reason everything so that it fits my idea of perfection. From my sheets to my name, I try to make it all my vision for what life should be. I can't do that with you. You aren't reasonable or controllable or perfect. You're better than that. You're you. And it's those little imperfect bits of you that make you the man I want. I don't need to be taken care of…I just need a partner. And I want you to be him."

He unbuckled his seat belt and pulled Hannah into the car, onto his lap, holding her close. "Hannah, I want so much to… I want to be your champion. To make everything easier for you. I don't want to be a burden."

"Do you want to know something? When I saw you having your migraine…when I held you against me…that was when I realized that I could be a mother. Not because I feel even remotely maternal about you, but because I realized that loving someone, being surrounded by the person you love, was so much more important than status. Than things. I've spent all of my life trying to fill this emptiness in me. I tried to do it by just giving in to whatever I wanted anytime I wanted it. Then I tried to do it by controlling myself. Controlling everything I did. I filled the void with things. With a penthouse with a view. But the satisfaction didn't last. It wasn't real. The one thing I've never had is love. And you've given it to me. You've shown me not just how it feels to be loved, but how beautiful it is to love. Eduardo, loving you could never be a burden." She pressed a kiss to his lips. "I wish you could feel it."

"What?" he asked, his voice rough.

"I wish you could feel what I feel. I feel like my heart was trapped in a cage. I wouldn't let myself have emotions. I wouldn't let myself care for anyone too deeply, wouldn't let myself have friends. I was strangling my heart, suffocating it. And you set it free." He looked at her eyes, pale and filled with tears, so sincere. "I'm free."

Something broke open inside of him. A stone wall that had been wrapped tightly around him. And he felt it, too. Felt like he'd walked out of a prison cell and into the sunlight for the first time in years. She'd spoken of that feeling once, and he felt it now. So real, so intense.

His heart thundered, his hands shaking as he stroked her hair. "Hannah…I… You love me?"

"Yes."

"Me. This me. Not the me that I was?"

"Eduardo, this man, the one you are right now, is the man I fell for. You're the one who changed me."

A wave of relief, so strong, so powerful, washed over him. "You want me like this?"

"Yes. Just like this. I don't think you're diminished, or wrong, in any way. You're just you."

He closed his eyes and rested his forehead against hers, his headache fading. "With you, Hannah, I imagine maybe I can just be me. The me I am now. I was…as afraid as you were of changing back into who you used to be, I was afraid I never would. But I think we were both being stupid."

"Do you?"

He nodded. "Like our past was a destination we could so easily get to. Like it was one I might want to get to. I thought that by bringing you back, by seeing your face, I would see the past. But now when I look at you I only see my future. I love you, Hannah."

She smiled, real, happy. "You mean, you really do want to be my husband?"

"Forever. I was just…too afraid. Of failing you. Of failing our child. I want to give you everything, and I'm afraid that I'm so much less than what you deserve. But I don't despise the man I am now… I don't want to go back. How can I when you love me? When you'll be in my future?" He took her chin between his thumb and forefinger.

"I will be," she whispered. "I promise."

"Sometimes I'll have headaches. I'll forget things. I'll make mistakes. But one thing I promise never to forget is how much I love you."

Hannah smiled, her blue eyes filled with joy. "I won't be perfect, either, but I will be myself. I will be committed fully to you."

"I promise the same."

Hannah looked around them, at the mountains, at the car, at him, and she laughed. "It's like making marriage vows all over again."

"Only these are very real," he said.

She nodded. "From my heart, I promise, Eduardo. I'll love you always. You know…no one has ever loved me before. But you were worth the wait."

His chest expanded, his heart overflowing with emotion, with love. "Never doubt that I love you. I do. More than anything. And our children will love you. Our lives will be filled with it."

"I want that, very much."

"And you will have it, my love." He leaned in and kissed her forehead. "I never imagined I could deserve such a strong, beautiful woman as my wife."

"Some might say we deserve each other, Eduardo," she said, a wicked little smile curving her lips.

"True."

"And it's a good thing we're both strong."

"Why is that?"

She pressed a kiss to his lips. "So we can take care of each other."

EPILOGUE

HANNAH looked up at the picture that had hung in their bedroom for the past ten years. When she'd first seen it, she'd thought the woman standing in the crowd looked alone. For some reason, she didn't think so now.

Maybe because she never felt alone. Just as Eduardo had promised, her life was filled with love now.

She looked down at the nightstand and opened up the drawer, and looked down at the letter that was there, a blue ribbon wrapped around the outside. The letter from Benjamin Johnson, who was now eighteen and headed off to college. The letter that thanked her. For giving him life. For giving him his family. She smiled down at the paper, her heart swelling with love, and slid the drawer closed.

"Mama!"

She heard screaming and shouting and a scuffle, then Eduardo's deep voice scolding in Spanish and four sets of little feet running, then a door slamming. She laughed and turned away from the painting just as her husband came into the room.

"Everything well with the troops?"

"Graciela had Juanita's doll. And the boys were simply choosing sides to create a scene," he said. "I sent them out. It's a nice day."

She turned to him, leaned against his solid strength. "I need your quarterly report," she said.

He dipped his head and kissed her on the nose. "I already sent it to you."

She smiled up at her husband, the father of her children, her business partner. "Well, now I have no reason to punish you."

His eyebrows arched. "You sound disappointed."

"I am."

"Thank you," he said.

"For what?"

He wrapped his arms around Hannah and she rested her head on his chest. "For being my partner."

She went up on her toes and pressed a kiss to his neck. "Always."

* * * * *

FORTUNE'S SECRET HUSBAND

KAREN ROSE SMITH

To my grade school friend Liz, who married young, too. We made it! Thanks for being my friend.

Chapter One

Lucie Fortune Chesterfield was late!

It was her own fault. She'd forgotten her phone and had to run back to the Austin, Texas, apartment she was subletting to retrieve it. In a rush now on her way out again, after disembarking from the elevator in the lobby, she stopped cold.

Was she seeing things? Was that Chase Parker leaving the building? Not possible. Just because he still invaded her dreams—

The doorman stood at his counter and she ran to him and pointed to the departing tall, broad-shouldered man whose Stetson was tilted at an angle she thought she recognized.

The doorman did a double take. "Lady Lucie, I thought you'd left."

Irving hadn't been at his station when she'd rushed

back in for her phone. "I forgot something and had to return to my apartment. Do you know who that man is?"

Lucie was very used to doormen and chauffeurs and pomp and circumstance. Born in England and living on the Chesterfield Estate, she was considered "almost" royalty. Her mother's adopted father had been an earl. Her own father had been knighted. In England and the United States, her family was sometimes hounded and followed by paparazzi searching for that money shot. After the scandal her sister had become involved in, Lucie was more than aware of her actions and couldn't just run into the street chasing a tall Texan who resembled a ghost from her foolish past, a ghost so secret not even her family had known all the details about her association with him.

Irving, in his fifties and balding, turned red to his scalp as he reached out to the shelf under the counter and retrieved a business card.

"I'm so sorry, Lady Lucie. I saw you the first time and assumed you'd left for the morning."

She'd been following a routine. Each morning after breakfast, she'd been scouting out properties for an office for the Fortune Foundation, which was planning to open a branch in Austin.

Irv, as he preferred to be called, went on to explain further as he handed her the business card. "The gentleman gave me this and said he'd be back later."

Lucie read the card aloud in a low tone. "Chase Parker—" There were two numbers listed.

At the idea of Chase being in close proximity, she felt a tremble race through her. At seventeen, she'd been on a youth trip to Scotland. And then…

She had to forget about Chase Parker, ghost or not,

and concentrate on this trip to visit her relatives in Texas. She had agreed to help the Fortune Foundation set up a branch in Austin for the benefit of children there.

"What do you want me to do if he comes back again?" Irv asked.

She fingered the card in her hand. What did Chase want with her now? He obviously knew she was here. Why hadn't he called first? Should *she* phone *him*?

No. He'd forgotten about her easily. The past was in the past. If he had a reason to see her, she'd find out soon enough what that was.

Answering Irv's question, she said, "If I'm in, buzz me just as you do with everyone else."

"As you say, Lady Lucie. There is one other thing—"

She really had to be going, but Irv looked worried about something, so she waited.

"That reporter's been out there again from the news station. I saw him yesterday afternoon, but he was gone until you got back."

"As long as he stays outside, there's really nothing we can do about him."

"I don't want him accosting you as you leave," Irv maintained, "or as you return. You know, we can always arrange for your driver to pick you up in the garage instead of at the front entrance."

"He'd soon catch on to that because he knows I'm usually out and about. I'll deal with him if I have to, Irv. Please, don't worry about me."

"But I do," Irv said with a boyish smile. "Somebody has to. With your relatives living in Horseback Hollow, you need somebody to worry about you here."

Everyone thought they knew her family's history—from the articles in the tabloids and in the more respectable media. Irv was right, though. Her relatives were in Horseback Hollow about five hours away.

"I have friends here, too. In fact, I'm supposed to be meeting them for brunch. So I really need to be going. Barry is waiting to drive me. You have a good day."

"You, too, m'lady."

The temperature in Austin, Texas, in March was around sixty during the day and went to a low of forty at night. Lucie had chosen a grass-green suit for this brunch, a professional look, since she would be visiting office spaces with a real estate agent afterward. The three-quarter-length sleeves of her jacket were perfect for the weather.

As she pushed her straight brown hair over her shoulder and stepped from the car, she checked the sky. All blue, not a cloud in sight.

Thanking Barry, telling him she'd text him when she finished brunch, she headed for the restaurant that her friends had chosen for this get-together. It was a bit of an elite location. Cavette's catered to a crowd that didn't have to worry what they spent on brunch, lunch or a late dinner. No paparazzi were allowed inside, and there was a security guard stationed in the restaurant who would react quickly if he had to. Celebrities in the area who often stopped in at Cavette's were assured of their privacy and a backdoor exit should they need it.

The restaurant was tastefully decorated with lots of real greenery. Lucie stopped briefly at the hostess's desk but spotted her friends at a table against the wall. Ella Thomas had recently returned from her honeymoon with Ben Fortune Robinson. Vivian Blair was engaged to Ben's twin brother, Wes. Ella spotted Lucie first.

Ella was a beauty with thick, long, wavy auburn hair

and blue-blue eyes. Lucie respected her. She wore minimal makeup and preferred to be admired for her brains rather than her body. She'd dressed today as she usually did, in dress jeans, a Western-cut blouse and expensive boots. In contrast, Vivian was taller than Ella with hazel eyes and honey-streaked brown hair that she wore pulled back today. She also wore glasses—very stylish ones. A computer programmer, she'd dressed in a navy pantsuit with a red blouse. She was shyer than Ella but smart and fun. Lucie liked both of these women immensely and was glad to call them friends. As she took a seat with them, she noticed they'd already ordered her a mimosa.

"You don't have to drive this morning," Ella counseled her. "Let loose. Champagne and orange juice are a good way to start your day."

Lucie laughed. "I can't let too loose. I want to choose the right office space for the Fortune Foundation. It has to be utilitarian, but classy, too, with just the right square footage to fit what they want to do."

"And what is that?" Vivian asked after a quick hug.

"What I'm looking for would mostly be a functional space. If we have programs for kids, they would probably be at other sites."

"Or maybe at a community center?" Ella offered. "I can see the Fortunes building one of those."

"Just how long are you going to be in Austin?" Vivian asked.

"I'm free until April, when I fly to Guatemala with my mother to start a project there."

"How do you like living in Austin? I know your sister likes living in Horseback Hollow."

Lucie took the napkin from her plate and spread it onto her lap. "Amelia loves Horseback Hollow. But truth be told, I prefer Austin. It's more metropolitan than Horseback Hollow."

Vivian and Ella both exchanged a look. "You won't get any arguments there," Vivian said. "In Horseback Hollow, everybody knows everybody's business."

"And in Austin," Vivian supplied, "they just know Lady Lucie Fortune Chesterfield's business. Any reporters lately?"

"Irv says one's been hanging around, but I haven't run into him face-to-face yet." She took a sip of her mimosa. "You both look good," Lucie said to them, narrowing her eyes. "Are you happy?"

Ella sighed. "I couldn't be happier."

"Me either," Viv agreed. "And not only with Wes. We think the app I developed, My Perfect Match, is going to continue to be a huge hit. I mean, after all, it brought me and Wes together, though not exactly in the way I intended."

Although she was listening to Viv, Lucie couldn't help letting her mind wander again to Chase leaving his card with Irv. "Just when you think you have life planned out, fate shoves it in another direction."

"Exactly," Viv responded. "And I'm trying to think of a way to balance My Perfect Match. Tell me something, Lucie. Do you think it's better to hook up with someone you know you're compatible with, or should you hook up with someone who sets your heart on fire?"

Wasn't that a question for the test of time? Because of her own experience, Lucie responded sadly, "Flames die down. Compatibility might be better long-term."

"That sounds like experience to me." Ella motioned to Lucie's mimosa. "Come on and drink that, and tell us who taught you about flames."

Lucie had slipped Chase's card into her jacket pocket. Now she touched it, and when she did, she remembered all too vividly the touch of his hands. Her cheeks grew warm, and she blamed that on the mimosa. What could it hurt to talk about it a little? "Come on," Viv coaxed. "You know all about *our* love affairs."

"What was his name?" Ella prompted.

"His name was Chase."

"Now, that's a good Texas name if I ever heard one," Viv noted. "But he couldn't have been a Texan if you were living in England."

"Oh, but he *was* a Texan. His father owned an oil company and they were wealthy. I was seventeen when we met in England at the start of the trip to Scotland. Chase was a group leader. I thought it was love at first sight, but I guess it was just lust at first sight. We got caught together in the hostel room. So much about it was against the rules. A leader consorting with one of the tourists, being in his room alone together, both of us undressed..." She trailed off. "Chase got fired, and I was sent home." At least that was the gist of the story.

Contrite, feeling disgraced in the eyes of her parents, Lucie had vowed to herself to never do anything so reckless again. She'd maintained that vow by pouring all of her energy into setting up orphanages with her mother in developing countries. Their lives were about helping needy children.

"You never saw or heard from him again?"

"I received a letter. I wrote him many, but I never heard from him after that first one."

"You didn't call him?"

"Not what a proper lady would do," Lucie answered

almost teasingly, though there had been other reasons not to call, too.

Should she tell them about Chase dropping off his card at her apartment? No. He might not even come back. She was sure nothing would come of it.

Lucie had learned early on the best way to turn attention away from herself was to listen to another's story, and she knew these women had stories to tell. Ella's husband, Ben, had recently found out he was a Fortune and that his father, whom he'd always known as Gerald Robinson, was really Jerome Fortune, who had disappeared years ago. Ben was now on a quest to locate other relatives. The Robinsons might be Fortune cousins.

"Has Ben gotten any further in proving that his father is really Jerome Fortune?"

"His father is thwarting him at every turn," Ella said with a frown. "His sister, Rachel, who uncovered the connection and confronted their dad, is sure their father is hiding something. Ben wants the truth. He has seven siblings who want to know about their roots, whether his father wants to deny the past or not. Thanks to you, he located Keaton Whitfield, who's his half sibling."

In one of those quirks of fate, Lucie had already known Keaton, an architect in London. He'd designed a house for one of her mother's friends, and he and Lucie had run into each other at a few parties. He was what the Americans would call a stand-up guy. When Ben had asked for an introduction to him, she'd readily complied.

"Hasn't he located anyone else who might be related?" Lucie asked. Apparently Ben's father had had several affairs.

"Right now he's on the trail of Jacqueline Fortune,

who may or may not be his paternal grandmother," Ella revealed.

"This is a mystery unraveling before our eyes," Viv said with enthusiasm. "I can't wait for the next installment."

Brunch was full of more Fortune stories, including the party Kate Fortune had planned for her ninetieth birthday. Lucie, Viv and Ella kept their voices low because Kate Fortune's residence at the Silver Spur Ranch near Austin was still a secret, except to the Fortune family. In the past, Kate had been the target of blackmail and kidnapping attempts. Now, looking for an heir for her company and not wanting media attention about it, she intended to keep her presence in Austin quiet.

When Lucie checked her watch, she saw the day was moving ahead without her, and she really had to get on with looking at properties. After goodbyes to Viv and Ella, she called the real estate agent who was advising her. They agreed to meet at the first location on Lucie's list and then tour the others together afterward.

By late afternoon, while Lucie sat in the car on her way back to her apartment, she was quite discouraged. None of the spaces had seemed quite right. She was becoming more and more sure that she might also have to help find satellite locations for the actual kids' programs themselves—summer lunches, music, art, sports. Building a community center might be a possibility, unless the foundation could find already established and deserving programs to fund.

Barry pulled up in front of her apartment building. She was tired and all she wanted to do was soak in her tub. After she climbed from the car, Irv came to meet her at the curb. That was unusual, since the doors had an electric sensor.

He said quickly, "Just in case you wanted to get back in your car and go in the other direction, I wanted to warn you, the man who was here this morning is waiting at my desk."

Lucie stood at the curb and peered through the glass doors into the lobby. Her heart began to beat in triple time. The man at Irv's desk *was* Chase Parker. She couldn't tell exactly how much he'd changed from when he was twenty-one. After all, he'd be thirty-one now. But she could tell he was still as tall and straight-shouldered. The Western-cut jacket he wore fit him impeccably, his black jeans and boots just as much so.

He turned toward her now, and that tilt of his Stetson told her some of the young man still remained.

"It's fine, Irv. Apparently he has some business with me, and I have to see what that is."

She squared her shoulders, forgot her fatigue and started forward to meet her past head-on.

Lucie walked through the glass doors and approached Chase, thinking his dark hair was still the color of the finest imported chocolate. His dark brown eyes seemed to take in everything about her all at once. Even in that wonderfully cut jacket, she could tell he was more muscular than he'd been at twenty-one but not too bulked up. He was long and lean and still looked like everything good about Texas.

Before Lucie took another step toward the unknown, she turned to Irv who'd come in behind her. "Not a word of this meeting to anyone, not anyone." After all, Irv knew Chase's name from the business card. If the press associated their names, if reporters started digging, a new scandal could erupt.

"Not a word, Lady Lucie. You know you can count on me."

"Thank you, Irv. You don't know how much I appreciate that. Was that reporter around here at all today?"

"I didn't see him…or the news van."

She nodded and stepped up to Chase. She felt as if all her composure had slipped away, though she knew that was crazy. After all, she'd practiced that her entire life.

With that stiff upper lip Brits were accused of having, she said simply, "Chase?"

"You've grown up." His gaze traveled over her suit, seemed to linger on her tiny waist, then idled on her long, straight brown hair. She wondered if he could see all the questions in her hazel eyes. She wondered if he had any idea of what seeing him again did to her—increased her heart rate and brought back vivid pictures of the two of them together, but, most of all, squeezed her heart until it hurt.

He nodded to the corner beside the elevators that was away from the doors, Irv's counter and everyone else for the time being. She walked with him and stood beside a potted palm.

Before she could ask a question, he inquired, "Do you know how hard it is to track you down, even though you and your family and your stories are spread across the tabloids?"

Lucie was flummoxed. So he'd kept up with articles in the tabloids as if they were true.

He went on. "I thought you were in London. Then I found out you were in Horseback Hollow. After consulting a PI, I learned you were here in Austin, where my father's company is located. If you only knew how much time I wasted—"

After all these years, he was acting as if seeing her was an emergency. "My life is full of people and activities, as I imagine yours is."

"I don't globe-trot. I was beginning to have visions of my traveling to some developing country to see you."

"Would that have been so bad?" she asked, sensing his agitation but still not understanding any of it.

He took off his Stetson, ran his hand through his thick hair and shook his head. "None of that came out right. I read the stories about your work with orphans and refugees. I know you and your mother are selfless in your cause. But I had to find you."

"Why such urgency?"

"Because…" he started. He leaned close and lowered his voice to a whisper. "We're still married."

Chapter Two

Chase felt as if he'd been kicked in the gut. Lucie Fortune Chesterfield was even more beautiful now than she'd been at seventeen. That glossy, dark-brown hair and those expressive hazel eyes… He remembered the dimple that only appeared when she smiled, but she wasn't smiling now. She looked worried and upset and very pale.

She confirmed some of his conclusion when she warned him, "Come up to my apartment so no one overhears us or sees us."

She was obviously worried about information getting into the wrong hands. He knew the paparazzi hounded her family. Put an earl in your background, or a sir, as in Sir Simon Chesterfield, her father, and the press thought the whole world wanted to read about you. Maybe they did.

Lucie pressed the elevator button with an impatient finger as she snuck a glance at him. He wanted to smile at her, but he had a feeling this was no smiling matter.

"We'll get it worked out," he said in a low voice.

Chase had been twenty-one and a group leader when he and Lucie had secretly married in Scotland. There, at seventeen, Lucie hadn't needed permission. However, another member of her tour group had caught them disrobed in Chase's hostel room and reported them. Chase's father had swooped in with a lawyer and confidentiality agreements with promises of an annulment. Everyone had been sworn to secrecy.

When the elevator doors swished open, Lucie didn't respond. Maybe she was so upset because of her sister's recent scandal. He'd read the tabloids about Amelia's status as a run-away fiancée and that she'd become pregnant from a cowboy lover. That had probably made Lucie even more skittish of public opinion. The tabloids ran with stories that weren't even true. He knew that. Though he *had* followed Lucie's engagement a few years ago with interest, and couldn't help being irrationally relieved when it had come to naught.

When Chase's elbow brushed hers, Lucie stepped away. He found himself taking a step closer. He was stabbed by the same desire for her now that he'd felt at twenty-one. Yet he was sure she must hate or resent him because of the way they'd been broken up...because of the way his father had handled it. After all, she'd never answered his letters.

When they stepped off the elevator, Lucie motioned to the left. Chase noted there were two apartments on the floor. "I'm surprised you don't have a penthouse. Then you wouldn't have to worry about nosy neighbors."

"I don't have to worry about nosy neighbors." She took her keys from her purse and unlocked her apartment door. "The other apartment is rented by a businessman who travels a lot. He's in Hong Kong right now for the month while I'm here. So I basically have the floor alone. Win-win all around."

She'd made her voice light and airy, but he had a feeling nothing was light and airy. There was a note of anxiety beneath her words.

After she unlocked the door and he stepped inside the apartment's foyer, he gave a quick glance around. "This doesn't look like you," he said automatically.

She gave him an odd look. "How do you know? You've had nothing to do with me for ten years."

That sounded like an accusation, but he didn't stop to wonder about it. The apartment was decorated in chrome and glass, black and white. There was a row of flowered throw pillows on the sofa and he wondered if Lucie had added those.

"You weren't chrome and glass at seventeen, and I doubt very much if you are now."

"I'm only going to be here a month, Chase. The sublet was furnished. Now tell me, why are we still married?" She went over to the sofa and sank down on it, motioning for him to do the same.

He rounded the long, glass-topped coffee table and lowered himself beside her, careful not to let any parts of their bodies touch. He didn't know why, but it just seemed to be the wise thing. Discarding that sentimental thought, he gazed into her eyes and wisdom seemed to fly out the window. This was Lucie, the girl who had stolen his heart. But then he snapped his thinking back to what it should be. She was a public figure now and here only for a month.

He explained quickly, "I applied for a business loan

separate from my father's company. It has nothing to do with him."

He saw the remembrance pass through her eyes that he'd once told her he'd never work for his father and never be anything like him. Circumstances had changed that, but now they were going to change again.

"After I filled out all the paperwork at the bank," he went on, "the loan officer called me to tell me I needed my wife's signature before they could put the payment through. I couldn't believe what I was hearing. My parents said our marriage was annulled. But then I did research of my own and discovered it is still on the books. I wanted to tell you in person in case the information leaked out and somehow made the tabloids. I know how much your family has been hounded by the media."

Lucie looked even paler. In fact, she looked ill, as if she might faint.

"Are you all right? Can I get you something? I don't want you to pass out."

She straightened her shoulders and tossed her hair back. "I've never passed out in my life, though this might be a good time."

Apparently she still had a sense of humor. Right now, though, he didn't think it made either of them feel better.

"Did you see the media storm my sister went through?" she asked.

Chase nodded. "I did. And I don't want us to experience anything like it. That's why I'm here. To tell the truth, I'd never be caught dead shirtless outside my house with a shotgun aimed at reporters like Quinn Drummond."

Quinn was Amelia's husband, a cowboy commoner in the eyes of everyone but Amelia and now her family.

"He was driven to it," Lucie protested. "You can't imagine what it's like living in a fishbowl with every decision or faux pas analyzed to death by the media."

Chase felt disgruntled at her assessment. Maybe he really didn't know what it was like. "I understand your concerns. My parents and I can't understand what happened with the annulment. My father maintains that he had the marriage dissolved. It must have been a snafu in the paperwork. He and I have spoken with our family's lawyer, as well as an international attorney. We're going to settle this as soon as possible. If I have to, I'll get a whole law firm on it."

Lucie wasn't looking at him but rather at the wall. She seemed to be in a daze. Maybe he should stay a little while. On the other hand, maybe he should go quickly. He handed her another business card.

She started. "I have your card."

But he shook his head. "You have my personal one. This is the ranch card. Note the address for the Bar P. It's about a half hour from here."

"You live on your parents' ranch?"

"I live in the guesthouse. That's going to change soon."

"And you work for your father?" There was surprise in her voice. He'd been right. She did remember.

"For now, but that too will be changing. It's a long story. You have all my numbers. If you want to talk anytime, just call me."

She studied the card and kept studying it as if she was thinking about him working at Parker Oil, as if she might be thinking about all the things that might have been.

He stood, believing she needed time to absorb the news. He had started to cross for the door when Lucie suddenly popped up from the sofa and rushed to him. She took his arm. The feel of those fingers of hers, even through his suit jacket, made his body respond.

He could tell she was a proper lady now when she said, "I'm sorry for my reaction. The shock of the news of being married to you really upset me. You must be just as upset."

"I'm not upset. I'm just concerned about what it means for you, too. When I couldn't find you, I panicked a bit. I didn't want this to come out without us talking first."

Talking. Not only talking but falling right back into memories. As he had in the elevator, he caught the scent of her perfume, light and airy. It teased him, even though she always tried to be so proper. She hadn't been proper in bed. That was something he'd never forget—their wedding night.

"Maybe after this sinks in and we absorb it, we can have lunch or something."

She was gazing up at him in that way she'd always had, and he thought he could tell she still felt drawn to him, just as he felt attracted to her. But it didn't mean anything. It couldn't. A wife was the last thing he wanted right now. He intended to buy property that was all his own and move the horse rescue operation he'd started on his family's huge spread to his own place. This project would be all his and have nothing to do with the Parker family name. He'd owe his dad nothing but a good day's work when he consulted with Parker Oil.

Chase stepped away from Lucie and toward the door. She didn't follow him. Maybe she'd decided a husband was the last thing she needed, too.

He opened the door, but he couldn't help saying, "Remember, if you want to talk, call me." He didn't wait for her response. He left before he stayed.

Once outside the apartment complex, he headed down the street. Unfamiliar with the building and its parking restrictions, he'd left his pickup in a public lot down the block. He headed for it now and made a decision. Instead of going to his family's ranch, which was about a half hour away, he was going to book a hotel room near Lucie. He'd give a call to his mother later and let her know he wasn't going to be back tonight.

His mother had persuaded him to live on the Bar P. She'd asked him to stay there after his dad's stroke several years ago. His dad had recovered, but she lived in constant fear he'd have another stroke. She wanted Chase to keep him from overdoing it, and that was what Chase had done on all levels for the past five years. But recently, when a college friend was killed, he'd realized he had to live his own life, not the life his parents wanted him to live. The horse rescue ranch would be a first step in that direction.

Thinking again about a hotel room, he felt he needed to stay close by Lucie so she didn't disappear again or fly off somewhere. The reason? He couldn't get his life restarted until their situation was cleared up.

What other reason could there be?

When Lucie's alarm woke her, she wasn't only startled by the sound; she was startled by the dream she'd been having. It starred Chase and was anything but tame. She was still married to the man! Her subconscious had apparently been trying to process that and had inserted him naked into her dream.

She remembered his body all too well. She recalled

every detail of the way he'd touched her—not simply in the dream, but on their wedding night.

"I'm still married to the man," she repeated aloud, remembering all too well everything about it, including being sent home in shame.

Her parents had known about her reckless affair with Chase, but not the marriage. Why hurt them with an impulsive escapade that had been erased from the books? Lucie had promised Chase's father she'd never breathe a word about any of it to anyone. After all, her family would have been embarrassed and humiliated even more if the word of her marriage ever got out. They were constantly in the public eye.

She had to talk to someone about it, and she had to talk now.

If she called her mother... First of all, she couldn't. Her mum was in a remote village without cell phone towers for miles. Second of all, she'd tell her mother in good time. After all these years, her mum might be hurt that Lucie hadn't told her in the first place.

Lucie sighed. The questionable decisions of youth. She'd thought the passage of time had healed all this, but she'd been wrong. Because the annulment had never gone through?

Yes, that was certainly the reason.

She'd call Amelia.

She didn't even bother to brush her teeth first. Amelia lived on a ranch with Quinn and she'd be up early. She had a baby, so *certainly* she'd awake. Thinking about her niece, Clementine Rose, made Lucie miss her. She picked up her cell phone and dialed her sister.

"You're up early," Amelia said without preamble. "Going to look at more office spaces?"

"I wish I was. I mean, I will be. I mean—"

Lucie heard a shout…a deep male voice.

Amelia called, "I'll be right there, Quinn. I'm on the phone."

He must have shouted something back.

"It's Lucie," Amelia called back. "Can't you get Clementine her breakfast?" A pause. Then Amelia asked Quinn, "She tossed all the cereal on the floor?"

Obviously this wasn't a good time for Lucie to have a talk with her sister, not about something as serious as a marriage Amelia knew nothing about.

She said, "Amelia, I'll talk to you later when you're not so tied up."

"Lucie, really, if you want to talk, I'm sure Quinn can handle this."

"No, it's okay. You two give my niece a big kiss from me. I promise I'll hug her soon. Have a good day."

"I'm coming," Amelia called to Quinn. "You, too," she said to Lucie, meaning it.

Lucie stared at the phone after she ended the call. Maybe her brother Brodie could help, in more than one way. He might be able to give her some professional advice. He was a publicist who would know how to handle this news, especially if it got out.

But when her call went through to Brodie, all she got was a voice mail message. Next, she tried her brother Jensen. He didn't have voice mail and he didn't pick up.

That left one person she could call. Her brother Charles, who was still in London. She found his number in her contact list and pressed Send.

"Hello, Lucie," he said cheerily. "You're up early."

It was around noon in London. "I have reason to be. Do you have time for a chat?"

"With you? Sure. What's wrong?"

"Why do you think something's wrong?"

"You're my sister. I know the tone of your voice. Spill it."

Charles was the youngest son, a bit of a playboy and charming. He sometimes had trouble being serious, but he was now as he waited for her to talk about whatever it was she needed to discuss.

"Do you remember when I went to Scotland when I was seventeen?"

"Of course I do. There was a ruckus when you were sent home. My sister, who was usually an angel, the perfect sibling, had gotten herself into a mess. Mom and Dad did some fast pedaling with the press, if I remember correctly."

"You mean, they managed to squelch the story that I was sent home from a trip because of a boy."

"That about covers it."

"Actually, no, that didn't cover it. Now don't say a word until I finish telling you everything."

"My lips are zipped."

Was she making a mistake telling Charles? She hoped not. "Promise me you will tell no one else until I say you can."

"Lucie, you're starting to scare me."

She plunged in. "I didn't just have an affair with Chase Parker in Scotland, I married him," she blurted out. "But when we were caught, his father flew in, didn't give either of us a chance to breathe and started paperwork for an annulment."

Charles whistled.

"I'm not done," she protested.

"Still zipped," he assured her.

She rolled her eyes. "Chase found me and came to

see me yesterday. The annulment never went through. We're still married."

She wasn't exactly sure what she expected from Charles, but she definitely didn't expect his burst of laughter.

"Oh, my gosh! Miss Goody Two-Shoes got herself into a mess. I didn't know you had it in you."

"Stop it," she warned him, "or I'll hang up right now."

His laughter simmered down to a smile in his voice as he coaxed, "Ah, you wouldn't hang up on me, not your favorite brother."

"Charles—"

"Oh, Lucie. So you made a mistake and it was never rectified. That doesn't mean it can't be now. A good lawyer will straighten it out. What does Parker say?"

"He says he has lawyers on it, that I should call him if I need to talk, that we'll figure this out. Charles, if this gets out to the press, Mum will be mortified. Think of the scandal. I was engaged while I was still married. All my work at the orphanages will be looked at as some hypocritical jaunt. I can't stand the idea of it."

"The paparazzi are one matter," Charles agreed. "But Chase Parker is another. Are you going to call him to talk about it?"

She remembered her dream. She remembered all the feelings that went with it.

"I don't know," she said in a low voice.

"Lucie, are you telling me everything?"

"What do you mean?"

"What did you feel when you saw him again?"

She went back to that moment yesterday, and she didn't want to admit what she'd felt.

"Aha!" Charles said.

"What do you mean, 'aha'? I didn't say anything."

"Exactly. It was never over with this man, was it?"

"Of course it's over. It's been ten years."

"Sometimes our hearts don't count time. More than anything else, Lucie, you'd better figure out what you want. You can't face the world with news like this with any uncertainty if it does get out."

"I have to think. I need some time."

Suddenly Lucie's bedside phone rang. From caller ID, she could see that it was Irv downstairs.

"Is that your phone?" Charles asked.

"Yes, I have to get this. It's the doorman. Someone must be downstairs. I have to go. Promise me, Charles, you won't breathe a word of this."

"I promise."

She ended the call with her brother and picked up the phone. "Yes, Irv?"

"Mr. Parker is here to see you. Shall I send him up?"

"Tell him to give me five minutes," she said, suddenly out of breath.

"Yes, Lady Lucie. I'll make sure he gives you five minutes."

She didn't have time to do much, but she did have time to brush her teeth. She was wearing pink-and-white-flowered sleep pants and a pink tank. No time to think about clothes. She ran a brush through her hair and grabbed a long pink satin robe, belting it tightly.

There was a knock at her door.

She ran to it and looked through the peephole. It was Chase. Today he was dressed more casually. His chambray shirtsleeves were rolled up, and he'd left his suit jacket somewhere. She undid the chain lock and then the dead bolt. When she opened the door, she just stared at him.

Breaking out of whatever spell that came over her

when she looked at him, her senses returned. "Did anyone see you down there?"

"No one was around but your doorman."

"We have to be careful, Chase. If we're seen together, there will be questions and gossip. If anybody finds out Irv is buzzing me to let you up, someone will investigate."

"I get it. We'll have to work something out," he said, as if seeing each other might become a common occurrence. Because of paperwork? Because of resolving their situation, of course.

"We can't be seen together here," he reiterated. "I understand that. But certainly there are ways you go out when you don't want to be recognized, right?"

"I have a wig."

He nodded. "Come to breakfast with me. I know a hole in the wall, otherwise known as a truck stop, where you won't be recognized and neither will I. There's wonderful food there. We can talk about all this and what we're going to do."

She thought about it. Sometimes she did feel as if she were a captive in her apartment. Having a normal life was tough in her position. In her family, it had always been that way. Maybe that was why she'd been so reckless in Scotland when she met Chase. She just wanted to be normal. Since then, she'd accepted the fact that her life would never be that.

However, today—

"We can't just walk out of here together," she warned him.

He took his phone from his belt, tapped on his picture gallery and handed her the phone. "That's a photo of my truck. It's a blue pickup. I'll drive into the parking garage and meet you up on the third level. Will that work?"

"That works, but I need at least ten minutes to get dressed."

He looked her up and down. "I don't know. What you're wearing works for me."

She blushed, and his grin and the sparkle in his eyes told her he was remembering when her being dressed in her robe or *without* her robe would have been just fine.

But that had been another time and place.

"I'll meet you up on the third level, parking row C," she confirmed.

"Got it," he agreed, then went to her door and opened it. As he left, however, he threw another look to her that told her that, dressed or undressed, he still found her attractive. Just what was she going to do about that?

Fifteen minutes later, Lucie had her wig firmly in place, her sunglasses on her nose and all her wits about her. She would not let Chase rattle her. She couldn't. There were too many consequences if she didn't control this situation.

Finding Chase's truck easily, she opened the passenger door and climbed inside.

Chase gave her a smile, nodded and started the engine. As he exited the parking garage, turned and drove down the street, he cut her a sideways glance. "You look hot as a redhead."

So much for not being rattled by him. She didn't respond.

She didn't recognize the route he took, but then she didn't know the city all that well yet. Ten minutes after they'd left the parking garage, he pulled up next to a gas station where several semis were fueling up. There was a restaurant attached—the Lone Star Diner.

Lucie had dressed in a more casual way than she usually did. After all, she didn't want to be recognized. She'd worn jeans and a T-shirt and a blouse on top of that. Her auburn wig was curlier and fuller than her own hair and the chin-length strands brushed her cheeks. She had to hurry to keep up with Chase's long strides as he led her into the diner.

"It's totally impersonal," he told her. "The waitresses rotate shifts, so the same ones are never on at the same time."

"Do you come here often?"

"There are times when I like to be nameless, too. When I agreed to stay at the ranch, I told my mom I wouldn't be there for regular meals. I didn't want anybody keeping tabs on my comings or goings. So I drop in here now and then. The waitresses seem to have a high turnover. I haven't run into the same one twice."

All of that was good to know, not that she'd be coming back here again.

"The thing is," he said in an aside to her, "this isn't a royal kind of place."

"I'm not a snob, Chase."

He sobered. "That wasn't an insult. I was just teasing."

Yes, her sister and brothers teased her, but no one else did. She wasn't used to it.

There were a few stools open at the counter, but Chase led her to a booth in the back, and she was glad of that. He was definitely aware of her need for anonymity.

The waitress arrived immediately and Chase said, "Two coffees and lots of cream for her."

When the waitress moved away, he asked, "You still take it that way?"

"I do. But, you know, Chase, I'm not used to a sterling carafe to pour it from. When I go to developing countries to help with orphanages, sometimes I physically help to build them. My life isn't all silver spoons and Big Ben."

After a long, studying look, he nodded. "Noted. I won't take the tabloid stories about you seriously anymore."

"I'm surprised you read them."

"Only when you're on the cover."

So he'd been curious about her and what was going on in her life? She was curious about him. "So, tell me what you've been doing for the past ten years. In Scotland, you explained you'd never work for your dad because he was manipulative and hard, and he had to control everything."

"Yes, I told you that. After Scotland, I joined a construction crew, but I found I missed the horses on the ranch. So I signed on as a trainer at a quarter horse spread. I liked the work, and I liked being separate from my family."

"But then?" she prompted.

"But then Dad had a stroke. At first we thought his one side would be completely paralyzed. But it's amazing what rehabilitation can do now. I helped him with it. He's so stubborn and independent that we set up a home gym. My mom asked me to live there and watch over him. When he went back to work, she asked me to be his right-hand man there again."

"*He* didn't ask you?"

"Are you kidding? He always expected me to work there, so that's where I've been the past five years. But it's time for a change. It's time for me to leave. My plans are in the works. That's where the loan and me finding out about our marriage have come into play."

Because Lucie had known Chase before, she felt she could read into his expression and his words. He'd felt trapped for five years, and he couldn't wait to break free. Now, however, he was trapped in a marriage he'd assumed had been dissolved.

"You want out. You want to be free."

His gaze locked to hers. "Don't you?"

She did, didn't she? In a month, she'd be in Guatemala working on a new orphanage. In a month, Chase would be putting his plans into action. At that time, they'd be going their separate ways. That was the plan, wasn't it?

Gazing into his eyes, she wasn't so sure.

Chapter Three

Lucie sat beside Chase in his truck as they drove back to her apartment. She folded her hands in her lap, and she could swear they were trembling a little. Why was that?

After their initial dip into what she was doing and what he was doing, they'd talked about mundane things. Maybe because both were afraid to go too deep into anything…maybe because the tension between them was evident to them both. There was tension for lots of reasons—regrets, resentment, something unfinished. Most of all, sexual tension remained. When his knee had brushed hers…when her fingers had tangled with his, reaching for a creamer…

Touch was taboo.

Suddenly Chase said, "You said you'll be in Austin for a month. Is that a solid deadline?"

"Yes, it is," she answered. "I'm meeting my mother

in Guatemala on the first of April. She has set up introductions to officials who can get the ball rolling as far as construction goes."

"You have a site picked out?"

"We do."

He changed the subject a bit. "So you're officially a Fortune?"

"Yes, I am. When my mother found out about her heritage, that she had a long-lost sister and brother, she changed her name to Josephine Fortune Chesterfield, and I changed mine. It seemed right. Her sister and her family have come to mean everything to Mum. Now that Jensen and Brodie and Amelia all live in Horseback Hollow, our visits can become more raucous than royal."

Chase chuckled. "Would you say your family's become closer?"

"Amelia and I have definitely become closer. I know that seems odd, with her living in the United States and me living primarily in England. But when we were growing up, there always seemed to be a wall between us. I'm not sure exactly why. Maybe because we had nannies and were at boarding school. Maybe because our lives were very formal."

"With her married to a cowboy, is her life as formal now?" Chase asked.

"Quinn is down-to-earth. With their baby, Amelia's just like any new mom. Maybe we all just seem more human in Texas. I don't know."

When Chase drove into the parking garage, Lucie was almost sorry. In spite of the tension, she'd enjoyed breakfast and all of their conversations. He was more mature now, with a broader view of life than he'd had at twenty-one. She could tell he wasn't as impulsive and he thought things through. He wasn't so wild, though she could still see deep passion in his eyes. His father's stroke had apparently changed his focus on life. Now he seemed to know what he wanted for his future.

Chase said, "I'll park and walk you back to your apartment."

"It will be safer if you don't do that," Lucie informed him. "You can watch me until I'm in the elevator if you'd like, but then I'll be safe from prying eyes or from a stray reporter. The wig and the clothes help, but anyone who spies on me regularly could probably identify me. We don't want anyone to identify *you* with me."

Chase was silent as he drove up to the second level, through the garage and around the bend and then followed the exit sign to another ramp. No cars trailed them. No one with a camera was evident. Chase should probably change the level he parked on if they ever did this again.

There was no reason to do this again. Legal documents could be sent back and forth by courier.

Instead of just pulling up outside the glass doors that led into the elevator bank, Chase slowed, braked and then backed into a parking place.

"What are you doing?"

"If I'm going to stay until you get on the elevator, I don't want to block traffic."

That made sense. She fingered her purse, a simple, natural leather bag that didn't snag anyone's attention. She knew she had to look at him. That was only proper. But she also knew that when she did, she'd get caught by the dark, knowing expression in his eyes.

Stalling, she unfastened her seat belt, but then she

angled toward him and realized he was already gazing at her. "I enjoyed breakfast."

"The chocolate chip pancakes there are the best."

"It wasn't just the pancakes," she admitted. "It was good catching up with you."

He unfastened his seat belt and turned toward her. She wasn't really so very far away from him. She caught a whiff of either soap or aftershave. Like lime, and manly. She fell under the spell of his dark eyes and the way his hair dipped over his brow. He'd tossed his Stetson into the back, and she could remember the feel of the thickness of his hair sliding through her fingers.

The tremble was back in her hands, and she felt she had to make conversation to hide her nervousness. "I like to do things that make me feel like a real person. This breakfast did that."

He moved only slightly, but he was big and the cab of the truck seemed small. He was closer to her now as he reached out a hand and smoothed strands of hair from her wig away from her face. "You are a very real person, Lucie Fortune Chesterfield. I've always known that."

"Even when the tabloids make me look like a cartoon?"

He smiled but didn't move his hand from her cheek. She was both hot and cold and afraid to move.

"You could never look like a cartoon. You're much too beautiful for that."

Her father had called her beautiful, and her mother told her she was. But they were her parents. She accepted compliments as the polite conversation they were, but this was different. This one came from a man she'd once loved and was still sorely attracted to. She didn't know what to say. Maybe it was better she said nothing, because they were both leaning toward each other.

Chase's thumb swept across her cheek. "Ten years have given you refinement, polish and a generous spirit."

He was going to make her cry. No, he wasn't. She wouldn't let him. When she found her voice, she whispered, "Ten years have made you wiser, stronger, motivated."

"So this really was a get-to-know-you breakfast."

"Maybe so."

But then she asked herself the important question: Why were they getting to know each other when they were going to end something between them?

As if he sensed that question flitting through her mind, he said, "We may be clarifying that there was no marriage between us, but that doesn't mean we can't have a friendship."

Clarifying that there hadn't been a marriage? But they had been married, and they'd done what married people do. How did you just wipe that away forever?

Now he reached out his hand to the other side of her cheek and held her face between his palms. "Are you happy?"

"We all define happiness differently. But yes, I am. I have every earthly need met. I'm helping children, so they can have their own needs met. My family and I are closer than we've ever been. Amelia's baby daughter is such a blessing, and I love her deeply. My only regret is that Dad isn't here to see it all. Sometimes I wake up and my heart hurts because I want him to be involved in all this, too. The Fortune Chesterfields are changing, and I want him to see that change and be as excited about it as I am."

"I can believe he's with you, Lucie. I can believe he nudges you in the right direction when you might go in the wrong one. Energy is energy and it doesn't disappear. Your father could be your personal guardian angel whispering in your ear."

"And who's *your* guardian angel?"

"My guardian angel is a college friend I lost. He died way too young, without accomplishing a quarter of what he wanted to. I feel him sometimes pushing me. Really, I do. And not in the direction my father wants me to go, but one that will give me the most fulfillment in life. Not money, but value. Value that can help horses and people, too."

"As I said, you've matured."

"And you have grown into a woman many men would be proud to be married to."

His face was before hers, and hers was before his. Neither of them were blinking. Neither of them were breathing. If she didn't breathe soon…

He brought his lips very close to hers. "Do you want to kiss?"

"If we kiss, we could be starting something instead of ending it. Is that what you want?"

"I want to know what's beneath the Lady Fortune Chesterfield facade."

Lucie thought about her task here for the Fortunes. She considered her upcoming mission in Guatemala and her responsibilities as a Chesterfield. She considered the way her mother had depended on her since her dad died. She didn't have time for a dalliance.

Chase ran his hands down over her arms and held her hands. "Do you want an annulment?" he asked.

There was only one answer. "Yes. I'm committed to

my life. I don't see it changing. What about you? Do you want it?"

"Oh, yes, I want it. Starting over at my own place, with no one telling me what to do but me, taking responsibility for it all, the horses, the finances and management, the vet bills. I've been counting the years until I could do this."

When he talked about the work, she could see it made him happy. "So one day you're going to leave your dad's and not go back again?"

"No, it won't be like that. I'm grooming someone in my office to take over my position. Jeff has been apprenticing with me, and he can do it. He just needs to have the confidence that he can. I'll stay part-time for a while until everybody gets used to the idea. Then I can slip away and just be used for consulting services."

"We're on the verge," she said softly.

With his gaze unwavering, he agreed, "We are. I enjoyed breakfast, too. Maybe we can do this again."

When he tilted his head, she thought he was going to kiss her. It wasn't full-blown. He kissed her on the cheek. She still felt it all the way down to the toes of her boots. She almost grabbed him and laid one on his lips, but she'd been taught better. Decorum could be everything. She'd never been forward and she wouldn't be now.

She hurriedly opened her door, slid over to it and dropped her legs around to take the giant step down from the running board.

When it seemed as if he was going to come around the truck, she shook her head vigorously. "No, you stay. I'm fine." Shaky, but fine.

She could feel his eyes on her as she walked through the glass door into the bank of elevators and greeted the security guard. She pressed the button and the doors swished open immediately. She stepped inside. Fortunately there was only time for a small wave before they closed in front of her.

She breathed a sigh of disappointment, regret, but also joy. She'd enjoyed being with him. She'd enjoyed feeling alive with him. She'd enjoyed the fact that Chase Parker still turned her on.

At his desk later that afternoon, Chase tried to concentrate on examining the work records, evaluations, and overall résumé of Jeff Ortiz. Jeff was now Parker Oil's CFO, and had done a bang-up job ever since Chase hired him three years ago. He was a good manager with great public relations skills. Not only that, he was intelligent, informed about the industry and would go far either at Parker Oil or for some other company who might try to steal him. He was Chase's pick to replace him when he left. The feat would be getting his father on board with the idea.

Turning away from his computer, Chase thought about breakfast as he had on and off all day. He couldn't shove Lucie out of his mind. Had it been easier ten years ago? He'd had no choice then. If she hadn't been so young, maybe things would have been different. If *he* hadn't been so, maybe he would have known better what he wanted.

He took his cell phone from his belt, pulled up his contacts and studied her number. She'd given it to him in case he had to reach her about the paperwork…about the annulment…about ending something that had hardly started.

He jabbed the green phone icon.

He half expected her voice mail. After all, she'd said she was going to look at more properties this afternoon with a real estate agent. But he didn't get voice mail. She answered.

"Hi, Chase."

Her tone was cautious, but at least she hadn't avoided his call. Without preamble, he asked, "Are you finished with business for the day?"

"I just got home."

He hesitated only a moment. "We have about an hour of daylight left. How would you like to see the ranch I plan to buy?"

Her silence lasted a few moments and he realized he was holding his breath. But then she answered, "I can be ready as soon as you get here. But you'd better pick me up on a different level this time. Let's try level two."

"I'll be there in ten minutes," he assured her.

When he ended the connection, he wondered how she lived her life like this. She had to think about every twist and turn in the road, and how the public would view it. When did she ever get to do what *she* wanted to do? Would she be wearing her wig again?

Standing, he pushed in his desk chair and realized he couldn't wait to find out.

Ten minutes later, when she ran to his truck and hopped inside, he saw instead of a wig she was wearing a baseball cap with a large bill that practically hid her face. Jeans, a plaid shirt and boots rounded out her outfit. She didn't look royal, and he supposed that was the idea. She used a persona for her public appearances.

Who was the real Lucie?

They didn't speak until they were well out of Austin. He noticed her checking the rearview mirror a few times. He had checked it, too. From what he could tell, no one had followed them. She seemed to relax the farther from Austin they drove.

Finally she said honestly, "I was surprised you called… about your ranch."

She was obviously wondering why he'd asked her to come along. He wasn't entirely sure. "Maybe I just want a second opinion on the place."

"No one else has seen it?"

"No one else."

"How many horses do you plan to run on this property?"

"I'm bringing five over from the Bar P. I adopted two out last month, but I'd like to triple or quadruple that. A lot has to happen first, though. Some horses have to be quarantined. Others need their own pastures. There are no wild mustangs, per se, in Texas. That's the way most people think about horse rescue. But in stiff economic times, people are abandoning horses on private and public lands. As far as the wild mustangs go, the Bureau of Land Management has adoption events in Texas. I purchased a few, gentled them, and then sold them."

"It's a wonderful idea. What made you start doing it?"

"Dad added property to the Bar P when I was a teenager. It was a rundown ranch. The owner was selling. Two of his horses were malnourished and hadn't been cared for. I convinced Dad to let me take them on that summer. I turned them around. One of them became Mom's favorite to ride. After Dad's stroke, I guess I needed an outlet for living there again, something else to keep me occupied while I was there. So I began rescuing horses."

"I looked you up online yesterday."

He cut her a glance. "Oh, you did."

"There's an article about you in one of the Texas magazines about being the most eligible bachelor in Austin."

He kept silent to see where she was going with this.

"It's just—with your money, looks and reputation, you could be leading the good life."

"Fast cars, bars, clubbing every night?"

"Something like that."

"That might have been me in my teens and early twenties, but it isn't now. Scotland changed me, Lucie. Didn't it change you?"

"Before Scotland, I was never impulsive or reckless the way you were. I think maybe I let you sweep me away to prove that I could be. The thing was, after the humiliation the whole episode caused my parents, being sent home from the trip in disgrace, I was never that way again."

Had she reverted to type, or had she just curbed her passionate tendencies? Maybe that was something he wanted to explore.

Lucie's face wore an interested expression as he veered onto the gravel lane to the ranch. Suddenly the thought that this was a bad idea assaulted him. The ranch was run-down. The main barn needed to be refurbished. The second barn with its apartment on the second floor needed a makeover, too. This property was certainly nothing like the Bar P or the Chesterfield Estate in England. He'd seen video clips of her home. What was she going to think?

"I have to repair the fence, of course." He nodded to the worn stakes and supports along the road.

"Lots of caretaking involved," Lucie commented as if she knew.

"It will be a lot of work at the outlay, but then upkeep won't be so bad. The land alone is worth the price. With the rest, I'll add to its value."

As the truck bumped along, the barns and then the house came into view. They could see the forest beyond now and Lucie was looking in that direction.

As they parked at the house, they both climbed out.

"I'm going to have the house sided, of course," Chase said. "I'm thinking tan with brown shutters."

She wrinkled her nose. "Pale yellow siding with black shutters would be more inviting."

He grinned. "I knew there was a reason I brought you along."

They went up the three porch steps to the house. The porch was a large one, rounding three sides.

"It's locked, of course," Chase explained. "But you can peek inside. It's empty, so you won't see much. The plank flooring is good, if a little worn. In time, I'll redo the kitchen."

Lucie peered in the window, devoid of shades or curtains. "The living room looks nice-sized," she noticed.

"There are four bedrooms upstairs. One's a little small. The whole place has that original ranch house feel."

She stepped back from the door and glanced toward the barn.

"Do you want to explore a little? The barns aren't locked."

"Sure. Old barns can be like treasure chests. They take you back into another era."

"Exactly."

They were on the same page with that. The early 1900s feel of the barns and the house was the reason he liked them so much. If he had his way, he'd restore all of them as much as he could and keep the original wood and architecture.

He went ahead of her and opened the heavy, creaking barn door. She came up beside him and when she passed him, the light perfume she wore teased him. Once inside, however, the smell of hay, old wood and rusting tools was evident. There was a loft with an old, rickety ladder propped against it.

"I wouldn't use that ladder to look around up there," she warned with a smile.

"I brought my own in to have a look around. But when I own the place, I'd like to replicate the original."

Basically the barn was one open space.

"You'll need stalls, right?" she asked.

"Oh, yes. Lean-tos and a fenced corral. I'm looking into enlarging the second barn."

"Wow. You have your work cut out for you."

"I do and I can't wait to start. I want to do some of the work myself, especially in the house."

They were standing close to each other near a support beam. He had one hand on the support and his other he dropped by his side. She was standing right in front of him, close enough to touch. Dim light shone in the foggy windows. Last light from a long day shadowed the barn. The hushed atmosphere inside made him aware of his breath as well as hers.

He tipped up the bill of her cap. "This really doesn't disguise you very much. The wig does a better job."

"It hides my hair, though, and part of my face. It works, Chase."

Her life seemed to be all about what worked, what fit in, what didn't stir the pot. What if he stirred the pot?

As he swept the hat from her head, her hair fell down around her shoulders. He couldn't help touching it. He couldn't help sliding his hand under her hair, along her neck. He couldn't help bending his head.

A beep made them both start. It was as if someone had walked into the barn and caught them there.

Lucie stepped away from him and said, "My phone. I'd better check to see who it is."

Slipping it from her pocket, she said, "It's Amelia. I have to take this. She and I never ignore each other's calls."

Chase didn't have a brother or sister, but he understood that if he did, he wouldn't ignore their calls either. He turned away and walked to the other side of the barn to give Lucie some privacy. The idea of kissing her had revved him up. Better if she didn't understand just how much.

Chapter Four

Lucie was abominably rattled. She knew Chase had been about to kiss her and she'd wanted him to do it. Good sense hadn't stepped in. Recklessness had almost taken over. Thank goodness Amelia had called.

She was breathless when she glanced at Chase, who'd turned away and walked across the barn. She answered her phone. "Hi, Amelia."

"I'm sorry I was so distracted yesterday morning. It was late last night until I realized I hadn't called you back. So I made time right now. The baby's sleeping and Quinn's out in the barn. Are you at your place?"

Her place. Only it really wasn't hers, because she'd be flying away again soon.

"No, I'm not at the apartment. I'm exploring a ranch."

Amelia sounded puzzled. "For the Fortune Foundation?"

"No, not for them. I'm with…" She couldn't go into a long explanation with Chase in the same room, so to speak. "I'm with a friend."

"I'm so glad you're making friends in Austin. Are you with Ella or Viv?"

"No, not them. Amelia, I really do want to chat. We have a lot to talk about. But now isn't a good time."

"I entirely understand. Maybe midnight would be better, when the day is calmed down. The problem is, then Quinn wants all my hours—"

She stopped as if she'd said too much.

"Of course he does. You're still newlyweds."

"It feels as if we are," Amelia admitted happily. "And truthfully I don't want it ever to end. You should try it."

Wasn't that a touchy subject? She couldn't talk about finding Prince Charming with Chase in the barn with her.

As if Amelia understood something was going on, she asked, "So you can't talk freely?"

"Not now."

"Okay, so you don't have any privacy, and I know you probably have a bunch of international calls coming in later with regards to your trip."

Lucie had almost forgotten about those. She checked her watch. She had told contacts who were donating supplies to call her after eight tonight. Or was it nine? Chase had her so rattled. The whole situation had her rattled. This wasn't like her at all.

"Have you heard from Mum?" Amelia asked.

"Not since last week. And now she's traveling in an area with no cell phone connection. Did she tell you about that?"

"Yes, she did. When I spoke with her last, she seemed

to be in her element again. She loves the work…just as you do."

Lucie's life had been about helping orphaned children. But had she chosen the work for the right reasons? Or because her mother had needed her to be just as involved as she herself was? The orphanages had become a passion project after her husband died.

Now she wanted to tell her mother about her marriage to Chase. She wanted to prepare her in case news of it got out.

"Text me when you're free," Amelia went on. We'll have that talk. We can video-chat."

"I'll text soon. Give Clementine a kiss for me."

"Will do."

After Lucie ended the call, her gaze found Chase. He was over at the loft looking up, maybe deciding what he wanted to do with it. He was acting all casual, as if he hadn't been listening.

But as he turned to Lucie, he asked, "So I'm a friend now?"

He'd obviously heard her conversation with Amelia. Suddenly frustrated with the whole situation, Lucie blew out a breath. In a fit of unusual pique, she said, "I don't know what you are. We're in a kind of limbo. We want to live in the now, but the past is interfering. Yet we can't resurrect the past—"

Apparently Chase believed the simplest thing to do to get her to stop thinking was to encourage her to stop talking. She noticed a moment of doubt in his eyes. Then suddenly his arm was around her, his hand on the small of her back, urging her closer. His gaze never left hers.

First she felt surprise, swiftly followed by anticipation. Would a kiss be as explosive as it had been ten years ago?

There was only one way to find out. She let it happen.

Chase's lips covered hers before she could second-guess her decision.

In his adult years, Chase had prided himself on his self-control. But kissing Lucie almost destroyed it. It was the scent of her, the softness of her, the feel of her in his arms again. He wasn't thinking about the past or the future as his tongue breached her lips, and he took the kiss deeper, wetter, more intense. The fire was still there—fire that burned away any reservations, fire that had urged him to propose to her. The main reason...she'd been a virgin. Now, when she gripped his shoulders and he felt the sweet clutch of her fingers, his desire ramped up until it was almost dizzying.

Nevertheless, as quickly as it had started, it ended. Lucie broke away, brought her hands to his chest and put a foot between them. When he gazed into her eyes, he saw she was reeling from the kiss, too. Past dreams had been resurrected just for an instant. However, reality had rushed in, and he could see her good sense was telling her to run. That was exactly what she did, if not literally, figuratively.

He heard her swallow hard. He heard her deep intake of breath. He needed a swig of air himself. He needed to calm sensations that he'd forgotten.

She said, "I have to go. Can you take me back to my apartment? I have incoming international calls that I'm expecting tonight, and I can't be late."

He couldn't help asking wryly, "Isn't that what cell phones are for?"

"They'll be coming in on the landline," she informed

him. "I want to make sure my conversations aren't cut off."

Sure she did. She was doing important work. She'd be leaving in a month to build another orphanage. She probably had suppliers to talk to, directors to engage, donors and sponsors to extract money from. And she was telling him in a not-so-subtle way that that kiss had changed nothing, that the past was in the past, that their lives were very different and separate now.

"Let's go," he said, motioning to the barn door. "I'll have you back in no time at all."

And he did. They drove in silence, and when she climbed out in the parking garage, she said, "Goodbye, Chase."

He watched her walk to the elevator bank. He watched her nod to the security guard, then disappear inside, regretting every word they hadn't spoken, regretting the fact that Lucie's life was headed in one direction and his was headed in another.

The walnut-paneled study at the Silver Spur Ranch was the perfect place for Lucie's meeting with Kate Fortune the following day. Lucie studied this icon, who had recently turned ninety, as she sat in a huge leather chair that seemed to swallow her up. Kate had ended up in the hospital recently and was still recovering, but she looked at least ten years younger than her age, maybe more. She had more wealth than anybody could make use of, thanks to the success of the Fortune Youth Serum, which she'd discovered and perfected in the '90s. She was a walking advertisement for the efficacy of the product. But the future of her company was on her mind and she was looking for the right person to run it. For some reason, the two of them had seemed to connect at Kate's birthday party and Lucie had accepted this invitation to coffee, glad to see this remarkable woman again.

"How are you feeling?" Lucie asked.

Kate waved her hand. "Better each day. As you know, I'm still looking for the right Fortune to work at my company. I can't seem to find someone with all the attributes that are necessary, though the family tree does seem to be growing."

Kate motioned to the coffee and pastries that a butler had set up on a tray near them both. "Eat, my dear. You're much too thin."

Lucie did eat, and she was fortunate that she didn't seem to put on pounds because of it. She picked up a petite cherry Danish and took a bite. "What about you? Are you going to have some?"

"I have to watch everything these days—sugar, cholesterol, caffeine. I suppose it all matters. This morning I'm just going to enjoy your indulgence in the pastries. Tell me what you think about Ben Robinson's claim that his father is a Fortune."

"Could it be true?" Lucie asked, unsure how to answer.

"Anything can be true, I suppose," Kate mused.

"I had brunch with Ella and Viv," Lucie said. "They both seem very happy. Ben and Wes both are their Prince Charmings."

"Prince Charming is one thing, a Fortune is another," Kate proclaimed. "Ben can be very bold, as he proved at my party, but I believe he's sincere. I've tried to contact his father since I've been out of the hospital to verify Ben's claim that his father *is* Jerome Fortune. But Gerald Robinson hasn't returned any of my calls or my emails. Ben might claim his father is Jerome Fortune, but the man doesn't seem eager to prove it. His children deserve to know the truth, and so do I."

"They also want to find any half siblings they might have," Lucie explained.

"You're the one who connected Ben with Keaton Whitfield, correct?"

"Yes. I happened to know Keaton. It was amazing, really, that Keaton confirmed to Ben that Gerald Robinson is his father, too." Keaton and Ben were now working together to uncover other possible blood relatives that Gerald might have sired. The Fortune family was complicated and messy, and if Gerald Robinson was truly Jerome Fortune, Kate would have a lot to sort out.

"I know what you're thinking, my dear—that maybe finding family and trying to control my legacy might just be too complicated for someone my age."

"I'm not thinking that at all," Lucie protested. "Maybe I would be thinking that if you were the type of woman who sat in a parlor with an afghan covering your lap, knitting all day." She waved to the study with the computer, the printer, and the state-of-the-art smart TV for video-conferencing. "But you're not that type of woman. You like to be in charge. You like to know what's happening. You want to have a finger on what happens after you leave. I think you're up to the task."

Kate laughed. "I'm glad to see someone's on my side."

"I'm sure lots of people are."

"I've been reading more about how you and your mother work together to build orphanages and provide schooling for children who don't even have the necessities. Emmett Jamison, the head of the Fortune Foundation, told me you're hunting for office space to open a branch of the foundation in Austin. How is the hunt for space progressing?"

"I've seen a few possibilities. Probably the best strategy is to tap into programs that are already running. If we set up the office, then on-site events for kids can be anywhere. For instance, if there's a sports program that needs funding, we can do that. If there is a music therapist involved in community action, we can help her find space and a place to teach. We could also help provide college scholarships for girls interested in science."

"Emmett told me you'd put a lot of thought into this. It will be a remarkable undertaking."

"We would have an Austin Fortune Foundation Central, so to speak," Lucie concluded. "Then all the outreach programs would be like satellites."

"That sounds practical," Kate agreed. "Any program that is worthwhile can apply."

Kate gave Lucie a sly smile. "I have no doubt you're capable of getting this ball rolling. But I have been wondering something."

"What's that?"

"You travel the world with your mother helping others, but that doesn't leave much time for a personal life, does it?"

"No, it doesn't."

"Do you ever intend to marry?"

Lucie didn't know how to answer that honestly, because the truth was, she was already married!

When Lucie seemed stumped for an answer, Kate went on. "It's none of my business, of course. Charitable work is wonderful. But you know, don't you, it can't replace the love of a husband and family."

Lucie wondered if Kate was right. On the other hand,

though, her mother had had both during her second marriage, as well as now, though now she spent more time and intensity doing her charity work. Lucie realized she would never want to give up helping children, even if she had a husband and her own family.

If she had her own.

Just what kind of father might Chase Parker be?

She pushed that thought out of her head.

"Would you like to go for a walk?" she asked Kate. "It's a beautiful day outside."

"A change of subject is in order, huh?" Kate smiled. "Sure. Let's go for that walk. You can tell me about your sister Amelia and all about Horseback Hollow. You can also regale me with stories about how your royal life is different from mine."

Lucie laughed. "You *are* a royal, Kate Fortune, and you know it."

Kate gave a slight nod, agreeing.

Chase's workday had seemed long and tedious for several reasons. Soon he had to tell his father his plans and was trying to figure out how to do that. His dad was away in Galveston meeting with cronies, checking on a branch of their office there. But when he got back, Chase would have to be honest with him. And speaking of being honest, his last encounter with Lucie was heavy on his mind, not to mention that kiss.

So when he got home from Parker Oil, he headed toward the barn. That was his place where he could work off stress, communicate with the horses and chill. At least that was what he hoped. After a quick change into jeans and a T-shirt at the guesthouse, he checked on one of the last horses he'd rescued. The owners had left the property and abandoned him in the pasture. Chase didn't know how people could be so cruel.

Now he went to the fence and clicked his tongue against the roof of his mouth. Dusty, a chestnut, loped toward the fence and eyed Chase.

"Well, at least you come when I call now," Chase said conversationally.

The horse snorted, pawed at the ground, then turned tail and headed in the other direction.

"Making progress?" a female voice asked from outside the barn door.

Chase turned and saw his mother. She rarely ventured out here. She went on rides now and then, but those were few and far between since his dad had had his stroke. Was she afraid to be away from the ranch house in case he was taken to the hospital again? When he was in the house, did she feel she had to be with him?

"You should ride more often," Chase said now.

"Do you think I need the exercise?"

"I think you need the escape."

There were so many subjects they didn't talk about. There were so many feelings they'd never expressed. That was just the way it had been between him and his parents. Somehow he'd gotten the idea that boys should turn into men like his father—buttoned up, stoic, inflexible. After the Scotland fiasco, he'd rebelled against everything he'd learned as a child. He'd found his own way with work and horses, if not with women. He'd learned what was important to him and how he should feel when he treated others rightly or wrongly. He'd learned there were many shades of gray, and black and white were just illusions that his father and mother lived under. Since his dad's stroke, all of it had become even clearer to him. All of it had led up to this point.

"You didn't stop in at the house or text me to let me know you were here."

"Were you worried?" he asked, really wanting to know.

"No, I suppose not. But you didn't come over to the house last night either. Is something wrong?"

Whether he liked it or not, his mother could read him. Maybe all mothers were like that. Still, he felt he had to deny it.

"Nothing's wrong."

"We haven't heard from Mr. Sylvan yet. There's so much red tape."

Mr. Sylvan had been his family's lawyer for years. He was the one uncoiling the complications with the international law firm.

"You told me that when you met with Lady Fortune Chesterfield, she said she wants this dissolution as much as you do."

He thought about breakfast with Lucie, as well as kissing her. He'd seen the resolution and commitment in her eyes when she asked him to take her back to her apartment. "Yes, she wants the annulment. She wants to get on with her life, too, a very public life. She was even engaged under the glare of the media. Imagine how it will look if the news of our marriage gets out."

"You've had your picture taken at society events with beautiful women on your arm. The same would be true for you."

Chase was already shaking his head. "It wouldn't be the same at all. We mere mortals don't know what the royals go through."

"The Chesterfields aren't exactly royals," his mother maintained.

"That all depends on the way you look at it. The way Lucie tells it, her mother was first married to a man who was an earl. Lucie's father, Simon Chesterfield, was knighted for his service in the RAF and gained the title of "sir." He was also as wealthy as Dad is. So her family is in the royal public eye. We don't have paparazzi on our property every other day or even once a week. Once in a while someone wants to do a story on us, like Norton Wilcox, who set up the interview with me about horse rescue. But if I had said no, he would have accepted that for now. It's not that way for Lucie. The press actually hounds her family. They even follow her. And if they're on public property, there's nothing she can do about it."

"So you've talked about this?" his mother asked.

"Not just talked about it, lived it, in a small way. I took her for breakfast. We went in my truck and she wore a wig and jeans so nobody would recognize her or connect her with me. Right now that's our big problem—not being able to be associated together. We have to meet up in secret."

"Why do you have to meet up at all?"

Chase sighed. Why indeed? Ignoring that question, he said, "Mom, there's something we have to talk about other than Lucie. I was going to tell you and Dad together, but maybe it's better if I talk to you first."

His mother's face looked drawn, the lines around her mouth and eyes cutting deep. She looked almost scared.

"I've given the last five years to Dad and I don't regret any one of them. I don't regret living here for a while to help take care of him, and I don't regret being on the property these past few years. I don't know how much closer it's brought us, but at least we have the illusion of being together."

"It isn't an illusion," his mother protested heavily. "We *are* together."

"Together, Mom, means talking. Together means understanding. Together means compromising to find the best way for everybody."

"And in your not-so-subtle way, you're trying to tell me you want to compromise."

"What I'm telling you is that I'm going to make changes. I'm going to leave the company in the CFO's capable hands. Jeff is trustworthy, intelligent and knows every aspect of what we do. Dad's never going to retire, and if he does, he can sell Parker Oil for a hefty profit. He won't need me to be there."

"And just what would *you* be doing? Riding around the great state of Texas, collecting horses that are left on private land?"

"Maybe. Maybe those horses can find homes with loving families. Maybe they can find the lives they were made for."

His mother gave a resigned sigh, as if she didn't approve, but also as if none of this was a great surprise. "I understand that you're determined to see a horse rescue ranch come to fruition, and now you're determined to leave Parker Oil. When are you going to tell your father?"

"When he returns from Galveston. I won't jump on him. I assure you, I'll wait until the time is right, once I'm a free man and can obtain my loan."

"Have you discussed your plans with Lady Fortune Chesterfield?"

"I've mentioned my plans, and she's told me hers. A

month from now, she'll be in Guatemala, helping her mother build another orphanage."

Again, all he thought about was the last time he'd seen Lucie. All he could think about was that kiss.

His mother watched his expression carefully, watched him poke his hands into his pockets, watched him walk over to the fence and stare at Dusty.

"I know you don't often go along with my ideas, but maybe you should listen to this one," she suggested. "How about if you ask Lady Fortune Chesterfield to come to Sunday brunch? We can all handle this whole dilemma with civility."

Chase wasn't sure what to think about that. But it would give him the opportunity to talk to Lucie again. After all, she wouldn't be staying in Austin that long.

Lucie had had her driver stop at the market on her way back to her apartment. She'd picked up everything she'd need for a chicken and vegetable stir-fry. Swishing it around in the pan on the stove, she added soy sauce and breathed in the aroma as it cooked. When her cell phone beeped, she thought about letting it go to voice mail. But she didn't.

Turning the burner down to low, she picked up her phone on the counter, spotting the name and number there. Her heart beat crazily. She willed it to slow down, to not act so foolish. She hadn't liked the way she and Chase had parted. Maybe he hadn't liked it either.

The only way she'd know was to answer the phone. "Hello," she said cheerily.

"Lucie, it's Chase. Did I catch you at a bad time?"

She stared at her simmering dinner on the stove. "Not at all."

Neither of them spoke for a moment; then Chase stepped into the void. "How would you like to come to brunch on Sunday at the Bar P?"

Brunch? That didn't sound like an invitation Chase had issued himself. A moment later, she found out she was right.

"My mother suggested I invite you."

"Your mother did," she repeated. "Can I ask the reason why?"

"She just thought it would be a good idea. She'd like to keep this dissolution friendly—"

Lucie cut in, "Friendly? It's not as if I've been friends with your parents, Chase."

She heard him blow out a breath.

"Heck, Lucie, I don't know what she's thinking. Dad's away and maybe she's just lonely, or maybe it's her way of getting me to brunch. But she suggested it, so I am offering the invitation."

"Do you want me to come to brunch? Do you care if I do?" She wasn't sure why she was pushing. She just wanted to know where everybody stood. That would make going forward easier.

"We didn't part last night on the best of terms, and I'm not even sure why. That kiss—"

In the minute that followed, Lucie imagined they were both remembering exactly what had happened when Chase had kissed her. She imagined she could still taste him. She imagined his arms around her. She imagined…way too much. Maybe she shouldn't go. Maybe she should just break off this relationship right now.

What relationship?

Trying to weigh the pros and cons in less than a second, she finally answered, "All right, I'll come."

"Do you want me to pick you up?"

"No. And I won't have my driver bring me. I'll rent a car myself. I've done that before."

"Can you drive in the US?"

"I have an international license and can usually manage to stay on the right side of the road." *With concentration,* she added to herself.

"Are you sure you don't want me to pick you up?"

Chase had always had protective instincts. She'd felt them ten years ago, and she felt them now. But she couldn't let him protect her or do anything for her. After all, he'd cut off their relationship by not answering her letters. That had hurt more than she'd ever admitted.

"I'm positive. What time would you like me to be there?"

"How's ten a.m.?"

"That sounds fine. Give me the address."

"Text me your email address and I'll send you directions."

"Chase, I'm sure the car I rent will have a GPS."

"I'm sure it will, but I want to make certain you don't get lost."

By the time she ended the call with Chase, she already felt lost—lost in the past, lost in a feeling she couldn't decipher, lost in the knowledge that Chase Parker was going to disrupt her life.

Chapter Five

"This is the smaller dining room," Florence Parker explained to Lucie on Sunday morning. "We have our more intimate meals here."

Lucie, Chase and his mother had passed the large dining room with its ten-foot table and twelve hand-carved oak chairs. This place could rival any British estate! The smaller dining room Florence spoke of hosted a table for six in deep walnut. White lacy place mats sat beneath the Spode china. Crystal juice glasses sparkled from the sun shining in the bank of windows.

Chase pulled out Lucie's chair and she sat. She resisted the urge to glance over her shoulder at him. If she did, this breakfast would indeed be more intimate. She was sure that wasn't what his mother had in mind.

Chase went around to his mother's side of the table and helped her with her chair. When she smiled at him, she looked about ten years younger. Florence Parker possessed classic beauty with her high cheekbones, patrician nose, blond-gray hair that curved just under her chin and wide blue eyes. Lucie imagined she'd had china-doll beauty as a young woman. For brunch Florence had chosen pale lilac slacks and a matching sweater.

Lucie hadn't known how to dress. She'd worn a flowered blouse and navy slacks. As an extra touch, the pearls her mother had given her on her sixteenth birthday lay around her neck, visible in her open collar.

A maid in a black dress with a white collar brought in a tray that was loaded with breakfast entrées—waffles, pancakes, bacon and scrambled eggs. She set the dishes on the table and Lucie could see they were going to be served family-style. That was nice. It made the room feel less like a restaurant and more like a home. As they'd passed through the grand foyer and entrance hall, wound around the curved staircase, passed the high-ceilinged living room, Lucie noticed the Western décor, lots of leather, cowhide and suede. But what she hadn't noticed were any homey touches. Was this house really lived in?

Since she didn't know where to begin a conversation with Chase's mother, she began with something easy. "Your estate is beautiful."

"It's a ranch, dear. You might have estates in England, but we have ranches in Texas."

"Mother," Chase scolded with a warning look.

Lucie, trying not to connect with Chase, even with her eyes, said, "Your mother's right to correct me. I'm still learning about idioms and Texas idiosyncrasies."

Florence Parker laughed. "Idiosyncrasies like wanting our steak rare?"

Lucie smiled. "I prefer mine medium-well."

"You don't have a heavy British accent," Florence noted.

"My mother tells me I once did, but we traveled so much I seemed to pick up intonations from every dialect."

"At seventeen, you were British all the way," Chase said in an undertone.

This time Lucie couldn't help looking at him, and when she did, their eyes locked, and a little tremble went through her. That had to stop.

"I should have traveled to Scotland with Chase's father all those years ago," Florence concluded. "Maybe then the two of you wouldn't be in the fix you're in. But he said he'd handle it, and back then, I guess I listened to him more than I do now."

Chase laughed at that. "What Mom's saying," he explained to Lucie, "is that she's grown independent over the years."

Florence smiled fondly at her son. "When I was first married, I hung on my husband's every word. I took it as law. I wanted to please him. It's not true, you know, that you don't find yourself in marriage. I certainly did, and I think Chase's father respects me more for it."

In a way, Florence reminded Lucie of her own mother. She had a bit more of an edge, but Lucie liked the woman's frankness. Maybe this brunch wasn't a trap after all, though she wasn't sure why Florence wanted to get to know her when she'd be leaving Chase's life.

"Tell me about your work with orphanages," Florence suggested.

For most of the brunch, that was exactly what Lucie did. Florence asked leading questions and Lucie didn't hesitate to answer them. Finally, when the maid poured cups of coffee all around again, Florence revealed, "I work with many charities, too."

That didn't surprise Lucie. Florence Parker probably had a high standing in the community and led fund-raising attempts.

"Word is going around that the Fortune Foundation will be opening a branch in Austin. Is that true?" she inquired.

"Yes, it is. I've been spending much of my time looking for office space."

"Not space to run programs?" Florence prodded.

"No. The programs will be satellite connections to the main office. We'd like to work within the framework of already established ones. That would stream funds to children quicker."

"I see," Florence said, looking thoughtful. "I like that idea. At present I'm trying to find funding for my church's after-school program. Money will soon run out and the minister might have to close it down. Would the Fortune Foundation be interested in something like that?"

Was this why Chase's mother had asked her to brunch? "I can ask Emmett Jamison, who runs the foundation."

"I didn't know if the Fortune Foundation's expansion to Austin was truth or gossip."

"I guess every town has its chatting chain."

"Chatting chain?" Florence asked.

"Grapevine," Chase interpreted with a smile for Lucie. When he smiled at her, her toes curled.

"Yes, this chatting chain you speak of is one of the reasons you and Chase want to get this annulment quickly, correct?" Florence determined.

Neither of them spoke.

Finally Lucie said, "It's in both of our best interests."

"I see," Florence murmured. "You of course mean because of the media attention?"

"Yes. I took a circuitous route to drive here today to make sure I wasn't followed. Usually I have a driver who does that, but neither Chase nor I want to bring embarrassment to our families if the word of our marriage seeps out."

"There's no embarrassment in getting married," Florence said with a sly look at her son.

"Don't start, Mom. You know I have too much on my plate to even consider getting married and having kids, though I know that's what you want me to do."

"I would like grandchildren before I'm too old to enjoy them." She studied Lucie. "Do you have someone special in your life?"

"I'm not dating anyone now," Lucie admitted.

"There was talk of an engagement a while back."

"That didn't work out."

"Can I ask why?"

"Mom," Chase said with exasperation.

Lucie laid her hand on his arm to stop his protest and then was sorry she did. Her fingers burned against his skin, and she quickly withdrew her hand. However, she said, "It's okay, Chase." She was practiced at this. A little bit of truth went a long way. She didn't need to reveal that Terry's dishonesty had left her doubting most men. As much as that, she didn't need to reveal that his critical attitude toward her at the end of their engagement had left her with insecurities that weren't easy to shake off.

"I thought about my broken engagement a lot. I was involved with orphanage work with my mother. Much of my relationship with Terrence was long-distance. Never-

theless, I don't think that was the problem. His family
knew mine. We had common interests. But I finally realized I didn't love him the way I wanted to love a man
who was going to be my husband and he didn't love me
the way a man should love a wife. There was no big
clash or conflict or anything like that, even though the
tabloids hinted that there was. We just weren't right for
each other."

Florence looked from Lucie to Chase. "Yes, I guess
one comes to realize who the right person might be as
one grows older, doesn't one?"

Lucie suddenly felt uncomfortable and wasn't even
sure why.

But then Florence changed the subject and addressed
her son. "You *are* going to show Lucie around the place,
aren't you? Do you have time?" she asked Lucie.

"I have time," Lucie assured her. "I'd love a tour."

"So it's settled," Florence said.

But Lucie wasn't sure anything was settled.

A half hour later, Lucie and Chase walked in silence
through gardens and finally along a path that wound
around the barns. He said, "Maybe we should have taken
my truck. There are roads through the ranch that lead to
the different pastures."

"You have three barns."

"Yes, we do. One leads to the pastures where we keep
the horses that have always been on the Bar P and any
new ones Dad might find that he'd like to ride. The second barn is for horses who might come in and out, and
we want to keep them separate from the others."

"And the third barn?"

"The third barn used to be for storage. But I cleaned
it out and now it's for my rescue horses. The stalls each

lead to fenced-in areas, in case they don't get along well with others or are afraid of them. It takes a while to gentle them sometimes. That's true of the wild mustangs, too. They can take weeks or months, depending on the temperament of the horse."

"Let's look at the third barn," she decided.

When she cut a glance at Chase, she could see the smile that slipped across his lips. Every time she looked at him, she remembered their kiss. Every time she looked at him, she remembered more than that.

His T-shirt accentuated his muscled arms. His broad shoulders never slouched. That told her he was confident in his stature as a tall man and as a person.

She was glad she'd worn slacks as they walked over packed ground and gravel and through some grass. Now and then, she had to hurry a little to keep up with Chase's stride. He was giving her a tour as his mother had suggested, not stopping to talk or touch. That was what she wanted, wasn't it?

The barn was only about twenty feet away when Chase increased his pace a little more, probably so he could open the door for her. She was looking at him, not watching where she was going. The stones were larger here and one turned under her foot. She gave a little yelp as she felt herself starting to fall, but she never hit the ground. Chase was there, his arms around her, helping her right herself on her feet. She just wished she could right herself in her heart and her head, because when she was standing in the circle of his arms, looking up at him, she felt as if her world would never go back to spinning normally again.

"Are you okay?" he asked, his eyes concerned.

"I'm fine. I should have worn sneakers."

"Did you turn your ankle?"

"No, I just basically slipped. Thanks for saving me."

They stared at each other for a long time, but then Chase blew out a breath. "Come on, let's see the horses. You can only get close to one of them—Gypsy. She's going to be a great riding horse for someone. I hope I can find a family who wants her."

Now Chase took Lucie's arm as they walked. She almost pulled away but decided what could it hurt? She liked the feel of his fingers on her skin. She liked having Chase that close.

"You don't keep any of them?" she asked.

"I'd like to keep them all. When you put time and care and gentling into an animal, you create a bond that really can't be broken. But practically speaking, I can't keep them all. I have to transfer that bond to someone else who will love and appreciate them."

"But if you find a special one—"

"You mean like Gypsy? Yeah, if this deal goes through for my own place, I might just have to keep her."

They stepped over the threshold to the barn. This structure had eight stalls, four on each side. No horses were housed there at the moment. They were enjoying the March day.

Chase opened one of the stall doors and beckoned for Lucie to come in. Walking through, Lucie could see the mare in her own little pasture. She was a gray with a silver mane.

Chase clicked his tongue and the horse came running to him.

He put his arm around her neck and rubbed her. "Hey, girl, how are you today?"

She nudged the back pocket of his jeans.

He laughed. "She knows I keep snacks in there." He took out what looked like a cookie.

"All natural," he said. "She's getting back the shine on her coat and the sparkle in her eyes."

"Can I touch her?" Lucie asked.

"She hasn't seen many people. Mostly me. Just approach her slowly and we'll see what she does."

Lucie did just that.

Chase handed her another piece of cookie. "Give her that. Just hold it in your palm. She doesn't bite."

Lucie's father had taught her to ride. She'd been around horses who were biters, horses that were gentle, and horses who would obey every command. In the Chesterfield stables, Lucie had a special horse, and she understood all about communication between mount and rider and bonds that had formed since childhood. Her horse, Mayfield, took her on trail rides and listened to all her woes and joys.

Holding her hand still with the cookie treat on her palm, she waited. Gypsy snorted and seemed to look Lucie over. Then she took a step forward, snuffled Lucie's fingers and licked up the treat. As she chewed, she stared at Lucie, and Lucie took another step forward. Gypsy didn't retreat and Lucie saw that as a good sign.

"Can I pet you?" she asked the horse.

Gypsy stood by Chase's side, not moving, so Lucie ruffled her fingers under the mane, slid them along the smooth neck and petted Gypsy's flank. "You're a beauty."

"Yes, she is," Chase said, but he wasn't looking at Gypsy. He was gazing at *her*. He gave Gypsy another treat and said, "I'll take you for a run later."

As they walked back into the barn, the magnetic pull

toward Chase was getting stronger and stronger, and Lucie knew there was only one way to break it.

"I really should get going," she said.

Chase didn't argue with her. "I'll walk you to your car."

Silence again stretched between them as they returned the way they had come. Once they arrived at Lucie's car door, she opened it. When she looked up at Chase, she wasn't sure how to say goodbye. Maybe he wasn't sure either, because he reached out and ran his thumb over her cheek. He brushed her hair behind her ear and looked down at her with longing that she so wanted to appease.

Suddenly he said, "We're in this mess because I convinced you to marry me ten years ago."

"You didn't need to work hard to convince me. It was as much my decision as yours. You didn't coerce me, Chase. I married you freely. We were reckless and impulsive, and now we just have to be mature about what we do next."

"Mature. Grown-up. Doing the right thing. Sometimes it's hard to know the right thing, isn't it? I thought I was doing the right thing by staying here after my dad's stroke. But now it's going to be that much harder to tear myself away. For them, not me. I don't want to hurt them, but I need my own life."

"You don't want to feel trapped," she empathized.

"And neither do you. You're trapped by the paparazzi, by the life you've led up till now, by a marriage that wasn't really a marriage."

"My life isn't going to change that much, one way or the other," she assured him. "I've accepted my role."

"Life should be more than a role," he advised her.

Perhaps he was right. She hated the fact that she didn't

know when she would see him again. But she shouldn't be looking forward to it. There were so many shouldn'ts in her life and maybe too many shoulds.

When she climbed into her car, Chase still didn't close the door. Lucie gazed up at the house and thought she saw a curtain move in a second-story window. Was Chase's mother watching them?

Chase leaned down and rested his hand on Lucie's shoulder. "You will look into whether the Fortune Foundation wants to fund the program my mother suggested?"

"I will look into it, then I'll give her a call." She wouldn't have to talk to Chase again, not really.

Maybe he saw the determination in her eyes, or maybe he just heard it in her voice. He leaned away and straightened. Then he backed up and shut the door for her.

That closure sounded like an end rather than a beginning.

That was the way it had to be.

The following morning, after Lucie spoke with Emmett, she called Florence Parker. She wasn't nervous about the call. After all, she didn't have to worry about Chase picking up. He was in the guesthouse. He would most likely not answer the phone at his mom and dad's residence.

She was right, because the maid answered. Lucie recognized her voice from the brunch the previous day.

"I'll fetch Mrs. Parker right away. Hold on please."

In no more than a minute, Florence Parker herself was on the line. "I'm so glad to hear from you. That was quick."

"Emmett answered my question immediately. He assured me the Fortune Foundation could fund the program you mentioned. But I need to take a look at it and make notes about the program itself. Would your minister be okay with me dropping in?"

"I'm sure he would if he has a little notice. When are you thinking about?"

"How about tomorrow after school? I just want to observe and make some notes about the age groups and their needs."

"What time were you thinking?" Florence asked.

"Around three?"

"I'm sure Reverend Stanhope will be fine with the idea once he knows he can get funding to keep the after-school program open. I'll call him, then call you back. Would that be all right?"

"That would be fine."

"I'll try to be there myself," Florence said. "I often volunteer and can show you around if the reverend is busy. Sometimes he's shorthanded, and that's one of the problems I'd like to cure. Volunteers are wonderful, but sometimes a paid position is necessary to keep it all running smoothly. Let me give you the address of the church."

"Is the program right on the premises?"

"It is, in the church's social hall. Do you have a pen and paper?"

"I do."

Florence rattled off the name of the church and the address. "Thank you so much again for taking this to the Fortune Foundation."

"I was glad to be able to help."

After Lucie ended the call, she felt as if she'd done something worthwhile. She would give the after-school program a thorough evaluation and then present her findings to Emmett.

* * *

Lucie arrived at the interdenominational church the following afternoon with a smile and her electronic tablet in her purse. She already had evaluation forms set up on there, and she could just type in her observations. She was excited about this first Fortune-funded project in Austin and ready to speak with the reverend and Florence Parker.

However, when she opened the door to the social hall and stepped inside, she didn't find Florence. She found Chase!

She stopped in her tracks, her mint-colored A-line dress swishing around her knees. She didn't think twice about asking, "What are you doing here?"

The first words out of his mouth surprised her even more than she expected. "Pretend you don't know me," he said in a low voice.

"What?"

Glancing over his shoulder to the room inside, where there was noise and commotion, he repeated, "Pretend you don't know me. My mother was supposed to be here to meet you, but she wasn't feeling well and she asked me to come in her stead."

Lucie had never known Chase to be anything but honest. As far as she could tell, he was being sincere now. But what about Florence? Did she really not feel well? She couldn't be trying to push them together, could she?

Knowing Chase was right and that no one could know their connection, Lucie forced herself to smile and extend her hand.

Chase took it and shook it, but he held on a few moments too long, and she felt the ripple of sexual awareness travel through her whole body. Pretend they didn't know each other? These would have to be Oscar-winning performances.

As if they had just met, Chase motioned her into the larger room and led her to the minister. After introductions, Reverend Stanhope, a tall, thin man with wire-rimmed glasses that fell down his nose, nodded to the children, who didn't seem to be organized well.

He pushed his glasses to the bridge of his nose. "I know you're here to evaluate our program. Please ask any questions you'd like. We're open to suggestions to make it better, even if you don't take us on as a project."

She was used to working with children at the orphanages. All ages. Here, she could see exactly what needed to be done first. There was one motherly looking woman at a table participating in an activity with the smaller children, encouraging them to color and draw pictures. But the rest of the kids were pretty much on their own and not doing a good job of keeping themselves busy. There was squabbling in one corner and raucous roughhousing in another.

"You just have one helper today?" Lucie asked.

"I do. I'm down two volunteers to the flu."

"The first thing we need to do is divide the children who are ages five to seven in one group and eight to twelve in the other. Do you mind if we do that?"

The minister looked relieved that someone had a suggestion he could incorporate. "I don't mind at all."

"I can take the older kids outside," Chase offered. "Do you have a ball?"

She admired Chase's desire to help and wondered if he'd be good with the kids. "That would be a great idea."

She clapped her hands to gain the children's attention, introduced herself and Chase to them and began to organize.

* * *

After an hour of dodgeball, Chase felt he'd had a workout. He rounded up the children and took them back inside. Once they'd chosen books from a shelf and settled in a reading corner, he directed them to choose a partner. They could read to each other.

Suddenly, he heard a little boy crying, and he looked over to see Lucie crouched down with one of the five-year-olds.

"But I can't find it," the little boy wailed.

"What color is it?" Lucie asked gently.

"Red with white letters. It says my name—Dave."

"Okay, Dave. Let's think about where you had it last. When was the last time you wore your cap?"

"I had it on before we were dancing. I had it on before we were singing."

Dancing and singing. Lucie was probably good at both. He could imagine her leading the kids.

"How about before that?" she asked the child.

Dave poked two fingers into his mouth. "I had it on before I played hopscotch." He suddenly grinned. "It's on the bench outside. It fell off and I left it."

"Come on," Lucie said with excitement. "Let's go see if it's still there."

Sure enough, two minutes later, when they both came back inside, Dave was wearing his cap. He wrapped his arm around Lucie and gave her a huge hug. "Thank you. My mom would be mad if I lost it. She bought it for me when we went to San Antonio."

"I'm sure she'd be more concerned that you were upset. But now you have it. How about drawing a special picture of that cap?"

Chase was aware of every word Lucie spoke to the

little boy, but he wasn't only aware of that. He was aware of her arm around the child's shoulders, the tone of her voice that was compassionate and ready to help any way she could. Sure, she'd had practice. She'd helped children around the world. Would she ever think about a life of her own and children of her own?

Parents began arriving to pick up their kids. Lucie saw the reverend say goodbye to his last volunteer, who was looking kind of pale.

The minister came over to Lucie and Chase, shaking his head.

"I think I'm going to have to close down the program for the next few days. I certainly can't handle this crowd on my own. My last volunteer thinks she's coming down with whatever is going around."

"Let me talk to Mr. Parker a few minutes before you make a decision," Lucie suggested to the reverend.

She and Chase went to a quiet corner.

"What do you have in mind?" he asked.

"I know this is awkward, and I know we have to pretend we didn't meet each other before, but do you think we can help the next few days? I hate to see Reverend Stanhope close down the program in the midst of deciding whether we're going to fund it or not. I've had background checks done for the work I do. I don't know if we can get you cleared or not."

"I know the police chief," Chase informed her. "Maybe he can get a background check through quickly for me. It only takes about twenty-four hours. I want to help you with this. And as far as pretending we don't know each other goes, we can pull it off."

They'd done a good job this afternoon, but she'd been inside and he'd been outside.

"Can you spare a couple of hours away from Parker Oil tomorrow?"

"It will be a good test for my CFO. I want to see if he can handle whatever comes up on his own. If he can do that, I'll know I'm leaving the company in good hands when I leave."

"And if he can't?"

"Then I'll find someone else. I trust Jeff, though. I don't think he'll let me down."

"So we're going to offer to help?"

"It's a done deal," he said, holding out his hand again so they could shake on it. This time she slipped hers into his and then quickly pulled it back again.

Chase's knowing smile said he knew what she was doing. She didn't fool him one little bit.

"Since you have your own car and I have my own car, why don't you follow me again to the truck stop? They have great breakfast-for-dinner specials."

Lucie knew she shouldn't. Chase Parker was a temptation that could land her in all kinds of trouble—with her family, with the press, with her life. On the other hand, chocolate chip pancakes and Chase were very hard to resist.

At the truck stop, Lucie didn't see Chase's car. He apparently hadn't arrived yet. She was overtaken with the knowledge that she shouldn't have come. She was sending Chase the wrong message that she wanted to spend time with him. Time with him was not going to help their situation. Time with him was only putting her in a tailspin. Time with him was reminding her of time in the past, when they'd held each other and kissed and made love.

She had stowed her wig in the car for emergencies and she put it on now, combing it into place. Exiting her car, she glanced around and then entered the diner, passed down the row of booths, finally taking a different one than where they'd sat in the last time…just because. Never do the same thing twice. Always do the unexpected. Don't give the media a pattern to follow.

Finally Chase came into the diner and slid into the bench seat across from her, wearing his sunglasses.

She had to smile. "I can recognize you even with the sunglasses," she said.

"And I can recognize you even with the wig."

Was it true that they still knew each other so well after ten years? Maybe so.

Lucie was grateful when a different waitress waited on them this time and took their order. A different shift. That was good.

When she said as much to Chase, he reached across the table and took her hand. "For ten minutes, Lucie, just ten minutes, forget who you are and what you have to do. Just enjoy your chocolate chip pancakes with the whipped cream and talk to me about whatever matters to you."

She wished she could just let go of everything that easily, but for ten minutes—"I'll try."

He nodded and squeezed her hand. She felt that squeeze deep inside, but then he let go and sat back. Taking off his sunglasses, he pocketed them.

She unwrapped her silverware, took the napkin and spread it on her lap. Silence hovered between them.

Lucie asked, "Do you really want me to talk about what's important to me?"

"I do."

"Those kids back there are important to me. I feel like I'm doing something worthwhile when I'm singing a song with them or teaching them a dance. You can see knowledge exploding in their eyes when you show them something new. There is so much innocence there and precociousness and curiosity. Don't you wish we could all keep some of that as we grow older?"

"I wish we could. But that seems to be impossible. Problems and stress weigh us down."

"But they have stress, too. They see their parents argue. They don't get along with a brother or sister. They're scared to come to school. They don't know how to play a game and they're afraid the kids will laugh at them. They don't seem like big stresses to us, but they are to them."

"You really know a lot about kids, don't you?"

"I've probably been with them more than adults over the past eight years, anyway."

The waitress brought them mugs of coffee. After she disappeared again, Chase put his elbows on the table and leaned in. "So, tell me about your life and your dreams. You obviously love children. How many do you want someday?"

To her amazement, she admitted the truth. "I haven't given it much thought."

"And if you did?" he prompted.

If she did… Her mouth suddenly went dry. If she had children, she imagined having them with him! Impossible.

She had to answer his question because he was sitting there, studying her, waiting for her response. "Thinking about it, I think I'd like three."

"Or four?" he countered with a teasing glint in his

eye. "Two girls and two boys, so none of them feel out of place or outnumbered. Of course, we'd have to throw in some horses, and maybe a dog or two."

She laughed, a genuine laugh that had nothing to do with the past or the future and everything to do with now.

As they discussed the kids in the after-school program and what activities they'd devise for the next day, their pancakes arrived.

They both dug in with gusto.

Chase downed his faster than Lucie did. He was finishing up when he reached across the table again. This time, not to hold her hand but to swipe a bit of whipped cream from the corner of her lip. His finger, his touch, was gentle but sensual. She wished she could touch him in the same way. She wished she was kissing him.

They couldn't seem to stop looking at each other.

They both started when Chase's cell phone buzzed. He took it from his belt and studied the screen. "Work," he grumbled.

"It's after hours," she said.

"There are no after hours in this business. I have to take this."

She nodded and didn't even try to keep from listening.

"I understand, Jeff," he said after about a minute of complete attention to his employee on the other end of the line. "He doesn't want to meet with you, he wants to meet with me. Do you want me to give him a call? Fine, you call him."

Chase checked his watch. "I can be there in a half hour."

There was a pause, and then Chase said, "There's no need to apologize. You can't dictate what someone else does or wants or demands. But I want you to sit in on the meeting, too. Channing is going to have to realize he has to trust you as much as he trusts me."

After Chase ended the call, he brought his gaze back to Lucie's. "I have to go."

"A crisis at work?"

"Something like that."

"Do you really think you can ever leave the company?"

Chase pulled his wallet from his pocket and took out a few bills. He laid them on the table with the check and then pulled out a tip, too.

"I can leave the tip," she protested.

"My treat," he insisted. Then he stood, loomed over her and answered her question. "I don't know if I can ever leave the company, but I'm going to try to make it happen. Maybe I'm deluding myself that I can change the course of my life, but I'm certainly going to give it a good try. I'll see you tomorrow at the church."

Lucie watched Chase leave the restaurant, her heart feeling heavy. She doubted if Chase would show up at the after-school program the next day. After all, an oil magnate had better things to do.

And if he did show up?

She'd have to pretend she didn't feel closer to him again. She'd have to pretend she wasn't attracted to him. She'd have to pretend that she didn't wish things were different.

Chapter Six

It was almost midnight as Lucie sat on her bed, her laptop adjusted so that Amelia could see her face through her webcam. They often video-chatted since she'd been living in Austin. It was one way of seeing each other face-to-face.

"Do you really have time to talk?" Lucie asked her sister.

"I do. Quinn helped me put Clementine to bed and then he crashed. He also said if I'm up late talking to you, he'll get Clementine up in the morning. Isn't he wonderful?"

Lucie couldn't help smiling. It was so good to see her sister happy. "Spoken like a woman in love."

"I am and always will be. So, what do you need to talk about?"

Now that the time had come to say it out loud, she didn't know if she could. She'd kept the secret for so long that she hesitated to share it. But that was silly. This was Amelia, her sister. She deserved to know. Just as her mother deserved to know, especially with Chase back in her life. Well, not really back in her life. Just sort of.

"I've been keeping a secret."

"Really? You don't keep secrets. You're an open book."

"Maybe not as open as you think."

Yes, she was the one who usually followed all the orders. She was the one who followed the rules. She was the one who was proper. Maybe not anymore.

"Do you remember that trip I took to Scotland when I was seventeen?"

"Barely," Amelia admitted. "I was involved with riding competitions that summer. I do remember you were sent home early and there was all kinds of hush-hush about it. Mum and Dad wouldn't talk about it. They just said you'd broken a rule."

"They didn't find out this secret. They only knew part of what happened."

"What happened?" Amelia asked, her eyes widening.

"I got caught with a boy in his room. Not a boy, but a man. Chase was twenty-one."

"And that's why you were sent home?"

"It was, and he was fired. He was from the US. Texas."

"Uh-oh. Do I know what's coming? Are you having a reunion?"

"Not exactly."

When she couldn't seem to find the words, Amelia jumped in. "So, what was the secret?"

"Before I was found in his room, Chase and I got married."

Amelia's mouth dropped open. Her eyes grew even

bigger and wider. She stared through the computer screen at Lucie as if she had two noses. "You got what?"

Amelia's voice had grown louder and Lucie said, "Shhh, you'll wake Quinn."

Amelia brushed that thought aside with her hand. "I might wake him on purpose after *this* conversation. So, what else happened? You got married and just came home?"

Lucie told Amelia about Chase's father and his oil company and his plans for his son that didn't include an English girl.

"So Chase's dad sent you home with a threat that he'd cause a scandal if you didn't keep quiet."

"That's pretty much it."

"And you gave in to that?"

"I had broken rules. I wasn't going to break any more. My time with Chase was an experiment that didn't work. I didn't want to cause more embarrassment to Mum and Dad."

"Would that ever have been a scandal across the tabloids! It would have involved two countries."

Leave it up to Amelia to look at it that way, but it was true.

"So, what brought all this to the surface now?" her sister asked.

"Chase tracked me down and found me here. It turns out, the annulment never went through. He and I are still married."

A frown immediately adorned Amelia's face. "Uh-oh. You were engaged to Terrence."

"Yes. This is another scandal in the making."

Amelia was looking down at her hands, so Lucie couldn't see exactly what she was doing. But she must have been looking Chase up online on her phone because she let out a little squeal. "Chase Parker. You sure know how to pick 'em, don't you? What a hunk. Almost as hunky as Quinn."

"Amelia—"

"So, what have you been doing with him? Is he the friend you were with the other night when I called?"

"Yes, he was. He's buying a ranch. That's how all this came up. In the paperwork. He took me there to show it to me. He wants to rescue horses."

"And you have a keen love of horses."

"I do."

"And?" Amelia prompted.

Should she reveal it all? Should she confide everything to Amelia in a way she hadn't before?

Her sister was perceptive, because she asked, "Are you telling me Chase found you, and the marriage isn't over?"

"It's not over legally."

"I'm talking about emotionally. Do you still have feelings for him? Have you thought about him all these years?"

"I have thought about him," Lucie returned quietly. "But they were merely dreams that came and went. I never expected them to materialize."

"But now they can?"

"Oh, it's not like that. We've had a couple of breakfasts together at a diner. I even wore my wig. If anybody connects us, we're in big trouble for his business dealings and my reputation. We're being very careful, but now things have gotten complicated again. His mother asked if the Fortune Foundation could fund a program at their church. I looked into it and they're going to. The volunteers there have gotten sick. Somehow Chase and I ended up volunteering today and played with the kids. We're helping there again tomorrow and maybe the next day."

"Is he good with kids?"

"He seems to be."

"That's good, because you're a natural. You need a bunch of your own."

Lucie went silent.

"What would be so bad about hooking up with him again? You need some fun in your life, if not someone you can dream about."

"We're intense when we're together. There's tons of chemistry. We're asking for nothing but trouble if we become involved again."

"You kissed him, didn't you?"

Lucie felt herself blushing. "*He* kissed *me*."

Amelia rolled her eyes. "Same difference in this situation. Tell me again why it wouldn't work."

"Because he's changing his life. He's separating from his parents and going out on his own with this new business venture. He's found his vocation just as I have. But mine takes me around the world. I don't want to give up what I do. It's important work. And our mother depends on me."

"Did you ever consider that she depends on you too much?"

"Is that possible? I work with her. She has to depend on me."

"It's more than that and you know it. Ever since Daddy died, she looks to you for emotional support. She's closest to you," Amelia said matter-of-factly without any jealousy.

"I'm beginning to wonder if it's good for her or me."

"I believe you have a lot to think about, my lady,"

Amelia decided. "None of this sounds like you. You really do have to tell Mum as soon as you can."

"Do you have any advice about Chase?"

"Not advice, exactly. I can tell you I tried to deny my attraction to Quinn and that didn't work. If you care about Chase, you shouldn't put the brakes on. You should see where it goes."

"And if it goes nowhere? Or if it takes a wrong turn and goes wrong?"

"Then you'll know. After what I've been through with Quinn, I know I can get through anything. You can, too."

"I'll think about everything you said. I promise. In the meantime, why don't you and Quinn come up here and go on a night on the town? I'll babysit. I'd love to spend some time with Clementine Rose."

"She goes through fussy spells for no reason sometimes."

"That doesn't matter. I'll be here for her and with her. You do trust her with me, don't you?"

"You know I do. You're so good with her." Amelia was silent for a moment—she appeared to be thinking about Lucie's suggestion. "Let me talk to Quinn. Maybe we can get away for at least a night. That would be nice. So, tell me when you're seeing Chase again."

"Tomorrow afternoon at the after-school program, but as I said, we have to pretend we don't know each other. This is going to take a bit of acting."

"You can do it. And after you're done acting?"

"I'll come back here and he'll go back to the Bar P. That's the way it has to be, Amelia, at least for now."

"Don't live in fear of what might happen. Live for what *is* happening. Got that?"

"I got it."

"I'll get back to you about an overnight, and you can tell me what happened. And I want full disclosure."

Lucie laughed. "Full disclosure. And, Amelia, please don't say anything to anyone else about this…except Quinn."

"I won't. I promise."

Lucie knew Amelia kept her promises. "I'll talk to you soon."

When Lucie closed her laptop, she thought about Chase and tomorrow afternoon. A thrill of anticipation bubbled in her stomach. She just couldn't help wanting to see him.

The following afternoon, Lucie knew she had to put on the brakes. She just had to. She felt as if her heart were careening down a highway going the wrong way.

A ten-year-old named Jasper quickly kicked the ball her way and she stepped sideways so she wouldn't be out of the dodgeball game.

Today the minister had taken the smaller kids inside, so unfortunately she was outside with Chase and the older children. They weren't anywhere near each other. He was across the circle. However, when their eyes met…

She expected lightning to strike—either from the chemistry between her and Chase…or the storm that was brewing in those gray clouds up above.

When parents began arriving to pick up their children, Lucie ducked inside the social hall. The kids didn't recognize her, but it was possible one of their parents might. She didn't want a three-ring circus to ensue. She busied herself straightening up the activity room until all the children were gone. At least she thought they were all gone. One little blond girl remained.

Reverend Stanhope checked his watch. "I have a meeting and Michelle Tillot, Chrissy's mother, isn't answering the phone number she gave me. I don't think she has a cell. She can't afford it."

"I can stay until her mother picks her up," Lucie offered. The little girl looked tired and maybe a little scared.

She looked up at Lucie and said, "Mommy always comes."

"She'll come, honey. I'll stay with you until she gets here."

"I'm not going to leave you here alone," Chase said. "I'll stay, too."

"There's no need…"

The reverend looked from one of them to the other, and Lucie knew she shouldn't protest too much. That would just raise a red flag.

Chase asked the minister, "Do you want the folding chairs taken down and stacked against the wall?"

Reverend Stanhope nodded. "That would be terrific. It's good that the two of you work well together. Chase, you tell your mother I hope she's feeling better soon."

"I'll do that."

"I'll check back here after my meeting to make sure Chrissy got picked up and then I'll lock up."

After the minister left, Lucie attempted to ignore Chase's presence as he began collapsing chairs.

She asked Chrissy, "Would you like me to read you a story? There are plenty of books over there. We can do that until your mom comes."

Chrissy poked a finger in her mouth and asked around it, "Can I sit in your lap?"

"Sure you can. Let's use that bigger chair over there."

It was the one the volunteer used for story corner that could easily hold her and Chrissy.

It wasn't long after Lucie began reading *Where the Wild Things Are* that Chrissy fell asleep. Lucie just held her securely, her chin resting on the little girl's head. When she looked across the room, Chase was watching her.

"You and children seem to go together," he said quietly.

She didn't comment because she didn't know what to say. Was he thinking of her with children of her own, and possibly imagining what they'd look like? She could imagine a boy with his dark hair and eyes.

Nope, she wasn't going there.

Fortunately she heard a car pulling into the lot outside. Chrissy's mom, she hoped.

Apparently Chase had heard it too and he went to look. A petite woman with light brown hair and dark brown eyes came rushing in. Spotting Chrissy in Lucie's arms, she looked relieved.

She introduced herself and began apologizing at once. "I'm so sorry I'm late. My car battery went dead and it took a while to find a Good Samaritan to help me jump-start the car. I'm afraid the same thing's going to happen when I start it up again. Is the reverend around? I was going to ask him if I could borrow some money from the emergency fund." Michelle looked embarrassed to have to say it.

"He had a meeting," Lucie said kindly.

Before she could say more, Chase took a card from his pocket, quickly went to a table where pencils were still strewn and jotted something on the card.

Then he held it out to the woman. "If you go to this

garage, a new car battery will be waiting. I'll make sure it is."

Chrissy's mom took the card, surprise in her eyes. "Are you sure about this? I'll repay you, I promise. I'm just short this month."

Chase was already shaking his head. "That's not necessary."

"I don't know how to thank you."

"No thanks necessary. When you have the opportunity, help out somebody who needs it."

Chrissy awakened, fluttered her eyes and saw her mom. Scrambling from Lucie's lap, she ran to her and hugged her around the knees. "Mommy, Mommy, you came."

"It's time to go home, sweetheart. How about macaroni and cheese for supper?"

Chrissy bobbed her head. Michelle mouthed another thank-you to Chase and Lucie and then left, holding her daughter's hand.

Chase stood at the door and watched them climb into the car that was still running. Apparently Michelle had been afraid to turn it off.

"I hope she can get to a garage in the morning," he said.

"Maybe she'll have a neighbor who can help her jumpstart it if it doesn't work. That was a nice thing you did." Lucie studied him.

He shrugged. "I couldn't see depleting the church's emergency fund."

"Do you do that kind of thing often?" She was so curious about him and his life and didn't want to be. She was still trying to figure out who he was now compared to who he had been.

"Probably not as often as I should. Giving to an impersonal charity foundation is one thing. Giving help to someone who really needs it, who was right in front of me, is another."

"I see."

"What do you see? Why did you ask?"

"I'm still trying to figure you out. I wondered if maybe you did that to impress her."

"Impressing anyone isn't high on my to-do list," he returned, almost angrily. "Do you do what you do to impress people?"

"Of course not."

"All right, then why suspect that of me?"

"Because I don't know what to believe where you're concerned. I mean, ten years ago, you asked me to marry you. I did. Then your father swooped in and I basically never heard from you again."

She could see the anger disappear from his face and he looked perplexed. "You're the one who didn't write back because your royal life got in the way."

"That's not true. I received one letter from you, and then nothing else."

They stared at each other, not knowing what to believe.

Why did Chase look confused? He'd written one letter and that was it. And why did he insist her royal life had gotten in the way, when she'd written time and time again? Apparently neither of them trusted the other. That was because ten years and a whole lot of history had passed between them. Maybe they hadn't known each other back then any more than they knew each other now.

"It doesn't matter." Lucie gathered up her purse.

Chase's pride seemed to kick in and he crossed his

arms over his chest in a defensive stance. "No, I guess it doesn't. After our marriage is annulled, we won't see each other again."

After their marriage was annulled… She might be flying off before that even happened. There was no point to this conversation. No point to what had happened and what hadn't happened. No point in standing in the same room with Chase and feeling a longing she didn't want to feel.

The gray sky had turned even darker and the wind had picked up. The last thing she needed was to get caught in a storm. "I want to beat the rain getting back to my apartment. Take care, Chase."

She'd call the minister later and see if any of the volunteers were coming back tomorrow. Although she thought she and Chase worked well together, she couldn't be in his presence again tomorrow. She just couldn't.

Chase let her leave without a word. What was there to say? Don't go? It was silly of her to even think he *could* say it.

To her dismay, Lucie didn't beat the rain. As soon as she pulled out of the church's parking lot, sheets of it beat down, heavy and thick. She really *wasn't* used to driving on the right side of the road, especially not with the weather front moving in.

Her conversation with Chase played in her head. Why had she said what she'd said to him? Maybe she just didn't trust men, and that was why she hadn't dated since her broken engagement. After all, hadn't Terrence lied to her on more than one occasion? Hadn't he told her he was having business meetings when he'd gone to his club? Hadn't she seen a text from more than one woman on his phone? Hadn't he admitted not enough sparks were there between the two of them, and he'd seemed to blame her because she wouldn't show cleavage, because her skirts weren't short enough, because she didn't wear enough makeup?

He'd implied all that, and part of her had believed him. Look at the way the tabloids characterized her sometimes. She meant it when she'd said to Chase that they made her into a cartoon. They constantly held up a distorted mirror. Chase had read those tabloids. That was what he'd known about her in the past ten years. He was far ahead of *her* because she'd known nothing about him, certainly not enough to trust his intentions and his motives.

Tears welled up in her eyes and she wasn't even sure why. Because she hadn't believed Chase seemed to be the man that he portrayed himself to be?

The rain was almost blinding now. She tried to take her time to remember where she was and how to drive in this mess. Suddenly, with another cloudburst, she simply couldn't see. The windshield wipers weren't fast enough. Her tires dipped into an immense pothole puddle. The car slid. She wasn't even sure which way.

All she knew was that she came to a banging halt with her shoulder slamming into the door frame. All she knew was that the car tilted sideways. All she knew was that she was in trouble, with no help in sight.

Chase was driving away from Austin toward his family's ranch when he decided to turn around. The weather was miserable and so was he. His pride had gotten the best of him, and he'd become too defensive with Lucie. He shouldn't have let her drive off into the storm like that.

Instead of having more regrets, there was something he was going to do about it. He was going to go after her.

Taking the first side road, he made a quick turn and headed back the way he'd come. The rain was pouring down with no regard for anything in its wake. That was nature. As he drove past the church, he saw that the lot was empty. No surprise there. Continuing toward Austin, he tried not to think. He was on a mission. He didn't know what the result would be, but it had to be better than what he was feeling now. Was Lucie in the same state of tumult?

His windshield wipers swiped as fast as they could, but had trouble keeping up with the downpour. He almost missed the car along the side of the road. Almost.

Thank the Lord, he didn't.

He recognized the shape and color of the vehicle that was barely visible through the rain. But a sixth sense had made him notice, and his gut clenched because he didn't know what he'd find when he pulled off the road.

It wasn't hard to tell that the car was firmly entrenched in a muddy ditch. He climbed out of his truck, ran up to Lucie's car and banged on the window.

When she opened the door, she looked scared and pale. "Oh, my gosh, Chase, you gave me a fright. I didn't know who you were at first."

"Are you all right?"

"I'm fine, but the car won't start and I can't get it out of here."

He was getting soaking wet, and she would be, too, until they got out of this. But there was no help for it.

"Come on," he said.

But when she tried to get out of the car, she winced and grabbed her shoulder.

"You're not fine. I'm taking you to the ER."

"No. The media will be down on this if you do that. Really, I'm just bumped up and bruised a bit. I need a hot cup of tea and my car rescued."

His arm around her now, he hustled her into his truck and helped her into the passenger seat. Then he ran around to his side and climbed in. "I'll get the foreman at the ranch to pull your car from the ditch. Tomás knows how to keep his mouth shut. I'm going to take you back there."

She bit her lower lip. "I can go back to my apartment." There wasn't a whole lot of force behind her voice.

"If you won't go to the ER, I need a second opinion, and Mom will give it. It's the Bar P or the emergency room. Your choice."

"The Bar P," she said with a sigh, giving him a look that told him she didn't like any of this.

They drove to the ranch with only the sound of the rain rat-a-tatting on the truck roof. Using his hands-free device, Chase pressed the button on his mirror and called Tomás. After giving instructions, he ended the call.

"Aren't you going to call your mom and warn her that I'm coming?" Lucie asked.

"I don't want her to worry before she has to."

"Spoken like a man," Lucie murmured.

Chase cut her a glance but didn't argue with her. He knew his mom. She was great in a crisis. But she worried up, down and sideways beforehand. They'd be there in five minutes.

"Is she still ill?" Lucie asked.

"She's feeling better." Though he suspected his mother hadn't told him the truth about the matter. He wasn't sure anything had been wrong with her. He didn't know why she'd wanted him to be at the church instead of herself. Certainly she wouldn't be trying to push him and Lucie together when she'd supported his father as he'd pulled them apart. Sometimes he didn't understand his parents at all.

By the time they reached the house, the two of them were soaked to the skin. Chase didn't ring the bell but walked right in.

"I could take you to my guesthouse, but I didn't think that would be proper…just in case anybody does find out about this. We want to go through the right channels so there's no reason for gossip."

"Gossip? We're married, Chase. There'd be gossip for the next three months about that."

"All right, so we're going to keep it from happening. Mom, you here?"

His mother came strolling through the dining room. "Of course I'm here. Where else would I be? Oh, my goodness! You've got Lucie, and look at the two of you. What happened?"

Chase wrapped his arm around Lucie's shoulders and took her over to the sofa. "Mom, can you get some towels, maybe a blanket? Her car hit a pothole filled with water, hydroplaned and went off the road. She's a little bumped up."

Lucie looked up at Chase's mom. "I hit my shoulder on the door. It's a little sore. With an ice pack, I'm sure I'll be fine."

Florence plopped her hands on her hips and studied Lucie carefully. "You, my girl, need some tender, loving care. Ice on that shoulder is going to make you cold. Coffee or tea?"

"Tea, please." Now Lucie sounded like a small child. That was the effect his mother had on people.

"And the seat belt probably cut you across the ribs. Are you having trouble breathing?"

"It hurts a little when I breathe."

"I wanted to take her to the ER, but she wouldn't have it," Chase explained.

"I can understand that. Come on, Lucie, why don't you come with me? Instead of making the sofa all soppy, I'll put you in the guest bedroom. You can get a warm shower, and I'll give you some spare clothes I have up there. I'll make tea and then we'll see about that ice pack."

"I don't want to put you to any trouble."

Florence waved her hand in front of Lucie's nose. "Nonsense. It isn't trouble. After all, you are still one of the family."

At that, Chase could see Lucie felt totally out of her depth.

"Go with Mom," he said. "I know how to put the tea-kettle on. You should probably eat something, too, something with salt. You're much too pale."

"I'm rattled," she responded vehemently. Yes, she was. First from their argument, and then from that slide off the road.

The two of them had forgotten for a moment that Mrs. Parker was listening.

"There will be time to fix whatever's wrong," Florence deduced wisely. "Come on, Lucie."

Lucie slipped off her shoes. "I don't want to leave marks on this beautiful floor."

"Juanita takes care of that," Florence said. "No need to worry. Chase, did you see to Lucie's car?"

"I did. Tomás will bring it back here and we'll see if there's any damage. He'll clean it up, too."

As Lucie and his mother walked out of the room, Chase headed for the kitchen. He had to keep his hands busy. He'd wanted to put them all over Lucie to figure out if she was okay, of course, but for more reasons, too. Her pale skin with the slightest amount of freckles on her cheeks, that dimple at one corner of her lip begged to be touched. Her hair, even though wet, was silky and sexy. He'd wanted to sling her over his shoulder, toss her into the back of his truck and make love to her right there. How stupid was that? It wasn't as if she was the type of woman who would do anything like that. It wasn't as if he had any right. It wasn't as if they had any reason other than lust for coming together.

No, he had to bury those caveman tendencies. They'd gotten him into trouble with her ten years ago, and he wouldn't let it happen again. He was also grateful his father wasn't home. Then he might have had to take her to the guesthouse and hide her!

A half hour later, his mother had brought Lucie back to the kitchen. They were almost the same size, except Lucie was taller. So the slacks she wore were a little short. But the peach-colored silky blouse hung on her just right. She didn't have a blanket around her, but his mother had apparently offered her one of her cashmere sweaters. It matched the blouse.

"Herbal tea or regular?" Florence asked her.

"Herbal would be nice. Something with cinnamon?"

"Orange spice."

Chase picked up a carafe that sat on an electric warmer. "Just the right temperature."

"You know about that?" Lucie asked, surprised.

"I've been taught by a master. Mom's an expert on tea making, brewing and choosing."

He found an ice pack in the refrigerator and wrapped it with a kitchen towel. Then he gently placed it on Lucie's shoulder while his mother poured tea.

"Just a bit of sugar," Lucie said.

Florence wrinkled her nose. "I like it straight."

Chase had made himself a pot of coffee. "And I like it black." He cast his mother a glance before he broached the next subject.

She seemed to read his mind, because she looked over at Lucie and nodded.

"I think you should stay here tonight," he said. "If those muscles around the ribs swell and you have trouble breathing, someone needs to be with you."

Chase could see the warm tea was calming Lucie down, and fatigue was setting in. Instead of protesting, she asked again, "Are you sure it's no trouble?"

"No trouble," Florence said. "I'll feel better knowing you're safe. Wouldn't you rather have us come to your aid if you need it than a doorman?"

Lucie targeted her glance at Chase. "You told your mother about Irv?"

"I told her he was protective, and that's a good thing."

Lucie had left her purse on the coffee table and now her phone rang inside it. She said, "I'd better check it."

When she did, she said, "It's my mother. She must have reached an area with cell phone towers."

"Do you need privacy?" Florence asked.

Lucie hesitated a moment. "No, I'm fine." She said it as if this were going to be a short call.

Chase guessed Lucie wouldn't be having a heart-to-heart about her marriage to him.

Florence walked away to give Lucie privacy. "I'll see what we have in the refrigerator that we can have for supper."

Chase, however, stayed right there in the living room with Lucie. He wanted to overhear this conversation.

Lucie answered the call. When she did, she pretended everything tonight hadn't happened. "Hi, Mum. How are you?"

Chase couldn't hear what her mother told her, but whatever she said made Lucie happy. At least until her mother added something that drained the color from her face again.

"Yes, I suppose I can do that," she answered. "I'll see where I am with the Fortune offices in two weeks and then I'll let you know. Arriving a week early shouldn't be a problem. No, nothing's wrong."

Uh-oh. Lucie's mother must have good intuition, too, if she'd asked what was wrong. Obviously she could sense something was up, but Lucie was giving nothing away. However, by the time she ended the call, Chase could see she was in turmoil.

"I thought you were going to tell your mother about our marriage the next time you spoke with her," he said.

"I just couldn't do it now."

"Why? You're here. I'm here. The accident happened. You didn't even tell her about that."

"I don't want her to worry."

"Famous last words," he muttered.

He crossed to the sofa and sank down beside Lucie, taking her hand. "Why didn't you tell her? Because I was here and you didn't have privacy?"

Lucie lowered her voice. "I didn't tell her for the same

reason you haven't told your father you'll be moving out and quitting Parker Oil. It's not an easy thing to do."

She was right. Soon they'd both have to deal with those harder aspects of their life. Soon they'd be signing papers dissolving a union that shouldn't have happened to begin with.

Florence called from the kitchen, "I found leftover roast beef and mashed potatoes that we can warm up to have with it. I can rustle up some fresh broccoli. What do you think?"

Chase thought food was the least of their problems. He had no appetite, at least not for what his mother would be cooking up in the kitchen. He had an appetite for Lucie, and he was going to have to deal with that soon.

Chapter Seven

Sun poured in the window of the guest room at the Bar P as Lucie awakened slowly, stretching to try to figure out what hurt. Her shoulder was a bit sore. Her ribs felt better.

Last night had been mostly a blur after the phone call from her mother. Maybe it was stress from the accident or stress from being with Chase. She wasn't sure which. He'd shown her to a pink and lilac room decorated with a luxury comforter and satiny cream-colored sheets. His mother had brought her an ice pack and a heating pad, too. Chase might have stayed, but Florence had insisted Lucie rest and get a good night's sleep. After some hesitation, he'd left. And she'd fallen asleep.

Until a few minutes ago.

There was a slight tapping on her door. She realized someone didn't want to wake her if she was still asleep. But she had to start her day and return to her apartment.

"Come in," she called, tensing a bit because she thought her visitor might be Chase.

However, it wasn't. It was Florence. Chase's mother wheeled in a tea cart that smelled wonderful. There was a large plate with a stainless steel cover, a teapot, a teacup and a plate of pastries.

"Are you hungry?" Florence asked.

"Now that I smell food, I am," Lucie said with a smile. "But you didn't have to do this."

"You didn't have much supper." She took the lid from the large plate that held scrambled eggs, bacon and a stack of silver dollar pancakes. "Warm syrup is in that little pitcher, and butter's in the cup."

"This is wonderful."

"How's your shoulder?"

"Not bad," Lucie said.

Florence reached to the shelf under the top of the tray. "I brought you another ice pack. I thought you might want to put it on before you get dressed."

"You've thought of everything."

Florence frowned. "Not quite. I'm sorry this happened to you. I never imagined you'd be hurt helping me with the church program. You don't have to worry about today," she added. "I called the minister, and he has volunteers again."

"Do you know if my car is ready?"

"You'll have to ask Chase about that."

"He didn't leave for work?"

"No. He always spends some time with the horses in the morning, especially when he's trying to figure things out."

"Figure things out?"

"He's making changes, and I'm not sure he's used to

the idea of them yet. I know *I'm* certainly not. I'm going to miss not having him in the guesthouse, and I know his father will, too. I just hope Warren doesn't explode when Chase tells him what he's going to do."

"I hope he doesn't either. That won't be good for either of them." She did not have fond memories of Warren Parker, and Florence seemed to sense that.

"Chase's dad isn't the ogre Chase makes him out to be sometimes. He's just very old-school and set in his ways. But he has a good heart, and he wants the best for Chase."

"He always wanted that," Lucie agreed, thinking about the plans he'd had for his son when Chase was twenty-one.

"Hmmm," Florence said to that, and that was all. "I'll leave you to your breakfast. Do you remember your way to the barn?"

"I do."

"Well, good. I'll be in my study if you want to say goodbye before you leave."

And with that, Florence left the room.

The food called to Lucie and she ate with a hunger she hadn't had in a while. Afterward she dressed, wishing she had fresh clothes. But she'd be back at her place soon.

A half hour later, she was finding her way to the barn, hoping Chase was still there. When Lucie found him, he was...mucking out stalls! She grinned as she approached him.

Seeing her expression, he laid the pitchfork aside and put his hands on his hips. "What?"

"This isn't quite what I expected you to be doing."

"Horses have needs, too, and clean stalls are one of them. At my own place, I'll probably be doing this even more than I do it here. How are you feeling?"

"Like someone put me in a milk shake mixer."

He chuckled. "Vanilla, strawberry, or chocolate?"

"Chocolate all the way."

He sobered and came toward her. When he reached her, he asked, "Are you sure you're all right? I can take you to my mother's private physician. He'd keep the visit quiet."

"There's no need. Really, Chase. I'll keep icing my shoulder and I'll be fine. Is my car ready?"

"Tomás has to wash it down yet. The truth is, I'm not sure you should be driving. Why don't you let me take you back to your apartment, and he can bring your car in and park it later?"

She was about to protest when he shook his head. "Don't tell me it's too much trouble. Those are words you use too often."

When he was standing this close, she couldn't think straight. "Maybe part of the problem is I don't want to owe you anything."

Really close now, he let his hand drift to her shoulder, then up her neck into her hair. "I don't think of *owe* or *not owe* when it comes to you."

She could hardly push the words out, but she wanted to know. "What do you think of when it comes to me?"

He nudged her closer, and she didn't pull back. "The same thing I was thinking of last night while I lay in the guesthouse and you were at my mom's. Which was probably a good thing because when I'm with you, Lucie, I want to take you to bed again. That's the long and short of it. Our fire didn't burn out ten years ago."

No, it hadn't, but how long could it sustain glowing embers? She and Chase were being pulled in different directions. How could any fire last that way?

"I thought about coming to your room last night," he said honestly. "Even if it was just to hold you through the night."

"My guess is, we wouldn't have just held each other."

His eyes blazed with that fire they were just talking about. "You're right. That's why I didn't come. I didn't want to take advantage of you being vulnerable."

She felt all too vulnerable around him. But when he laced his hand through her hair and came in for a kiss, she didn't protest. Chase's kisses had always been filled with excitement and fervor, and demanded an answering response from her.

When his tongue swept her mouth, she held on to his shoulders as if her life depended on it. As his thumb caressed her cheek, his tenderness swept over her with repercussions she didn't even have the sense to consider. She remembered his kiss all those years ago—the very first one. She recalled how she'd trembled as soon as his lips touched hers, how his coaxing ardor had led her to press against him, the way she was pressing against him now. His jeans weren't that much of a barrier against his passion. Feeling it, she knew she'd welcome satisfaction as much as he would. Chase's arms were as possessive as his tongue was seductive.

He'd just laid fresh hay in the stall next to this one. She'd seen it.

What was she thinking?

A truck door slammed outside, and with that noise, the web of passion around them was torn asunder.

Chase released her, then shook his head and muttered, "Whew. We keep that up, we'll light the barn on fire."

"If we keep that up, we're both going to get hurt."

Chase's gaze raked over her face. "Why didn't your engagement work out?"

She blinked because the change of subject was so abrupt. But the truth was, she didn't really want to talk to Chase about it.

"It just didn't. I'm sure you've dated women and then decided they weren't right for you."

"I've never gotten as far as an engagement. That's serious. What made you decide he wasn't right for you?"

"For one thing, I was traveling and we had distance between us."

"That's not insurmountable if two people care."

He was going to probe and probe until she gave him something, she just knew it. "He lied to me. He went clubbing and wasn't alone when he did."

"Honesty is everything," Chase agreed. "But there was something else, wasn't there?"

"Chase, I don't see why we need to talk about this."

"Tell me the reason you broke up with him wasn't because of the fire we'd experienced. Maybe you just couldn't match that and you didn't want to accept less."

Was that the true reason her relationship with Terry hadn't worked? Maybe with Chase she would have felt sexy, coy and flirtatious. Maybe with Chase—

Flustered now from him delving too deep, she shot back quickly, "You don't have much ego, do you?"

"This isn't about ego, Lucie. I know I've been looking for that same kind of passion ever since."

"We were young…with raging hormones."

"And what's our excuse now?" he asked wryly.

"Maybe when we know we can't have something, we want it even more. Isn't that human nature?"

Chase glanced around the barn, and then he looked

back at her. "Maybe it is. I'd better get you back to your apartment and I'd better get to work. Dad will return within the next few days, and I want to make sure everything at Parker Oil is ready for my departure."

"You've decided on your replacement?"

"I have. Jeff will be perfect. I just have to organize the paperwork with all his accomplishments, so Dad can see my point. Do you need to go back to the house before we leave?"

"I really should say goodbye to your mother. She was so kind."

"All right, then. I'll finish this last stall and meet you in front of the house."

As Lucie left the barn, she felt as if she'd been dismissed. She didn't like that at all, but she knew what Chase was thinking. He had a lot of hard work ahead of him. He would be trying to juggle a new venture while still keeping his foot in at Parker Oil. She'd be building an orphanage in Guatemala. A night in bed, or a tumble in a stall, wouldn't make divergent life paths suddenly coincide.

Lucie couldn't help feeling defensive on the ride back to her apartment. She and Chase could always find things to talk about, but the sexual tension between them was difficult to deal with. This day, conversation didn't come easily. She was aware of his solicitous glances every once in a while, and in a way she resented them. She'd been taking care of herself just fine for the past ten years. If she had a sore shoulder, she'd take care of it. He didn't have to worry.

But he didn't seem to believe that.

By the time they neared her apartment building, she couldn't wait to hop out of his truck. However, about a half block from the building, Lucie noticed a red car with a news station logo on the window. She murmured, "TXLB. I wonder if he's in the lobby."

"TXLB?" Chase asked. "The TV station?"

"Yes. The reporter's car is parked right back there."

"I'll be doing an interview with Norton Wilcox at TXLB for his talk show *About Austin* in about ten days. The station's highlighting the horse rescue. I'm going to reveal all my plans and hopefully encourage public support."

"Wilcox is the reporter who phoned me for an interview. But then he began hanging around. He doesn't want to take no for an answer. He keeps showing up, hoping I'll change my mind."

"He didn't give *me* a hassle. But then, I said yes to the interview because it will help my cause. Maybe I could act as a buffer for you."

She shook her head. "I don't need a buffer. I'll handle him."

As they neared the entrance to the garage, Lucie said quickly, "Keep on going."

As Chase passed the garage entrance, he asked, "Why?"

"Just go around and let me out a good block away. I'll double back."

"Okay, so you don't want a buffer. But if you need me to act as your bodyguard to lead you to your place, I will."

"I don't need a bodyguard. And unless you want your life turned as topsy-turvy as mine is, we need to do this my way. Just think about Amelia and all those tabloid photos. Do you want your face plastered on the front of one of those? Do you want this reporter associating you with me and digging up our marriage?"

"I don't like this, Lucie. I don't like letting you off a block away. You were hurt yesterday, whether you want to admit it or not."

She sighed. "I'm a little sore, that's all. Please, Chase, just do this for me."

As he rounded a corner to take the detour around the block, his jaw drew tense and his lips tightened into a straight line. Finally he agreed. "All right. I'll do as you ask under one condition."

"What?" she asked warily.

"Call me as soon as you're inside your apartment. Not five minutes later, but as soon as you're inside."

"That doesn't sound like a condition. It sounds like an order."

"You are a very frustrating and stubborn woman."

"And you're reaching into territory you shouldn't be."

"Maybe so," he agreed without apology.

She could see he wasn't going to back down. He might not let her out of his truck if she didn't agree.

"I'll call you as soon as I'm inside, I promise. I'm going to walk straight into the lobby and deal with whatever I have to deal with. You can expect my call in about five minutes. This is a good spot. Just let me out here."

Chase pulled over to the curb a block down from her apartment complex. Neither of them said a word as she climbed out. She did so quickly so no one would notice, and soon she was incognito in a line of pedestrians going their separate ways. She didn't glance back over her shoulder. She didn't see if Chase pulled away. She guessed he would, though. That was the smarter thing to do. But he might just drive around the block again until she called him.

Picking up the pace, she neared her apartment building and took a long, deep breath. Irv was standing at his counter and she immediately recognized the other man standing there with him—Norton Wilcox.

After he'd called for an interview, she watched his spot on the evening news. That hadn't changed her mind about sitting down with him. Irv was frowning, but Wilcox was smiling. It was one very fake smile, but it was an attempt. Wilcox had on-air anchorman good looks, or at least he thought he did. His hair was brushed to the side and gelled. He was wearing a suit with an open-neck shirt and no tie. The casual professional look. She wished her clothes hadn't seen her through an accident, but she squared her shoulders and stood as tall as she could.

Wilcox's blue eyes were alert as Lucie walked toward him. He studied her down to the purse in her hands.

"Hello, Lady Fortune Chesterfield," he said in an ingratiating way. He extended his hand. "It's good to meet you in person. I'm Norton Wilcox from TXLB. I called you a week ago to ask you for an interview, but you declined. I've been trying to connect with you since then, but I keep missing you."

Being as civil as she was able, she said, "Yes, I declined because, as I told you then, I'm not looking for publicity."

"Your charity could use it."

"That's possibly true," she agreed, awarding him the point. "But I'm not on a fundraising mission."

"What mission are you on? Rumor has it you're looking for office space for the Fortune Foundation. Why don't you tell me all about it?"

"No interview, Mr. Wilcox." She didn't know if the foundation was ready to go public until the programs were up and running.

His smile slipped from his lips. "Where were you already this morning? Looking for office space? I ran down a lead that you'd contacted a real estate agent. Or maybe something personal came up?"

The worst thing she could do was become defensive. In her sweetest voice, she answered, "I had an early errand."

His face took on a look that said he was determined to search out the truth. "You weren't here last night either when I asked your doorman to buzz you."

Keeping her composure, she stated blandly, "I must have been in the shower. Have a good day, Mr. Wilcox."

Then she walked quickly to the elevator, punched the button and was grateful when the door swished open. The doors closed and she sagged against the back wall. She'd dodged that bullet. So far so good as far as Chase was concerned, she hoped.

Once inside her apartment, she took her cell phone from her pocket, found Chase in her contact list and pressed the number for his cell phone. When she did, she remembered his expression as she'd left his truck. She remembered their conversation in the barn. She remembered their kiss.

He answered immediately. "Are you in your apartment?"

"I am and all is well." Though she knew it really wasn't for one very important reason. She was falling in love with Chase Parker all over again.

There was momentary hesitation on his end. "Hold

on a minute. I'm going to pull over and park. I like to concentrate on my conversations."

Just what did he have to concentrate on? This conversation was over, wasn't it?

"I'm parked," he said. "So the reporter left?"

"I hope so. I made it into the elevator and I imagine Irv got rid of him."

"He'll be back if he's good."

"Maybe." She sighed. "I can always pull some strings and quiet him, but I don't want to have to do that, at least not yet."

Suddenly Chase asked, "How would you like to run around with your wig on again tomorrow?"

"We'd be tempting fate."

"No, not with what I have planned."

"And what would that be?" In spite of herself, she was interested. In spite of her better judgment, she liked being with him.

"The South by Southwest Conference is in full swing. No one will recognize us in a crowd at the music venues, especially if we wear disguises. If you wear a wig or a baseball cap, you'll be good."

The thought of being free enough to enjoy a music festival intrigued her. "And what disguise will you wear?"

After a moment, he answered, "I'll find a fake mustache and wear cheap boots."

She couldn't help laughing. "I know I shouldn't do this."

"But you want to."

Yes, she wanted to. She thought about the reporter, about having her every move scrutinized. What if she could escape that for a day? "All right," she agreed. "But this time *I* have a condition."

"Uh-oh."

She could tell he wasn't happy about that. "If your foreman brings my rental car back later today, I'll drive myself tomorrow, and I'll meet you on a back street. I really don't think you should be seen anywhere near here."

"You have a sore shoulder."

"By tomorrow, it'll be even better than it is today."

"I don't like meeting you on a back street," he protested.

"We have to meet somewhere where there aren't any security cameras. Convenience stores have them, grocery stores have them, big box stores have them."

"Your knowledge base is a little different than most people's," he grumbled.

"I'll tell you what. I'll let you pick the location, since you're familiar with Austin. Just pick a street where we can both park. I don't care how far we have to walk. I just don't want to be noticed."

"As soon as I'm at my office, I'll check a map and I'll email you."

"That sounds good. And wish me luck today. I'm hoping to find the right space so I can start the paperwork and get the Fortune Foundation office set up." She'd made another list and was determined to find the right space.

"I wish you luck."

She smiled at the sincerity in his voice. "Email me the location and time you want to meet and I'll be there."

"That's a promise?" he asked.

"It's a promise," she vowed.

"I'll see you tomorrow." There was a sexy huskiness to his words that made her anticipate the time with him as much as she anticipated a short time of freedom.

Their conversation stayed with her as she ended the

call. It stayed with her as she searched her contacts for the real estate agent's number. She wouldn't be able to forget about Chase easily today…or their plans for tomorrow.

South by Southwest, a music and media conference in Austin, was a huge event. Lucie had read up on it last night and she understood it was full of aspiring song-writers, from almost-making-it stars who sang their hearts out to musicians who just wanted to play music. A singer might play four live sets in twenty-four hours to get noticed, to engage an audience, to elicit applause. Refreshments were plentiful, from jalapeño margaritas to the best barbecue sandwiches. There were indoor and outside stages, private parties and plenty of public brou-haha. It was one big party, and Lucie found herself grin-ning from ear to ear as she met Chase.

He seemed to know all the ins and outs and exactly where he wanted to go. He had a printout and a back-pack, water bottles and hats emblazoned with a South X Southwest emblem for both of them.

"It seems like I'm going to be taking a trek into the wild," she joked, feeling at home in her wig and her gauzy blouse and skirt…at home with him.

"It can get pretty wild."

"Do you come every year?"

"I try to."

Lucie found herself letting go of anxiety and worry they'd be discovered when Chase hooked his arm into hers. They stood at showcases, listening to everything from indie rock to hip-hop. Most of the time they couldn't talk because the music was loud and the crowds were thick. They walked around Sixth Street and hopped in and out of restaurants as well as a few bars to hear alternative and traditional music.

"I'm glad you took my advice and wore flat shoes," he said, studying her espadrilles.

"I always take good advice."

Chase laughed.

After having to use earplugs at one venue—Chase had thought of those, too—they stopped at a shop for iced coffee and then walked some more.

Music, food, people of all shapes and sizes in all types of attire abounded.

Country music poured from a restaurant they passed and Chase snagged Lucie's arm and pulled her inside. There, they found a high table for two.

After they ordered ribs and cheese fries, Chase said, "We could go somewhere with more refined fare, but I thought you'd want to stay in the center of the action."

There was a small dance floor filled with people. Chase nodded to them. "Have you ever danced the two-step?"

"I've never learned that one," Lucie admitted, eyeing the couples warily.

"It'll be a while before our food gets here. Come on." He stood and grabbed her hand.

"Chase, I don't know. I don't want to make a fool of myself. I know how to waltz and fox-trot, but—"

He eyed her and interrupted her protest. "Don't you ever try anything you're not sure you're good at?"

"Not usually," she confessed.

He laughed out loud. "Well, today's a first. Come on."

Standing, he held his hand out to her. Finally after a few seconds, she took it and let him lead her to the dance floor. When Chase's arm went around Lucie, she felt electrified. They weren't even that close. He took her right hand in his; his right arm came about her, his hand resting on her shoulder blade.

"I'll lead. You follow," he said with a smile.

He kept a few inches between them, and that seemed to be even more enticing than being smack against each other. His hold was light but firm, and she didn't think she'd ever enjoyed a day as much as today. She caught on quickly to the four steps—two quick, and then two slow. It was easy to follow Chase, just as it had been ten years ago.

She found they were in line with the other couples moving around the perimeter of the dance floor. The whole thing felt so natural she couldn't believe it. She jumped into the spirit of it, truly enjoying herself. They were dancing so fast at one point that when Chase executed a spin with her, her wig slipped. Chase righted it for her and they both laughed as they gazed into each other's eyes as she felt stirrings she'd never felt with another man.

When the number ended, Chase directed her back to their table. They sat around the corner from each other and Chase reached out, straightening a few wayward strands of her wig. Now they were close as his hand lingered on the side of her face. Everything they'd done together from the past until today seemed to surround them.

Chase leaned forward and she moved toward him. His kiss was soft, sweet, with a touch of his tongue. Then he backed away.

Just in time, too, because their waitress brought their meals. She winked at them. "You're a cute couple. Enjoying your time here in Austin?"

So, many of the festival-goers weren't local. Lucie answered, "Very much."

But when she and Chase locked eyes again, the realization hit that they weren't a couple.

Picking up one of her cheese fries, Lucie looked away from Chase and outside the plate glass window. But the person she saw out there made her cringe. She grabbed Chase's arm.

"Chase, I think that's Wilcox out there. Do you think he could have followed us?"

"I don't see how that would be possible."

The window was the type that seemed to be darkened glass. The patrons inside could see out, but anyone standing outside couldn't see in.

"If he comes in here, I'm going to have to hide in the ladies' room."

"Hold on," Chase said, keeping his hand on her forearm, keeping her in her seat. "We're not going to let him spoil dinner if we don't have to."

"But Chase, if he sees us together—"

"I don't see how he could recognize us," Chase twirled the end of his mustache and slipped his sunglasses back on.

As they waited, Lucie held her breath. Wilcox pulled open the door and Lucie was all set to run. But Chase kept her still. There were so many people, so much noise, such loud music. After a glance around, Wilcox stepped back outside and headed away from the restaurant.

Lucie breathed a sigh of relief, yet she knew it was possible they were still in jeopardy.

Chase gestured to her ribs. "I know you're worrying that he's lying in wait. Let's eat our dinner, and then I'll find a back way out. He can't be two places at once."

"I don't like this, Chase. Do you think it was a coincidence?"

"I don't know, but we'll evade him. You should come back to the ranch with me. If he *is* trying to follow you, he'll end up at your apartment again. Besides, I'm not ready for this day to end, are you?"

No, she wasn't.

If she went with Chase to the ranch, she'd be digging herself deeper into love. But she didn't know how to stop. She hadn't experienced a day quite like today since… Scotland. She liked…no, *loved* being with Chase. What could it hurt to indulge herself for a few more hours?

Chapter Eight

Chase and Lucie stood by the paddock fence, watching Gypsy. Dusk was starting to fall as the shadows in the pasture began melting together. The sun was tipping over the horizon.

"You don't think Wilcox saw us run out the back door, do you?" She must have asked Chase that about ten times, but she needed reassurance. She'd left her wig and baseball cap in the car after they arrived at the Bar P, but she almost felt as if she should be wearing her disguise even here.

"I'm sure he didn't. There's no way he could have recognized you in that crowded bar, let alone suspected we'd run out the back. There were so many people everywhere, Lucie. There was no way he could have seen you or kept track of you."

"It couldn't have been sheer coincidence he was there, and you know it."

"Maybe, maybe not. It could have been bad luck we ended up in the same place as he was. He was probably all over Austin looking for stories at the festivals."

She sighed. "I hope you're right. I'd hate to think he was tracking me."

He rested his hand on her shoulder. "You're safe here. We both took such a circuitous route, I'm sure no one followed us."

She could feel the heat of his hand through the fabric of her blouse. She looked up at him, feeling that thrill she always felt when she was with him. "Your mom seemed interested in the festivals. Doesn't she go?"

"Too much walking, too many people. At least that's what she tells me. But I don't think she wants to go alone."

"She doesn't have friends she could go with?"

"She did before my dad's stroke. But since then, she's devoted herself to him, all her time and all her energy. When she did that, friends dropped away. She still has contacts on charity boards and at church, but those aren't the kinds of friends you want to run around South by Southwest with."

"No, I imagine you want a close friend for that, one who appreciates all of it as much as you do."

Today she'd felt close to Chase. She'd felt as if they were on an adventure again together as they had been in Scotland. They'd communicated, bonded and laughed together.

He must have been thinking about that, too. "You're even more beautiful now than you were ten years ago," he murmured.

"And you're…" she started. "You're as sexy and as

hard to resist now as you were back then. Even without your fake mustache."

His lips twitched up in a smile, right before he bent his head and wrapped his arms around her. She was surrounded by sensations that almost made her tipsy. There was the scent of Chase, the evening muskiness of damp earth and pine. A light breeze stirred her hair as Chase laced one hand in it. She savored the idea of his kiss as much as she wanted it. The anticipation was a heady aphrodisiac.

He must have thought so, too, because he wasn't rushing anything. He rubbed his cheek against hers and she could feel his evening beard stubble. She breathed him in again, waiting for the inevitable. He began with a nibble at the corner of her lip that left her hungry for him. When his lips finally took hers, she'd ringed her arms around his neck and held on tight.

Chase's tongue dashed against hers, then returned for a lighter stroke.

She responded, giving the same as he had given her. She curved her fingers into his taut shoulder muscles and remembered how he'd looked shirtless. Everything about Chase turned her on.

Their kiss became their world.

Lucie was so involved in a passion she'd almost forgotten that she barely heard the rustle of grass, the crunch of boot heel on stone, Gypsy's quiet neigh.

"What in the blazes, Chase, do you think you're doing?" Warren Parker suddenly yelled. "Your mother told me you were out here with…her. We could have handled this without you getting in touch with her. There was no need for you to see her, and now to find you like this—"

They'd broken apart at the first sound of his father's voice. However, they stood shoulder to shoulder now, facing him as Warren sputtered and fumed.

Lucie was all but fuming herself. The man had been rude ten years ago, and apparently his temper hadn't improved.

"Hello, Mr. Parker," she said evenly, hoping in the dimming light he couldn't see she looked well and thoroughly kissed.

"I hear you're a Fortune now," he said, but not as if he respected the idea. "I read about your mother being united with her long-lost sister—Jeanne Marie Fortune Jones—but I didn't know if it was true. Florence tells me that it is. Apparently you have family on top of family in Horseback Hollow now. Such a quaint two-horse town."

"Yes, it is true my mother and her sister, as well as their brother, were reunited," Lucie responded quietly. "And I have family in Horseback Hollow now."

"Well, bully for you. None of that means anything to us."

"Dad," Chase said sharply.

"Well, it doesn't, Chase. Your marriage is going to be dissolved. Why would you want to consort with an airhead royal who cares about pomp and ceremony and getting her photo all over the news?"

Her temper well past the boiling point, Lucie didn't know which misconception to address first.

But she didn't have to address any of it because Chase stepped in. "You're wrong about everything," he insisted before she could. "First of all, Lucie's anything but an airhead. She's highly intelligent, and she's finding office space for the Fortune Foundation in Austin so they can expand their programs here. Point two—when she's building orphanages in developing countries, the last thing she cares about is pomp and ceremony. She cares about the children she's helping. Point three—as far as getting her photo in the news goes, do you think she wants her life laid out like that?"

But Mr. Parker didn't seem to have heard anything his son had said. He was jabbing his finger at Chase. "You need to be single-minded about your career at Parker Oil as I have been all these years. An up-and-coming CEO needs to have a woman by his side who's an asset, not a disadvantage because of scandal and innuendo being printed about her at every turn of the tabloid page."

Apparently Chase had had enough. He stepped forward, boot to boot with his father. "I didn't want to do it this way, but you're leaving me no choice. I told Mom, and I was waiting until the time was right to tell you."

"Tell me what?" his father snapped.

"I'm leaving Parker Oil to establish a nonprofit horse rescue ranch. I didn't want to merely buy property with my loan for some distant future. I intend to do something worthwhile with it right now. I put down earnest money on the old Schultz land."

"You did *what*? That place is falling down!"

"Not entirely. It needs work, but it'll be worth it, and I'm going to do it."

Warren Parker had been a burly man who'd lost weight since Lucie saw him last. He wasn't so burly now. He looked older, much older. His Western-cut suit was of superb quality, but the jacket was wrinkled, and so was his shirt. That didn't stop him puffing out his chest and blustering.

"I didn't put an end to this romance before to have it rise from the ashes again."

"You didn't put an end to the romance. The annulment did that," Chase concluded. Yet something in his father's expression must have alerted Chase that Warren might have schemed further. "That is what you mean, isn't it?" Chase asked.

"You mean the annulment that didn't happen? Sending *her* back to where she belonged?" Warren scoffed. "That wouldn't have been enough. I saw the way you two looked at each other. I intercepted your letters, and they never went out to her. I got hold of her incoming ones, so you never saw them. That was putting an end to a dalliance that never should have happened."

Lucie saw Chase's jaw stiffen, his mouth press into a straight line. But more than that, she saw his eyes widen, and the look in them hurt her, too. He was stunned by what his father had done, and she imagined he was feeling totally betrayed.

Her suspicion was confirmed when he took her hand and pulled her toward the barn. "Let's go," he said.

His father called, "Chase, you come back here. We're not done."

Chase threw over his shoulder, "We're more than done. I was going to stay on part-time and then consult at Parker Oil. You can forget about that."

And then he was almost running with her. Outside the barn, he took keys from his pocket and headed to a red pickup truck that was close by. There was a ferocious look on his face and she realized he was just as angry as he was betrayed.

"Where are we going?" she asked.

"For a drive. Get in."

"But this isn't your truck…"

"It's a ranch truck Tomás usually uses. He won't care."

She didn't argue. She'd never seen Chase look like this before, and it scared her a little. Yet she wasn't going to let him drive off alone. They were in this together.

As soon as she slid onto the bench seat inside the older truck, she fastened her seat belt. Chase took off. She didn't ask again where they were going, because she suspected he didn't know. He just wanted to drive out of frustration and hurt. He was a controlled man in many ways, or at least he'd learned to be. That control was worn thin tonight, and she suspected he wanted to yell a few things, too, but wasn't doing it because she was with him.

"Say whatever you need to say, Chase."

"Your ears couldn't handle it."

"My ears have handled a whole lot more than you think they have."

He cut her a quick glance, put on his high beams and roared down the back road of the ranch, straight into the forest.

"I guess you know where this leads." No matter where or how fast he drove, she oddly trusted him.

"It leads into another back road and then another one after that. This property is large enough to need its own map."

"Is this helping?" she asked as he zoomed down the road and bumped over a pothole.

"Not much."

They had to be at least a mile from the house now, maybe two. She could feel the vibrations still pulsing around Chase like a ferocious aura that couldn't be quieted. His hands had a death grip on the steering wheel.

Finally she said, "Chase, we can't fully blame your father for what happened."

At that pronouncement from her, he slowed the truck, pulled over to the side of the road and braked. "What do you mean we can't blame *him*? He intercepted our letters."

She needed to be closer to him and she couldn't do that with the seat belt on. She unfastened it and angled toward him on the bench seat.

"If I had had less pride, fewer insecurities and more common sense, I would have contacted you somehow. The same goes for you. Why did you give up without a fight? Why did I? There could only be one reason. We weren't ready for a relationship, let alone a marriage. Not if we could let go that easily."

Chase switched off the ignition, unfastened his seat belt and moved closer to her. "Easily?"

When she gazed into his eyes, she saw so many things. He was devastated by what his father had done. The loyalty Chase had given to him, the years of his life—he might now feel they were wasted.

He reached out and caressed her arm. That was the tenderness she liked so much in Chase.

"I'm sorry for what my father did," he said huskily. "I'm sorry you got caught up in his need for control."

Then without warning, Chase was kissing her. It was wild and took her back ten years. It was so like their first kiss, unbridled. It was so like the first time they'd made love.

Darkness was falling with a vengeance now. The forest surrounded them. His hands touched her as if he wanted more than a kiss as he leaned her back against the door. She found herself pulling his shirt from his waistband. She wanted to feel his skin. She needed to. Their day together reminded her how much she loved being with him, how infatuated she'd been, how hard she was falling again.

He broke away only long enough to murmur, "I have a condom in my pocket."

She didn't stop to think about that. Had he known this was going to happen? Had she, deep down, known, too, because of desires she'd kept secret all these years?

"Are you sure?" she asked him. "Are you sure you're just not angry and frustrated at your father and you want to get back at him?"

"Lucie, this has nothing to do with getting back at my father. Believe me. Do you know how many nights I've dreamed of doing this again?"

Yes, she did. Because if she was honest with herself, she had dreamed about it, too.

In no time at all, he unzipped his jeans. Somehow she divested herself of her panties while he tore open the condom packet. Then he was pulling her onto his lap. He was holding her as she faced him. This wasn't roses and champagne. It wasn't a hostel in Scotland. It was a pickup truck on the Bar P and she knew it. She also didn't care. This was a side of her Chase brought out. This was a side of her she wanted to be free.

She maneuvered herself up until he slid inside her; then she lowered herself onto him. With his groan, she knew she felt the same satisfaction he did. With her moan, he was sure he was pleasing her. He had a condom, and even though they were using it, if he hadn't had one, she'd still be making love with him like this.

He found his release as she reached for the stars and grabbed them. Delicious prickles ran through her whole body and after they ebbed away, she felt boneless. Chase was embracing her, and she was so glad he was. Still, as the night breeze blew through the windows, both of them were silent.

The colder night air made her shiver, and Chase said, "I'll give you a little room to get…straightened up. I'll be right back." He helped her onto the seat and then he stepped out of the pickup.

She wondered what was going through his head. She hadn't known for ten years, and she didn't know now.

He gave her a good five minutes. Her cheeks had cooled down, and so had the rest of her body by the time he climbed back into the truck.

Staring out the windshield, he said, "Maybe that will give us closure."

"Is that what we needed?" She had a feeling what they'd just experienced would never bring closure.

Since Chase's silence told her he obviously wasn't ready to express his thoughts or his feelings, she sighed. "I'd better get back, not only to my car but to my apartment. I don't want rumors floating around that I'd been out all night. And you—you need to make sure your father's okay."

Instead of looking out the front window now, Chase faced her. "How can you even think about my dad?"

"I can think about *your* dad because I lost mine." Not a day went by that she didn't miss him.

"I never want to go back to our ranch."

Softly she offered, "But you will. You're that kind of son." It was one of the reasons she admired him so.

They didn't speak on their return drive. Lucie could see some of Chase's excess energy had subsided. He was definitely calmer and not in as much of a hurry. Eventually they pulled up at the barn at the Bar P.

Lucie said, "I'll come inside with you, just to make sure everything's okay."

Chase wrapped his arm around her, pulled her in for a tight hug and then let go.

They climbed out of the truck and met at the back. They didn't hold hands as they walked up to the house. In fact, in some ways, she felt more separated from him— maybe because they were both confused, maybe because too much was happening at once.

Chase's mom met them in the living room. It was obvious to see she'd been crying. Lucie saw the guilty look on Chase's face and then he masked it.

Florence wasn't accusatory when she said, "Warren told me what happened, and he's in his den. Chase, I did *not* know about the letters. Please believe me."

Lucie could see that Florence was afraid Chase would pull away from her, too. He would associate his dad with his mom and think of them as a unit that had tried to destroy his happiness.

But apparently Chase could easily see that she was telling the truth. "I believe you, Mom."

"Please don't let this put a permanent wedge between you and your dad."

"I don't know how it won't."

Lucie lightly touched Florence's arm. "I think the two of you should talk this out. I need to get back."

"I'll walk you out and make sure you get on your way safely," Chase said firmly.

He did that without reaching for her, without touching her, without kissing her.

At her car, he suggested, "You call me once you're back inside your apartment. I want to know you're safe."

"I'll call," she agreed without protest, not only to ease

his mind, but to ease hers, too. Maybe by the time she called, he'd know how to proceed with his parents. She meant what she'd said to him about making things right with his father. You never knew how long you had someone you loved. Chase would deeply regret that he didn't fix this if something happened to his father. The time was now.

On the way back to Austin, Lucie was determined not to let happen what had happened the other night—getting distracted while driving. She kept her concentration on the road, not on Chase. The traffic wasn't light, but it also wasn't so heavy that she'd feel insecure driving. She was exhausted, though. The day of sun and music and walking, the night of emotion that had blown up in their faces, had worn her out. She was sure Chase was tired, too.

She traveled up the ramp into the parking garage and around the first level into the second, then pulled into her assigned space. It was about twenty car slots down from the elevator. She'd walked it many times and wasn't the least bit nervous about it. Tonight, though, she suddenly stopped walking.

Had she heard footsteps behind her?

She listened. She heard nothing. She was becoming paranoid.

She hurried to the bank of elevators, nodded to the security guard, entered the car, then took the elevator to her floor. Once inside her apartment, she went to her sofa and sank down on it. She pulled her phone from her pocket and dialed Chase. He answered immediately.

"How are you?" she asked.

"Shell-shocked," he answered succinctly.

Just how much had their lovemaking contributed to that?

"How's your dad?"

"I haven't talked to him, but Mom checked on him. She even took his blood pressure. He seems okay. I don't know when we'll hash things out."

"Chase, do it soon, for your sake, as well as his. Don't let this fester. It will only make the situation worse."

"I don't see how it can be much worse. He wants to control my life, and I'm not going to let him. One of us has to win."

"Instead of winning, instead of trying to be right, can't each of you find what will make you happy?"

"Not if we don't agree on what happiness is. Lucie, this isn't your battle. I'm sorry you got mixed up in it."

Was that a dismissal? Was that an I-don't-want-to-think-about-this-anymore end to the conversation?

They were both exhausted, and that had to factor in.

"Chase, try to get a good night's sleep. That will help. Things have to look better in the morning."

"No, they don't have to. But someone like you always thinks they will. It's just another reason I like you, Lucie. I had a great time today, and it's not something I'll soon forget. I hope you enjoyed the day, too."

"I did."

They could talk about the day, but not about what had happened in the pickup truck. Their silence became the end of their conversation. Chase said, "Good night. Take care of yourself."

"You, too."

He ended the call.

There was no talk about seeing each other again, no talk about further conversation. She'd have to see him to sign the annulment papers, wouldn't she?

Time would tell.

She made herself get up from the sofa, take a shower and go to bed.

Everything would look better in the morning; she was sure of it.

Wasn't she?

Chapter Nine

Lucie had finally found the perfect office space Saturday morning, filled in all the details and had all the paperwork sent to Emmett Jamison at the Fortune Foundation headquarters. She would help him set up the office quickly so that the funding could flow. To celebrate, she'd called Ella and was meeting her at an out-of-the-way but excellent deli for lunch. Ella arrived first, and happily waved when Lucie walked in. Her friend had chosen a back-corner table where they'd be pretty much out of sight. It was early for the lunch crowd, so the deli was quiet enough for them to have a decent conversation.

Lucie plopped her purse on the table and said, "I want the works today. Barbecued pork club, cheese fries and sweet peach tea. I'm forgetting the salad in celebration."

Ella laughed. "A job well done. From what you described, this space sounds perfect."

"Two main closed-door offices and plenty of room for cubicles," Lucie added. "Now all they need are more programs to funnel the funds to. I'll be on the lookout for those while I'm still here."

"Now that that task is off your shoulders, tell me what's been filling your time. You said you wanted to talk to me about it. I get the feeling it's a *who*, not a *what*."

"How could you know that?"

"I know women, and I'm getting to know you. It's the sound of your voice. I'm right, aren't I?"

Lucie had told Ella she wanted to discuss something personal with her. She could talk to Amelia, but their snatches of time were so limited that she'd decided to confide in Ella.

"There's a man from my past who's been a secret for ten years."

Ella's eyes widened. "Give me the details."

So Lucie did.

Ella listened intently, not interrupting even once. By the time Lucie was finished, she was surprised she almost felt like crying. Because she didn't know what to do next?

"So your pickup-truck interlude yesterday—was that serious for him, too?"

"I don't know. He was in such turmoil about what his dad did."

"Don't you feel betrayed, too?"

"I feel manipulated, but his father did that from the beginning, so intercepting the letters doesn't come as a huge surprise. If I'd been sure of my relationship with Chase, if I'd been older, I might have flown back here to Texas to see him. But I didn't and he didn't. Neither of us acted."

"And you take that as a sign you weren't meant to be together?"

"Not then," Lucie admitted.

"But you two are headed in different directions now." Ella could see the obvious problems.

"We are, but maybe I shouldn't keep thinking about what my mother expects from me and my responsibilities. Maybe I should think about how I feel."

"Seeing what I've just been through, I think you should take any risk for love. Would you consider settling in Austin permanently, stopping your work, maybe finding something as important to do here?"

"It's a lot to think about," Lucie said, confused by it all. "I suppose I'll figure it out eventually." She sighed. "There's no solution now, so let's talk about something else. Is Ben still on his hunt for other Fortune relatives?"

"Actually something sort of monumental happened."

"Tell me," Lucie coaxed.

"Ben went to meet with Jacqueline Fortune, Gerald Robinson's mother."

"What did he discover?"

Ella shook her head and frowned. "Unfortunately the woman is in a nursing home and suffers from dementia. When she heard the name Jerome Fortune, she started yelling, 'There is no Jerome Fortune. Jerome Fortune is dead.'"

"Oh, my goodness. Ben must have been so disappointed," Lucie sympathized.

"He's not stopping there. He believes there's more to the story. He's working with Keaton to get more information."

"So Keaton's in the area?"

"Actually he's in Austin. Why?"

"I have a charity event to attend and I need an escort. Of course, I wish Chase could take me, but that's not possible, not without everything splattering all over the tabloids and newspapers and cable channels. But since Keaton's here, maybe he'll escort me."

"Go ahead and give him a call now. I'll go place our orders. It's not like I can forget what you want for lunch."

Lucie laughed and pulled out her phone. Checking her contacts, she found Keaton's number, not expecting him to answer. But he did.

"Keaton, this is Lucie Fortune Chesterfield."

"I heard you're in Austin finding space for the Fortune Foundation's new office."

"I've accomplished that. How are *you* doing? I heard that you just started a job at a brand-new firm that only handles the most prestigious projects. Is that fact or fiction?"

"It's fact," he responded. "I'm just taking a break before I start."

"I'm glad you're in Austin. I have a favor. Can you take me to the Museum of Plein Air Artists' fundraising gala tomorrow night? Are you possibly free?"

"Of course I'm free for you. I don't have an active social calendar right now."

"Do you want me to text you the details?" Lucie asked.

"That sounds good. Do you want to meet there or do you want me to pick you up?"

"Do you mind the publicity if you pick me up?"

"Not at all. We'll be seen together at the gala, and I'm sure there will be photos, maybe TV coverage. We might as well go all out."

"Thank you, Keaton."

"Anytime. I usually have my phone on, so text me whenever you want."

When Lucie ended the call, she felt...odd. Her date—if you could call it that—with Keaton would help cover up what was going on with her and Chase. She was debating with herself about how she should tell her mother the whole story. But her mum was out of cell phone contact again and she'd said she'd call when she was back in civilization.

Lucie was beginning to hope that would be sooner rather than later.

Back at the apartment, Lucie was worried about Chase and his dad, about the annulment, about everything. She only knew one way to appease some of her worry. Picking up her cell phone, she went to her contact list and pressed Call for Chase's cell phone number. He answered on the first ring.

"How are you?" he asked, forgetting about small talk.

"I'm good. How are *you*?"

Evading her question, he responded, "I'm getting ready to leave for Masey's Horse Auction Center. Would you like to come along?"

"Where is it?"

"About a half hour from here. I can pick you up, you can come to the ranch, or I can meet you there."

She thought about the implications of all three choices. "Will you be there long?"

"Probably a few hours."

She considered being followed and what she could do to prevent that. If she used her driver, that car was a definite target. She might be better off in the rental again.

"I'll meet you at the auction house. Does that work for you?"

He gave her the address. "That works just fine. Are you thinking you can make sure you're not followed?"

"Exactly."

"And you feel comfortable driving there?"

"Chase, stop being protective. I'm fine. I only got into trouble the other day because of the rain and the potholes and…our argument. I'm not distracted now and today's a sunny day. I'll text you when I arrive at the auction house and you can text back where to meet me."

"Sounds good."

An hour and a half later, her wig in place, her jeans hugging her hips and legs and an oversize green T-shirt completing the ensemble, Lucie parked on the gravel parking lot of the auction house. She texted Chase and he wrote back that she should meet him at the snack cart right outside the main entrance.

I'm wearing my wig, she told him in a return message. He sent her back the thumbs-up sign, and she smiled.

She doubted he'd be wearing his mustache and sunglasses. If they ran into somebody he knew, he could introduce her as his new girlfriend or as a long-lost relative. She'd worn a lot more makeup than she usually did, outlined her lips a little more. Her wig and her clothes should throw anybody off her trail. She'd made sure she wasn't followed to the auction house by taking a winding route.

Lucie couldn't believe how happy she was to see Chase when she spotted him. She found herself wanting to run to him, to be held in his arms. But she couldn't do that. She considered what she *could* do. *Could* she have an affair with him during the time she had left in Texas?

As he gazed down at her with one of those Chase

smiles, she thought it was a definite possibility. Her head was telling her one thing—*No, no, no*—but her heart was telling her another—*Yes, yes, yes.*

"Come on," he said. "I really shouldn't buy any horses today with everything in flux, but there's one I'm going to bid on. She's pregnant."

He looked absolutely excited by the idea. This really was his passion.

He went right up to the barricade and gestured to a beautiful bay with an almost black mane. She was dusty and looked as if she needed more than one good meal.

Chase obviously understood that, because he assured Lucie, "She'll be a beauty when she's taken care of."

Looking over the horses, Lucie wished she could bid on one or two herself. They all needed care and gentle hands and love.

She touched Chase's arm. "I could sign on the dotted line for you right now. You could get the loan and buy the ranch."

He shook his head. "Word would get out, you know it would. Our marriage would be public. We'd have to explain not only that, but the annulment, too. It would be a nightmare. But thank you for the thought."

He wasn't even questioning that they were getting an annulment. She shouldn't be either. Didn't they both want to start over with a blank slate?

But at some point in her life, she wished she could just throw up her hands and not care what anyone said or thought, not care about what was printed or recorded, not care about rumors and innuendos and the public peeking in behind closed blinds. Would that happen when she was fifty, sixty or seventy…eighty or ninety? Could it ever happen?

She hadn't been raised not to care, and that was the problem. She always thought about her family and how what she did would reflect on them. Obviously Chase cared about his family, too. He wouldn't have stayed at the ranch after his dad's stroke if he didn't. He wouldn't listen to his mother's worries if he didn't. That was why she wondered what would happen now that his father knew he wanted to leave not only the ranch, but Parker Oil.

As they walked over to the bleachers to take a seat for the auction, they settled next to each other on the hard bench. Her leg fell beside his and she didn't move away. Neither did he. Pictures played in her head—legs against legs, his chest against her breasts, his mouth on hers. When she cut him a glance, he was looking at her, and she knew he was remembering, too. So she talked about what had led to what happened between them.

She'd leaned in close to him, and almost spoke into his ear. "Have you ironed out everything with your dad?"

When Chase shook his head, she wanted to run her hand over the strong line of his jaw and ease the creases from around his eyes. But they were in public, and even though she wore a disguise, it would be a foolish thing to do.

"I can't talk to him, Lucie. I'm still so angry about what he did. And he's made no move to talk to me. There's a silent wall between us now. He went into work today and I didn't. I gave Jeff instructions about everything that had to be done. He's going to deal with Dad today, whether Dad likes it or not."

"But you could act as a buffer. You could ease the way for their relationship."

"That's what I intended, and yes, I could. But do you think Dad's going to let me? He's going to bluster and yell until he has everyone in a tizzy. On Monday, I'll go in and talk to Jeff and see what can be done about the whole situation. But I'm beginning to think that the sooner I leave, the better. The sooner I move out, the better."

And that meant, the faster the annulment happened, the faster Chase could get his life back on track.

"Since you found an office for the Fortunes, what else are you going to be doing?" he asked her.

"I'm supervising the setup. I've chosen the computers and they're going to be delivered next week. Painters are coming in, too. Everything's going to be a light robin's-egg blue and yellow, both soothing and enlivening, don't you think?"

"So now you're a decorator?" he asked with a grin.

"I wear many hats," she assured him. "I'm wearing my fundraiser hat this week. There's a charity gala I'm going to tomorrow evening. The Museum of Plein Air Artists wants to fund a children's wing. Art programs are being cut in schools and this could be a benefit for children's education."

"Art and music aren't just extra subjects that can be tossed by the wayside," Chase agreed.

"No, they can't."

They were quiet for a few minutes as they watched all the activity, the bidders filing in and out of the bleachers, the horses milling about the pens, the desk where the winners of the auction could pay up.

"Is this gala a black-tie-and-ball-gown type of occasion?" Chase asked, looking straight ahead as if he weren't really interested in the conversation.

"It is," she said simply.

"Are you going alone?"

Was that the basis of his question in the first place?

She hesitated a moment but then told him the truth. "No, I'm not going alone. Keaton Whitfield is taking me. He's an architect I know from London. He's in Austin now on family business. I needed an escort and he agreed to be it."

"How old is he?"

"He's in his thirties. Why?"

"No reason."

But Lucie knew there was. She nudged his elbow. "Why are you asking?"

"Maybe I'd hoped he was sixty and bald."

He hadn't looked at her when he said it, and maybe she was supposed to take it as a joke. But she could take it another way, too. Maybe Chase was jealous.

He said, "After the auction, I'll be taking the horse home with me in the trailer. Do you want to come back to the ranch?"

Could she have an affair with Chase? she asked herself again. Could she throw caution to the wind? The more they were together, the more likely it was someone would let something slip or someone would find out.

"I don't think that's a good idea, on several levels. I don't want to make things worse between you and your dad. My presence on his ranch would do that. You know it would."

"My mother would welcome you."

"She wants what's best for your father, too. And, Chase, seeing each other again… It's not a good idea, is it? I mean, even today is a risk. Yes, I'm disguised. But if someone looked really hard at me and then at you, they'd learn our secret."

The secret that she was falling in love with him again?

Her secret that maybe she didn't think an annulment was the best way to go?

Possibly all of the above.

"You're right," Chase said. "Maybe we are being foolish."

The bidding was about to start, and Lucie was glad of that. They couldn't talk their way out of this situation. Discussing it every which way wasn't going to help.

She didn't know what would. Because going their separate ways just seemed like a mistake.

Chase glanced at the news clip on the big-screen TV for the second time that evening. It had run fifteen minutes earlier at the top of the program. The charity fundraiser at the museum with its glitz and glamour had been a good way to capture the interest of the audience. It had sure captured his, especially when he'd seen someone push a microphone in front of Lucie's face. The thing was, it wasn't only Lucie who had caught his attention. It was the man beside her, his arm linked in hers. This Keaton Whitfield she'd spoken of was tall with dark brown hair. He was a good-looking guy. When the camera zoomed in, Chase could see he had blue eyes any woman might go for.

Lucie had looked beautiful in a black sequined gown, her hair shiny and sleek. She was *so* beautiful. She hadn't seemed at all awkward with Whitfield, and they'd looked like a couple.

Chase had been pacing for the past fifteen minutes with an idea bouncing around in his head. Probably not the best-framed idea he'd ever had, but one he was going to act on. Lucie wanted to be wise about seeing him. He could be wise about seeing her.

Had Lucie gone home with Keaton Whitfield? Had the night been more than a convenient date?

He dialed her cell.

"Chase! Hi. I just got in."

"Is Mr. Whitfield there with you?"

Maybe taken aback by the blunt question, she didn't answer for a moment. But then she responded, "No. He walked me to my door and then he left. Why?"

He wasn't going to explain the thumping jealousy he'd felt. He wasn't going to make excuses either.

"I want to see you, and we don't have to be foolish about it. It just takes a little planning. How about if I come over for a nightcap? I'll use the parking garage and the service elevator. No one will notice me."

After a few seconds' hesitation, she said, "I can make sure the security guard sends you right up. Are you hungry? I didn't have much for supper and I'm ravenous. I was going to make an omelet."

"I never turn down food," he said with a smile in his voice. "I'll be there in a half hour."

"That'll give me time to change into something more comfortable." As if she realized what she'd said, she went on. "I mean, I don't want to sit around in this sequined gown while we have omelets."

"I'll keep that in mind," he responded ambiguously, thinking about himself unzipping her gown, thinking about the garments she might be wearing underneath, thinking about Lucie naked.

Chase nodded to the guard at the elevator after he'd arrived at Lucie's apartment and parked. Lucie must have given the guard his description, because he nodded, yet still asked for ID. After Chase flashed his driver's license, the guard tipped the bill of his cap and said, "Have a good night, sir."

Chase didn't know what this night was going to bring. He just knew he wanted to spend time with Lucie.

He rang her doorbell and when she answered, she was dressed in a swirling multicolored garment with a scooped neck, winglike sleeves and a length that went to her ankles. It had all the colors of the rainbow. Her lipstick still looked fresh, her eyelashes long with mascara, her brown hair as silky as it had looked on TV. But she wasn't on TV. She was right in front of him.

He reached out and tapped the sparkling, dangling earring at her ear. "I saw you on TV. You looked beautiful tonight."

She put her hand to the earring. "Oops, I forgot to take these off. It's fun to get all dressed up and act like a princess once in a while."

He followed her inside the apartment as she removed the earrings. "Go into the kitchen. I'll be right in."

When she came back, he asked, "Those were diamonds?"

"Yes, a gift from my father. I wear them whenever I can."

So she didn't just like wearing jewels. She liked wearing jewels with memories, or maybe anything with memories. He was still learning facets of her personality.

In a glance, he'd taken in the frying pan on the stove, the bowl with what looked like whipped eggs, the chopped pepper and tomatoes and onion.

"How about ham pieces in with all the rest?" she asked, motioning toward the ingredients.

"Are you telling me you know how to cook?"

"Of course I do."

"Haven't you always had servants?"

"We have, but they didn't keep me out of the kitchen. After all, don't you know I'm well-rounded?"

As soon as she said the words, she blushed, and Chase couldn't help taking advantage of the moment. He took off his Stetson and tossed it to the table. Then he closed in on her, his hands teasingly sweeping down her shoulders, down her arms to her waist and then over her hips. At her hips, he stopped, his hands moving the silky material of the caftan and slipping around the back.

"Well-rounded, huh? Everything happened so fast the other night, I couldn't even tell."

She stood perfectly still, and he wasn't sure what she was going to do. Pull away? Push him away? Run? But maybe accepting the inevitability of what they had between them, she didn't do any of those.

All she said was "Chase" in a way that made his blood run hot and his sexual hunger for her increase. The sparkle in her eyes said she was ready for his kiss and whatever came after. After all, she wouldn't have invited him to come over if she didn't have the same thing in mind that he did.

Still, he wanted to make sure. When he kissed her, he caressed her back and rocked her hips into his. It was obvious what he wanted. Did she want it, too?

She pressed against him, chased his tongue into his mouth, and moaned deep in her throat.

He wanted to yank her silky garment off her, but he wouldn't resort to caveman tactics. No, he was a civilized man, right?

His hand went to the zipper at her neckline. He slowly pulled it down, metal on metal, making a sound that was obvious in its purpose. When he reached her waist, she did push against him then, and he thought maybe the night was over.

Smiling, she wiggled her arms and the fabric fell, leaving nothing to his imagination. She'd been naked under the gown and she wanted him to know it. He hadn't been alone in what he wanted for tonight. Apparently she was with him all the way. He cupped her breasts and bent his head to one of them. She cried out when his tongue circled her nipple...when he teased it and then seriously kissed it. She hung on to him as if he was everything she'd ever desired.

Scooping her up into his arms, he carried her through the living room into her bedroom.

After he gently laid her on the bed, she looked at him and teased, "You're overdressed."

While he shucked off his clothes, she pulled back the covers. Soon they were entwined on the high-thread-count sheets, kissing and touching, remembering and making new memories. Chase took it slower than he had done in the pickup truck. He wanted to give her as much pleasure as he could. From her sounds and her smiles and her kisses, he knew he did.

He left her for only a few moments to reach into his pants pocket for the condom. She helped him roll it on, and he felt as if his whole universe was in her eyes. As he entered her, he was electrified, excited, consumed by passion. With Lucie he felt ten feet tall, strong, a master of the universe. She clung to him and he held on to her, never wanting the moment to end.

Chapter Ten

The sound of her doorbell woke Lucie and she had trouble orienting herself. She was wrapped in Chase's arms! But she was in her bed.

Why was the doorbell ringing without Irv buzzing her first? Or had he done so and she hadn't heard?

No, he wouldn't have just sent someone up.

Last night with Chase had been…exquisite. She couldn't think about the repercussions from it now, not with someone at her door, and not with Chase still in her bed.

"What do you want me to do?" Chase asked, his deep baritone in her ear. He was already alert and thinking about their compromising situation.

"Just stay here. Leave the door open a crack so you can hear who it is. I can't imagine Irv wouldn't have buzzed me first."

The doorbell rang again.

She quickly extricated herself from Chase's arms, grabbed her robe, slipped it on and belted it and then remembered she was wearing nothing underneath. That wouldn't do.

She quickly shucked it off, pulled on a nightgown from her closet, slipped her robe on top of that and belted it. So much for fashion. Nothing matched.

When she went to the door and peered through the peephole, she gasped. It was her *mother*.

She tossed a glance over her shoulder and called to Chase, "It's my mum. There won't be any hiding you, so you might as well get dressed and come out. I have to explain all this sometime anyway."

Then she threw open the door, happy to see her mother no matter what the circumstances.

Josephine Fortune Chesterfield took one look at Lucie and her eyebrows arched. "Give me a hug before you explain to me what's going on."

"How do you know something's going on?" She hugged her mother and then pulled away, trying to fortify herself for this explanation.

"Because you never come to the door looking like this!"

Lucie sighed. No, she didn't. She always made sure she looked properly royal first!

Just then, Chase emerged from the bedroom. He didn't hesitate to come forward and extend his hand. "Lady Fortune Chesterfield, I'm Chase Parker."

It only took a few seconds for Lucie's mother, who had a memory that could rival any genius's, to make a connection. "You couldn't be *the* Chase Parker from ten years ago, the one who sullied my daughter's reputation?"

Again Chase didn't hesitate. "Yes, I'm that one."

Josephine looked from her daughter to Chase and then back to Lucie again. "I think you'd better get dressed and make a pot of tea."

Chase laid a hand on Lucie's shoulder, and she remembered everything they'd done last night. He asked, "Do you want me to stay or go?"

Lucie studied her mother's expression, which was cautiously patient. All the feelings Lucie had experienced last night when she and Chase made love, slept and then made love again were careening around inside her. It was really hard to think straight. Having Chase here while she was trying to explain would cause even more turmoil and be even more confusing.

She dredged up a smile for him and suggested, "Why don't you go? I know you have to get to work."

He looked as if he wanted to take her in his arms again. He looked as if he wanted to kiss her. Yes, she wanted to kiss him, but certainly not now in front of her mother. Certainly not now, when everything was so mixed up.

Were they having an affair? Where was that going to go?

Chase went to the kitchen for his hat, which was still on the table there. Returning to the living room, he said, "It was good to meet you, Lady Fortune Chesterfield."

"Good to meet you, too, I think," Lucie's mother said politely, without a hint of a smile.

Then Chase was leaving. But Lucie wanted to pull him back inside.

However, after he closed the door, she faced her mother. "I have so much to tell you."

Her mother stared into the kitchen where all the dishes

and vegetables were still splayed across the counter from last night. She waved at it. "Your dinner was interrupted last night?"

"It wasn't dinner. It was a late-night snack. Keaton took me to a charity function and brought me home, and then Chase came over and we were both hungry—"

She was rambling and getting all tangled up in events.

Although her mother was wearing a casual, pale blue pantsuit, she said to Lucie, "Go get dressed. I'll start cleaning this up."

"You don't have to do that."

Josephine waved her away.

Lucie blew out a breath and headed for her bedroom.

Ten minutes later, she was back in the kitchen with her mother. Her mum had started the teapot on the burner.

"You didn't have to straighten up," she said, noticing even the counters were empty and cleaned off.

"No problem. I like to be useful. You know that."

Lucie pulled two cups and saucers from the cupboard and set them on the table. "Are you hungry? I can whip up something."

"I take it you didn't have your breakfast?" her mother asked with a wise look.

"No, not yet."

"Then by all means, you have something."

"Why didn't you tell me you were flying in?"

"Because I wasn't sure when or where I'd be in. I did send you a text when I landed late last night."

Lucie's phone was somewhere around here, but she didn't know where, and she certainly hadn't heard it. "Mum, I'm sorry. You probably wondered what was wrong when I didn't text back."

"Yes, I was a bit concerned, and that's what I told your

doorman, Irv. Apparently he knew who I was from the tabloids, and when I showed him ID, he was definitely certain of that. He didn't even hesitate to let me come up. Was I wrong to do that, Lucie?"

Her mother was giving her a probing look, and Lucie felt like a teenager again. "No, you weren't wrong. Chase and I... That was the first night he stayed."

The teapot whistled and Josephine crossed to the stove and took it from the burner.

"I only have teabags," Lucie told her mother, "but they're herbal."

Again Josephine just gave her an arched eyebrow. "You really haven't moved in, have you?"

"I knew I'd only be here temporarily."

Her mother nodded. "Yes, that is the plan. Now, why don't you start at the beginning?"

Lucie closed her eyes for a moment, her throat tightening with emotion. The beginning seemed like yesterday, yet so far away, too. She began with falling in love with Chase in Scotland, their days of touring and talking... their attraction. Finally with difficulty, she described marrying him and what had happened afterward.

She'd never seen such surprise on her mother's face as Josephine asked, "Why didn't you tell me? All these years and you've kept it to yourself? Didn't anyone else know? Does Amelia know?"

"No, no one knew. That was the agreement I had with Chase's father. He would dissolve the marriage and we'd act as if it never happened. He would get his son back on the track he'd planned for him, and I wouldn't have a scandal. You wouldn't have a scandal. He hushed up everything at the school about what happened and you hushed it up at home. You told the press I had the flu and cut the trip short. Just imagine the splash if they'd known I'd married. So I kept to the agreement with Mr. Parker and all went as smoothly as it could."

"You were the one who always played by the rules," her mother said, studying her. "Your father and I were shocked when you were sent home in disgrace. I thought the travel program somehow managed to keep it all quiet. I see now Chase's father had a hand in that."

"I'm so sorry I didn't tell you. I thought keeping the secret was for the best. I had been so foolish. I loved Chase, at least I thought I did, but I was too young to know what love and commitment were. That episode, my confrontation with his father, all of it taught me to always control my emotions, never act impulsively. It brought home the truth that I should think about the big picture, not just my part in it. I thought I was doing what was best for everyone." Her voice caught because she realized how much her mother might be hurt by being left out of the loop.

After a deep breath, she went on to explain to her mother how Chase's father had intercepted her letters to Chase and his to her.

Her mother shook her head and frowned as Lucie ended. "Mr. Parker probably thought he was doing the best thing for everyone, too. *He* was looking at the big picture," Lucie said as she finished.

"That's all well and good, Lucie, but sometimes truth is better than a good public relations spin. Sometimes truth can be liberating. If Chase Parker was here all night, it sounds as if old feelings are all stirred up. What are you going to do about that? You have responsibilities. You have a life of traveling to help the greater world. Certainly you're not thinking of giving that up."

Was she? Without knowing exactly how Chase felt? She did have responsibilities that couldn't easily be delegated. After all, she was Sir Simon Chesterfield's daughter. However, she responded honestly, "I don't know. The lawyers are going through with the annulment."

Her mother reached across and took her hand. "Lawyers, annulment, a marriage that was too early to take hold. The feeling in our hearts can't be dictated by lawyers or due process. You made a foolish decision ten years ago, but you have to be careful you don't make another one now. You have a lot to think about because you have a lot of responsibilities. I depend on you, Lucie. You know that."

Yes, she was the dependable one. She was her mother's confidante, sidekick, helper. Chase was starting a new life. That ranch would take his attention night and day.

Trying to shake off last night's hold on her heart, as well as the vivid, sensual memories from it, she remembered who she was and what her life and her mother's was all about. Just what part did the feelings in her heart play in this?

She couldn't let her mother down, not for a romance that might not have any place to go. "I'll be flying off to Guatemala in less than two weeks. The annulment is going to go through any day. I'll be keeping my commitments, Mum."

Yet Lucie's heart felt as if it was breaking. Leave Chase? It was the wisest path to take. Yet it didn't feel wise at all.

After spending the day with Lucie, her mother had left for Horseback Hollow and her condo there. Lucie felt drained. They had spent a good portion of their time together going over plans for their Guatemala trip and the to-do list once they were there.

Lucie had cooked them dinner and then her mother had left, her driver picking her up out front. Lucie had accompanied her downstairs to say goodbye and had no sooner returned to her apartment than her cell phone beeped.

She saw the caller was Florence Parker.

"Hi, Florence. How are you?" Lucie asked conversationally, but not feeling like engaging at all.

"I'm fine. I have a favor to ask."

Lucie braced herself for whatever was coming. She hoped it had nothing to do with Chase, or her resolve to resume her regular life would weaken.

"Reverend Stanhope didn't want to impose on you himself, but I told him I'd call you. He'd like you to attend Family Day at the church on Saturday. You can meet the parents of the children you're helping with the after-school program."

There was no reason she couldn't do this for the church, and for the Fortune Foundation, as well. Except..."

"Will Chase be there?"

"Probably."

"If he attends, we'll have to pretend we don't know each other."

"I'm sure he understands that," Florence said.

"I'd call him," Lucie responded, "but I'm not even sure our cell phones are secure." Her mother had brought up that point, and she was right.

"I understand, Lucie. Really, I do. And I'm sure Chase does, too. Don't worry. I'll make your wishes clear to him."

Lucie just wished her wishes were clear to herself.

* * *

Had a reporter like Norton Wilcox followed Lucie to Family Day at the church, all he would see would be her enjoying the day with children and their parents. He might be able to dig up the fact that the Fortune Foundation would be funding the church's after-school program, but that was it.

When Chase's mom had called her, asking her to come to this event today, Florence understood full well that Lucie couldn't be associated with her or Chase in the public's eye. Lucie was the Fortune Foundation's representative, and she'd be attending on those grounds. She'd stay only a short time and if anyone recognized her, she'd simply wear her busy public persona.

Simple. Besides, if anyone did do a story about this, more programs that needed help would come forward and the foundation could select where the money would be best spent.

Win-win all around.

At least that was what she thought until she spotted Chase in jeans and a T-shirt, his Stetson tilted at that just-right angle, hauling hay bales onto a wagon. She imagined the minister needed help with all sorts of things, and Chase could provide strong manpower.

She attempted to keep her distance from him at every turn. She avoided eye contact with him. There were a few awkward moments when she ran into Chase's mother and father and she made polite small talk. "Isn't this a wonderful event? It's a beautiful day. Have a great time." Then she moved on.

No one seemed to recognize her, because she was out of her element. She was wearing jeans and an over-size blouse. She wasn't on the Chesterfield Estate. She wasn't in a foreign country building an orphanage. She wasn't dressed in a gown as she had been for the gala. She was trying to be just Lucie for a short while and get away with it. She was fine, really, she was, until one of the mothers recognized her.

With a wide smile, the woman rushed over to her and said, "You're Lucie Fortune Chesterfield, aren't you?"

Lucie put her finger to her lips. "I've tried to keep that under wraps, but yes, I am."

"I heard the Fortune Foundation was investing in our after-school program and I put two and two together. I knew you looked familiar."

Lucie gave her a conspiratorial smile. "I'd like to keep everyone else from doing that. The attention today is on parents and their children, and I'd like to keep it that way."

"Oh, I understand completely, except…could I bribe you to sit next to me on the hay ride? I promise I won't tell a soul, but at least I can say I sat next to Lady Fortune Chesterfield."

Lucie didn't want to make a scene. She didn't want to prolong the conversation. On a hay ride, children would be scurrying about and their parents would be focused on having them behave. No one would be looking at her.

"It's about to take off again." The woman motioned to the hay wagon. "Come on, please?"

Lucie couldn't say no. She followed the mom over to the hay wagon, but then stopped cold. Chase was climbing in. He sat on a hay bale with a small child beside him. The boy must have been about four. When their gazes met, he gave her a shrug and a *what can I do?* look. Maybe Chase was watching the little boy for his parents.

What could *she* do?

The woman hopped into the wagon in front of her and motioned to one of the large bales, where the two of them could sit side by side. The problem was, it was right next to Chase. She was getting a headache...or maybe a heartache.

The hay wagon soon filled up with kids as well as adults. As Lucie had predicted, the adults were busy keeping the children in line. No one paid any attention to her, except the woman on the bale next to her. She chatted, "I've seen your estate on TV." In a lower voice, she said, "Does it really have stables and everything?"

"It does," Lucie assured her. "I learned to ride when I was small."

Her gaze met Chase's again, and just that contact rocked her. Anybody watching them could feel the electricity between them. She quickly directed her attention to the small child across from her who was trying to scramble into his mom's lap.

When her phone buzzed, she wasn't going to answer it. But she decided any distraction would help. As the wagon bumped along, it jostled her and the woman beside her, making the kids giggle, making her even more aware of Chase.

She slipped out her phone. The text was from Chase. This is ridiculous!

She quickly texted back, This is the way it has to be.

She didn't look at him. She didn't dare. She just hoped this was going to be one short hay ride.

Florence Parker had convinced her husband to attend the church's Family Day. Since his argument with Chase, he'd been sullen and in a bear of a mood. But she was hoping today would change that.

They'd each picked up slices of homemade apple pie and carried them to a picnic table set in the shade. The hay wagon was just returning from another run. She'd been so glad to see Lucie climbing on when Chase was already on it. Serendipity?

She hoped so.

"They're pretending not to know each other, and that's fine as long as they don't look at each other," she said as she cut off a bite of pie with her fork.

"It's the stupidest thing I've ever heard of," Warren said. "But what else can they do?" he muttered. "I don't think Chase would care about a scandal anymore, but *she* certainly would. Her family's hoity-toity with their fox-hunts, royalty for guests and highfalutin parties."

"You don't know Lucie, Warren, you really don't. I've had a chance to spend a little time with her, and she's nothing like you suspect. I don't know why you had your mind set against her from the beginning, when you knew how Chase felt about her."

"How he felt about her," her husband scoffed. "He was too young to ruin his life with the wrong woman. They were an ocean apart. You know that never would have worked."

"He would have gone over there to live. You know he would have."

"And that's why I had to squelch it. Besides, she was too young to know her own mind."

"When she looks at him now, do you think she's too young to know her own mind?"

"She's not looking at him," Warren noted, as if he'd been watching their every move this afternoon, too.

"Every once in a while, they can't help glancing at

each other. Don't you remember when we looked at each other like that?"

Warren pushed his pie away as if he'd suddenly lost his appetite. Then he looked at her, really looked at Florence, as he hadn't in many weeks, maybe even months. "I'm not the man I once was. That's why we don't look at each other that way."

Was this what her husband had been thinking since his stroke? Was this the reason he didn't come close to her at night? Florence reached out and touched his hand with hers. "I still see you as the young man I married. I still look at you that way because I love you. You're the one who sees yourself differently. Is that why you can't let go of Chase, because you're afraid you'll need him again?"

Warren pulled his arm back, and she was afraid she'd erected a new barrier between them. But then he directed his focus toward the hay wagon. He watched Lucie jump off; then he saw Chase lifting a little boy onto the ground. When their son straightened, his gaze seemed to meet Lucie's. They were frozen, only for a moment. But as Chase's father, Warren seemed to recognize what that moment meant.

"Maybe I *am* afraid to let go of him," he murmured. "What if something happens to me and the company can't survive without him? What if I have another stroke and he's not here for you or here for me?" he murmured.

"We raised our son to be a caring man with a good heart. He wouldn't want to start the horse rescue ranch if he didn't have a good heart, if he didn't care. The fact that he still cares for Lucie after all these years tells you something about him, too. Just because he leaves the company, just because he tries to find his own life, doesn't mean he'll forget about us."

"What if he flies off to England to be with her?"

"If he's chosen the right woman, they'll figure it out, don't you think?"

"I planned his life. I separated them so he would find his full potential."

"He *is* finding his full potential, but in his way, not yours. If you don't let him go, Warren, he won't come back to us. I've come to realize that, and you have to, too."

She took his hand again and squeezed it. "We do love each other. And we've been happy, haven't we?"

"Those first years were rough, when the company wasn't doing well and we didn't have much. But yes, we've been happy."

"How can you deny Chase that?"

"You know I don't want to deny him anything. That's the whole problem. How can he find happiness with her when she's not even in the same country?"

"Her sister lives in Horseback Hollow with her rancher husband. Don't you think Lucie is made of the same kind of stuff?"

"They're pretending they don't know each other. Chase hasn't stopped the lawyer from proceeding with the annulment."

"Maybe that's because they're not listening to their hearts yet. Maybe the time's not right. But that's not for us to decide. Think about giving your son your blessing, would you?"

Warren sighed and pulled his pie back in front of him. "I'm sure you won't let me forget thinking about it."

Her husband's voice was resigned, but his mood seemed lighter.

Watching a child find his happiness could do that.

* * *

It was noon on Sunday when Chase tried to coax one of his rescue horses to eat from his hand. He wasn't having much luck. The horse could feel the tension oozing all around him, or the frustration. The situation with Lucie had him tied up in knots. Pretending not to know her yesterday had seemed like sheer stupidity.

When you gentle a horse, you have to be calm, he reminded himself. He wasn't calm. He'd wanted not only to talk to her yesterday, but to kiss her silly. Especially after they'd finished the ride on the hay wagon. But she'd disappeared, practically vanished into thin air. He'd texted her, but she hadn't texted back. That was her way of dealing with their situation. He had to be levelheaded about it and respect her wishes, but he didn't like being levelheaded, not after the night they'd spent together. He wanted a repeat. Didn't she?

His mother had reminded him conversations could be overheard on all phones for someone like Lucie. Who knew what devices were out there that a tech-smart press spy could use? With Lucie's mother in the country probably reminding her of her Chesterfield duty, her sister's fiasco not all that far behind her, Lucie was trying to be supercautious.

Chase heard the sound of tires on gravel and figured it was Tomás's truck. But after another attempt to feed the chestnut mare and getting nowhere, he heard a male voice determine, "She's not ready for that yet."

Chase spun around, and when he saw he had a visitor, he smiled, immediately left the fence and approached Graham Robinson, Ben's brother.

"I came to see how your plans are coming along," Graham explained.

Chase nodded to the doorway leading into the barn. "Let's go into my office in there, and we can talk about *your* plans, too."

Graham was six feet tall and every inch a cowboy. He wore his light brown hair short under his Stetson. Even though he was only thirty-two, the lines around his blue eyes told a story that had sobered the man because of an unfortunate teenage escapade. Graham's best friend had died in his arms when they were only teenagers. Graham's father, Gerald Robinson, hadn't been the best father, so Graham had sought out another role model, his best friend's dad. They'd helped each other through the grief, and now Graham was working with Roger Gibault on the Galloping G Ranch. The two men had developed the same dream and wanted to help troubled teenagers find their place in the world.

Once in the office, Chase sat behind the battered desk in an old-time wooden chair that creaked as he adjusted his weight in it.

Graham took a seat on the other side of the desk.

"It's been a while," Chase said. "Would you like a beer?"

"Sure," Graham agreed, and Chase pulled two from the small refrigerator back in the corner. He handed the long-necked bottle to Graham.

"I've been busy," Graham said. "Roger and I are trying to get the place in shape. We're remodeling a bunkhouse and thinking about adding a cabin or two. We're going to have kids coming in around June first and we want to be ready."

"Do you feel ready to handle troubled kids?"

"I once was one."

Chase nodded sagely, not pushing. He knew Graham would say what he wanted to say in his own time.

Graham removed his Stetson, ran his hand through his hair and plopped the hat back on his head. "Roger and I are consulting with a professional, too. We're smart enough to know there are a lot of things we don't know."

"Good idea," Chase agreed.

"How about you?" Graham asked. "I heard you're buying the old Schultz place. I thought maybe we could help you out, take a horse or two off your hands once they're ready to go to a good home. If kids have something to care about and care for, it helps. Gentling a horse could teach them a lot of life lessons."

"I have one or two now that you might be interested in. Maybe by June I'll have my ranch up and running, and we'll have more to choose from. I hit a roadblock that's stalled me."

"Something serious?"

The Galloping G wasn't that far from the Bar P. He and Graham had known each other for a long while. In fact, Graham was one of the few men he'd consider a friend, a friend he could trust. Maybe he could cope with the whole situation a lot easier if he could talk to someone about it.

"Can I trust you to keep what I tell you confidential?"

"You know you can," Graham assured him.

"I'm married. I have been for ten years and didn't know it. We both thought the marriage had been annulled, but it wasn't. When I tried to get a loan approved, I found out."

Graham gave a low whistle. "So this isn't just a business mess."

"No, it isn't. And to make matters worse, this woman

is in the public eye. If our marriage leaked out, it could cause a major scandal for us both."

"You've got to be kidding."

"Nope." Chase blew out a breath. "The marriage happened in Scotland. A lawyer's trying to get it resolved, but we have to keep everything quiet or there will be a scandal to end all scandals. I haven't been celibate and she was engaged."

Graham's gaze suddenly fell on the printout that lay on the corner of the desk. "Why are you printing out ads for engagement rings if you're seeking dissolution of your marriage?"

"It's complicated."

"Believe me, I understand complications."

There was a look in Graham's eyes that told Chase much was going on beneath the surface. But Graham would tell him what that was when he was ready.

Obviously not wanting to talk about himself, Graham asked perceptively, "Are you thinking about staying married?"

Chase shook his head. "It's an impossible situation. She's leaving Texas in a week. She has commitments. I can't ask her to stay to see what develops because her work's her life. Even if we could somehow compromise on that, if she gives up her present job, wouldn't she resent me for it?"

Graham took a long swig of his beer, then shook his head. "I never thought about getting married myself, and I can't see that ever happening. But I sure wish you luck whichever way it goes."

Chase suspected he needed a lot more than luck.

Chapter Eleven

Amelia's long dark hair swayed across her back as she cooed and rocked Clementine on Sunday evening. "Who's the cutest little girl in the whole wide world?"

Quinn Drummond, who claimed he was a small-town rancher who merely wanted a simple life, responded for his child. "*You* are, Clementine Rose Drummond, and no one else." His thick dark brown hair fell over his sun-tanned forehead as he said it, and his hazel eyes twinkled.

Clementine Rose wiggled and wiggled until her mama put her down. She toddled over to Lucie and held up her arms.

Lucie, of course, obliged, sweeping her off the floor. "So, what hotel are you staying at?"

Quinn answered, looking smug, "We're staying at the Dominion."

The Dominion was an old Austin hotel with lots of

history and a presidential suite and bridal suites that could rival any posh resort.

"I reserved the bridal suite for a mini second honeymoon," Quinn said, looking proud of himself. "I got a fine deal on it, too. An old friend from high school is in a management position now. This was last minute because they had a vacancy and a cancellation, and he wanted to fill it."

"Your bargain is my good luck," Lucie said, nuzzling Clementine. "We'll have a grand time here and you'll have a grand time there," she teased.

A look passed between Amelia and Quinn that said it all. They were still deliriously happy.

"Since Mum is back in Horseback Hollow, she offered to babysit." Amelia rooted in her purse. "But I told her you wanted to spend time with the baby, and we'd be back tomorrow night and she could see Clementine Rose all she wants then. She's catching up with Jeanne Marie and everybody else while we're out of town. She likes her place at the Cowboy Condos to have people in for an intimate conversation or to have a group party. She's much less stuffy than she used to be, don't you think?" Amelia asked Lucie.

Quinn came up behind Amelia and wrapped his arm around her shoulders. "You're much less stuffy than you used to be, don't you think, princess?"

She wrinkled her nose at him. How many times had her sister told Quinn she wasn't a princess? But he still treated her like one anyway.

He said now, "Amelia is a wonderful mother and doesn't take a break from Clementine, except to do chores. So now and then, I like to indulge us both."

"Taking care of Clementine and helping you make the

ranch succeed is what I intend to do with the rest of my life," Amelia assured him.

Clementine pulled on Lucie's hair and babbled. They all laughed.

"Are you ready to go?" Quinn asked Amelia.

"We have such little time to visit," she said to Lucie, handing her a sheet of paper. "This has all the emergency numbers. You have my cell and Quinn's, but this is the hotel number, too. And a pediatrician in Austin who I spoke with, just in case Clementine would need a doctor."

"Look at her," Lucie advised. "She's perfectly healthy. It's just going to be overnight. We'll be fine. I have all the food you brought for her in the refrigerator and on the counter. Quinn set up the crib in my bedroom and I have this cute little collapsible play set in here that she can nap in, too. I have the monitor set up in the bedroom so I can hear her if I'm in here and she's asleep. Her toys practically filled up her crib. She has enough clothes for the next three weeks."

Amelia brushed Lucie's conclusion away. "Don't exaggerate. Babies can go through three or four outfits a day. Just wait until you feed her. You might not only have to change her outfit. You'll have to change *yours*, too."

"You didn't put red beets in as part of her diet, did you?"

"They're an essential part. I gave you a variety of foods to use. I marked them breakfast, lunch and supper, and you can vary them."

Lucie checked with Quinn, "Does she plan this much with you, too?"

"She tries to, but most of the time, I get her to roll with the punches. Just go with the flow, Lucie, and you'll be fine. Clementine does have a fussy time, though. When she's like that, we just carry her around and try to entertain her, no matter when it is."

"I'll remember that. I have a couple of lullabies up my sleeve."

Quinn said to Amelia, "Time's a-wastin'."

Amelia gazed over at her baby daughter. "I want to be with you, but I hate leaving her."

"Call me whenever you'd like," Lucie said. "Or text me."

After waves all around and blown kisses, Amelia and Quinn left.

Lucie half expected them to pop back in, but they didn't.

Clementine toddled over to a stuffed toy Amelia had left for her on the sofa. She picked up the pink dog and gurgled at it. Just as Lucie was about to pick her up again—she loved holding her niece—her cell phone beeped. When she glanced at the screen she saw an unfamiliar number. She could let it go, but the call might have to do with her trip.

She answered. "Hello."

She was surprised to hear Chase's voice when he said, "I bought a burner phone that can't be traced. You should, too. I want to see you."

She thrilled at the words. But she was hesitant to repeat them back. If she and Chase kept up an affair, they were going to get hurt.

"I'm babysitting Clementine," she told Chase, regretful yet also, in some ways, appreciative for the excuse.

After a few moments of silence, he asked, "Does that mean you're tied up, or would you like a visitor?"

"You can visit if you're ready to babysit. Clementine

Rose needs all my attention." That type of dedication usually warded off men's attention.

"I've never been around babies," he admitted in a low voice.

She expected him to back off. Some men were downright afraid of babies because they considered them to be little alien creatures. You never knew what they were going to do next. Chase had been good with older children, but this was different.

However, this was Chase Parker, who didn't seem to know what backing off meant. "I'll borrow Tomás's truck so no one recognizes mine, and I'll sneak in the back way."

Lucie's heart sang a little that he was willing to join in her babysitting efforts. Or was he?

"Chase, I really meant it when I said Clementine needs all my focus. We can't—" She stopped, unable to put their passion into words. She had no doubts that if they were here alone, they'd be in each other's arms in her bed.

"I understand, Lucie, I do. And it's all right. I'll be there in a half hour."

Keeping to his word, Chase arrived precisely at her door a half hour later. She laughed when she opened the door to him. He was wearing a baseball cap instead of his Stetson, and he had that fake mustache pasted on above his lip again.

"You went all out," she joked.

"I did."

Once inside, he captured her shoulders and gave her a kiss on the forehead, his mustache tickling her skin. Then he leaned away and said, "Introduce me to Clementine."

Amelia and Quinn's little girl didn't seem to mind strangers, maybe because of the big family in Horseback

Hollow. She was used to many people fussing over her as if she were a little princess. She was too young to be really spoiled yet; Amelia and Quinn thought that was okay and so did Lucie. Children needed to know they were loved, and Clementine Rose did.

Chase took off the ball cap and tossed it to a nearby table. Then he peeled off the mustache and stuffed it in his pocket. "I'll let you see the real me," he teased as he approached Clementine.

"Have I seen the real you?" Lucie asked as Chase smiled and held out his hands to the little girl.

"You saw the real me on that country road after I learned about my dad's betrayal."

Yes, she did. She'd seen the Chase who really cared and was passionate about family and loyalty and maybe everything else.

He picked up a green elephant that rattled and wiggled it in front of Clementine. "What do you think of this, honey?"

Clementine grabbed at it and he laughed. Then he picked her up at the waist and held her high in the air. "Do you like it up there?"

Clementine giggled.

Maybe he'd never been around babies, but he sure had a way with them. Lucie suddenly felt…odd.

Almost to herself, she said, "The tabloids have called me conservative and stiff, or maybe even a little frozen. Sometimes I feel that way when I'm around you."

He cast her a quick glance over his shoulder and plopped Clementine into the crook of his arm. Instead of saying, *Oh, no, the tabloids don't see you that way,* he asked, "Do you see yourself as conservative and stiff?"

She considered his question. "I see myself as unusually cautious, and I try to stay calm, no matter what the circumstances. I never know when my photo's going to be shot, even from a long-lens camera. So almost every moment I'm outside and with people, I have that in the back of my mind. Hence, the pasted-on smile that might look frozen."

"Your smile is anything but frozen," Chase said vehemently, "and as for seeing the real you, that night on the country road, you were pretty free yourself. Don't beat yourself up over the *public* you and the *personal* you. As long as you're genuine with the people who love you, that's what matters."

She'd always thought that, but she wasn't so sure sometimes. "I try to be genuine when I do an interview, but almost every word is turned upside down and sideways, so it's hard."

"I saw the one you did after your father died. You were quite genuine, and the reporter thought so, too. She even had a tear in her eye. Don't you see your public life as a job?"

"Do you show one personality at work and another at home?" she inquired, really wanting to know.

He thought about it and sat with Clementine on the sofa. The baby was suddenly fascinated by the buttons on his shirt.

"I try to be professional at work and watch my words. So yes, I guess I'm different there than I am at home. Maybe that's another reason I want to run the horse rescue ranch. I can just be who I am."

She liked who Chase was and who he'd become.

"Speaking of the press," he said, "I'm doing that interview tomorrow with Norton Wilcox."

"I forgot all about that. Is there anything you have to prepare for?"

"No. It's going to be all about the horse rescue, so there shouldn't be any curveballs. I was talking to a friend yesterday about the ranch. He's the manager of the Galloping G, and they're going to be taking in troubled youth starting in June. We might coordinate some of our efforts. Giving kids a horse to gentle could solve some of their problems, too."

"That sounds like a plan. It also sounds like something the Fortune Foundation might want to help fund."

"I don't know. You're talking about proud men here, who want to run a program their own way. If you accept money from a foundation, there are usually strings attached."

She didn't think these funds were going to work that way, but what did she really know? All she was doing was setting up the office and suggesting programs to aid.

"I think it's time we started supper," she suggested. "Amelia provided baby food, but she also said Clementine liked mac and cheese, so I thought we'd have that, burgers and green beans. With you here, it'll be that much easier to put it all together. I wasn't sure if Clementine would sit in her high chair while I did it."

"I'll keep her occupied. That sounds like a great dinner."

"You're looking at me again as if you're surprised. I am a normal person, Chase. I really do cook. I even knit."

He blinked. "You knit?"

She just rolled her eyes. "I knitted Clementine a baby blanket. What do you think I do on long plane rides?"

"Read," he said with a straight face.

"Come on," she said, motioning him to the kitchen.

"Clementine likes to play with the pots and pans. You can help her clang lids together."

In the kitchen, Lucie made sure she kept at least three feet between her and Chase. That wasn't hard as he raced after Clementine, made sure she was occupied and Lucie started dinner. She also made sure she didn't look at Chase too often, because if she did, she'd want to kiss him. No, Clementine couldn't carry tales yet, but Lucie was very aware she was Clementine's aunt and didn't want to do anything untoward when she was in her company. Chase seemed to realize that and respected it. Except…

There were times they couldn't avoid touching. Lucie dropped an onion. He scooped it up. When he handed it to her, their fingers almost entwined. A muscle memory, that was all it was.

Lucie's version of macaroni and cheese involved a white sauce, melting the cheese in it, then pouring it over the macaroni to bake. After that was in the oven, she patted the burgers and inserted them under the broiler.

"Are steamed carrots okay for you?" Lucie asked. "Clementine loves them."

"Carrots are fine with me."

"And for dessert, we have cookies Amelia baked, something with oatmeal that's supposed to be good for Clementine."

"Do they taste like dog biscuits?" Chase asked.

Lucie cast him a look that was in the least scolding, at the most maybe a little coy. "No, they don't taste like dog biscuits or horse biscuits. They have cinnamon and raisins. If Amelia says they're good, I'm sure they are."

"Do you believe everything she tells you?"

"Mostly. Why?"

"I just wondered how that was between sisters."

"We bonded together against the boys."

"Your brother Charles isn't married either, is he?"

"No, the tabloids have gotten that right. He's been engaged twice."

"The reason for the breakups?"

"He's not ready. Charles is a go-with-the-flow kind of guy, and I'm not sure he wants to seriously be tied down."

"Maybe nobody does," Chase said. "Maybe everybody wants what they want when they want it. Do you actually know many men or women who could compromise? Just in my work alone, we sometimes have to navigate decisions as if we were in peace negotiations."

"I know what you mean, but a marriage shouldn't be about negotiation. It should be about giving on both sides."

They stared at each other while Clementine clinked lids together, like cymbals, cymbals that were going off in Lucie's head. How did they get into this discussion?

"Can you watch the burgers for a while?" she asked, changing the subject. "I'll take Clementine to the bedroom and change her. After that, dinner should be ready."

"You know, I can cook, too."

"Main dishes?" Lucie asked.

"Burgers and tuna fish sandwiches."

They both laughed.

"We could probably put a weekly menu together," she teased and headed for the bedroom.

Chase had never had more fun, had never enjoyed conversation more, had never realized a child was a constant energy suck. But an adorable one. He and Lucie had spoken hypothetically about having kids, but tonight, acting like a couple with a child, he could actually see himself in the role. What would it be like to come home to Lucie and a little girl, or a little boy? To fit everything else around their children because they would be the most important beings in their world?

The whole concept was foreign. If this deal went through on the Schultz property, he'd have mega-renovations to do, and that was going to take time. What woman would put up with having her place torn apart, piece by piece, room by room, floor by floor, appliance by appliance? Lucie was used to the best of everything. Oh, she might go on trips to foreign places and make do while she was there, but when she came home, she came home to conveniences and things she might never even ask for, like walk-in refrigerators, the highest-quality ranges.

He wasn't sure she knew what she had. She just expected it to be there. He wanted to renovate the ranch house nicely, but not at the highest cost he could find. He wanted to be economical and practical about every renovation he made. And if Lucie chose to live there—

He blanked that thought away. She wouldn't. That was the end of it.

By the time Lucie brought Clementine back to the kitchen, the little girl was fussing.

"I think she's just hungry. Let's get it on the table and see if she'll eat."

Lucie and Chase tried to please Clementine. They really did. But the little girl had missed her nap, and Amelia had warned Lucie that might mean she would be cranky. But Lucie hadn't wanted to believe it. So she tempted Clementine with bites of burger, spoonfuls of macaroni and cheese, steamed carrots soft enough for her to chew. Their meal was constantly interrupted by a spilled dish, an overturned spoon, macaroni in Clementine's hair.

Clementine was squawking now as Chase tried to wipe cheese from her hair.

"She's going to need a bath, isn't she?" he asked.

"Probably so. I don't know how much fun that's going to be. But Amelia included her little bathtub and her toys, so it might calm her down a bit. Do you want to postpone coffee and dessert until I try it?"

"That sounds like a good idea. I can get the bathtub set up."

"Okay, but not too hot."

"I'll check it with my elbow."

"Where did you learn that trick?"

"Some program I was watching one day. I'll test the water on my wrist, too, and make sure it's just right. Don't worry, Lucie, I've got this. While you're giving her a bath, I'll clean up."

They were negotiating, sort of…or were they just compromising? Whatever the case, if Chase kept it up, he'd be a darn good husband. Could he keep a compromising attitude?

Clementine was not warm and snuggling after her bath, and not even one of the oatmeal cookies could quiet her. Her voice started in a low cry and then built until she was practically screaming.

Lucie walked her back and forth in the living room. "Amelia told me she sometimes gets like this. She's overtired. She's in a strange place with strange people."

"She's going to make herself sick," Chase muttered, taking her from Lucie's arms. "We can't let her keep this up."

"I hate to do it, but I'm going to call Amelia."

Amelia answered her cell, sounding breathless. "Is something wrong?"

"I'm sorry to interrupt, but I don't know what to do with Clementine. She's crying and won't stop."

"She has a fussy spell sometimes after supper. Did she eat?"

"Yes, she did. Some."

"Well, good. That's important," Amelia explained. "Now all you have to do is get her to sleep. Put her on the phone."

"What do you mean, *Put her on the phone*?"

"Just bring her to the phone. Quinn will sing her a lullaby and she'll fall asleep."

"Just like that?" Lucie asked.

"Just like that."

Lucie told Chase what her sister had said. He shrugged and carried Clementine to Lucie, who put the cell phone to her ear. She was still wailing at that point, but after about a minute, the sound began to diminish. Lucie could just hear Quinn's baritone over the speaker phone as he sang to his daughter. Finally the cries vanished into little hiccups. Her eyes started to shut, and Lucie cradled her in her arms.

When the baby was quiet, Lucie said to Quinn, "You're a magician."

"No, I'm just a dad who knows what to do to make his daughter fall asleep. Now, if that happens again, and sometimes it does, call your friend Chase and have him sing to her."

Lucie looked up at Chase, and she couldn't lie to her sister and brother-in-law. "He's here."

"Well, good," Quinn said. "Then you definitely don't need us. We'll see you tomorrow, Lucie." And he hung up.

Lucie stared at her phone. "I think I feel like a baby-sitting failure."

Chase shook his head. "You're not a failure unless you have to call them again. That is the last thing you want to do."

"Hopefully I won't have to. Let's put her down for the night."

Putting Clementine down for the night lasted for about fifteen minutes. Lucie and Chase had tiptoed out of the bedroom and gone into the kitchen to have a cup of coffee. Lucie was pulling cookies from a container on the cupboard when Clementine began crying again. She and Chase exchanged a look.

Then she said, "I'll see if I can quiet her."

But there was no quieting Clementine Rose when she didn't want to go to bed, when she didn't like sleeping in a strange room, when she wanted her mum and dad.

Soon Chase peeked into the room. "Bring her out here again. If we play with her for a little while longer, maybe she'll fall asleep on her own."

"Wishful thinking," Lucie murmured, standing with the crying baby and rocking her back and forth. "Come on, little one. Let's go see what other toys your mum picked out to send with you."

On the sofa, Clementine stuck her thumb in her mouth and held her stuffed elephant, her cheeks still wet from tears. She smiled, however, when Chase took out a hand puppet and danced the dog across her knees. She pulled her thumb from her mouth to yank on the dog's ears.

Lucie said, "I'll get us both some coffee. I think we're going to need it."

And they did, because Clementine just wasn't going to

sleep. Every time they tried to put her down, she began crying.

Finally Chase decided, "She's manipulating us, and if she doesn't sleep tonight, I have a feeling she'll be a holy terror in the morning."

"You know what we haven't tried yet," Lucie suggested.

He sighed. "Me singing her a lullaby. All right. Why don't we both cuddle on the bed with her and we'll try it?"

Lucie gave him a long look.

"Seriously. We'll all be comfortable and if she falls asleep, we'll just let her sleep."

It was almost 2:00 a.m. "You don't mind staying the night?" she asked him.

"I don't mind." His voice was low and sexy, and she couldn't help wishing he was staying for another reason other than singing a lullaby.

Bringing a few of Clementine's toys with her, Lucie sat on the king-size bed—Clementine in the middle. Chase crawled onto the other side, propped up on two pillows. It should seem odd, having him in her bed. In some ways it did. But in other ways, it felt very natural. That scared her. Everything about her situation with Chase scared her. She might as well admit it.

Clementine picked up rattles, one in each hand, and began shaking them.

"What lullabies do you know?" Lucie asked him.

"I don't know any, but I do know a couple of nursery rhymes. Doesn't everybody? Let's try 'Twinkle, Twinkle, Little Star.' But you have to promise not to laugh."

Lucie crossed her heart with her hand. "I promise."

After a shake of his head and a long, blown-out breath, he began the first line.

At first Clementine didn't respond, but then she looked over at him as if somehow recognizing a male voice with a tune in it. Lucie lounged against the pillows too and began rubbing Clementine's back the way her mum often did hers and Amelia's when they were little. It was a soothing motion that had settled tears and fears and bad dreams.

After Chase finished with "Twinkle, Twinkle, Little Star," he began with a Disney tune, "When You Wish Upon A Star." Maybe he thought the heavenly-body theme would put Clementine to sleep.

To Lucie's surprise, it did. Clementine was soon nestled in the crook of Lucie's arm, and her little eyes were closed.

But would she stay asleep?

Chase sang for a little longer, then shrugged. In almost a whisper, he said, "She probably doesn't want to be in that crib all by herself. We should take advantage of her sleeping now in case it doesn't last long."

Chase moved over closer to Lucie, turned on his side and ran his hand through her hair. She could have purred.

Leaning in even closer, he gave her a deep, long, wet kiss that could have led somewhere else if a child hadn't slept between them. When he broke away, he was breathing raggedly, and so was she.

Finally he said, "You're going to make a wonderful mother."

Lucie couldn't help thinking, *And you'll make a wonderful dad*. But she didn't say the words aloud. If she said them out loud, that could be a dream waiting to come true.

Was it a dream she should try to capture? Or should she let their marriage be annulled? Should they go their separate ways?

Maybe in the morning after a few hours' sleep, the answer would become clearer.

Chapter Twelve

When Lucie awakened, Chase was no longer in bed. Had he left?

Clementine was sleeping soundly. Still, Lucie didn't want to leave her on the bed when she went to check in the rest of the apartment for Chase. As gently as she could, she lifted Clementine and laid her in the portable crib. The baby seemed unaware of the move. She stuffed her little fist near her chin and made a sighing sound. Lucie made sure the monitor that Amelia had brought along so she could hear Clementine if she was in the other room was turned on high.

Chase had found the pods to brew coffee and was making himself a mug. He gave her a crooked smile. "Is she still sleeping?"

"She is. I put her in the crib."

She didn't know what to say to him about last night. It had been nice. More than nice, really.

Lucie had brought her cell phone into the kitchen. and now she said, "I wonder if I should text Amelia and tell her everything is okay."

Chase shook his head. "If you don't call her, she knows everything's okay. Let her and Quinn have this time together."

"You're right." Lucie glanced at her phone, where she saw she had a text. She tapped it. It was from Keaton. He wondered if she'd like to have lunch sometime.

"Is that from Amelia?" Chase asked.

"No. I must have missed this last night. It's from Keaton."

Chase frowned. "The guy who took you to that charity event?"

She nodded.

Chase took a few steps closer. "What did he want?"

Her mouth suddenly went dry at the look in Chase's eyes. It was a possessive look.

"He wants to have lunch."

"Are you going to go?"

"Possibly," she answered, not sure at all what she was going to do or even what she should say.

Chase took the phone from her hands and set it on the counter. Then his hands caressed her shoulders and brought her closer. He didn't say he didn't want her to have lunch with Keaton, but that look in Chase's eyes—

"So Clementine is sound asleep?" he asked in a husky murmur.

Lucie nodded to the monitor on the counter. "I'll hear her if she wakes up."

Lucie was already trembling, anticipating his kiss. Last night had been comforting and warm, but this electricity she felt whenever Chase was near her was definitely even better—exciting and extraordinary.

Although he was close enough to kiss her, he didn't. He said, "Lying next to you in that bed last night and not being able to really touch you was torture."

She did know exactly what he meant. Getting close, yet unable to be totally intimate, created an insufferable longing.

"We're close now," she whispered.

"I have to be at a meeting with Jeff and my father in forty-five minutes. All hell could break loose."

"Maybe you need a little bit of heaven first." She couldn't believe she was being this bold. Charles would never believe it of Miss Goody Two-shoes.

Chase, on the other hand, grabbed on to believing it. He slid his hands into her hair, tipped her face up to his and took her lips in a consuming kiss that forced her to think about nothing but him.

She was entranced by his taste—coffee and Chase— by his male scent…but mostly by his passion. Her blouse was fashioned with buttons down the front, and now she wished she'd worn something easier to take off. Chase's fingers fumbled on the cloth buttons as he pushed them through the holes.

They were standing in bright daylight in her kitchen, and she could hardly believe the sensations rippling through her. He was looking at her as he undid the fastenings, at her face, and then down to her breasts, back to her face again. His eyes were hungry, full of smoky desire, and she couldn't wait to fall into it.

This was impulsive, maybe even reckless, but she felt she needed it. She felt she needed *him*. She never knew when might be the last time they could be intimate. He didn't finish the bottom two buttons, simply helped pull her blouse from her shoulders so she could tug out her arms. Somehow she knew he would just rip it open if it got in the way. And even that excited her.

He was staring at her bra, a little champagne number that seemed to go with everything. She liked lace, what could she say? And he seemed to like it, too.

He just stared, ran his finger over the edge and shook his head. "I wanted to go slower this time, but I don't think I can."

"Slow is definitely underrated," she assured him.

When he removed her bra and cupped her breasts in his palms, his gaze was on hers. She knew her eyes grew wider because she couldn't hide what she was feeling. He set the base of his palm on her nipple and rubbed, and she couldn't help moaning. She couldn't let him watch her melt in front of him. She needed the same kind of power. Now she reached for the buttons on his shirt, and much more quickly than he had, she unfastened the placket. When his bare chest was before her, she placed her hands on it and splayed her fingers. His curly chest hair popped up between them, and she slid them up to his shoulders.

"Oh, Lucie, you're driving me crazy," he groaned.

"Isn't that what I'm supposed to do?" she asked innocently.

At that, he scooped her up into his arms and carried her to the sofa. She lay there, staring up at him, as he took a condom from his pocket and laid it on the arm of the couch. Then he unzipped his jeans and let them fall. When he sat down beside her, he pulled off his boots, then the rest of his clothes.

"What about you?" he asked. "Are you just going to watch?"

"I can't just watch," she said. "We only have a limited amount of time. I'm ready to participate."

With a laugh, he helped her rid herself of the rest of her clothes. He stretched out on top of her and kissed the hollow at her neck, the V between her breasts, each of her ribs.

"Chase, we don't have that much time." She was panting, and being so vulnerable, so open with him, scared her. It must have something to do with the daylight. Seeing each other's every expression, hearing each other's every sound.

"Are you embarrassed by me kissing you everywhere, Lucie? Certainly other men have."

"Other men haven't kissed me naked. Only you have, Chase. Only you."

He looked astounded by her words, and then he looked just plain pleased. He kissed lower and lower, until her navel caught his attention. He ran his thumbs along her mound, touched her intimately, and so seductively, she felt like swooning.

Then he asked, "Are you ready for me?"

"Yes, Chase. Yes, I am."

Taking her words to heart, he rolled on the condom, positioned himself and then thrust into her. She wanted to be as close as she possibly could be. She wrapped her legs around him, rocking with him on that sofa. Bringing them both countless seconds of pleasure was all that was on her mind. She wanted to give as well as take. She wanted to take with him, knowing she'd return it all over again. They seemed to want to make up for ten years of being apart. Chase didn't hurry, but pulled in and out to give them both the most ultimate friction and superlative pleasure.

Lucie didn't think she could take any more. Her breaths were coming so fast. Her body was so overheated. Yet still she wanted more. She wanted *him*. She loved *him*.

Chase's thrusts became longer and harder until finally the pleasure overloaded all her senses and she felt as if she came apart in his arms. If he hadn't been holding her, she wasn't sure what would have happened to her. She called his name, and when she did, he found his release, too. They clung to each other breathing raggedly, letting their bodies cool, letting their breaths fall into a more normal rhythm. Somehow he gathered her into his arms and they lay like spoons, tight against each other, holding each other.

"I'd stay here all day with you if I could, but this meeting is important. I'm going to convince my father that Jeff is the man for the job, and it's time for me to go."

"Clementine will probably wake up soon. Amelia and Quinn are going to pick her up after lunch and head back."

Even though she was still in a bit of a daze because of their lovemaking, she realized they weren't talking about what was important—the two of them.

"You want to settle this with your father before you do that interview with the reporter tomorrow, right?"

"Yes. I don't want anything coming out during the interview that would be new information to Dad. I owe him the courtesy of telling him all about my plans first. On the other hand, he has to be willing to listen. That has never been his strong suit."

Lucie suddenly wondered what would happen if she could prolong her stay in Austin, if she could give herself and Chase time to figure out a life…if they could have one together. But her mother was depending on her. The orphanage was depending on her. She had to put her personal life on the back burner, didn't she? She *could* come back to Austin after the orphanage was built.

She had so much to think about.

And when Chase was quiet, she assumed he did, too.

From the monitor on the end stand, she heard little cooing sounds. That turned to babbling, and the babbling turned to a cry.

"She's awake." Which meant there was no time to talk now. No time to talk before his meeting, and no time to talk with a little one needing attention.

"Do you want to shower?" she asked.

"There's a shower at Parker Oil, and I have a change of clothes there. I often have to go from work during the day to an evening meeting."

"I see," she said. Chase's life had been a high-powered one. How easy was it going to be to rev it down to ranch work instead?

They both dressed quickly. Chase made a stop in the bathroom while Lucie picked up Clementine. She was settling the baby in her high chair when Chase came back to the kitchen and said, "I've got to go."

The awkwardness was there again that always came when one of them had to leave. What was it from? Not knowing when they'd see each other again, not knowing what to say, not knowing the feelings would change in the course of an hour or five or a day?

He picked up his cap from the table and plopped it onto his head. "Tell your sister and brother-in-law that their little girl is the cutest in the world."

Lucie smiled.

He kissed her lips slightly, from one corner to the other, and then he pulled back. "I've got a full day today, with the meeting and odds and ends I want to clear up.

Tomorrow's lighter. Why don't I give you a call after my interview? Maybe we can hook up again."

Hook up. Was that what she wanted?

"Chase, what are we doing? Having an affair before our marriage is annulled? It's dangerous and potentially explosive."

"When are you leaving?" he asked, looking as serious as she'd ever seen him.

Her mouth went dry. "Next Monday."

He waited as if he wanted her to say more. But what could she add?

"Are you telling me you'd rather not see me again before you leave?" he asked.

She was so confused about what was propitious, what was best, what was right.

"What do *you* want, Chase?"

After a moment, he responded, "I want to start my new life...one way or another."

With or without her?

Clementine was crying full out now and Lucie had to go to her. Responsibility versus heart's desire. Swallowing hard, she said, "It would probably be best if we end this now."

Chase looked stoically accepting as he nodded. "I'll call you after the annulment goes through."

Then before she could take either a step toward him or Clementine, he was gone.

Out of her life.

Chase couldn't stop thinking about Lucie. That was just the way it was these days. Especially after this morning and the way they'd parted, she was definitely on his mind. At work, he showered and changed, feeling disconcerted about her, but prepared for the meeting with his dad. This wasn't a matter of *ready*. He was simply going to tell his father what he was going to do.

He went to one of the conference rooms to prepare. For the first part of this meeting, Jeff would join them and give the presentation.

A few minutes later, Jeff entered, looking nervous. But he pointed to the interactive whiteboard. "I'm ready for this."

Chase gave him a thumbs-up. "Good. Don't let my father see you sweat. If he sees a weakness, he'll exploit it. Just be honest with him and stick to the facts."

"Will do," Jeff agreed with a nod.

When Warren Parker came in, he looked from Chase to Jeff to the whiteboard to the laptop. "You're not going to give me a chance to convince you not to do what you want to do, are you?"

"No," Chase said with conviction.

"With all due respect, sir," Jeff interjected, "I have a presentation ready that will show you where I intend to take the company. These are ideas I've developed with Chase over the past six months. Of course, you'll have to confirm every venture I want to start."

"What if *I* want to start a venture?" Warren Parker asked with some vehemence. "Don't think you're going to take over. I'm not going to be just some figurehead."

"Of course not, sir," Jeff assured him. "I just want you to know I have ideas to share—about everything, from new projects to overhauling our software system."

Warren rolled his eyes. "So you're leaving me with someone young and eager?" he asked Chase.

"And intelligent and forward-looking."

Warren lowered himself into one of the chairs. "All right, let's get started."

A half hour later, Chase's dad wasn't asleep or barking that he didn't approve of any of it. He was looking pensive.

"All right, Jeff," he said. "You've shown me you have backbone and you're imaginative. Why don't you meet me in my office after lunch around one?"

Jeff knew he was being dismissed. He nodded, closed down his laptop and left the room.

Chase studied his father, unable to read him. "He'll be good for the company, Dad, trust me on that."

Warren eyed Chase and then said, "I'll agree to try Jeff in your shoes for the next three months. If he works out, wonderful. If he doesn't, you're going to have to find me someone else. And the only way I'll agree to this whole thing is if you'll consult with Parker Oil. I'll put you on the books as a consultant, and you can arrange your schedule accordingly."

"Not for the first month," Chase said, negotiating with his dad as he hadn't done before.

He almost thought he saw a twinkle in his father's eye. "Agreed," he said. "One month, and then we'll negotiate what projects I want you to work on."

"Maybe everything will be flowing so smoothly that you won't need me at all," Chase countered.

His father just arched an eyebrow. His face took on a very somber expression. "We have to talk about ten years ago."

Chase thought about what had happened then and what his father had done. He also thought about the fact that his dad wasn't fighting him now about leaving. Maybe because he knew he'd lose him for sure if he did?

"What's done is done," Chase said, ready to forgive because that was right to do. But he wouldn't forget.

"I didn't apologize for it, and that's because I don't know if I did the right thing or the wrong thing. Marrying someone so young wasn't right for you back then."

"Dad—" Chase warned.

Warren raised his hand. "I know. I should keep my mouth shut. Your mother tells me that all the time. But I'm going to say this. Lucie Fortune Chesterfield is a beautiful woman. She was a pretty girl ten years ago and that beauty has just increased. I can see why you fell head over heels then, and why you could now."

Chase didn't protest because he didn't want to lie to his father. Something had happened again now. He just wasn't sure what to do about it or how to handle it. His heart thumped madly whenever he was near her. He was excited whenever he saw her. He wanted to spend as much time with her as he could. Could it really be love?

"Over the years, I have learned a thing or two about women, mostly through your mother. If Florence likes Lucie, then the girl must have a head on her shoulders as well as a pretty smile."

Chase couldn't help being a bit amused by his father's assessment. "She does have a good head on her shoulders."

Warren stuck out his hand. "I know everything can't be forgiven. Nothing's that easy. But maybe we can have a new start. What do you say?"

Chase extended his hand to his father, and as they shook, he felt closer to his dad than he had in years. Would it last? He didn't know, but he hoped it would.

* * *

The following morning, Norton Wilcox introduced himself to Chase in the greenroom about ten minutes before their interview at TXLB began. Chase hadn't given the reporter much consideration because he was still thinking about all the details he had to handle at Parker Oil before he left, as well as his confusion over Lucie leaving. Norton—the man had said to call him by his first name—had been made up with his hair gelled, his navy suit and red-and-blue tie perfect for an interview. Chase had worn black jeans, a white shirt and a bolo tie, knowing he had to look professional as far as the horse rescue ranch went.

Once the lights in the studio were glaring and the interview began, Norton's questions started easy enough. He said, "You're an oil man by experience and family history. Why did you want to get involved in rescuing horses?"

As Chase had explained to his father last evening as they'd talked over dinner—really talked—he related, "When I was a kid, I went to the barn when I didn't get my way or when I had a problem that needed to be solved. I never thought of a horse as just a vehicle for a trail ride. Like any other animal, a horse responds to voice, to touch and to kindness. I learned that early. They are intuitive creatures if you tap into their souls. I like doing that. I felt fulfillment, being able to communicate with them. And when I see one neglected, it makes me angry. That, however, doesn't serve much purpose. My reaction to it does. I rescue the horse and coax it to trust humans again."

Norton looked totally surprised by his answer. "You make the connection sound almost mystical."

Chase shook his head. "Nothing of the sort. Just as people have to learn how to communicate with each other, I had to learn how to communicate with a horse. But once I did, I wanted to use that for good. Gentling horses can benefit us all."

"How so?" Norton seemed to be truly interested.

"I have a friend who's going to be involved with helping troubled youths. When a kid makes a connection, he's helped. Gentling a wild mustang might not solve a teenager's problems. but it can pull him out of himself. It can teach him how to feel productive and worthwhile."

"So you plan to open a nonprofit ranch on the old Schultz homestead?"

"I do. I'm going to refurbish the house and the two barns and soon get started."

"But you can't get started right away, can you?"

A prickling began at the back of Chase's neck and he knew he wasn't going to like what was coming. He kept silent.

Interviewers hated dead air time, and Norton rushed to fill it. "There's a glitch getting a loan for the place, right?"

Chase still remained silent.

Again Norton hurried to fill the air with words. "Apparently you had a secret marriage ten years ago that you thought was dissolved. But it wasn't. You're still married and you need your wife to sign those loan papers. I think our audience would be very surprised to learn who that wife is. They're seeing the photo of you and Lucie Fortune Chesterfield on a split screen now."

Chase glanced toward the monitor. The photo was one of him and Lucie at the South by Southwest Conference.

"Haven't you been dating Lady Fortune Chesterfield again since she's been in Austin?" Norton pressed.

Chase could easily grasp the fact that the photo was a long shot. Lucie was wearing her wig, sunglasses and ball cap. Chase's disguise made him almost indistinguishable. Only one thought occupied his mind. He had to protect Lucie and her family.

He tried to be as nonchalant as he could be. "As your audience can see, Mr. Wilcox, the two people in that photo look nothing like me or Lady Fortune Chesterfield. I don't know where you've gotten your information, but you're mistaken."

Norton studied him with a scowl. "I took that photograph that day myself," the interviewer said in a huff. "And I've been shadowing Lady Fortune Chesterfield. I spoke with someone who saw the two of you at a church function."

This Chase could explain and he could even add some truth to the interview. "If you've done your research, Mr. Wilcox, you know that Lady Fortune Chesterfield is in Austin, setting up a branch of the Fortune Foundation. My mother asked her to evaluate the after-school program at our church to help with the funding. Lady Fortune Chesterfield was at the function and so was I. But we weren't together. Maybe you should have talked to me about this before the interview, so we wouldn't mislead your audience."

"You're the one who's misleading my audience, Mr. Parker."

"I imagine your audience tuned in today to find out about my horse rescue plans. They haven't been misled in the least. I'm sure your station will post the information on your website, but if anyone is interested in the

program or has a horse in need of rescue, just email me."
Chase rattled off his email address.

The tech was giving a signal for Wilcox to wrap up
the interview. Trying to paste on a recovery smile, the
reporter said, "Thank you for coming in today, Chase.
I'm sure our audience appreciates your forthrightness on
everything we discussed."

Chase felt a flush come to his face. He didn't like *not*
being forthright. But for Lucie's sake, what else could
he do?

Chapter Thirteen

After watching Chase's interview, feeling for him as he was ambushed by the reporter, Lucie came to several realizations. She *was* irrevocably in love with Chase. Because she loved him, she couldn't let him put his reputation on the line. He probably didn't realize what was going to happen next. There would be so much fallout that there'd be an absolute media scramble to find out the facts. There would be rumors about their marriage and affairs and engagements, and everything in between. Chase had no idea what was coming.

But she did.

What did Chase feel for her? Did he just want her in his bed? Or did he love her? Did he want their marriage annulled? She didn't, but she wasn't in this alone. If Chase didn't love her, it would hurt and be almost unbearable. But because she loved him, she'd give him the annulment and let him go on with his life.

However, neither of them could continue without the truth. It was about time she followed her mother's advice and let the truth be liberating. She knew the best way to do that was to contact her mother's public relations secretary and let her set up a press conference. But first she'd call her mother and tell her what she was planning.

Chase was pacing his office, realizing that wily reporters, let alone investigative ones, could probably access his phone records to see if he and Lucie had talked. Should he call her and tell her he hadn't known what else to do except fall back on denial?

While he was considering that, his own phone beeped. Taking it from his pocket, he didn't recognize the Texas number. "Chase Parker here."

"Mr. Parker? This is Josephine Fortune Chesterfield. We met briefly last week."

"Yes, we did," he confirmed, wondering why Lucie's mother was calling him. Then a horrible thought hit him. "Has something happened to Lucie?"

"You mean, by way of an accident or that type of thing? No, no, no. I'm sorry if I worried you in that way."

Worried him in the least? If something happened to Lucie, the light would go out of his life. This realization stunned him. Chase's heart had almost stopped when he realized how his world would fall apart if harm came to Lucie...because he loved her. It had taken him too long to realize it. Was he too late? "How can I help you, Lady Fortune Chesterfield?"

"Lucie saw your interview and so did I."

He was silent because he absolutely didn't know what to say.

"Chase?" she asked.

"I was there to talk about the horse rescue. I didn't expect the rest."

"No, of course you wouldn't. You're an honorable man. Mr. Wilcox was out for the ratings. Lucie is terrifically unhappy that you were put in that position."

"That's not her fault."

"I'm so glad you don't blame her. Other men in your position might."

"It is what it is, Lady Fortune Chesterfield. She can't help that the press hounds her and her family. The truth is—I didn't know what to tell him. I'm sure with investigation all of this is going to come out. But at least with notice, you and your family can prepare what you want to say. It gave you a little time if nothing else."

"I see now that that was your plan," Josephine said. "Thank you. Lucie is wasting no time dealing with this and that's why I called. She will be giving a press conference in about an hour at the Crown Hotel's ballroom. I thought you might want to be there."

"Why didn't Lucie call me and tell me?" Was she too upset about what he had or hadn't said?

"My guess is that Lucie doesn't want you to be embarrassed if you don't like what she's going to say. Personally I think you two need to communicate better."

There seemed to be much Lady Fortune Chesterfield wasn't saying, but Chase understood loyalty, and she would be true to her daughter no matter what.

"I don't know whether to be worried or relieved she's giving a press conference," Chase said honestly. "Do you *know* what she's going to say?"

"She hasn't shared everything with me, but she did say she was going to tell the truth. You can infer from that what you may."

"Will you be there, Lady Fortune Chesterfield?"

"No, I'm still in Horseback Hollow. I won't be able to get there in time. But I will be watching."

"Then you'll see me there. I'll be as close to the front as I can get."

"I thought you'd want to be there. Lucie's going to need all the support she can get. After she makes a statement, the press will bombard her with questions."

"I'll protect her. No matter what she says."

"I was counting on that," Josephine said with a smile in her voice. "I've depended on her a bit too much since her father died. I think we're both coming to realize that. She's a woman with her own mind, and I have to stand back a bit now and let her do what she must."

After Chase ended the call, he thought about what Lucie could say, might say, might feel.

Then he headed for the elevator. He had a stop to make before he attended that press conference.

Lucie knew she had to do this. She absolutely had to. If she brought the tabloids down on her family, well, so be it. They'd been through it before. They'd survive. Her mother had accepted her decision and hadn't tried to talk her out of it. Maybe she'd realized she had to pull back a bit. Maybe she'd realized Lucie wanted a different life from the one Josephine envisioned for her. Lucie had realized that she had to find her own life, no matter what happened with Chase. She simply knew she couldn't let him take the fall for their history and what had happened between them the past few weeks. She didn't want him to have to evade or be dishonest. Neither of them had done anything wrong.

To Lucie's dismay, the ballroom of the hotel seemed

to be filled. There were press members with their lanyards and ID badges, cameras and cords, and people everywhere. The cacophony of voices almost made Lucie's head spin. But she emerged from the shadowy corner and walked up to the podium, prepared for whatever happened next.

After she adjusted the microphone, she tapped on it and closed her eyes for a moment against the flashes of light. Taking a bolstering breath, she opened her eyes and put on her best smile.

"Hello, everyone. I'm glad you could join me here today. Ever since Norton Wilcox's airing of *About Austin* yesterday, there have been rumors and gossip about me and Chase Parker. I'd like to settle those rumors and give you the truth."

Any chatter in the room stopped. For so many people gathered, the atmosphere was as silent as that of a church. But Lucie wasn't nervous anymore. She wasn't anxious either. She was doing the right thing.

"I have a tale to tell you and it's not very long."

Reporters held up microphones. She knew some of the people in the folding chairs were recording and photographing with their cell phones. She continued. "It's the true story of a girl who hadn't known much about the world. That girl was me. I'd been fairly sheltered, sent to the best schools, taken care of as if I were royalty. But at seventeen, I felt it was time for me to venture a bit on my own. I signed up for a trip to Scotland. I thought I was ready to be an adult, away from my parents and family. I was enjoying some freedom. My trip leader was Chase Parker. He was twenty-one, and from the first moment we looked at each other, there was attraction there. So much so that we were both a little overwhelmed. So overwhelmed that when Chase asked me to marry him right there in Scotland where I didn't need permission, I said yes."

Many of the reporters in the crowd gave a gasp, and Lucie couldn't help smiling genuinely this time.

"Our marriage was short-lived, however," she went on, "because when Warren Parker, Chase's father, found out, he persuaded us both the best thing to do was to have the marriage annulled. I was sent home from that trip in disgrace because I'd been caught with a boy in a hostel room alone. No one but Mr. Parker, Chase and I knew that boy was my husband."

Again there was a buzz vibrating through the room. But it stopped when she began to speak once more. "Because of circumstances that occurred after that, Chase and I didn't see each other again, not for ten years, not until a few weeks ago, when he visited me and told me he'd just found out that our marriage had never been annulled. He said lawyers were working on putting it right, but he wanted to tell me in person in case the news got out. Chase and I have seeing each other since that day. We've gotten to know each other better than we knew each other ten years ago. And I want to make one fact perfectly clear. When I was seventeen, I fell in love with Chase Parker, and…I'm still in love with him now."

Oohs and aahs went up from the crowd.

"Yes, the annulment is in the works," she went on, "but if it's up to me, we'll stay married forever."

Chase had been sitting about ten rows back. He knew Lucie couldn't see him in the crowd, especially not with the lights and the flashes and everyone wanting her attention. When he heard the words *When I was seven-*

teen, I fell in love with Chase Parker and I'm still in love with him now, it took him a moment to absorb what she was saying.

Reporters began firing questions. "When did you last see Chase Parker?"

"Have you been intimate with him?"

"Did his horse rescue ranch bring all of this to light?"

Chase was not going to let Lucie handle this herself, and he knew what he was going to do. There was no question about it in his mind...or in his heart.

When he stepped out into the side aisle and moved forward, security that had been hired for the occasion stopped him. But Chase took out his wallet and flashed his driver's license.

"I'm Chase Parker, and I have something to say to Lucie."

The burly man's eyes grew wide. He stepped to the side to let Chase pass, and Chase heard the man call, "Good luck."

Yes, he needed luck, but he needed more than that. He needed Lucie to change her life the way he would change his. Would she do it?

Chase pressed his way to the front of the crowd and shouted above all of them, "Lucie. What happens next isn't just up to you. It's up to me, too." Then he ran up the steps to the stage.

She was staring at him as if he were a ghost. "Where did you come from? How did you know?"

"Your mother phoned me," he said with a grin. Then, knowing exactly what he had to do, what he wanted to do more than anything else in the world, he dropped down to one knee.

Immediately the room grew quiet once more.

On his way to the press conference, he'd stopped at the jewelry store. Removing a velvet box from his pocket, he opened it. "From the moment I met you, I was smitten with you. There was something so strong between us that years and distance couldn't erase. When I realized we were still married, one of the things I felt was…hope. I looked forward to seeing you again. Reuniting with you was the most life-altering moment I ever experienced. Because I loved you then…and I still love you now."

Then, his voice ringing out loud and clear, he asked, "Lucie Fortune Chesterfield, will you agree to not unmarry me?"

A genuine smile broke out on Lucie's face, and he could see tears brimming in her eyes.

"Yes, I'll agree to not unmarry you. I'll stay married to you forever."

Rising to his feet, Chase slipped the ring on Lucie's finger, took her into his arms and gave her a resounding kiss. The applause in the background registered only slightly because he had his world in his arms…and that was all he cared about.

Epilogue

One Week Later

Lucie and Chase sat on the fence, watching the horses trot in the larger pasture and in the separate runs from the barn. Chase had settled on the ranch, and his dad had let him borrow hands from the Bar P to quickly make necessary changes for the rescue horses. The sign for the Parker Rescue Ranch had just gone up the day before. Chase wrapped his arm around Lucie's shoulders.

"We're going to take a real honeymoon. I want to take you someplace you've never been." That could be difficult, considering how much Lucie had traveled, but he didn't think she'd ever been to Curaçao or Bali.

"We *are* on our honeymoon," she reminded him.

He laughed. "Sleeping in sleeping bags the first two nights until we had furniture moved into the house wasn't exactly what I had in mind."

"Making love all night, whether on the floor or in a bed, is *my* idea of a honeymoon," she teased.

"Besides trying out the stall in the barn and settee in the sunporch and—"

She jabbed him in the ribs.

He leaned close to her and kissed her temple. "I never thought you'd agree to stay in Austin…to starting a life here with me."

"When you first told me we were still married, I couldn't comprehend giving up the life I was leading. I had so many responsibilities to so many people. I guess I finally realized I don't have to carry the world's concerns on my shoulders. And…Mom and I need a little bit of distance, too. Neither of us really realized what happened after Dad died, the way we held on to and depended on each other, and didn't make a move without the other's approval. It was like we were afraid we'd lose each other, too, so we did everything we could to hold on. But that kind of love soon feels confining. It didn't let either of us stretch our wings. We both realize that now."

"And your mom's not upset you found someone to take your place in Guatemala?"

"No. She knows Jenny Preston. She's worked with us on many projects. She knows as much about the details as I do and about the process. She and Mom will work well together."

Suddenly there was a honking of horns and the sound of cars on the gravel lane.

"Everyone's arriving," Chase said with a broad smile. "This barbecue might not be the best organized in the world, but the important thing is we're sharing our happiness with our family and friends."

"Exactly."

She and Chase hopped off the fence and ran to the front of the house. As they passed the front porch, Chase caught the scent of newly sawed wood. He'd been cutting new baseboards. The inside of the house needed lots of work. He and Lucie had painted some walls and sanded the living room floor. It was work they enjoyed doing together.

As he rounded the lane and peered into the backyard, he grinned. It was ready for company, with picnic tables, benches and canopies. He'd had new appliances delivered to the kitchen two days ago, so that room was ready.

A limo drove up first and he knew his mother-in-law would be ensconced inside. She'd postponed her trip until after the barbecue.

Lucie waved at the couple in the second car and Ella stuck her head out the window. "Are you ready for us?" she asked.

"More than ready," Lucie assured her.

A third SUV parked beside the others. It wasn't long before Amelia, Quinn and Clementine were rushing toward Lucie and Chase.

Chase said, "Come around back, everyone. There's beer, sweet tea and plenty of food."

It wasn't long before Chase's parents arrived, along with Josephine's sister, Jeanne Marie, and her husband, Deke, as well as Josephine and Jeanne Marie's brother, James Marshall. Lucie's brothers and their wives were there, too. All except her bachelor brother Charles, who couldn't get away from London yet.

Quinn said to Chase, "There's a news van parked out at the end of the lane. But I saw you had two burly guys in a truck watching them."

"I hired security for today so we could have privacy. This is the reception Lucie and I never had, never dreamed we'd have. I'm not going to have it ruined by the press."

Lucie and Amelia, Josephine and Jeanne Marie went into the kitchen and soon had the food organized, bringing it all outside to a large buffet table.

Chase heard Jeanne Marie say to Lucie, "I understand you're going to keep working for the Fortune Foundation."

"I am. I'm not giving up my work with children. There are lots of needy kids here in Austin. I'll be helping the Fortune Foundation fund the best ways to aid them."

Chase wrapped his arm around Lucie's waist. "And soon maybe we'll have kids of our own."

They'd talked about that at night as they'd held each other in their arms. They both wanted children, at least three and maybe four.

Lucie's cell phone buzzed and she took it from her pocket. Chase could see her press her video-chatting app. Her brother Charles's face appeared on the screen.

"Hi, Luce. I wish I could be there with you, but I had to congratulate you and tell you I'm happy for you."

"Oh, Charles, I wish you could be here, too."

"I'll visit Texas soon. I just wanted to tell you I was thinking about you. Love you, sis."

"Love you, too, Charles."

After Lucie pocketed the phone, she looked up at Chase and said, "I'm the happiest woman in the world."

He took her hand and pulled her away from the crowd into the kitchen. "What do you think about the Caribbean for a delayed honeymoon, possibly in a month or so?"

She laughed. "I'm thinking anywhere with you would be heavenly."

"After we get the house in order, I'll hire a manager

to live in the apartment above the barn. Then we won't be tied down here twenty-four-seven."

She wrapped her arms around his neck. "I don't mind being tied to you."

He kissed her soundly, certain they were going to have the best happily-ever-after a couple could ever have.

* * * * *

JOIN US ON SOCIAL MEDIA!

Stay up to date with our latest releases, author news and gossip, special offers and discounts, and all the behind-the-scenes action from Mills & Boon...

 millsandboon

 millsandboonuk

millsandboon

t might just be true love...

MILLS & BOON

THE HEART OF ROMANCE

A ROMANCE FOR EVERY KIND OF READER

MODERN

Prepare to be swept off your feet by sophisticated, sexy and seductive heroes, in some of the world's most glamourous and romantic locations, where power and passion collide.
8 stories per month.

HISTORICAL

Escape with historical heroes from time gone by. Whether your passion is for wicked Regency Rakes, muscled Vikings or rugged Highlanders, awaken the romance of the past.
6 stories per month.

MEDICAL

Set your pulse racing with dedicated, delectable doctors in the high-pressure world of medicine, where emotions run high and passion, comfort and love are the best medicine.
6 stories per month.

True Love

Celebrate true love with tender stories of heartfelt romance, from the rush of falling in love to the joy a new baby can bring, and a focus on the emotional heart of a relationship.
8 stories per month.

Desire

Indulge in secrets and scandal, intense drama and plenty of sizzling hot action with powerful and passionate heroes who have it all: wealth, status, good looks…everything but the right woman.
6 stories per month.

HEROES

Experience all the excitement of a gripping thriller, with an intense romance at its heart. Resourceful, true-to-life women and strong, fearless men face danger and desire - a killer combination!
8 stories per month.

DARE

Sensual love stories featuring smart, sassy heroines you'd want as a best friend, and compelling intense heroes who are worthy of them.
4 stories per month.

To see which titles are coming soon, please visit

millsandboon.co.uk/nextmonth

LET'S TALK

Romance

For exclusive extracts, competitions and special offers, find us online:

 facebook.com/millsandboon

🐦 @MillsandBoon

📷 @MillsandBoonUK

Get in touch on 01413 063232

For all the latest titles coming soon, visit
millsandboon.co.uk/nextmonth